SHADOWWAR

SHADOW WAR

SEAN
McFATE
& BRET WITTER

𝒲𝓂

WILLIAM MORROW
An Imprint of HarperCollins*Publishers*

SHADOW WAR. Copyright © 2016 by Sean McFate and Bret Witter. All rights reserved. Printed in the United States of America. No part of this book may be used or reproduced in any manner whatsoever without written permission except in the case of brief quotations embodied in critical articles and reviews. For information address HarperCollins Publishers, 195 Broadway, New York, NY 10007.

HarperCollins books may be purchased for educational, business, or sales promotional use. For information please e-mail the Special Markets Department at SPsales@harpercollins.com.

FIRST EDITION

Designed by William Ruoto
Frontispiece courtesy of trekandshoot/Shutterstock

Library of Congress Cataloging-in-Publication Data has been applied for.

ISBN 978-0-06-240370-4

16 17 18 19 20 OV/RRD 10 9 8 7 6 5 4 3 2 1

TO OGUN, THE ORISHA WHO LOOKED OUT
FOR ME WHEN I WAS RAISING ARMIES IN
THE FIELD

It is not the critic who counts; not the man who points out how the strong man stumbles. . . . The credit belongs to the man who is actually in the arena, whose face is marred by dust and sweat and blood; who strives valiantly; who errs, who comes short again and again . . . but who does actually strive to do the deeds; who knows great enthusiasms, the great devotions; who spends himself in a worthy cause; who at the best knows in the end the triumph of high achievement, and who at the worst, if he fails, at least fails while daring greatly.

THEODORE ROOSEVELT, 1910

With lies, you may go forward in the world but you
may never go back.

RUSSIAN PROVERB

SHADOWWAR

PROLOGUE

Libya

May 10, 2014

"Target ahead," my team leader, Jimmy Miles, said from the lead car.

"Copy that, Alpha One," I replied into my headset, as the outer wall of the abandoned outpost began to emerge from the desert half a mile away, a dark shadow against a dusty brown hill so slight most people wouldn't have noticed it was there.

I scanned the horizon. Nothing to the east but dunes and distant mountains, the same thing we'd been seeing for the past four hours and two hundred miles. Nothing in front but a dust track in a desert. The hill to the west was maybe fifteen feet at its highest point, rising at a consistent low gradient. It wasn't much more than a tilt of the horizon line, but out here, it could hide an army.

The perfect place for an ambush, I thought, although that didn't mean much. Every building in this rocky corner of the south Sahara was perfect for an ambush, since they were all built in wadis or against small cliffs to escape the wind. Our contacts, the Tuareg, were the legendary bandit-warriors of this harsh world; they knew every foot for five hundred miles. But they didn't have GPS, so you couldn't global-position a meeting. You had to meet them at a spot like this.

This was kinetic country, like the old Wild West: banditos were common and law came out of the barrel of a gun.

"Steady speed," I said. "Eyes open."

The call had come in seventeen hours ago from a new contact in Benghazi. A tribe of Tuareg had two cargo trucks full of weapons, and they wanted to deal.

"Why?"

"They were in Mali last year," the contact said. "They fought the French paratroopers at Gao." I could almost hear the shrug. "Now they need money."

My instinct was to turn the opportunity down. Too many variables. Maybe the contact sensed my hesitation.

"It's not small arms, I assure you," he said. "It's what you want."

Finding AK-47s and rocket-propelled grenade launchers was easy. The world was awash in them, especially Africa. But surface-to-air missiles, antitank rockets, 20 mm cannons: those weapons were gold. You laid your hands on them whenever you could.

"When?"

"Tomorrow. Fourteen hundred. Deep southwest, near the Algerian border. I'll shoot you the coordinates."

The two hundred thousand euros had arrived five hours ago, on a fishing trawler. The boat had probably come from Malta, our primary Mediterranean financial hub since the collapse of the Cypriot banking sector, but that wasn't my concern. What mattered was the courier. He had been late, so now I was late. I had intended to arrive at the rendezvous by noon, two hours early, but . . .

"They're here, Charlie One."

"Copy that, Alpha Two," I said flatly, biting off my frustration at the sight of the off-road trucks. I trusted my team—six Alphas (my team) wearing earpieces, and four local recruits—but I didn't like the Tuareg having the jump. I wouldn't be able to scout the location or position marksmen on surrounding dunes.

This was how the accident happened, I reminded myself.

"Fifteen," Miles said, counting men, as the compound came into view, two crumbling buildings surrounded by a six-foot earthen wall. Sand piled on the west side; the roofs clearly collapsed. It was probably the most habitable permanent structure for a hundred miles.

"Eighteen," said Tingera "Tig" Butuuro, our spotter. "Three against the rise."

Based on the satellite imagery, I had intended to set up between the warehouse and the rise, but the Tuareg were already there. That left my team with the bunkhouse and the earthen wall. At least the Tuaregs' cargo trucks—two canvas-covered deuce-and-a-halfs that looked like they'd been in use since Indiana Jones slid under a German version eight years before D-Day—would be between us.

"Plan B," Miles said, seeing the same thing. "Use the deuces for cover."

Miles's white Toyota Land Cruiser, obviously stolen from the United Nations and bought by me ten days ago on the black market in Tripoli, left the road and swung wide, giving him a better view into the Tuareg position. Our other two identical vehicles, also bought on the black market, followed.

"Twenty," Tig said, still counting men.

"Twenty-two."

"Jesus," I muttered, as the two Tuareg sentries stood up to announce their positions. At least the deuce-and-a-halfs were facing our convoy. That meant the Tuareg were planning for us to drive them away, as agreed. Or maybe it didn't mean anything.

"Lock and load," I said, as we approached firing range. "Stay frosty."

Manners were important to the Tuaregs. This was a planned meeting; it had to be approached with respect and trust. That meant guns pointed down. Out here, respect meant security . . . if you crossed a line, quite literally, the knives came out.

"Roger that, Charlie One," Miles replied.

I didn't need to tell him anything else. I was the mission leader, but Miles, as always, was in tactical command. He chose the men, mixing and matching skills as mission parameters required. These Alphas were all Tier One operators recruited from the elite of the elite: Navy SEALs, Army Delta, British SAS, Thai special forces, Ugandan Presidential Guard, El Salvador counterdrug hit squad, the best money could buy. I had worked with some of them for years, others just this month. But we understood each other. In this line of work, danger breeds respect and respect breeds love, faster than a fungus. At this point, they were practically family. But even if they'd been strangers, I trusted Miles. He was my brother-in-arms; he'd been protecting my ass since 1992, when I was fresh meat out of officer training and he was my platoon sergeant. Twenty-two against ten, if it came to that, wasn't particularly dangerous for this team. But it was poor operational planning, and that was on me.

"Move to staggered formation," Miles said. "Alpha Three on overwatch. Alpha Two on me."

The Land Cruisers fanned out, the drivers approaching at a flat angle to face the Tuareg, then turning and stopping in unison with their grills facing the way we had come. In a combat situation, parking mattered. You never wanted to back up. You always chose cover. The embankment would offer protection for our two most important assets: men and engine blocks.

I checked my pistols, being an ambidextrous shooter. Everyone else was kitted out with body armor and heavy weapons. I was wearing mercenary business attire—sunglasses, desert boots, 5.11 cargo pants, a web belt, a super 80 button-down Oxford shirt, and bespoke blue linen sport coat from Jermyn Street in London. No Kevlar vest or assault rifle. A few years ago, I was a Tier One operator, too, but I was corporate now.

I adjusted my earpiece and slid the nine-mils into their dual holsters at the small of my back, the only place my sport coat would hide them. Corporate, but not foolish.

"Ready?" I asked the interpreter. The man nodded weakly. He was in his fifties, dressed in cheap slacks and a short-sleeved button-down shirt. He looked like what he was: a linguistics professor forced into this dangerous job by the ongoing disintegration of Libyan society.

Another weak link, I thought. But what I said was, "Don't worry. You'll be fine. This is a friendly transaction."

I stepped out of the Land Cruiser and walked toward the warehouse, trusting my men enough to keep my eyes on the Tuareg. A few older fighters, but mostly young men. Kalashnikovs slung, but close at hand. There were a few traditional sky-blue robes, beautiful in their simplicity, but most of the men were wearing mismatched desert fatigues. All but one was wearing a black turban. This wasn't religious. The Tuareg weren't zealots. In this climate, turbans were a necessity against sand and sun.

I was disappointed but not surprised they hadn't brought their camels.

"*As-salaam alaykum,*" I said, greeting the Tuareg at the entrance. The building had no ceiling, but faded Italian graffiti was still visible on the walls, probably from the soldiers condemned to live in this hole when Mussolini tried to control this desert.

The man nodded, pulling aside the rug that shielded the empty doorway. I stepped inside. The Tuareg had swept the room, strung a cloth tarp for shade, and placed five rugs in a circle in the center of the space. Three men in blue robes were sitting on the rugs, watching me. They seemed to have been sitting for days.

"*Marhaba*," the old man in the middle said, and touched his forehead in the traditional greeting. His face was grizzled and his teeth rotten. That was typical of the Tuareg, who drank mostly sugared tea.

The man gestured to an empty rug, and I sat cross-legged before him. The interpreter sat beside me. It was traditional to take off your shoes, but I had no intention of removing my desert boots. I noticed the Tuareg hadn't removed theirs.

We waited, watching each other, saying nothing. These were among the fiercest fighters in the world, but also the most civil. They had survived in this desert for centuries, and their customs were ancient, especially compared with the West. Patience was the Tuareg way.

Finally, the leader nodded. A man appeared from the doorway, carrying a long, slender brass pot. He squatted beside us and lined up four small glass cups on the ground. He placed a lump of sugar in each one, then poured boiling tea slowly over each lump from the long brass spout.

He waited, then poured the tea back into the pot. He repeated the process, this time raising and lowering the ornate kettle as he poured, arcing the tea into the glasses. My interpreter spoke to the Tuareg leader, and the man to his right responded, but there was no need for translation. It sounded like small talk. Perhaps the interpreter was wondering about his lack of a cup. But he wasn't a person here, only a mouthpiece. That was also the Tuareg way.

Finally, after ten minutes of pouring, the teasmith passed out the cups. I took my tea. It was scalding hot, but I drank it without expression. It was sweet and minty.

Sugar cookies followed, then another round of tea. The Tuareg sipped and munched silently, their eyes alert, their battered but well-oiled Kalashnikovs at their sides.

Arms deals are dangerous, I reminded myself. *Arms deals are points of contact. All points of contacts can go wrong . . .*

The teasmith bowed. Then he stood, took his empty pot, and exited. The three Tuareg began speaking softly. I sat silently. I would wait until one of them addressed me, and then enter the conversation.

Don't lose focus. Don't forget the danger . . .

"American?" the Tuareg leader asked.

I nodded solemnly. "A colleague," I replied, stopping to allow the interpreter to repeat my words in Berber. "We have traveled far to meet you."

The Tuareg nodded. They had also traveled far. "Where are you fighting?"

"In the north. Beyond the desert. This is not our fight."

It wasn't the Tuaregs' fight, either. It had been forced on them by European boundaries and the implosion of Gaddafi's regime. This desert was their homeland, and also where the Libyan army dead-enders had withdrawn when there was nowhere else to go. The weapons cache outside had almost surely been Gaddafi's at one time.

The old Tuareg nodded approval. The man on his right spoke.

"Let's go to the trucks," the interpreter said, clearly relieved.

There was no need to negotiate. The terms had been fixed by our mutual friend in Benghazi. No doubt we had overpaid.

Outside, it seemed as if no one had moved, but I spotted Miles in the lead position and surreptitiously extended three fingers on my right hand, telling him all was as planned. Speaking through the earpiece would have raised Tuareg suspicion.

I walked to the two cargo trucks. They were 1960s Soviet, probably taken from Algeria in a past skirmish. I peeked inside the steel cab. The mechanics looked good, and the keys were in the ignition. The doors were rusted, and the canvas over the beds was covered in dust and patches, but the desert tires and metal rims looked new. They would run for miles, even if fragged.

A young Tuareg in an Atlanta Braves baseball cap stepped forward. He was wearing a Bob Marley shirt under his camos, probably thrown in a donation box by a stoner college kid back in Vermont. He dropped the tailgate and smiled, his teeth already rotten. Societies that forbade alcohol, like the Tuareg, were often insatiable for sugar.

The wooden crates were piled two deep, three wide, and four high. I climbed inside and opened two boxes. SA-18 shoulder-launched antiaircraft missiles, known as "Grouse" to NATO and "Iglas" in their country of origin: Russia. With these, amateurs had brought down helicopters in Bosnia, Syria, and Egypt. An SA-18 was rumored to have shot down the Rwandan presidential airplane as it approached Kigali International Airport in 1994, triggering the Rwandan genocide. Throw a few in the trunk of a car, park within a mile of a runway, and a terrorist could bring down a 747 at almost any airport in the world.

The other truck held twelve Soviet KPV-14.5 antiaircraft guns, wrapped in Tuareg blankets. The weapons were used but passable: well oiled, the action unclogged. When mounted on the back of a Toyota HiLux pickup truck to create a "technical"— the workhorse of modern warfare—these guns were devastating. In and out in minutes, killing everything within peripheral vision. I'd seen it in West Africa too many times.

The SA-18s would probably need new coolant units and the

AA guns some parts, but they were a great catch. I nodded to
Miles as I climbed down from the tailgate and walked over to
face the Tuareg leader, a sign of respect, but also a warning. If
anything went wrong, I wanted this man to know he wouldn't
get away.

"We accept."

The interpreter spoke at surprising length. The Tuareg nodded. Two of my Libyan freelancers emerged from a Land Cruiser,
each with a large Pelican case. They walked over and placed the
black molded containers on the ground at my feet.

The leader signaled, and the Tuareg in the baseball cap came
forward, flashing his brown teeth. He bent down on one knee
and popped the top of the nearest case. He lifted out a plastic-
wrapped brick of crisp, new hundred-euro notes. The poorer
the people, the more they appreciated freshly minted money.
He counted the bricks. The leader nodded, and the young man
pulled a long, curved knife from his belt.

"Tangos on the east perimeter."

The shout exploded in my earpiece, just as the knife sliced
into the plastic. A second later, I heard the *bip-bip-bip* of an
Israeli Tavor assault rifle. Our medic Boon's gun.

"Two Tangos"—meaning targets—"at seven o'clock."

"Eight o'clock."

"Taking fire."

I heard Miles's assault rifle firing in controlled bursts, and the
flat repeat of a semiautomatic pistol somewhere behind me.

I leapt forward and knocked the young man unconscious
with one swing of the collapsible metal baton I kept on my web
belt. In an instant, I had his knife. I looked up, locked eyes with
the Tuareg leader, and knew he hadn't double-crossed me. This
was third party.

I thought about grabbing the closed Pelican case anyway, but turned instead and sprinted for the cab of the first deuce, my earpiece echoing with commands.

"Shooters in the east building."

"Suppressive fire."

"Cover down on Charlie 1."

"Roger."

I grabbed the door handle and swung into the driver's seat, knowing the key was in the ignition. I turned it, and the engine sputtered.

I pumped the gas, the engine revving and then dying. The desert was full of the light popping of automatic fire, never as loud or chaotic as the movies made it seem. I could make out the audio signature of each of my team's weapons, with limited returning shots, mostly AK-47s by the sound of it. We had caught the assailants out of position, probably maneuvering for an ambush, so my men weren't targeting them. They were too well trained for that. This withering barrage was designed to keep enemy heads down, so they couldn't fire back. Only assholes counted kills.

I turned the key again. This time, the engine turned over. I pumped the gas, and the deuce belched smoke. I double-clutched and shifted. The gears ground, but the truck didn't move.

"Where are those shots coming from?"

"Tangos on the southeast dune. No vehicles spotted."

So how did they get here?

"The Tuareg are heading out. I repeat, the Tuareg are on the move."

I looked in my side mirror; both Pelican cases were gone.

"They're taking fire."

I heard the gears grinding on the other deuce, but I didn't look to see which one of my men was behind the wheel. I had one job now, and that was to drive my truck onto the egress route.

I slammed down on the gearshift and heard it crunch, then muscled it into first and felt the deuce lurch, then start to roll. I shifted to second, cranking the wheel to straighten it on the road. I heard bullets ripping into the wooden crates and cursed my stupidity in trusting the perimeter to the Tuareg. My cargo of SA-18 missiles wouldn't explode in a firefight, but they could be punctured and ruined.

"Fire in the hole," Miles's voice barked in my earpiece, as I shifted into third. I felt the explosion, then heard it, and a moment later, the dust cloud enveloped the truck. That was the end of a hundred-year-old Italian outpost.

"Pop smoke," Miles yelled. That was what I wanted to hear. Behind me, the Alphas were throwing smoke grenades and laying down fire to cover our escape while someone, probably Frank "Wildman" Wild, British ex-SAS, howled over the headset with delight.

At three hundred meters, outside the dust and the effective range of an AK-47, I looked back. The second deuce was straggling behind, two tires shot out, our Thai ex-paratrooper Boon at the wheel. I could still hear the popping of automatic fire.

Then I saw the Toyota pickup angling over the hardscape at the back of the incline. There were four—no five—men in the back, firing AK-47s as they came. Maybe local bandits tipped off to the sale, but more likely Libya Dawn or Dignity, the local jihadist groups.

Nothing dignified or dawning here. Nothing Western but their weapons.

A man stood up and lifted an RPG to his shoulder. It bounced as the truck caromed over the rocks, but the man needed only a second to line it up in my direction. The distance was a hundred meters and closing; there was nothing I could do. Hitting anything with the notoriously imprecise RPG was little more than chance anyway, and this man had probably never fired anything like it in his life.

I pounded the gas pedal and held my breath.

Misfire.

I couldn't hear the click, but I saw the man lower the barrel. *Now,* I thought, jerking the steering wheel toward the hardscape and careening back toward the Toyota. Bullets ripped through the canvas and steel, but I focused on a spot just behind the truck's rear wheel, hit the accelerator, and heard a tremendous crunch as the deuce crushed the rear flank of the Toyota. It spun sideways and flipped, launching the men into the dirt. The deuce sputtered, but I ripped the gear down to second and threw the wheel hard to the right.

A moment later, I was back on the dirt road, the Toyota a worthless hunk behind me. My rear tires were dragging, and blue smoke was spewing from under the hood, but the exit route was clear. Only another truck could catch me now.

"Charlie One clear," I said into my headset.

"Alpha One clear," came the response.

"Alpha Two clear."

"Alpha Three clear."

"What about the Libyans?"

"All clear, Charlie One." It was Miles, confirming the count.

"Even the interpreter?"

There was a pause, then I heard Wildman's Welsh accent in my ear. "I nabbed 'im, boss. But God, he smells."

Miles laughed. I knew that laugh anywhere, even though I couldn't see his face. I didn't even know where he was for sure. Behind me somewhere, covering my ass. "Number one or number two?" he said.

"Both."

More laughter over the headset, as the tension eased. Everyone shits their pants the first time the bullets start ripping.

"Any more trucks?" I asked.

"One," Miles said, "but it's after the Tuareg. Probably an inside job."

I thought of the Atlanta baseball cap. Maybe.

I eased back on the accelerator. With only one truck, the Islamists, or dissident Tuareg, or whoever they were, wouldn't give chase. It may not have been clean, but we had the weapons we'd come for.

Another victory for the good guys, I thought as I pushed the deuce into third, then fourth. I could barely see the road through the diesel smoke, but there wasn't much to see. It was all dirt and rocks anyway.

Eighty kilometers later the deuce died. Boon's truck, which had been blowing smoke for the last forty kilometers, limped up beside me. It was time to ditch the deuces. The men stripped our three Land Cruisers of excess weight—spare tires, pioneering kit, survival gear—and started to load them with the weapons, while Boon attended to the interpreter, who was in a state of shock. Thai paratroopers as a rule weren't shit, but I'd hired Boonchu "Boon" Tipnant four years ago because he was a combat medic. Turned out, he was an expert at stealth extraction and hand-to-hand combat, and a hell of a good guy, too.

"Lose the crates," I yelled, as the Land Cruisers filled up. "And the 14.5 millimeter ammunition." I could easily source the ammo in Romania.

While the team jammed the weapons into the Land Cruisers—they would enjoy driving the last hundred kilometers with heavy weapons drooping off the tailgate—Miles and I stepped into the desert. I lit a cigar from my portable humidor and activated my sat phone, then lit Miles's cigar, too. It was a ritual we'd picked up in Airborne in the 1990s, half a lifetime ago, and we'd smoked a thousand cigars together since, from Sicily to the drop zone at Fort Bragg to the jungles of Liberia.

"Lucky," I said, walking through my mistakes in my head. Unknown broker. Late arrival. No lookouts. I was getting sloppy.

"It's not lucky if you're good," Miles replied.

"That doesn't make it right."

"That doesn't make it wrong, either," he said. Miles was grinning. He was past fifty, and he looked like a dentist, but if I was in a death cage match with a crocodile and fighting for my life, he was the first man I'd chose to be with me.

The sat phone beeped. I looked down. I was surprised to see I'd missed several calls. I walked away a few paces for privacy, puffed on my cigar, and dialed the familiar number. A familiar voice answered.

"Monday, 0800."

"I'm in the middle of something."

"It's off. Come home."

CHAPTER 1

I straightened my red Hermès tie in the bathroom mirror, then brushed lint from the right shoulder of my dark blue Harvie and Hudson suit, the battle armor of the corporate world. I checked my shave, realized I'd missed a spot on my neck, and dry-shaved the stubble.

Then I went to my closet. On the right were ten suits, blue or gray, and stylishly cut. On the left were a dozen colorful robes and kaftans, gifts from grateful people I'd worked with in Africa. Crammed between them on shelves and utility hooks was my gear. Three sets of boots—black, tan, and olive green. Action slacks in the same three colors. My web belt, my six-inch folding knife, and my collapsible baton, the extendable steel club I'd used to knock the Tuareg unconscious less than thirty hours ago.

I checked my seventy-two-hour "go bag." I always kept two packed—one for the developed world, one for the rest. My third world bag had been depleted in Libya, so I restocked it with sterile syringes, malaria tablets, batteries, codeine, and other items prized in a war zone. Then I packed my personal essentials: the ivory chopsticks I'd picked up as a teenager backpacking around the world, my portable ten-cigar humidor, and an iPod crammed with classical music.

I had arrived home seven hours earlier after a twenty-eight-hour journey that involved driving the weapons to the desert camp, choppering to Tripoli, and buying a ticket to Rome with cash. I'd showered in the first-class lounge, waiting two hours, then bought a ticket to Washington, DC, and slept on the plane. I figured I'd have a day in DC, at most, and then it was back to the grind.

That didn't bother me. It was standard procedure. I was accustomed to flying twelve hours for a two-hour meal with a client or source, and then turning around and flying home. The information shared on such assignments couldn't be written down. It had to be delivered in person, or not at all.

What bothered me, as I locked my apartment and drove my thirty-year-old diesel Mercedes through Adams Morgan, my Washington neighborhood, was the Libyan operation.

I wasn't worried about the firefight. That was a known business risk. And besides, I'd acquired the weapons at the agreed-upon price, losing only two deuce-and-a-halfs in the process, and cargo trucks were essentially worthless. Yet, by the time I got back to base, my desert training camp was already being dismantled by one of the "cleaning" teams my employer, Apollo Outcomes, used to scrub evidence of an operation.

It wouldn't show, and I'd never let the bosses know, but I was pissed. I had spent six months planning the Libyan job. I had been back and forth between Washington and a fashionable conference room in Houston, Texas, a dozen times. Could this job be done? *Should* it be done? How long would it take? How much would it cost?

I had been the Apollo man in Africa for more than a decade: raising small armies for U.S. interests; preventing a genocide in Burundi with twelve competent soldiers; defeating a warlord in Liberia without firing a shot; "shaping the environment" in Sudan to make way for American foreign policy. Standard stuff.

The Libyan operation was different. In Libya, my goal was to seize, protect, and operate major oil fields, on foreign soil, for an American oil company, in the middle of a civil war.

It was un-fucking-precedented.

That was what traditional soldiers never understood, even my old paratrooper mates, the ones who called me merc like it was a dirty word. Working for Apollo wasn't about the money, which was less than most people thought, or the power, which was incidental and fleeting. It was about doing the shit I couldn't do in a uniform. No red tape. No political constraints, like I'd have in the public military. This job wasn't about licking boots in Washington. It was about being assigned mission impossible and getting it done. It was being dropped into the middle of a war zone with my rucksack and my wits and nobody to look over my shoulder . . . and changing the shape of the world.

I understood the geopolitical implications of the Libyan operation. I had sat through endless meetings in top floor conference rooms overlooking Houston, discussing the big question: what if the world found out?

But the circumstances, as I'd arranged them, were airtight. The drilling station had been abandoned for more than two years. The location was remote. The pipeline ran through uninhabited desert or controllable towns. AO, as Apollo was known in the field, even had a long-standing contact inside the port at Zawiyah, where we would load the oil onto tankers, and Zawiyah was truly a city where no questions were asked.

The light turned green, and I turned past the massive brick hotel onto Rock Creek Parkway, slipping out of the urban environment and into the leafy gully of Washington's hidden highway.

The operation was a shit pile, I thought as I passed under arched road bridges reminiscent of Roman aqueducts. It was a box of mismatched puzzle pieces. It should never have fit together. The job had been, by any reasonable estimate, too much to ask.

But I'd done it.

Three weeks in-country, and I'd already seized the drilling station, recruited a few hundred local fighters, and set up a desert camp to train them. We had more than enough light arms and "liberated" black market UN Land Cruisers. Thanks to the Tuareg, we had acquired the firepower to equip helicopters and technical. Already, we could defend a hundred miles of pipeline, and it was still two days before the Houston wildcatters arrived—the craziest bastards on planet earth, even worse than the Navy SEALs—and slammed the station into working order. If anything, I was ahead of schedule.

So where had it gone wrong?

Not the ground game, I thought, as Rock Creek Parkway bottomed out along the Potomac River. I had gone over every move during my layovers and flights, and my end was clean.

Was the operation compromised? Did someone in Tripoli or Houston leak to the press? Was a major shareholder concerned?

But even if a reporter started sniffing around—and I was sure no reporters had, yet—there was nothing to latch on to. I'd drawn my team from the elite forces of a dozen different nations. My indigenous recruits were loyal to tribal strongmen, who knew nothing of the overall operation. My management group, mere figureheads, were the cousins and other assorted confidantes of connected Libyan businessmen, the type of shady characters paid good money to do nothing more than take the fall, if it ever came to that. All financial transactions were layered through them, then routed through the British Virgin Islands, whose banks were more secretive than Switzerland's. It would be next to impossible to trace anything back to Houston, especially given the cutouts and shell companies I'd created. That was why the Fortune 500 hired Apollo.

What about the U.S. government? I doubted USG was involved, but I knew one phone call from State or Defense could shut down a company operation anywhere in the world. That's the power of handing out thirty billion a year in military contracts.

I downshifted as I passed the Kennedy Center, the giant Kleenex box where I got my opera fix whenever I had the misfortune of being in town, and eased into the bridge traffic. The Washington Monument was behind me, and the Jefferson Memorial off to my left, but the skyscrapers of Arlington, Virginia, rose in front, looming over the low treeline of Roosevelt Island. God, I hated going to Virginia, with its consulting firms and tract mansions and glistening office parks for the military-industrial complex. I distrusted it even now, on a clear morning, at the ass end of rush hour, on a reverse commute, and sure enough, the traffic snarled at the first big bend in U.S. 66. There was only one industry in Washington, and these office jockeys, like everyone here, were policy dependent: consultants, attorneys, think tankers, and advisors, a living army of opinions and analysis.

And yet few of them would understand the Libyan operation. They would insist that we don't seize foreign assets for profit . . . not in the sixty years since the United Fruit Company conquered Central America using the CIA, anyway . . . or since Prescott Bush brokered an oil deal with the Saud family.

But that was merely ignorance. This was the way the world worked. A place like Libya—or Syria or Afghanistan—wasn't a sovereign country in any modern sense. Even before Gaddafi was overthrown, the desert regions had governed themselves. In the end, the self-proclaimed "king of kings of Africa" was little more than the mayor of Tripoli. Now Libya was shattered, and everything from oil fields to "tax stations" along desert camel tracks were run by whatever local racketeer had the muscle and imagination to control them. The Sahara was the American West of 150 years ago: a lawless land where unemployed soldiers, smugglers, natives, and criminals took what they could, sometimes by cunning, usually by force.

Half the world was like that now. West Africa. Congo. Yemen. In South Sudan, I spent four months helping a local strongman with ties to a U.S. congressman destroy a rebellious rival. The strongman's reward was an appointment to the Ministry of Natural Resources. The reward for our client, a large energy firm, was the exclusive right to drill oil in Block 5A—at a hefty price, of course.

I had believed in that operation. The rebels were butchers. I had seen it myself. Then, three months later, I heard the strongman had slaughtered a thousand "Islamic terrorists," most of them women and children.

My Libyan operation cut out the local middleman. A middleman who was most likely a murderer, rapist, and thug. In my opinion, Libya was a step toward a more civilized world, not away from one. It was naïve to think otherwise.

So where had it gone wrong?

Somewhere along this damn interstate, I thought, as someone laid on a horn behind me, and somewhere up ahead another car answered. The traffic was completely stopped, and even the Virginians, who lived with this every day, were getting antsy.

Just get me back to Africa, I thought, as I heard the pounding opening to Verdi's opera *The Force of Destiny* on the classical station, WETA. It was one of my favorites: two men who fought as mercenary brothers-in-arms, now pitted against each other by fate in a fight to the death. A nice reminder that my occupation was as old as civilization and, like Verdi's opera, often didn't end well.

It wasn't my job to question Apollo or its clients, I reminded myself, as the traffic started moving. I was a high-end fixer. I was paid to solve problems in war zones, using whatever means I could get away with. And for the creative mind there were so many means.

Whatever happened after . . . well, it was only rumors, anyway.

CHAPTER 2

Thirty-eight minutes later, I pulled into the parking lot of a non-descript building in one of the endless office parks near Dulles International Airport. I parked my ancient Mercedes in a long line of similar cars and stared at the man-made pond and the picnic table no one ever used, letting the Verdi wash away my traffic-related stress.

This area was the heart of the mercenary-industrial complex. G4S, a competitor, supplied thousands of security guards to the U.S. military from these buildings, and tens of thousands more to domestic malls. DynCorp pulled down more than three billion a year, although much of that was from military-aircraft maintenance. Blackwater became Xe Services, then Academi, then merged with Triple Canopy, a rival, to beget Constellis Holdings, all in the space of five years. My employer, Apollo Outcomes, had been cleaning latrines on army bases in the 1990s. Now it was a private army with yearly revenues of $3.7 billion, most of it courtesy of Uncle Sam, according to their most recent Securities and Exchange Commission filing.

The mercenary business, to put it in technical terms, was hot. The industry had exploded during the Iraq War, not just because of contracts in Iraq and Afghanistan, although those were massive, of course. Just as important, with every national asset focused on those countries, there was no one left to deal with the other terrible things happening in the world. For the U.S.

military, that was the opportunity cost of waging two simultaneous wars. For the mercenary industry, it was a once-every-three-centuries opportunity.

Now, less than fifteen years after the Third Infantry Division rolled into Baghdad, contractors like me were the forward arm of Western power, fighting in every rat hole, brutal dictatorship, and economic backwater in the world. It was, quite simply, the biggest change in the military since the heyday of the *condottieri,* the infamous contract warriors of the Middle Ages. But you wouldn't know it from these shabby surroundings and nondescript office parks, where Apollo and its competitors abutted low-level consulting firms and industrial printers.

And that was all by design. The lack of media attention, the bland buildings in boring locations, the forgettable corporate names and artless logos—it was a strategy. Because to draw attention in this business, even positive attention, was to fail. That was why Blackwater was a pariah, before being sold and renamed three times. The military performed the covert actions the White House would neither confirm nor deny. We took care of the clandestine ones, those the government disavowed if they were ever spoken aloud. Our only competition was the CIA, but we were cheaper. And, in my opinion, far better, because we were so deep undercover that half the time, even the CIA couldn't find us. If you wanted to be a player in the Deep State—the shadowy coterie of big business, politicos, media, and other elites who ruled behind the headlines, beyond government oversight, and across national borders, regardless of who was formally in power, the world where private armies like Apollo thrived—never let them hear or speak your name.

There was a time, five years ago, when I might have been a power player here, a man who contracted operations instead of performed them. I was invited, groomed, *introduced to soci-*

ety . . . whatever you want to call it. But I hated the DC scene: the economy of favors, the double-dealing, the endless scheming in pursuit of a compromised version of a shining ideal, while the shabby duck on the fetid retention pond shed feathers like the plague.

I was a soldier, not a bureaucrat. I chose Africa.

Now I came back three, maybe four weeks a year. Many mercs in the field never came back at all. We were freelancers, hired by the job: cash on delivery, no health insurance or 401(k)s. Old mercs don't retire, they disappear, maybe to some unknown corner of the world, maybe to an unmarked grave. The ones I knew kept busy, taking job after job, so they wouldn't have to face this life, and the people left behind. But I was a mission leader, the point of contact between the men in the field and the suits in the office. My role was to plan the assignments and assemble the teams, so I came here just barely often enough to recognize the frosty attendant at the front desk, the one who never smiled.

"Hello Jane," I said. It had taken me two years to remember her name. She didn't even pretend to remember mine.

I slid my company ID into the bioscanner and held it for three seconds, waiting for the green light, and then placed my index finger on the fingerprint reader. Jane checked her monitor, confirmed my identity, and waved me to the employee turnstile, the one with the NO TAILGATING placard on it. The thick Plexiglas doors swished open. Next to the doors was a metal detector and X-ray machine, with two armed guards. Typical postterrorism precaution, Apollo always said. Only an expert would notice that the guards changed every few days and carried Heckler & Koch MP5SD6s with integrated suppressor barrels.

Beyond the metal detector was a wall—reinforced steel under plaster—with a huge company logo. I walked through a curved white tunnel called a waveguide, a security measure that emptied into a windowless cubicle farm. Cable trays and monitors hung from the ceiling, as kids in their twenties took phone calls in foreign languages. I had no idea what they did, but they seemed younger every year. When I started here in 2002, the cube dwellers were retired older men from the military and intelligence community, whose pants refused to acknowledge their extra pounds. They were refugees from the great defense layoffs of the 1990s, out here by the airport, playing out the string.

Now the cube ranchers were mostly women, because they make better intelligence analysts, and mostly younger than the Cold War–era coffee stains on the old guys' shirts. I assumed that meant they were going somewhere in life, besides the suburbs.

"Tom Locke. Good to see you. How was the flight?"

The speaker was David Wolcott, my handler for the last five years, lurking as always. Wolcott had the look of those old middle managers, right down to the bald spot and the belt that went underneath his belly instead of around. I figured he had a wife and kids somewhere in the suburbs, a barbecue grill, baseball equipment, and one of those fences with the support poles on the outside so the homeowner can sit in a lounger and look at the pretty side.

"It was first class," I said. As always.

Wolcott had called me home, but that was not something we would discuss. He was a middle manager, and this wasn't a business with postmortem meetings or after-action reviews. If Libya still bothered me a few months from now, I might try to figure out what had happened on my own. Otherwise, I left the past alone.

"Coffee?" Wolcott asked.

"No thanks."

"I don't blame you, Tom. It's garbage. No one has cleaned the pot in a year."

We passed the cube farm and turned down a hallway, where I left my cell phone on a table with twenty others, as required. The next door was steel, with a large combo lock, keypad, and camera. Inside was the Tactical Operations Center, or TOC, a large, windowless room of computer monitors running mission status updates, live team feeds, satellite imagery of areas of interest, and video conferencing with company managers around the world. The TOC was a 24/7 war room, complete with top secret government clearance and immediate access to every operative in the world, and it was the worst job at Apollo: cramped, dark, underventilated and underpaid.

Ten paces further, Wolcott stopped in front of an office suite, opened the door, and motioned me through without a word.

"Brad Winters," I said, as Wolcott closed the door and stayed outside, leaving me alone with my former boss. It wasn't often I was caught by surprise, but this was one of those times.

"Good to see you, Thomas," Winters said, rising from his chair.

I had instinctively straightened and brought my arms to my sides, a military sign of respect, but Winters came around the table to shake hands. This man had recruited me into Apollo Outcomes; we had worked closely together for six years; he had taught me, molded me, broken and invested in me, and then he'd invited me to join him, as his right hand, in Apollo's executive suite.

But I'd gone back to Africa instead, and I hadn't heard from him since.

That was the last anyone had heard from him, really. Brad Winters had transformed Apollo during the gold rush of the Iraq and Afghanistan wars, when the Department of Defense was handing out $300 billion a year to companies with any sort of link to military logistics or firepower. He had almost made a name for himself. And then he had disappeared.

I knew that meant he'd either fallen out of power, or ascended into the realm where only a hundred or so people needed to know your name. Clearly, it was the latter, and I wasn't surprised. Brad Winters was a dinosaur; he would always be around, even if it was just as an oil slick.

And I wasn't surprised that he looked exactly as I remembered him. That was the man's greatest asset: a manner so bland, he could disappear into any crowd. Winters had gotten his start in the 82nd Airborne—that was a big part of our connection, because I'd earned my jumpmaster wings there, too—and had come and gone from Wall Street before coming to Apollo. His grip had gotten firm in his time upstairs, but the only other change I noticed was the stitching on the lapel of his blue suit.

"I have a tailor, from Panama," Winters winked, following my gaze. "I see you're still shopping Jermyn Street."

My first trip with Brad Winters had been to Brussels to brief NATO officials on a security situation in Africa. When we met at Dulles airport, he had eyed my Brooks Brothers suit and tasseled loafers and finally said, "That won't do."

We got off during a stopover at Heathrow and took a cab to Jermyn Street, off Saint James Square, the ground zero of gentlemen's clothing. We walked into several modest-looking shops, where the staff greeted him by name.

Several hours later, I had four bespoke suits on order, nine tailored shirts, an overcoat with a velvet collar, two pairs of John Lobb shoes, a breast pocket wallet, and some Hermès ties and sterling silver cufflinks. It cost me two months' salary, including danger pay, but at least Apollo paid for the connecting flight we'd missed.

Now Winters laughed, and I realized I'd glanced down at his shoes. Most men skimped on footwear, because it was expensive. The shoes I had on this morning cost more than what a Washington bureaucrat takes home in a month. Winters's shoes cost even more.

"I'm glad you haven't turned your back on everything I taught you," Winters said.

I let the remark slide, made a mental note to be more careful with my gaze, and took a seat. If Winters had come down from the mountain, this was important. But I didn't expect to find out a damn thing about it here. In the army, it had been two-hour mission briefings, with a thick PowerPoint presentation and six outside experts. It was death by detail.

At Apollo, it was eight minutes if you were lucky. And no note taking. The company's unofficial motto was: "Figure it out."

"That was solid fieldwork in Libya," Winters said. "I'm sorry it didn't pan out. I know your other recent missions have been . . . less than satisfactory."

It had been a rough few years of muscle work, the kind of cheap intimidation and sudden violence that was beneath a man of my skills. I had started to wonder if I'd been forgotten, or taken for granted. Winters was telling me, straight off, that I hadn't.

"I recently talked to State," he said, tipping his chair back in a show of disdain for that august department. "There's an opportunity in Ukraine. Short term. Creative. Off the books. Your kind of mission, Thomas."

"Why me?"

I had operated in the Balkans during the '90s as a soldier in U.S. Special Operations Forces, and later transacted arms deals in Eastern Europe for Apollo, but my area of expertise was a thousand miles and a continent away.

"You're the best man for the job," Winters said, like it was a simple statement of fact, which of course it was. "The U.S. and its allies are getting run over by Putin"—*That's an understate-*

ment, I thought, *the man just straight out stole Crimea*—"and clients are being dragged down. This conflict is bad for business."

We must be in a new business, I thought, but I said, "I'm no Putin man, Brad." First name. Power move. You don't intimidate me, old mentor. "Surely you have someone in-country." Vladimir Putin was a field of study. There had to be a dozen company operatives, at least, whose careers were built on him and his cronies. And if I knew Brad Winters, he probably already had a half a hundred Tier One operators in the combat zone.

"This is improvisation, Thomas. I need a military artist. The last thing I want is a Putin man."

I thought of the first time I'd talked to Brad Winters. I was walking across Harvard Yard in the fall of 2001, a year out of special operations forces and a month into my first term as a graduate student at the Kennedy School of Government. "The Army's no place for a young man like you," my commanding officer had advised me. "It's all peacekeeping and politics now. You'll be wasting your career. Go to school. Spend a few years studying. There's a position at State waiting for you." By State, he meant CIA.

A week in, I was bored to tears. I wanted to be where the action was, not doing problem sets for my econometrics class. Then the planes hit the Twin Towers, and all my plans came crashing down. I was outside the Widener library when I received the call.

"You don't know us," Winters said, "but we know you. How would you like to save the world?"

What is this, a joke? I thought.

Two days later, I was drinking cognac in the presidential palace of the Central African country of Burundi. Hutu extremists were massing along the border. They were planning to assassinate the president, the small prim man sitting quietly across from me, and reignite the Hutu-Tutsi conflict that had ravaged neighboring Rwanda years before. I had six weeks, at most, to prevent a genocide, and nobody trusted the Burundian army. Nobody trusted the presidential guard. Nobody, even the U.S. ambassador, thought it could be done. That was why the CIA had turned down the job.

Sometimes, "best man for the job" just meant the least informed. And in Ukraine, I would certainly qualify.

"Who requested me?" I assumed this was a BNR—By Name Request. A client had asked for me.

A slight hesitation. Interesting. "I did, Thomas. This one is important. I'm handling it personally, and you'll be reporting to me directly."

I sat up a little straighter. I didn't care if Winters noticed, since there was no use pretending I wasn't intrigued. Even if Winters hadn't been my old mentor, he was a powerful man. You don't turn down pet projects. Or complete operational freedom.

"No chain of command?"

Winters nodded. "Just me."

"Nothing through official channels?" That was the telling detail of U.S. government work. On a straight USG contract, even a classified one, everything went through the embassy— cover, communications, money, weapons. I held a top secret clearance for this purpose, even though, these days, most jobs didn't go through the embassy.

"No USG contact. No company contact."

"A kite?" Kites were operatives that could be cut loose in the event of compromise. The riskiest assignments were always the most prestigious.

Winters nodded again.

Given the lack of actual information, company briefings were about understanding the unspoken. This mission was black, outside even Apollo's compartmentalized command structure.

I doubted if anyone outside of Winters, Wolcott, and the client would know I was on the ground.

"Who's the client?"

Winters slid a manila folder across the table. It contained one page: a picture of a middle-aged man. He was dressed in a Savile Row suit, with a stylish pocket square and a platinum Lange & Söhne precision watch, but he had questionable teeth. He was either minor British royalty or Slavic nouveau riche.

"Kostyantyn Karpenko," Winters said, "a Ukrainian oligarch and member of parliament. He's been our man in Ukraine for the past ten years." It was unclear who *our* was referring to, although Winters had dropped a mention of the State Department earlier. Still, you could never be sure.

"He's a patriot, Thomas. A believer in freedom. He impressed me during the Orange Revolution in 2004, and we worked with him again during the Euromaidan protests that toppled Putin's puppet government three months ago." Meaning Apollo Outcomes sent organizers, or provided tactical assistance, or both. We were experts at manufacturing so-called color revolutions.

"We expected Karpenko to be minister of energy in the new government. President if everything went right. It didn't. Russia invaded—unofficially, of course—and the place went to shit."

I knew Putin was using strong-arm tactics—fifth-column irregulars, soldiers out of uniform, mercenaries—to destabilize the country. Oligarchs and strong men loved instability; that was why the world was unstable. Putin had done the same thing in Chechnya in 1999 and Soviet Georgia in 2008, and both had almost ended in genocide. Fortunately, Apollo was built for these kinds of shadow wars.

"Our job," Winters continued, "is to reintroduce Karpenko to Kiev power politics. To do this, we need to deliver him a victory. The kind ordinary citizens can rally behind."

A symbolic victory, I thought. *Something public.* It had worked in the Eastern Bloc before. Lech Walesa had freed Poland from Soviet rule with a dock worker's strike. "Storm the palace? Parliamentary assault?" I guessed.

Winters shook his head. "Natural gas."

He handed me another file. It contained a photograph of what must have been a natural gas transfer station. It appeared to be mostly pipes.

"Russia and the West are fighting for energy security, the Pipeline Wars, as we'll phrase it for the press. Ukraine is the battleground. Specifically its liquid natural gas lines. Two days ago, Russian soldiers disguised as a separatist militia occupied the Donbastransgas trunkline station in the eastern Ukrainian city of Kramatorsk. A strategic location. We estimate between ten and twenty men. Karpenko needs help taking it back."

Straightforward enough. "Assets in place?"

"Karpenko has twenty-five loyal men left. And there is a pro-Ukrainian militia twenty kilometers away, the Donbas Battalion. CIA contract, Apollo execution. They're all volunteers, mostly policemen, teachers, the usual patriots. Two hundred men at last count."

More than enough, even if poorly trained. But I could see Winters's hesitation: never trust schoolteachers against trained soldiers, no matter the odds. Especially when the target was filled with a few hundred cubic tons of highly flammable gas. I'd seen it in Africa. Someone taps the wrong pipe, and the explosion levels a hundred huts. You can't even count, much less identify, the bodies. Better for the shooting to be over before the amateurs arrive.

"I want prisoners, not corpses, Thomas. Pretty pictures for the press. We'll charter two helicopters from Kiev for the media, and lure them with the tagline: evidence of a Russian military invasion."

"And the real story?" I said, knowing that ink was too slim to cut through the clutter of cable news.

"Karpenko's victory speech, which we're writing. It will be his Yeltsin moment."

In 1991, hardliners in the Soviet army surrounded the Russian White House. Boris Yeltsin, then in a power struggle with other reform leaders, stood on a tank and gave a rousing speech against the coup. The troops defected. Four months later, catapulted to a new level of popularity by his speech, Yeltsin became president.

That kind of moment was hard to engineer. I knew, because I'd tried. But it was worth the risk, since leaders mattered. If the Ukrainians lacked a focal point, they needed their own George Washington. But in a pinch, a Boris Yeltsin would do.

"Time frame?"

"Saturday," Winters said.

Five days. Tough.

"I know it's tight. And the window of opportunity is small. There will be less than an hour between the arrival of the Donbas Battalion at 0600 and the press at 0700." If either showed up on time, that is, and militias and reporters rarely did. "This is an active war zone. We don't want to give the Russians time for a counterstrike."

I sat back. This wasn't how Apollo operated. We took our time. We planned things carefully. That was how we stayed out of the news, not to mention the morgue. Someone was running hot on a unique opportunity, as Winters had called it. Maybe the U.S. government. Probably a business client. Someone was willing to gamble on a desperate man sitting on a lot of natural gas. I couldn't quite figure out, though, why it should be me.

"It's doable," I said, "if the Donbas Battalion will follow Karpenko."

"They'll follow him," Winters said, "I can promise you that. He's partially paying them. You just need to get him there."

I didn't like the sound of that. "Karpenko isn't with the Donbas Battalion?"

Winters laughed. "If he was, would I need someone like you?"

He was flattering me. Making me think of whatever he said next as a challenge, instead of a foolish risk. It wouldn't work. Not this time.

"Where is he?"

"In hiding," Winters said. "Bank accounts frozen. Warrant out for his arrest. A bounty on his head from the Kremlin, under the table of course, but enough to keep him on the run."

"Then how can I help him?"

"We have an inside man—"

"And why?"

That was the difference between being a soldier and a merc. In the army, you did what your commanding officer told you to do, no questions asked. A mercenary could turn down work if he didn't like it, logistically, morally, or for any other damn reason he pleased.

So I expected the hard sell: the importance of stopping Putin, Apollo Outcomes as the hand of the West, even Hitler-and-the-Sudetenland. Winters was a master talker, and this was the moment. Closing time. But instead of pumping me up, he stared into the distance. I couldn't tell if he was contemplating what to say next, or chewing a dramatic pause.

"There are children, Thomas," he said finally. "Young ones."

I thought of Burundi. The new president was the ideal leader for a war-ravaged country: a capable man, a humanitarian. That's why the opposition was desperate to assassinate him. The odds were he'd be dead in a month, everyone knew that, especially him, but he was willing to risk his life if it meant a small chance of a better life for his people. Ten years ago, Winters had handed me exactly what I wanted: a chance to make the world a better place. And I was going to turn it down, because keeping this noble man alive *was* impossible.

Then his eight-year-old daughter walked in and gave her father a hug.

Had I told Winters that? I must have—we were inseparable at one time, and I wasn't as careful about revealing myself then as I was now—because Winters was drawing a line: a line visible only to me. Ukraine now is Burundi then. Karpenko is a good man, a *family* man. This is a war-torn nation's best chance.

"Extraction or protection?"

"Extraction. Their passports have been revoked and Interpol is watching. But we have a window, three nights from now, and an An-12 on station in Bucharest."

A military cargo plane, I thought, mulling the possibilities. The Antonov-12 could take a family out, but it could also bring things in. The kind of things difficult to get through customs. The kind of things you needed for an assault on a hardened natural gas facility.

"How do I find them?"

Winters rose and walked to the door. Wolcott was waiting outside. Winters was the pitchman. Wolcott provided the details.

"We've set up a Sherpa," Wolcott said, wasting no time. "John Greenlees. Former CIA station chief in Kiev, retired in place. He'll meet you at the Hyatt Regency in Kiev at 1400 tomorrow."

He placed a box of business cards on the table. "Green Lighthouse Group. Business: facilitation services in frontier markets. You're the president, CEO, and only employee. We've created a legend. Articles on business blogs, old press releases, the usual. The website has been up since yesterday, but it looks like it's been up for months."

Wolcott placed a thick envelope beside the business cards. I knew what was inside: a debit card and €10,000, the maximum allowable without being declared. You broke the law in this business only when you had to. A fake passport meant arrest, a false identity, a hooded car ride to a Siberian prison. You could talk your way out of a two-month-old consulting business.

Besides, there was no hiding from the Internet. If anyone Googled me, it was all there: paratrooper, special warfare training. I even had a blog, the Musical Mercenary, where I wrote opera reviews. I had been interviewed about it on NPR, of all places. It was best, in this day and age, to own your past.

"The debit card is loaded with €50,000, for expenses. Greenlees will have another €50,000 in cash when you arrive. We'll subtract out for your plane ticket and equipment." They were making it look like I paid my own way. That was new. The company always ran cover for action, but not this deep. "Karpenko will pay additional expenses once you link up with him, anything you need."

Wolcott dropped a gold necklace with thick links on the table. It was old school. If things got bad, I could snip off a link at a time and barter my way out of the country.

I didn't like it. Apollo Outcomes was a corporation, not an Old West saloon. They took taxes out of my paycheck. My employment contract was fourteen pages long, for God's sake—and I was a freelancer. You should see my 1099 tax forms.

"You'll get your standard rate," he continued. "Four weeks worth, plus a 50 percent bump up for danger pay, and Mr. Winters is adding a 50 percent completion bonus." That came out to about $80,000 for a week's worth of work. Arguably, my fee should have been higher. But you don't haggle within the company, and if things went pear shaped, I knew Winters would get me out. Trust is worth more than money when your life is on the line.

"And," he continued, "you get a team."

I smiled, thinking of Miles and the boys. Having good men at your side was the only thing in the world more important than trust.

"I know you, Tom," Winters said slowly, stepping in. He always knew when to step in. "I understand why you stayed in the field."

He didn't. He never had.

"You're right," he said, as if reading my mind. "I don't understand. But I believed you when you said you thought you could do more good there."

He paused again. The man used pauses better than Beethoven. "I know this is unusual. I know it's outside your area of expertise. But it's the big one. The 'good job.' The one we've been waiting for. Forget Africa and look at the big picture. If we shift the balance of power in Ukraine, we stuff Putin back in his box. It's good for our clients and better for the world. Break Russia, Thomas, and we don't just win a victory. We change the future. Even for Africa."

There it was, the Hitler speech, soft-pitched, but unmistakable: *History needs us. We're the chosen ones. This is your purpose.*

He was stroking my ego. Manipulating me, like he always had. But so what? There were pieces missing here, explanations that were incomplete, but my job wasn't to see the forest, it was to cut down trees. If I didn't believe in myself, and my missions, on some deep fundamental level, why had I been risking my life all these years?

Winters rose and knocked on the door. Wolcott entered and handed me a flight itinerary. I glanced at it briefly. One way to Kiev. Three hours from now. Just enough time to head home for warmer clothes and a few appropriate downloads, such as Tchaikovsky's Second Symphony, known as the "Little Russian," after the nickname for Ukraine during the reign of the Czar.

Wolcott handed me another piece of paper. It had my exfil-tration data, handwritten: a time, date, and grid square location. I committed it to memory and handed the sheet back. Wol-cott put it back into a folder with the photo of Karpenko. They would be in the shredder by lunch.

"A company helicopter will extract your team," he said. "Fifteen-minute window. Don't be late."

And that was it. The operation was set. There would be no file, no photos, no written mission brief. And despite the cubicle gerbils toiling fifty feet away, no useful information. There never was.

"I'll see you in a week," I said, standing up and straightening my suit.

Winters stood up. I thought he was extending his hand for a shake, but instead, he slipped me a phone number. "My personal line," he said. "You'll know when to call."

CHAPTER 3

Three hours later, at almost exactly the time Locke was boarding his flight to Kiev, Brad Winters laid his knife and fork across his plate at the Occidental and pushed away the last of his steak. It was just past one P.M., but he had been here for more than an hour. It was time to get moving.

"You got the talking points?" he said to Tom Hagen, the man sitting across from him. Hagen was the only thing more synonymous with Washington, DC, power than a private government contractor: a law firm partner without a law degree.

Hagen's story was one Winters had heard a hundred times, with slight variations. Undergraduate at Georgetown (sometimes they were Ivy); Senate staffer at twenty-three (after one or two years of "charity work"); chief of staff at thirty; then a permanent member of a prestigious Senate or House committee; and, finally, a filthy rich lobbyist by the time the midlife crisis kicked in at forty. After that—at least in Tom Hagen's case—came the long, slow decline, something Winters had long ago decided was attributable to a lack of both ambition and imagination. He'd seen it too often, from too many people who had cashed out and lost their way. Never make your goal something you can achieve.

"I've got them," Hagen said, knocking back the last of his Sancerre. "It's more than stopping a tyrant. It's energy security. Ukraine has Europe's third largest shale reserves. Putin is imperiling the world economy."

"Freedom gas," Winters said slowly, as you would while teaching a toddler. "Ukrainian gas means freedom from the Soviet threat. Freedom gas."

"I'll start with members from Texas and Louisiana," Hagen said, ignoring the condescending tone. "We'll establish the Friends of Ukraine." Politicians were forever creating informal groups around newsworthy issues—the Friends of the Farmer, the Friends of Coal, the Friends of Real Americans.

"I know a crisis communications firm on K Street for the public angle. We'll create a 501(c)(3) non-profit organization called . . ." Hagen paused, thinking ". . . the U.S.-Ukraine Democracy Alliance."

"Good." Throwing democracy in a name was always a good idea.

"It will be a media platform and attack dog, going after the White House and critics, saying things Congress won't. Don't worry, the firm is clever, founded by ex-CIA. They do oppo research, media hit pieces, muddy reputations. They even infiltrated Greenpeace."

"Make it AstroTurf." Meaning the "nonprofit" should look and feel and, most importantly, sound like a legitimate grassroots organization. "When's the press conference?"

"When do you want it?"

"Tomorrow afternoon. So we get ahead of any breaking news. I want four senators, at least." Hagen started to object, but Winters cut him off. "Addison is already onboard."

Hagen nodded. Addison had pull. "Ten and four," he said, meaning at least ten from the lower house—they were easy—and four known names. "And then—"

"I'll see what I can do with Shell."

Shell Oil held the rights to the eastern Ukrainian gas fields, and they were halfway through an estimated infrastructure investment of $410 million, but they had pulled back because of violence in the area. A Putin victory, or a government collapse in Kiev, would put their leases and infrastructure investments at risk. It was a hazard of the modern world economy and, since the pull-back in government contracts at the end of the official Iraq War, Brad Winters's main engine of growth. Hagen would kill, almost literally, to have a fat oil company like Shell as a client.

"Are you sure you don't want to go through State?" Hagen said, trying to prove his worth. "I can get you in at the DepSec level." The deputy secretary was the alter ego of the secretary of state and the power behind the policy throne.

"I think it's best if I stay out of it for the moment," Winters said. He had no interest in going anywhere near this political charade until it was safe. That was why he needed Hagen.

"As long as it's for the good of the country," Hagen said with a knowing smile.

Winters figured at one point the phrase had meant something, but it was so de rigeur by now it had become a punch line.

"Right now," he said, putting his napkin on the table and pushing back from the table, "I'm in the process of saving our asses."

Hagen glanced up, surprised by Winters's serious tone. "You're a patriot, Brad," he said, standing to shake his hand. "Just like the rest of us."

The waiter appeared with the dessert menu, stepping deftly aside as Winters turned. "On my tab," Winters said, as his eyes scanned the room.

"Bodegas Hildalgo Napoleon, thirty-year," Hagen said absently, as he watched Winters glad-hand a few familiar faces as he left, the hundreds of black-and-white portraits of Washington players behind him on the walls, portraits that seemed to retreat farther and farther away the longer Hagen stayed in town.

CHAPTER 4

I'd seen the lobby of the Kiev Hyatt Regency a hundred times in a dozen different countries. The glass façade and square beige furniture were standard business class, the clean, modern lines not fashionable so much as what corporate architects and factories in China churned out to meet the needs of the world's discerning travelers. Even the painting on the wall—red and green interlocking salamanders, either fucking or forming a faux native pattern, I wasn't sure—could have hung on any hotel wall anywhere in the world. The only thing that would be unique, I knew, was the requisite sky bar on the top floor—this one was on the eighth—and then only because of the surrounding city. Fortunately, my suite had a firm mattress, always a pleasant surprise after three weeks on a cot, and a view of the gold onion domes of Saint Sophia's Cathedral (according to the bellboy) to remind me that I wasn't in an upscale area of Juba, South Sudan, or Wichita, Kansas.

The lobby bar was even more comfortably familiar, filled as it was with the usual conflict carrion. People assume upscale accommodations are deserted in war zones, but in the modern world, where economics trumped politics, reliable chain hotels like the Hyatt Regency quickly became de facto embassies. This is the place where conflict entrepreneurs, recently arrived from Lebanon by way of London or, if I had to guess, the more Eastern European sections of Brooklyn, swapped tips on how to "exploit" the situation, a word that wasn't just a positive, but a life mission.

The diplomats, meanwhile, were slumped into their drinks, waiting for whatever it is diplomats spend their lives waiting for. I spotted two squared-off Germans drinking pilsner in the corner; three Frenchmen at the bar with mineral waters and Gauloises; and two Brits in overly wide pinstriped suits with a little coin pocket above the regular pocket on the right side. Only English tailors bothered with that pointless little pocket.

"Woodford Reserve on the rocks," I said, nodding to the Germans and leaning on the bar between the businessmen and the French. Every nationality has a drink, and the bourbon would mark me as American, something I didn't mind. The dozen or so obvious undercover agents hanging around the lobby had already noticed me; the only question was whether they were working for the Ukrainians or the Russians.

Besides, I liked Woodford Reserve.

"Keep it," I said, sliding twenty euros to the bartender and shrugging off the glance of a barfly with blond hair and augmented assets. She was a professional, but she wasn't working for money. In a war zone, information was more valuable, that was what made hotels like these hothouses of intrigue. Everyone wanted a piece of everyone else. She'd probably be outside my room tonight, hoping to catch me in a moment of weakness.

Her, or another one like her.

I sighed. It was 1340 local time, twenty minutes until my meeting with Greenlees, and I'd been traveling for forty-two out of the last fifty-six hours. Despite a nap in my suite and on the Lufthansa overnight, I could feel the fatigue. But it was a virus I'd been living with for years. I was so used to it that I could sit perfectly at ease at a bar in a strange part of the world and use the reflections in the backsplash to pigeonhole everyone in the room.

There were the misfits: maybe tourists caught in the wrong place, maybe missionaries, who always managed to appear awkward. There were a few wealthy locals waiting for visas or other arrangements they needed before leaving the country. They'd probably been here for weeks, holed up inside except for shopping trips on whatever strip was considered the Fifth Avenue of Kiev. Their children looked so bored, I could image them chewing the upholstery. These kids weren't used to slumming it at a four-star hotel.

At the end of the bar, a small group of international journalists was gathered over gimlets and rye. They were all drunks, so it was too early for sloppiness, but I knew they were already telling the same endless war stories they'd been exaggerating for years.

The young reporters were buzzing, chatting each other up or eavesdropping on conversations. There were fewer of the old guys every year, with their set sources and set ideas and focus on the economics of delivering glass to mouth, and more of the youngsters, although *young* was a relative term. The right word was *underemployed*. Most of these reporters were freelancers, either locals or here on their own dimes—the lucky ones were on a daily allowance—hungry for any story they could sell.

That was why they gravitated toward the nongovernmental organizations, or NGOs, the swarm that followed modern war like the slatterns followed General Hooker's army. The two groups had a symbiotic relationship: the reporters gave these humanitarian organizations press, and the NGOs showed them suitable horror stories for the websites back home.

Even in the reflection of the bar back, I could smell their self-righteousness: their stylishly unkempt hair; their imperious manner, as if they were here to correct the wrongs men like me inflicted on the world; the colorful shawls they'd picked up in the last conflict. Humanitarian workers had an addiction to third world garb, as if pieces of cloth could make them locals, instead of a "warmonger" like me. Humanitarians liked to wear their internationalism on their sleeve.

Just like being home, I thought as I picked up my drink. A job is a job, and even though Ukraine wasn't my area of expertise, all I really needed to feel comfortable was a quiet corner where I didn't have to worry about eavesdroppers and ten quiet minutes with my bourbon.

And then I saw her, sitting with a group of twenty-somethings, their bags sprawled around them on two lobby sofas. Her curly hair was darker and pulled back; her elegant nose just visible in profile. But I knew it was her. I could feel the heat in the pit of my stomach, just from looking at the curve of her neck. Last I had heard she was in Bulgaria working on one of her sex trafficking stories. But that was a year ago. Now here she was, in Kiev, leaning into one of those good-looking, classically un-kempt video-journalists, while staring into the viewfinder of his handheld camera.

Instinctively, I paused, the bourbon coming down to the bar without reaching my lips. I looked down at the glass, collected myself, and looked up. There I was in the backsplash, staring back at myself. The metal was golden, and it gave my face a wavy look, like I was viewing myself through the top of a tanning machine. Even so, I could tell I looked tired.

I grabbed my drink and tipped it back, unsurprised to see her reflection getting larger as she approached, until the only thing I could do was turn around.

"Alie," I said.

"Tom," she said, putting a hand on my shoulder and swinging into the seat next to me. "I hope you weren't planning to ignore me."

"I just got here."

"I know. I saw you come in."

She had lost her roundness and looked harder than the last time I saw her. More sure of herself, maybe, and more fit. I missed her softness, the half inch of give when I caressed her arm, but that didn't mean she didn't look good.

"You look great, Allison. What's it been, eight years?"

"At least," she said, although we both knew exactly how long it had been. "What are you doing here? I thought you'd be in Africa."

"I thought the same about you."

She was sizing me up, and I couldn't help but wonder what she thought of my face, ten years later. What had she expected? Oh right. The way I left, she probably hadn't expected to see me at all.

"Are you still with that little company," she said. "I can't remember the name. Umm . . . Harvard University?" She was digging at me. That had been my cover story, but she knew my real work.

"Are you still with Catholic Relief Services?"

She smiled. "No. I burned that bridge a long time ago."

I wondered if I was part of that.

"You look good," I said, then realized I'd said the same thing thirty seconds before.

She checked me up and down with her legendarily direct stare, but didn't say anything. I hated myself for glancing, but she wasn't wearing a ring.

"Still trying to save the world?"

"You know me," she said, but I didn't. I'd only known her when she was twenty-four, with the life experience of an eighteen-year-old, and nobody is themselves at twenty-four.

"Double vodka," she said to the bartender. "On my friend."

I nodded, to tell him I'd cover the charge.

"So really," she said, glancing around the room, probably to ward off the blonde, who was lingering, no doubt sensing the waft of valuable intel coming off my bourbon and rocks, "what are you doing here, Tom? I'm sure there are plenty of problems in Africa for you to meddle in."

There was an edge in her voice, one I hadn't quite anticipated, and it struck me like a hammer that Alie resented me. Maybe because I left her behind. But maybe because it had been ten years, and while I'd been blowing up oil facilities and killing terrorists, she'd been . . . what? Trying to rescue young girls.

No, that wasn't right. She had gotten famous for those blog entries on Magdelana, a Burundian refugee trying to make it to Europe, but that was six or seven years ago. She'd bumped up to the *Guardian* after that, and she'd made a reputation for herself as a champion of the underclass, especially women. For a while there, she was humming. Sex trafficking. Human slavery. Almost won a Pulitzer, or so I'd heard. But then what? A slowing down, a falling away, followed by a quiet pink slip, or maybe she'd just faded back to the deep Internet and the unsourced pages, the things that would never get past the fact-checkers and lawyers because they were too unspeakable and, therefore, mostly, too true. That was why good-looking college dropouts asked her to look at their unedited documentary film footage— and that was why she did it, even though it was something no sane person would ever do. Out here, with this crowd, Alie was still a groundbreaking reporter.

And I wasn't an ex-lover. I was an exclusive.

"It's not a good time," I said, feeling resentful, as if she was disrespected our past, even though I knew that wasn't fair. She wasn't playing me, not necessarily. She was just leaning on the bar, wearing her confidence like a shawl. I wanted to reach out and touch her shoulder, and tell her I was sorry.

But instead I glanced over her shoulder, ostentatiously checking to see if anyone was eavesdropping. "Let's meet later," I said, knowing she would understand that this conversation, in this bar, wasn't a good idea. The last thing either of us wanted was for someone else to know I was a merc.

"Dinner."

"You choose the place." I handed her my business card, which included one of my real phone numbers. She smirked when she saw it.

"Green Lighthouse Group, Nice," She grabbed a small notebook from her jacket pocket. "Meet me at my room," she said, tearing off a sheet and handing it to me. Number 12, 8:00 P.M.

"First floor? I thought that was all conference rooms."

She laughed. "I'm not staying here. I'm at the Ibis with the rest of the do-gooders. Isn't that what you always called us?"

I thought about inviting her to my suite, with its world-class view, but I'd learned through painful experience never to let an unknown variable into my room. That was why I was meeting Greenlees in the lobby in . . . I glanced at my watch . . . two minutes.

"I have to run," I said.

"It's what you do," she replied.

She downed the double vodka and walked away without looking back, and I couldn't help but watch her go, the roll of her hips just like I remembered it, the heat turning the ice in my bourbon to water.

Then I turned and walked to the farthest corner of the lobby, where it was hardest for others to eavesdrop, and took a seat facing the door. I opened the *Financial Times,* knowing its unique salmon color and English-language format would be a beacon to Greenlees, and let my eyes wander aimlessly over the pages, trying to focus as my mind faded out to the sunset over

Lake Tanganyika in Africa, and the French restaurant at the top of the hill, and Alie MacFarlane stepping out of her dress in my little room beneath the palm trees, the freshest girl I'd ever seen, so clean and bright, like they'd taken her out of the package just for me.

CHAPTER 5

Two minutes later, exactly on time, an older gentleman walked through the rotating door of the Hyatt Kiev. He was wearing tan slacks, a golf shirt, a blue blazer, and well-worn loafers, his thin gray hair impeccably combed. He looked like a retiree on a junket, but he was clearly Greenlees. He had an ease most Americans can never pull off when they traveled, especially abroad.

He glanced around, then walked directly toward me. This was a public meeting in a busy hotel. Caution would only draw attention.

"Dr. Locke, I presume."

"That's right."

"John Greenlees," the man said, extending his hand.

"Pleased to meet you sir," I said, folding the *Financial Times* and giving him my Green Lighthouse Group business card, more for show than anything else.

"Call me John," Greenlees said, taking the other seat. "How was the flight?"

"Not bad. I slept."

"And the cab ride? The drivers can be maddening, I know."

He had a vaguely British accent and aristocratic manner, as if channeling a John le Carré double agent from 1963. Even his teeth had gone British. I had seen it before in Americans who built careers abroad, a subconscious separation from their old lives. It was the CIA's version of wearing an Indonesian shawl.

"Traffic was light," I said.

Greenlees flagged a waiter and ordered in Ukrainian. Turning to me, he said, "I'm having a vodka with lemon. And you?"

I raised my bourbon to show I had a finger to go. A high alcohol tolerance was mandatory in this business.

"To eat?" the waiter asked in English.

Greenlees looked at me, and I shook my head. "No thank you," he said. Then, as the waiter walked away, "How long have you known Dave Wolcott?"

"Five years," I said. "And I've never seen him smile."

"That's him," Greenlees said with a grin. "Droll. But a good man. I served with him in Nicaragua in 1986, before your time, I'm sure."

"I wasn't aware."

"Oh, it's hush-hush, as they say," Greenlees said with a shrug, although no one ever said that. "I was under diplomatic cover. He was military intelligence. Just a title, of course. Nobody ever referred to Dave Wolcott as intelligent."

I laughed. It was true. "You were supporting the Contras?"

"And covertly mining the Nicaraguan harbors." His smile was genuine. It was a fond memory.

"I was in Panama," I said.

"A paratrooper, I hear, then later in a special mission unit in the Balkans." Special mission units, or SMUs, were elite forces trained for the nation's most secret and dangerous work. SEALs. Delta. They were the pinnacle of the military pyramid. Or at least they used to be. Now they served as the Apollo Outcome's favorite recruiting pool.

"82nd Airborne Division," I said with pride.

"What regiment?"

"504th, under Abizaid, McChrystal, and Petreaus, before they made general."

"I remember Abizaid in Grenada," Greenlees mused, refer-ring to the U.S. invasion in 1983. "He ordered his Rangers to drive a bulldozer into a line of Cuban soldiers."

"So I've heard."

"You must know Bernie McCabe from your time in the Balkans." I recognized the tradecraft. It was a question to qualify me. There were no code words or secret signals between colleagues, that was fiction; common points of reference authenticated contacts.

"I know him, but Colonel McCabe wasn't in the Balkans. He commanded Delta Force when I was at Fort Bragg, then went private sector. He ran Sandline International with Tim Spicer, and put down the RUF in Sierra Leone."

"I hear they hired a Hind helicopter for that one," Greenlees said, shaking his head. Hinds were Soviet flying tanks. "Good God, what a mess."

"They got the job done."

"A good man," Greenlees said, perhaps too wistfully. "They were all good men."

I leaned forward, glancing over my shoulder. Alie was across the lobby with a group of charity workers, openly staring at us. So was the blonde. And a couple squared-off local goons. "Do you have somewhere else we can talk?"

Greenlees caught my eye, but didn't turn. An old mission girl, I almost said, meaning a temporary sex partner you pick up in some remote location. But there was no reason to share this in-formation, and besides, I couldn't use that phrase for Alie. Mis-sion girls are women you forget; but with Alie, it had been the opposite. Our time together had grown more important to me, the farther I'd drifted away.

"I have a car," Greenlees said, downing his vodka and rising elegantly from his seat. "Let me show you around."

CHAPTER 6

We bypassed the hotel's parking valets and went straight to the street, where Greenlees had a car waiting. It was a late-model BMW, with tinted windows and evidence of a Berlin green zone sticker scraped off the inside windshield. It was probably stolen in Germany and sold in Eastern Europe, a common fate for luxury cars. Either Greenlees liked to shop the gray market, or someone had given him an expensive gift. A shady-looking local was behind the wheel.

"My wife's brother," Greenlees assured me, sliding into the front seat. Free agents like Greenlees often made their trade a family business to deter enemy infiltration.

"Saint Sophia's Cathedral," he went on, pointing across the plaza. We turned north and passed a pastel-blue palace with golden roofs, straight out of a little girl's fairy princess set. "The Golden Dome, a monastery in a former life. Now, sadly, the oldest building in town."

We passed several nondescript blocks of apartments with the sagging façades of neglected city neighborhoods, then merged onto a major road lined with hotels and businesses. Before long, the Dnieper River was crawling on our left, the hills steep on the far bank. Somewhere over those hills, Putin's hired goons were tearing Eastern Ukraine apart, but from here, Kiev seemed like any other post-Soviet city.

"What do you know about Karpenko?" Greenlees asked,

breaking the silence. This was the real conversation, and there was no safer place for it than his personal car.

"Only the name, I'm afraid."

"He's an oligarch," Greenlees said, "but you probably guessed that, or you wouldn't be here. There are perhaps twenty of them in Ukraine, and together they control over 90 percent of the wealth. Factories, natural resources, even chocolate."

The concrete apartment blocks gave way to a large, leafy park, an archlike Soviet-era monument hanging desolately in the background.

"They're all gangsters, born from the ruins of the USSR. Often, they just showed up at a factory with a private army and claimed it."

Our line of work, I thought.

"Who was going to stop them? The locals? They were terrified. The old party officials? They were bought. Or shot."

It was the story of the world. The strong do what they want; the weak suffer what they must. Two decades in the field, and I'd never known a country any different.

"It was a capitalist's dream, Locke. For twenty years, the oligarchs were off-loading duffel bags of cash from private jets into Cypriot banks, until the European Union shut that down. They buy mansions all over the world to keep their money abroad. That's why London's so bloody expensive." He emphasized the British slang, and talked like it was a personal affront.

"Power makes them daft," he continued. "Igor Kolomoisky keeps a shark tank in his office. When he doesn't like what's being said, he presses a button that drops crayfish meat to his pets."

"Subtle," I replied. It reminded me of Africa. Or James Bond. That was the kind of idea that starts in a movie, then spreads around the world.

"You heard about Yanukovych?" Viktor Yanukovych was the

recently deposed president of Ukraine, and was now under Russian protection in Crimea.

"I heard he had a kitchen shaped like a pirate ship."

"Not a kitchen, Locke. A restaurant. At his private compound. With pirate-themed waiters." While half the country starved, I figured he'd say next, but Greenlees surprised me. "While the price of bribes for medicine went through the roof," he said.

That's the difference between Africa and Europe. Here, a fight between billionaires doesn't mean ten thousand starving children.

"What about Karpenko?"

"He's the youngest oligarch at forty-two, the son of a miner in the central city of Poltava. He was a finance student in Kiev when the Soviets collapsed. Two months later, he owned the mine where his father worked. Sasha Belenko, an old-school oligarch, brought him into the upper tier: factories, energy infrastructure, banking. Karpenko is worth $2 billion on the books, probably triple that in reality."

Probably ten times that, if he was like other strongmen I'd known.

"He's second wave, so he's more refined. He's not above aggressive litigation, debt enforcement, hostile takeovers, but he tries to stay clean. The older oligarchs, the ones who spent most of their adult lives under Soviet Russia, wanted to be Robin Hood. Lovable outlaws. Karpenko wants to be Rockefeller. The Karpenko Group, you probably haven't heard of it, but it was the first Ukrainian conglomerate on the London stock exchange. The traders loved him. Until Crimea. Two billion is the new valuation."

And next week, the way things were going, it might be zero. I wondered what percentage Winters was getting for my troubles.

"What happened?" I asked.

Greenlees glanced at me with his head tilted, like a bookstore owner looking over his glasses at a questionable customer.

"Besides the obvious, I mean."

"He bankrolled the democracy movement."

"And Putin wasn't happy."

"Some of his fellow oligarchs weren't happy. Russia has made them rich. Turning toward Europe will make them richer, but why take the risk?"

Because you were never satisfied, I thought, remembering my six months as Winters's protégé in Washington. There was always something more. That's how you became a billionaire—or a president—in the first place.

"Nobody expected Putin's response. After Ukraine's Orange Revolution in 2004, he let the democracy movement destroy itself with infighting. It took him four years to install Yanukovych. But you know that they say about doing the same thing twice?"

"It's for idiots."

"It's for Americans."

Greenlees paused, looking out the window at high-end apartment blocks along the Dnieper. We passed an enormous McDonald's, half a block wide, a beautiful woman sitting in the front window sadly raising a burger to her mouth as we floated by.

"Do you know who benefited most from the Iraq War?"

Apollo and others like it. Within three years, it had gone from cleaning latrines on military bases in the Balkans to a private army powerful enough to overthrow half the countries in the world.

"Vlad Putin, that's who. Ten years ago, he didn't have the courage to conquer Ukraine. Then the world got bogged down fighting medieval Arabs who lop people's heads off in the name of Allah"—I winced at the characterization—"and Putin seized the future. Chechnya, Georgia, Crimea. Those were all . . . groping. Ukraine has always been the goal. And after Ukraine . . ."

He looked at me, and I could see it in his eyes. Greenlees was a lone wolf, a voice crying in the wilderness. He'd probably been giving this speech for the last decade, with nobody to listen. Conspiracy was the last refuge of failures.

So how did we end up in this car together?

Greenlees sighed. He looked tired. "You don't know anything about what's going on here, do you?"

"I'm sorry. I work in Africa."

"Typical," Greenlees muttered, as we turned onto a wide pedestrian street. Several streetlamps were painted blue and yellow, I noticed, and blue-and-yellow Ukrainian flags hung from a few windows. We passed a woman dressed in some sort of peasant garb, clearly traditional, but wearing high heels. The country had reverted to Ukrainian spellings after Euromaidan, I had heard, such as *Kyiv* instead of the Russian *Kiev*. We are a free people, they were saying. Look at our words. Look at our clothes. We have a history that is ours.

"This isn't a war between Russia and Ukraine," Greenlees said, following the patriotic businesswoman with his eyes, "so put away your quaint notions of country. It's about economics and oil. ExxonMobil or Gazprom have more power than Belgium ever did."

I didn't bother to tell him I'd put away that notion long ago. Or that Belgium had once slaughtered five million people in Congo.

"Ukraine is a battleground between East and West. The Romans and Slavs; the Polish and Russian empires; Hitler and Stalin; NATO and the Soviet Union. And now, Putin. The oligarchs are taking sides. The people are, as usual, the victims of history."

As they say in Africa: when the elephants fight, the grass gets trampled.

"That's why the world is sitting on its hands, even as covert Russian troops pour over the border. Because this is nothing but a buffer zone to them." He paused. Sadly. "And because there are no good options. Every leader in Ukraine is crooked."

"Except Karpenko."

"In the most optimistic view, I suppose."

He stopped, staring out the window once again. "The Verkhovna Rada," he said, pointing toward a building strangely reminiscent of the Jefferson Memorial. "The house of parliament. In the West, they use money to buy politicians. Here, it is more honest. Every oligarch simply becomes a parliamentarian."

We turned right, along a street clearly intended by the Soviets as a parade route. The apartment buildings were so massive, they made the lives inside them seem small. I saw more traditional outfits, loose white tops with beadwork and aprons.

"Instytutska Street," Greenlees said. "Yanukovych's police shot forty protesters here. You can still see the bullet holes in the tree trunks. And the videos on the Internet."

I could hear the sadness in his voice. "What happened to Karpenko?"

Greenlees turned with a sigh, as if I'd asked the wrong question. "His mentor, Sasha Belenko, went over to the Russians six days ago. The next night, so-called Ukrainian patriots seized the Donetsk Iron and Steel Works, a centerpiece of Karpenko's empire. They raided the offices of his Financial-Industrial Group in Kiev." Greenlees gave me a knowing look. "Corruption, of course. That's the official charge."

"Belenko sold him out."

"Three days ago, there was an assassination attempt at a house in Poltava. Full frontal assault with RPGs and demo. Nobody claimed responsibility, but it was Spetsnaz." Russian special forces. "The operation was too precise to be anyone else. Rumor has it there was inside help. Fierce fighting amongst his men. Karpenko barely got out alive."

Three days ago, I was buying arms in the Sahara.

"Maidan Nezalezhnosti," Greenlees said, signaling for the driver to double-park in the busy street. "The center of the struggle. Ten thousand gathered here for two months, until Putin's puppet fell."

Maidan Nezalezhnosti was a concrete park, with a pond at the far end and trees along each side. Under the trees were makeshift tents and barricades, occupied by serious young women and older men in off-the-rack camouflage. I could see sand bags, Cyrillic graffiti, the burned remnants of radial tires. I didn't know what war these people thought was being fought, but whatever it was, this wasn't part of it.

"Where are the young men?" I asked.

"At the front. Hundreds have gone."

"But they'll be slaughtered." I had seen it too many times: untrained men and boys run over by trained troops.

"I know that," Greenlees said, "and so do they. I suppose that's why you're here."

He paused. He wanted me to say he was right, that things were being taken care of. But he wasn't right. I was here for five days, to do two jobs. Maybe they would matter in the grand scheme of things. I trusted they would. But either way, by next week I'd be gone.

"The Trade Unions building," Greenlees said, pointing out the car window toward an empty space of blackened debris. "The Russians burned it down with protesters inside. Seventy-seven people gave their lives. Seventy-seven. And what does the world care?"

Count your blessing, old man. It takes one thousand dead

Africans before anyone in the West even notices. Ten thousand, at least, before the cavalry arrives.

"Thirty-five years," Greenlees muttered. "Half my life. And this is victory?"

I looked out the window, past the shoddy barricades and piles of golden threadlike wire, the steel belts in burned-off radial tires. I liked Greenlees, and I trusted him, even if his jacket wasn't pressed and his shirtsleeves were showing signs of wear. He was a gentleman, one of those old hands who seemed like a throwback to a more subtle time. But his information was useless, something I could get in half a minute from anyone at the U.S. Embassy. And he was clearly compromised. *Us? We? Our?* The old man had "clientitis." He'd gone native, a cardinal sin for a field operative. I knew the company had to go outside its usual sources for work this black, but if this mission was so important to Winters, why would he saddle me with a sentimentalist?

I looked up. The driver was staring at me in the rearview mirror. Sloppy. He was probably a plumber, before Greenlees brought him onboard.

"We're being followed," I said. "Black car, halfway down the block."

"Don't forget about the tan four-door that passed us thirty seconds ago." Greenlees was right. I had been so focused on the black car, I hadn't looked farther.

"Russian FSB?" The FSB was the new acronym for the KGB.

"One's probably Russian. One Ukrainian. They're following each other as much as they're following us."

"I assume my room will be tossed when I get back."

"At least once, probably twice. For effect, mostly. I assume there's nothing to find."

"Of course," I said, as the car started to roll.

Greenlees handed me three prepaid mobile phones to be used

and discarded. I checked them. They were clean. I handed them back. We hadn't used burners in the field in ten years. They were a dead giveaway. My cell phone had been programmed by the company with the right amount and type of contacts.

"I'll stick with a sat phone," I said, not making a big deal of Greenlees's error. "You have the Berettas?"

Beretta Nanos were my favorite pistols for this type of work, small and easy to conceal. No silencers. Noise suppressors reduced range and accuracy, changed the gun's balance, and never muffled noise as advertised. If you want to kill silently, get a crossbow.

Greenlees nodded. "And the other supplies."

I had sent the list through Wolcott before leaving Washington. The Berettas were on it, but so were other necessities for an airlift: infrared lights to outline a landing strip, marker beacons, aviation radio, laser range finder, broadband scanners, and night-vision and field glasses. For an operation like this, supplies were often the most difficult part.

He handed me an envelope of euros, probably the €50,000 Wolcott promised. I shook my head and handed it back. "I'm set for now." There was a decent chance the goons would pick me up on suspicion of being suspicious, and I didn't want to give them a reason to detain me.

"I'll pick you up here at 2100," Greenlees said, as we pulled up in front of my hotel. "Wear your fine dining attire."

Nine o'clock. Damn. I thought about the dinner date I'd be missing with Alie and felt a tinge of guilt. I wanted to see her. I wanted to explain myself. Who I was. Why I left. Maybe, if she didn't walk out after the first glass of wine, I'd tell her that I hadn't forgotten her, even after all these years. That she always meant something to me.

But she was a reporter. I was clandestine. I was never really going to meet with her. Was I?

CHAPTER 7

We drove silently through the sparse night traffic, Greenlees's brother-in-law watching me with quiet disdain in the rearview mirror. No trouble with the FSB, Russian or Ukrainian, so I'd had a chance to shower and nap before changing into field clothes, and I was feeling fresh. Greenlees was wearing the same retiree-on-vacation outfit he'd been wearing before, but now with extra wrinkles, both in his shirt and under his eyes. He looked like he'd been at it for an extra ten hours, even though we'd only been apart for six.

Alcoholism, maybe—it was a common malady in the field. Or maybe he'd been compromised. It wasn't unheard-of for these old Cold War warriors to lose their way when the world changed.

"I was visiting with . . . someone," he said, by way of explanation. "I made promises, you see . . ."

"It doesn't matter," I said, not wanting the old man to struggle on. It was clear that his young Ukrainian wife (judging from the age of his brother-in-law) and decade (at least) in retirement had softened the man Ronald Reagan had sent to lay mines with Dave Wolcott in Corinto. We hadn't even left Kiev, and it looked like my Sherpa was coming apart.

What have you gotten me into, Winters?

We took the long route, stopping several times and making several left turns at red lights to see if anyone was following us, which they were. Eventually, we pulled up at a restaurant, walked through the dining room, and out the back door to another car. Old school. Like 1950s old school. So old the goons following us might even be fooled. At least the new driver was a professional. By the time we pulled up to a field somewhere beyond the outskirts of Kiev, even I didn't know what direction we'd gone.

The helicopter appeared less than a minute later, flying low against the dark sky, its lights off. It was an AgustaWestland corporate model, intended to ferry business executives on short commutes. Limited range. Unarmed. Seating for seven at most. It might have been Karpenko's, but more likely, given that Karpenko was a wanted man, it had been rented in the last few hours.

"Grigory Maltov," Greenlees whispered, as a burly man stepped out. "Karpenko's fist."

Maltov was a classic enforcer, maybe a former bodyguard, probably a thug jumped up to the inner circle because of his extreme efficiency at disagreeable tasks. Every organization had a man like this, and twenty more waiting in line to take his place. The key was finding out whether the boss enjoyed his company or treated him like a necessity.

"Grigory," Greenlees said, stepping forward and extending his hand. Maltov didn't shake it. He just frowned at us, clearly unimpressed. But that meant nothing. This kind of man was always unimpressed. That was his job.

"The fixer?" Maltov said, and I knew from the phrase that he was a fan of Western action movies.

"Tom Locke," I said, extending my hand. Maltov tried to crush it. He clearly understood that in America, he would have been cast as the villain. And not without reason.

"Get in," he said.

We retrieved our bags from the trunk of the car. Greenlees had packed lightly, in a 1990s-era stretchbag that had clearly come out of mothballs.

"We have equipment," Greenlees said, indicating the trunk.

Maltov grunted.

"This wasn't his idea," I muttered to Greenlees, as Maltov packed the radios, beacons, and landing lights without bothering to balance the weight

Within minutes, we were airborne, the ground passing swiftly below us, a dark, endless countryside of flat fields that could have been Kansas or the more fertile upland of Eritrea. I was half asleep by the time we banked steeply and dropped low, a few meters above the treetops. My stomach hit my throat as the pilot skimmed the treeline. It was a common military tactic to fly nap of earth, using natural features to evade radars and missiles, but not like this. The pilot was a cowboy.

"We're near Poltava," Greenlees said into the headset, the first words any of us had spoken for an hour. I wasn't surprised. Karpenko was a wanted man. Contrary to popular wisdom, wanted men usually stayed close to home.

When we swung over the road, I suspected we were close. Even in the dark, I could see it was dead straight with open fields on both sides and a compound at the far end. The edges had been cleared, probably recently. No power lines, meaning they had been buried. We slowed as we approached the compound: a house, a barn, and two outbuildings surrounded by a perimeter fence and six, seven, eight men with AK-47s and dogs.

It would take an army to storm this place, I thought, as we bounced down in the formal garden. I wasn't until I stepped into the mud that I realized this garden wasn't shrubs and flowers, but two-foot-tall weeds.

"Traditional dacha," Greenlees said, sliding up beside me.

"Summer home from the Imperial Period, original Russian Empire. Probably abandoned during the late Soviet years. This isn't one of the homes on our list."

Karpenko owned eight homes that Greenlees knew of, including the Poltava mansion that had been assaulted last week. This one was either a recently purchased safe house, or an early purchase on the way up. Karpenko came from a poor background in Poltava; owning this local emblem of wealth was probably the culmination of a childhood dream.

Until reality outstripped that dream a thousand times over.

Now he was a prisoner to that wealth, with two guards at the front door and a keypad security system. Five number. No scrambler. Amateur.

Inside, there was a security room, with two men monitoring camera feeds on laptops, then a second door made of steel. A guard with a handheld metal detector was waved away by Maltov, telling me even Karpenko's own men were probably being checked. And that this wasn't a job interview. Karpenko hadn't even met me, but I was already hired. He was desperate.

"Captain Locke," a man said, entering the room. He was tall and thin, a generation older than Maltov, wearing forest green fatigues and a 9 mm pistol. I could tell by his bearing he was ex-military, probably Ukrainian special forces. He was almost surely Karpenko's head of security.

"Colonel Sirko," Greenlees whispered, as the man and I shook hands.

The colonel nodded. "Come," he said, like a man who knew three words of English, and had just exhausted his supply.

There were no guards in the inner sanctum, but there wasn't much else to make it feel like home. The rooms were elegant, but damp and musty, with hardly any furniture. The enormous fish tank along one living room wall held dirty water . . . and a large pile of mobile phones. I thought about what Greenlees had hinted at: that the assault in Poltava had been an inside job. So now Karpenko was confiscating cell phones. Good. That meant he was learning.

If the oligarch was paranoid, though, it certainly didn't show. He entered the room moments later, seemingly at ease. He looked like who he was: a businessman. He was wearing a casual suit, tapered cut in the London style, with no tie and unbuttoned cuffs. He was my age, early forties, in Western shape, probably a member of a fancy gym or three, but he wasn't wearing anything flashy except his expensive watch, the same one from the file photo back in DC. Aside from a simple iron wedding band, his hands were clean. I knew he was eaten up inside by the recent turn of events—I wouldn't be surprised if he had ulcers so bad he was shitting blood—but he could have been interviewing a cake decorator for his daughter's birthday party, he was so languid and calm.

I liked him immediately, at least as a client. There was nothing worse than working with a pompous strongman. They had too many ideas, and too much faith in brutality. A man like Karpenko, I suspected, would leave the important work to the professionals. That was probably how he had gotten to the top in the first place.

"Mr. Locke," Karpenko said in a Kensington accent—London School of Economics, perhaps? Hadn't someone mentioned he was an economist by trade? He took the large leather chair; Greenlees took the only other seat in the room. I didn't mind. I preferred to stand. Sirko was standing behind Karpenko, in a protective position. Maltov was standing by the door, a power move, judging by Sirko's sour expression.

"Mr. Karpenko," I said, with proper respect.

"We've been waiting. How was the trip?"

"Long."

"You came from America." He picked up a bottle of translucent brown liquor and poured three glasses. He was checking my connections.

"From Washington, DC," I said, taking a glass.

"You met with Mr. Winters then? He filled you in on the situation?"

"I'm fully up to speed," I lied.

He raised his glass in a toast, *"Bud'mo!"* he said, and I wondered as I knocked back the translucent liquor how he knew Brad Winters by name, since nobody knew Brad Winters by name. But this was a BNR. Winters had named me to Karpenko. Maybe the oligarch was a friend. Or someone with a shared interest, which was as close to a friend as a man like Winters ever had.

"He says you are the best," Karpenko said, watching my reaction to the burning liquid.

"He said the same about you."

Beside me, Greenlees sputtered, then coughed. The liquor really did burn. "Lovely," he muttered, putting down his glass.

Karpenko poured another round. *"Horilka,"* he said. "Home-made herb-infused vodka. A Ukrainian specialty. You won't get anything like it in America."

That's for sure, I thought, as we downed another glass. Greenlees drank in silence this time.

"So what is your plan?" Karpenko asked.

I glanced at Sirko, then Maltov, who were eyeing each other.

"Don't worry," Karpenko said. "I trust these men with my children's lives."

It wasn't an idle phrase. That was exactly what Karpenko was doing.

"I'll exit your family by plane," I said. "Tomorrow night. The plane will come in low, no lights, undetectable by radar . . ."

"Yes, yes," Karpenko interrupted, "I know. But where will it land?"

The question threw me. Had Winters told him the plan already? When? And how?

"We don't have the landing coordinates set. We'll scout the location tomorrow . . ."

Karpenko said something in Ukrainian.

"It's the best way," I said, cutting any objections short. "I have locations in mind based on a map recon and GIS satellite imagery, but I won't commit until I've seen them in person. The plane's landing zone doesn't have to be set until twenty minutes prior to arrival. If the Russians tip their hand, we want to have a backup plan."

This wasn't true. Once we launched the plane from Romania we were committed. It was a one-shot deal. But American military prowess was a power tool. Clients usually believed anything I told them. Enemies usually believed anything they heard.

"Besides," I said, gambling based on the rumor of betrayal and the cell phones in the fish tank, "the longer we wait to commit, the less chance of a security breach."

Karpenko snapped to Colonel Sirko in Ukrainian. "No one has left the compound since they arrived," Greenlees translated. "No one is allowed to leave now."

"Smart," I said. "But that's why Greenlees and I have to scout the landing strips. We need to know what is going on out there. And I need eyes on the landing zone."

Karpenko stared at me quietly, as if waiting for something to sink in. I'd seen that look before, from men accustomed to power, but I never knew what they were thinking. Trusting their gut, I guess. Or seeing if I could be intimidated. It seemed like kindergarten to me.

"Take Maltov," Karpenko said, and I saw a wince cross Sirko's face. He didn't trust Maltov, and he wanted me to know it. Or maybe he just didn't like him. The enforcer and the security chief never liked each other.

"Perfect," I said. "I need your best man. And a car. And a driver."

Karpenko snapped in Ukrainian.

"Maltov has a driver," Greenlees said.

"How many men do you have?" Karpenko asked, looking me in the eyes, something he'd either learned in business school or during a basement torture session. I was guessing business school.

"Just one. How many do you have?"

Karpenko didn't answer.

"Forty," Maltov said, and I wondered how much English he knew. More than Sirko, that was obvious.

"Good. We'll need them tomorrow night."

Maltov nodded.

"What about cars?"

"Fourteen."

"Trucks?"

He looked confused. Greenlees translated.

"Six," Sirko said, butting in.

"What about all-terrain vehicles?"

"What about guns?" Karpenko interrupted. "What about . . . SEALs?" He gestured at Greenlees, then me, then said something in Ukrainian that made the older man drop his eyes. "Do you know how many men Belenko has?"

"More than us," I said, because that was obvious from Karpenko's tone.

"So what are we going to do about it?"

"Stay calm," I said. "And trust each other. Winters sent me for a reason."

Karpenko rose, turned calmly, and said something to Sirko in Ukrainian. Then he turned, looked at me, and walked out of the room.

Typical. Rich men always had unrealistic expectations.

Sirko motioned for us to follow. He took us down a dark back hallway perfect for servants and assassinations. At the end, we entered the servant's kitchen. On a small wooden table were two loaves of brown bread, a bowl of lard, and some cured bacon.

"Eat," the colonel said, turning on his heel.

I was so famished, I fell into the bread, tearing off a huge corner chunk, slathering it with lard, and shoving it into my mouth before I realized I didn't have anything to wash it down.

"What did Karpenko say?" I asked, when I'd finally choked down the crust.

Greenlees looked glum. He hadn't touched his food. "He said he should never have trusted Winters."

"He's right."

"Because I'm old, and you're out of shape, and you don't even speak Ukrainian."

I started to laugh, then tore off another hunk of bread. "Don't worry," I said as I reached for the lard. "I'm definitely not out of shape."

CHAPTER 8

Sirko returned a half hour later, no doubt after a rocky chat with Karpenko. It wouldn't have been his idea to hire Apollo, but he had clearly given his assent, and that was all Karpenko needed to blame him for any problems. Like the cavalry arriving and consisting of a retiree and a guy in a suit.

Fortunately, he had an unmarked bottle of liquor, which turned out to be vodka, so I pushed the last heel of bread aside.

"98th Guards?" I asked, noticing the tattoo on his forearm when he gave me a glass. It was a blue shield featuring a yellow arm, clad in chain mail, holding a sword.

Sirko nodded. The 98th were Soviet paratroopers, but Sirko was pushing sixty, so of course Ukraine had been part of the Soviet Union when Sirko was coming up.

"I'm airborne, too," I said, pounding my right fist on my chest, where I had worn my jumpmaster wings while in uniform.

Sirko smiled and thumped his chest. It was the universal brotherhood of military airborne: paratroopers, rangers, Russian Spetsnaz. Beyond the tough training was the shared suffering, topped off by secret initiation rituals like "Blood Wings" and "Prop Blast." The U.S. Army put a stop to them in the 1990s after CNN caught Canadian paratroopers pounding jump wing pins straight into new member's chests—thus "blood wings"— but to old dogs like Sirko and me, the rituals would never die.

"Airborne," he said, lifting his glass.

We drank.

"Were you in Bosnia?" I asked. The colonel didn't answer. I doubted he understood. "I was in Srebrenica, summer of 1995."

The images came back to me: the beautiful valleys of northeastern Bosnia, the two Serbian "Red Berets" we captured on the road, the terrible beating we gave them, the first time I'd shattered teeth. It wasn't right, but I was raw and eager, and we were hunting Scorpions, a vicious Russo-Serbian militia that referred to Bosnians as cockroaches. Yugoslavia had shattered into ethnic violence, and the Scorpions, among others on the Serbia side, had elevated that disagreement into ethnic cleansing. Even the Red Berets were more afraid of their allies than they were of us, thus the missing teeth, but they finally gave up a location: Srebrenica. It was only forty clicks away. I radioed in the intel, and requested a change of mission to Srebrenica.

The response from military special ops command was instant and clear.

"Negative, Falcon 2-0. Charlie Mike." Meaning *continue mission*. "Drina Valley is UN safe area and no-go zone."

I locked eyes with Miles, my noncomm. "Your call, Captain," he said.

I made the call. I followed orders. We stayed away from the valley. The next day, the thunder started to the east, the unmistakable sound of artillery, but headquarters refused our requests to investigate. For the next five days, I ignored the thunder and Charlie Mike'd like a good soldier, sticking to our original mission, my men angry and mutinous, until I finally said, "Fuck it. We're going in."

I will never forget the town of Srebrenica: the smell of smoke and corpses; the burned houses; the destroyed Dutch troop carrier smoldering in the road. It was desolate, even in the center of town, but there were women in the wreckage, traumatized and starving, just as the Serbians intended.

We walked in double-wedge formation with Miles on point, nobody saying a word. On the north end of the town, the destruction was thicker. We saw the back wall of an old zinc factory, covered with blood. The ground was soaked in it, a long line of individual pools. We stayed off the road. Three hundred meters farther, we came to a fresh mound of dirt. Culver, one of the young buck sergeants on my team, started digging. Within seconds, a hand was sticking out. A child's hand.

Culver stopped. He looked up at me. He didn't say it, but he didn't need to. I could see it. *Fuck you, Captain.*

Later, Miles put a hand on my shoulder. "It's all right," he said. "It's my fault. I'm the NCO. I should have told you to fuck that order."

But it wasn't his fault, and it wasn't all right. Eight thousand Bosnians were executed in and around Srebrenica, mostly men and boys, but for me, it only took one. I lasted another four years, but that was the end of my army career. Every time someone asked me why I'd gone merc, I thought of that dead boy, and HQ insisting I stay the course, and how I could have saved him . . . if only I'd had the freedom or the nerve.

"Srebrenica," Sirko said slowly, pronouncing each syllable. He didn't understand English, but any military man in the Eastern bloc understood that word. "Srebrenica. Bosnia. Dah. I was there."

He said something in Ukrainian, and I looked to Greenlees.

"He says that's when he left."

I remembered the calm on the boy's face when we dug him out. There was a bullet hole in his forehead with powder burns around the entry. Barrel on bone. How much worse would it have felt, I wondered, if I had been on the same side as those butchers?

I raised my vodka glass for another round. Sirko poured. We

drank in silence, each of us lost in our thoughts, until Sirko put down his glass and spoke.

"He asked if you have a plan," Greenlees translated.

"A thin one," I said. "Mostly assumptions."

Sirko nodded. "That's what he figured," Greenlees said, as Sirko pulled out a worn tactical map case with a faded Soviet star on the front and slapped it on the table. Inside were old Soviet army maps of the Poltava area, complete with an acetate overlay showing military graphics and enemy units. In the side pockets were an orienteer's compass, a map protractor, a small maglite with a red lens for night vision, a few markers for the acetate overlay, and two chem lights. A true soldier's kit.

I pulled out my tablet computer and, while Sirko watched, punched up some GIS satellite maps with movable three-dimensional overlays of the same location: population density, satellite imagery, topography, and militia movements, courtesy of the gerbils. My tablet was security encrypted, ruggedized for field deployment, and completely sterile. I would never use it for writing, and it contained no identifying information. It was simply a traveling reference library. It had its own solar panel and could locate a GPS satellite, but it wasn't Bluetooth or Wi-Fi enabled, and it would never connect to the Internet or a cell phone tower. There was no such thing as cybersafety. I had often tracked prey by remotely locating a smartphone. The only way to stay secure was to stay off the grid: Sirko and I represented two means of doing just that.

"Now," I said, as the maps opened. "Where the hell are we?"

Sirko pointed to a blank spot three kilometers from any road, in the middle of the countryside. He had set up this safe house three years ago, he told us with pride. Hired the old couple in the false farmhouse that fronted the main road. Built the fence and laid in a power supply. Even Karpenko didn't know about it. That caution had probably saved Sirko's job, maybe even his life, when the assassins hit Karpenko's mansion a few days ago. Security chiefs don't usually survive security breaches.

"What happened in Poltava?" I asked.

Sirko grimaced. "Bad partners," Greenlees translated. "But they are dead."

I waited for Sirko to say more.

"He told Karpenko to run after the first night here," Greenlees continued. "Before the enemy could regroup. But Karpenko wouldn't go. He wanted to wait for you."

Not for me, for Winters. At this point, apparently, the oligarch trusted his American friend more than his most trusted security man.

The colonel pushed the map forward, pointing to the Poltava airport. Change the subject, the motion said. Let's talk about the future, not the past. So I did, and for the next two hours, Greenlees earned his money translating between us.

By then, I was exhausted, the last sixty hours finally catching up to me. Or maybe it was the buzzing lights, and the linoleum kitchen, and the dead fly that had somehow burrowed into the lard.

"What should I know about Maltov?" I asked, folding up my tablet. I was reluctant to cut Sirko loose; he was a kindred soul.

But the old colonel smiled, or maybe he grimaced once again. "Maltov is . . . *krysha*," he said. "Only *krysha*. Ho *hrabr*."

"*Krysha* means 'muscle,'" Greenlees translated, knocking back a vodka nightcap. "Maltov is only muscle. But he is brave."

Greenlees looked at me, wondering at the deeper meaning. *Maltov clearly saved his ass during the assassination attempt*, I wanted to explain, but Greenlees looked tired beyond caring, and I felt guilty as I watched the old man shuffle behind Sirko toward one of the outbuildings. The exhaustion was coming over me, though, and my sympathy felt fuzzy and weak. It was dusk, and frogs were calling from the trees, and my mind slipped into the pastoral beauty of "At Night," a song from Delius's *Florida Suite.* The music took me out of Ukraine and back to my childhood home, where I used to sit at my window at five years old and listen to the frogs. That was before the divorce. Before my sister went to live with another family, and I talked my way into Saint Thomas Choir School, a boarding school in Manhattan for musical savants. That was back when I would listen to Beethoven and the frogs, and wonder what it was like to live free, on your own. I knew exactly what it was like now, and it wasn't anything like I had dreamed it would be.

"Oh hell," I said, when I saw the bunks.

Greenlees threw his bag on the bottom. "Too old to climb," he said.

It wasn't even midnight, but I dry-brushed my teeth, jammed the door with a chair, and closed my eyes. This was a plum assignment, I reminded myself. Winters was watching. Six years in the bush, and he'd called me back. I needed to keep quiet and figure it out, to come up with a plan for tomorrow, but instead of focusing on the operation, my mind kept drifting back to my first run in an An-12 cargo plane, more than ten years before.

I was bootstrapping a planeload of weapons from Bulgaria to Liberia with six pilots who were drinking homemade Slivovitz, chain-smoking Caro cigarettes on ammo crates full of RPGs, and using a car GPS suctioned to the windshield to navigate the Sahara. We stopped for fuel at an unmarked Algerian military base deep in the desert, and a caravan of camels delayed our departure as they meandered across the runway. We were leaking so much hydraulic fluid by then that I figured we were going to crash, and at least three times we almost did. It was one hell of a ride.

For some reason, it made me think of Alie.

But that wasn't right. Alie and I hadn't crashed and burned, like my parents. We hadn't even bootstrapped to a destination. I'd just gotten out in the middle of the journey and walked away.

CHAPTER 9

Chad Hargrove checked himself in the reflection of the china cabinet's glass doors and straightened the tablecloth—*classy touch,* he thought—one last time. He had been out for drinks with the chauffeur of a second-term Kiev city council member, and his half-finished cable for Langley was still on the table.

The doorbell rang again.

Leave it, he thought. He liked the idea of looking busy.

"Allison," Hargrove said with a smile, opening the door to his spacious duplex on the ten-acre U.S. diplomatic compound in Kiev. If he lived in Washington, DC, on his junior CIA salary, he'd be marooned out by Dulles in a cramped one-bedroom. In the field, everyone lived like kings.

"Thanks for meeting me on such short notice, Chad," Alie said, sloughing off his appraising glance at her body, since this happened all the time to every woman she knew. Hargrove had a young man's bulk and a Matt Damon smile, with blazing white teeth he must have bleached twice a month.

"My pleasure," he said, motioning toward his only chair. He was straight out of "the Farm" by way of Colorado State, or so he'd told her the first time they'd met at one of those American gatherings—a bar or an official function, she couldn't remember which. They had been circling each other ever since, but this was the first time she'd had a look at his life. It was clear the CIA had provided this standard-issue Colonial furniture, but he'd probably bought the big television out of his first paycheck. Everything was typically American, except for the ugly shirt, which he'd no doubt bought at some boutique on Khreshchatyk Street to blend in with the locals. But there was no way Chad Hargrove could pass for a local. Not with those aspirational teeth.

"Glass of wine?"

Maybe, if they were both still here in a few months, she'd ask him for a good dentist. She couldn't remember the last time she'd been to the dentist.

"How about Scotch?" she said.

He smiled and grabbed a bottle of Bowmore, a beginner's top-shelf brand. His father had probably introduced him to it back in—where was he from? Suburban Denver?

"Neat," she said, as he dropped a few pieces of ice in a glass.

She checked his bookshelf as he poured. *Clash of Civilizations. The Tragedy of Great Power Politics.* Some well-thumbed Kissinger and a less well-thumbed Stiglitz. York Harding. They were the kind of books young men read in college; the kind that never mentioned a woman, unless it was Margaret Thatcher.

"So what do you need?" Hargrove asked, handing her the Scotch. "I assume this isn't a social call."

She lifted her glass in a toast. "To information," she said.

"You know I can't tell you anything."

She smirked. So FNG—Fucking New Guy. They loved being secretive.

"Don't worry, this is off the record," she said, pulling out her smartphone. "And only a photo. Just wondering if you know this guy."

Hargrove studied the photograph. It was the Hyatt lobby. Two men talking in the corner, distant and out of focus, but recognizable.

"I don't," he said, "but he's American. Must be new in town. Never came to the embassy to check in. Probably a businessman, judging by the suit. I assume he's a douchebag, otherwise you wouldn't be asking." He flashed the teeth. "What did he do, beat up some hookers in Bangkok?"

Alie smiled to hide her anger. She was still known for her investigative reporting on sex slavery and refugees, even if she hadn't broken a story in years. In some circles, that made her a hero. But in others, it was a joke. Women's issues. *Hookers.* Aren't they funny?

"Not him," she said. "The old guy."

Hargrove looked back at the image, relieved that this wasn't competition. The old guy was American, too, probably the younger man's father, maybe on vacation or some sort of find-your-ancestors-before-you-die . . .

"Wait," he said. "That's Greenlees."

"Who's Greenlees?"

"John Greenlees, an old station chief, put out to pasture ages ago. He comes into the office every so often to talk to Baker, the deputy station chief. They must have worked together, but I don't know, he's in the wind. Nobody has cared about him in years. I only recognize him because I happen to have an office next to Baker."

An office? She almost laughed. She knew Hargrove stamped visas in the morning and spent his afternoons in a cubicle, typing up Baker's cables. It was the fate of all greenhorn case officers who were undeclared.

"What's Greenlees up to?"

"Nothing, as far as I know."

"He doesn't work for, um, your people?"

"Greenlees? No, he's out of the game. But he's got contacts, I'm sure, since he's been around forever. He's burned at the organization, though. Left under a cloud, not too happy about it, I hear. Something about a local mistress."

"Everyone has a mistress," she said.

Hargrove shook his head. "He left his wife for her. A CIA station chief doesn't leave his wife for a sex worker. It's blackmail material. And it's not professional."

She'd heard him use the word before. Professionalism was a sacred concept to earnest young men like Hargrove.

"Sex worker?"

"Whore, I guess. That's the word Baker used."

Which could mean anything. *Whore* was a generic insult used by old glad-handers like Baker, a way to put a woman in her place. Underneath.

"He may have been compromised. That's not something for print, of course," Hargrove said, "although I can't imagine anyone would care. That was years ago. And I assume nothing was proven, or they would have pulled his passport. But you know how rumors are. They can ruin a career."

She knew he intended to stay clean, but she also knew he wasn't above exploiting a rumor or two, if the timing was right. That's what reporters were for.

"Any idea where to find him?"

Hargrove shrugged. "At the embassy, I suppose. He comes in every now and then. I could ask Baker."

"No," she said too quickly, and saw Hargrove hesitate. He was an ambitious FNG; he wouldn't miss the implication that this was important to her. But there was no use not nailing it down.

"Can you just let me know if he comes in?" she said too casually.

Hargrove reached for the bottle of Scotch. She had been right about him, she thought as she watched him pour. He was well built. Wide, but in a bulldog way, unlike Locke, who was lean.

And Hargrove was fresh. Clean. He had good instincts and a sharp eye, and he wanted to learn. He was a young man who could be molded—who *wanted* to be molded—if a woman knew how to handle him.

"So who's the other guy?" he said, handing her a glass.

It was almost too easy.

She handed him Locke's card, with its bullshit consulting business. "It seems legit, but he's ex-military. I knew him years ago. In Africa."

"Knew him?"

She shook her head. "Just because I used to be a nun—"

"I know," Hargrove said.

And I know you love it, Alie thought. She licked her lips and sipped her Bowmore. "Everybody makes bad decisions, right?"

She was laying it on thick, but what the hell. She had been flirting with Hargrove for weeks, practically since he arrived in Kiev, and the longer something like that goes on, the more inevitable it becomes. And besides, she was lonely. It was a hard life on the road, where every story was temporary and every relationship short-lived. If she didn't sleep with sources like Hargrove, who would she sleep with? Those were the only people she knew anymore.

"You don't think he's a merc, do you?" she asked. One of the CIA's new jobs was supervising the contractors hired to do what the Agency used to do.

"You know I can't talk about that."

Which meant he had no idea who Locke was. "I'm just saying, Chad, you wouldn't believe some of the things this guy did in Africa."

"You wouldn't believe some of the things I've done."

Like getting drunk with mistresses and junior staffers? Or taking mental notes at cocktail parties? Or paperwork? First-year agents were so enthusiastic about their paperwork. Spotting new agents to recruit. Running human networks. They never realized the bosses back in Langley didn't read reporting by FNGs.

She let it drop, turning her back and wandering the room, fingering a few of his books. He wasn't brilliant, but he was a hard worker. Very organized. Passably neat. Probably boot-strapped himself to top of his class at the Farm. Even though he spoke Russian and Ukrainian, he probably wanted an assign-ment to the Middle East, because everyone did, that was where the promotions were. Europe was over. Nothing but old-timers. But then he stumbled into this Ukraine crisis, and all those old movies came back. Dead drops in Nyvky Park; midnight meetings under bridges; surveillance of Soviet operatives. There was something romantic about fighting the Russians. It was the KGB, after all, who killed that poor man in London with the poisoned umbrella.

And all he had been doing for the past three months was stamping visas in the consular section and meeting with schnooks. Then Locke comes along, and she drops an opportu-nity right into his overeager lap.

If she'd stopped to think about it, she would have realized she was in a similar place: jammed in a career cul-de-sac and latching on to Locke as a way out. But Alie had stopped think-ing about her motivations years ago. It was less painful that way.

"I'm doing you a favor," she said.

"What?"

Wrong tactic. Let him think he's doing the favor. "I said don't forget me, Chad. When you're in the field."

"I can't take you into the field, Alie."

We'll see, she thought, setting down her drink. She knew it was time to leave. There wasn't much more she could do to set the hook. She already had the first half of what she'd come for—Greenlees's name—even if, when she'd arrived, she hadn't been acknowledging the second.

Even now, it didn't cross her mind, at least not the conscious part, that her next decision had anything to do with Thomas Locke standing her up three hours ago.

But Hargrove understood. He was grinning behind his Bowmore, contemplating what to say next. She almost rolled her eyes. *You can't let them think everything is their idea,* she thought, as she put down her glass and stepped toward him.

"I've never been with an older woman," he said, sliding his hand around her waist.

Don't blow it, she thought. *I'm only thirty-four.*

CHAPTER 10

Nikolay Balashov, known as the Wolf, squinted as he entered the dark club in downtown Poltava. Last night, it had been thumping so loudly it could have shaken the radar installations in Stalingrad, he thought, with quick nostalgia for that old town name. This morning, it felt like this hole of a country: dreary and depressing, the bartender half asleep, the women slumped apathetically at the tables.

He walked slowly along the empty bar, the bartender not even moving from his slouch, until he saw what he was looking for: the red dress, the one so short that it barely covered her. She was with Ivan in the back, as he knew she would be, four men and two women, drinking *horilka* at 7:45 A.M.

She looked up and saw him. For a moment, she held his gaze. He didn't change his pace. She leaned in and said something to Ivan, who laughed.

He didn't care what she thought of him. She was an idea, one that recurred every few months in a dozen different faces. Dark hair, small nose. Hard bones. He didn't care about her red lipstick or her short dress, and he didn't mind her vicious smile. She was a denizen of this world, but then again, so was he. He liked the idea of some rough, violent romance that would shatter that part of her. A romance that would never occur, and that he would never act upon. Not *and,* he thought, *because* he would never act on it. He would never even ask her name.

"La Rus," Ivan said with mock surprise, as the Wolf approached the table. Ivan was enormous and blockheaded, so he never had any use for subtlety. He was Belenko's enforcer; he came with the oligarch's contract to find the traitor Karpenko. The million-dollar reward being offered by Putin's FSB, though, was the Wolf's real reason for being here.

"I'm shutting it down. The club is off-limits."

"Why, La Rus?" The Wolf wasn't sure where Ivan had heard that phrase for Russians, but it was an insult. "Are we finally going to do something?"

Typical. Foot soldiers always thought of the fight as the work. It was the part, after all, that was glorified in the old Soviet film footage. The stand outside Leningrad. The tanks on fire. The endless fistfights and car chases of American movies.

But it was these moments, the maneuvering before the encounter, when a true soldier thrived. The Wolf had learned that lesson from Sun Tzu and practiced it himself, in every battle of the last thirty years, from the mountains outside Kandahar to the shattered apartment blocks of Grozny and Tbilisi.

He was from the lost generation, the foot soldiers who had fought in Afghanistan in the late 1980s, at the tail end of the world's last great empire, when troglodyte commanding officers had plowed relentlessly ahead, in the old Soviet style, leveling villages and slaughtering the population to kill a few insurgents. He had watched helplessly as men like Andrei Sirko, his commanding colonel, turned the tribes against them and good Russian soldiers to heroin, and even now, thirty years later, he hated those incompetent commanders for the humiliation: the greatest country on earth, with the greatest weapons in the history of the world, brought low by primitives with a few Stinger missiles.

And then, a few months after their retreat from Kandahar, the Berlin Wall had come down, and the Soviet Union soon after. He had spent a month on his army base in Bolgrad, getting smashed on vodka and cursing men like Colonel Sirko. He spent the next two months thinking the Soviet Empire was better off dead, and the next two years watching corrupt politicians sell state-owned factories; corrupt senior military officers sell off state munitions; and hardliners in the Red Army stage a coup for the honor of the Motherland . . . only to be upstaged by Boris Yeltsin, the Politburo's drunk.

After the coup, he lost hope. The army was in tatters. The KGB and security systems dissolved. He considered joining the new society, working as a bodyguard for the emerging capitalist class, but Sirko saved him. He had seen one of the new oligarchs on television, not Karpenko but one of the Russian bears, and behind him, for a moment, he had glimpsed Col. Andrei Sirko, with his rigid military bearing, and he knew that world wasn't for him.

So he lit out for the Balkans when Yugoslavia collapsed. He was the Lone Wolf then, *odinokiy volk*, quarrelsome and surly, fighting for the Serbs but fighting, really, without cause or country. He didn't fit it in the new world, he had decided, and he didn't want to. He was a soldier. Fighting was his life.

But he discovered something else in Bosnia, besides the cleansing power of war. He discovered that there were others like him. Thousands of others. Tens of thousands, even, young soldiers cut loose by the collapse of the empire, angry and lost, looking for money and adventure and trained in the rudiments of war.

By Chechnya, five years later in 1999, Nikolay Balashov was the Wolf, a conflict entrepreneur. He had a way of drawing other displaced men to his side: old Soviet soldiers and KGB officers, pro-Moscow Chechyans, fighters from the Caucuses and the "Stans." It was a slaughter in Chechnya; they had shelled

Grozny like the Nazi's shelled Stalingrad. They had terrorized the populace and burned the rebel provinces to the ground. But that was what his generation needed. They needed to purge.

That was what Putin understood. That the old structures had to be torn down. That his base of power was a lost generation looking for a hard hand to guide it . . . empower it . . . and turn it loose. It didn't matter anymore that the Russian military was a mess. Russia had Putin now, and Putin knew there were better ways.

Chechnya. Georgia. Crimea. Ukraine. Putin's wars, but also the Wolf's. Together, they would take back their empire, one destroyed country at a time, because that was what they had been born to do.

Young men like Ivan, they would never understand. They weren't soldiers; they hadn't been raised with honor. They were thugs, born into the new world the Wolf had created. They valued nothing but money, worked for no one but the businessmen. They didn't love the rough, violent romance of war, like true soldiers. They didn't know how to maneuver before a fight.

"Give us an hour, La Rus," Ivan said, calling the Wolf back to this club, this dirty town, this fight. "What can that harm?"

"There's always time for one more," the woman in the red dress said lasciviously.

"Never speak to me," the Wolf snapped. He could feel his heat rising—at the woman for speaking, at Ivan for his ignorance. What was the point of living like this? Without pride or purpose?

"One hour," he said. "Make sure your men are ready."

He turned and walked away. He wasn't worried. Ivan would follow orders. And in the end, he would get his fight. Karpenko was a hunted man. He needed to get out of Eastern Europe, to Vienna at least, and Vienna was 1,300 kilometers away. Even

Warsaw, not safe but a doorway to the West, was seven hours. An oligarch would never risk such a drive. He would go by air, by the helicopter that the Wolf's men—his real men, not Belenko's goons—had heard landing somewhere north of Poltava last night. And anything that could be flown out could be shot down.

All it took was professionals, and an intelligent plan. The Wolf was eager to show his old commander, Colonel Sirko, that this former foot soldier had bested him in both.

CHAPTER 11

"Good morning," Karpenko said, as I walked into the kitchen. It was 0600 and not yet full light. I hadn't expected to see him this early. But what was life without surprises?

Maltov handed me a cup of coffee. Karpenko looked sharp, clean-shaven and bright-eyed, dressed in a custom-tailored plaid blazer, English cut. This was the business Karpenko, the man who took meetings in the Square Mile of London and blended in at swank Belgravia restaurants. Or almost blended in. The only people the London upper crust looked down on more than the Eastern European nouveau riche were African princes who bought their Ferraris with humanitarian aid money.

"I apologize for last night," he said, surprising me again. Warlords never apologized. Even Winters never apologized. Unless there was an angle. "I have been under stress, I admit." His slightly stilted English was unnerving, like a serial killer. I glanced at Maltov, but the enforcer didn't blink. "But of course you know that. That's why you're here." He paused. "Are you a father?"

Not in this life. "No."

He smiled. "The sacrifices we make."

We walked outside into the chilly morning air. In an alley between the barn and an outbuilding, where they would be impossible to see from beyond the perimeter, stood a line of twelve black Range Rovers and two bulletproof black Mercedes, a businessman's motor pool.

"No Maserati, I'm afraid," Karpenko said. "My fleet is built for safety, not speed."

So the Maserati is in London . . .

A young Ukrainian with a Kalashnikov, probably in his teens, opened the barn door. Inside were two beater cars, a winch truck, a tractor, a rusty pickup of Soviet extraction, a three-ton truck, and the AgustaWestland helicopter. A farmer's fleet, plus the bird. If the shit hit the fan, that was the backup plan.

"I'll take that one," I said, pointing to an early 2000s four-door Opel with an eight-cylinder engine and a large trunk. It was the worst car in the lot, meaning it was the car no one would suspect. By the time Greenlees wandered out, looking disheveled in the same golf shirt and loafers, the young Ukrainian—Maltov's driver, as it turned out—had loaded the trunk with our kit. Five minutes later, we headed out, stopwatch in hand.

Three minutes to the iron gate at the end of the entry drive. Click.

Nineteen to the entrance road of the Poltava Airport. Click.

Eighty seconds to the terminal.

We sat in the short-term parking lot. The airport wasn't crowded. In fact, it was almost deserted. Which made it almost perfect.

Too perfect, really.

According to Sirko, Belenko had twenty to twenty-five men in the area. They had moved into a hotel in the center of Poltava, across the street from the city's best brothel. Karpenko's brothel. By two in the morning, any morning, they were mostly drunk. But if they had anti-aircraft missiles, their aim didn't have to be perfect. In fact, it didn't even have to be good.

"Let's check the airbase," I told Maltov's protégé. "Take the back way."

Sirko had pointed out the secondary airfield, a former Soviet air force base. Most people had forgotten it, Sirko told me, but he had checked it himself several months ago, and the runway was usable. I was sure Belenko's men had checked it, too, but the location was still ideal. The airbase was eighteen kilometers from Poltava's town center, and only twelve from the dacha.

We skipped the main entrance—Poltava Museum of Long-Range Aviation, by appointment only, Greenlees translated from a small sign—and found a dirt track that cut through the forest a few hundred meters away. The forest was thick, but it took less than a minute to reach the edge of the parking lot. On the left was a low concrete building, with an abandoned flight tower behind it. On the right was the entry road, a metal gate, and a decrepit guardhouse. There was only one car in the lot, a beat up Soviet-era Lada, but halfway down the entry road, on a blind corner, a Škoda was sitting in the weeds. Belenko's sentries, taking the lazy approach.

As we watched, an old man and an older woman, themselves relics of the Soviet era, got into the Lada and drove away. Belenko's men watched them go, then walked around the parking lot and checked the lock on the front gate. Three minutes later, their car was filled with cigarette smoke.

"Lucky," Maltov said. "No appointments today."

We circled through the forest to the back of the building, then climbed onto the roof. The parking lot in front was surrounded on three sides by forest. The two-lane entrance was gated, and the two-lane exit emptied onto the landing strip. Nine Soviet aircraft were exhibited in a horseshoe, eight imposing strategic bombers and a lone Antonov-26 cargo plane, the two-engine version of the An-12 Brad Winters had chartered.

I surveyed the surroundings through my field glasses: waist-high weeds, a few abandoned buildings and aircraft bunkers, an obsolete radar array, and decaying gun parapets, presumably for air defense artillery. Weeds poked through cracks in the tarmac, but the runway was long, wide, and serviceable. Winters's An-12 was an antique, even by Soviet standards. It had four turbo-props, a glass nose, and 1946 technology, but it was tough and could land almost anywhere, as long as the ground was solid and flat. I'd used the An-12 to ferry guns and other supplies around Africa many times, and we'd landed on worse.

I scanned the open fields. The rusty barbed-wire fence was worthless against vehicles, but the meadows were so rutted that only a ruggedized off-road vehicle could cross.

"You could fly a convoy in here," Greenlees said, staring at the Tupolev 160, a massive Soviet bomber that was the museum's star attraction.

"Flying in isn't the problem," I said. "It's flying out."

Maltov was talking with the teenage Ukrainian, patting the building beneath our feet. "It's good," he said. "Concrete."

"What about the flight tower?" Greenlees asked. It was squatting between the parking lot and the landing strip, as if guarding the bottleneck there.

"Too dangerous for shelter," I said, "but that doesn't make it useless."

It was a good setup: one narrow ingress route from the main road, with a blind corner and thick forests on each side. A sharp turn and a gate at the entrance to the parking lot, which weren't prohibitive, but would slow an attack. Nothing but a narrow road from the parking lot to access the landing strip. Forty men could hold off 150 here, if they were smart.

But Karpenko's men weren't smart.

And there was still the question of antiaircraft missiles. Some-times, a rutted field was an obstacle, and sometimes it was noth-ing more than four hundred meters of clear sight lines.

"Let's check the forest," I said. Greenlees's shoulders fell, but

Maltov nodded to his protégé. He seemed to understand that, unlike in his line of work, precision was my stock in trade. I needed to understand every angle, calculate every distance. Men were going to die tonight. That was certain. Now was the time to get the details right, because once the shooting started, everything would go wrong.

By the time we finished, the sun was straight overhead, and Belenko's men had been relieved by a second shift. We watched them drive around the airbase once, then park right back where they had been before, as unprofessional as the first crew.

It would be tricky. And dangerous. But it could be done.

"Do you have a friend in the city?" I asked Maltov. "Someone nobody would know to watch."

He nodded.

"What about cargo trucks?"

"I can get what you need."

"C-4?"

He smiled. "How many kilos?"

We drove by an indirect route through the industrial section of Poltava, sticking to residential roads. There were hardly any cars, and steel metal shutters covered the windows. The town was a shithole in the faded industrial style, all rust and concrete and scraggly vegetation, the kind that absolutely refuses to die. No wonder so many people looked back on the Russian years with fondness.

"Here," Maltov said.

Maltov's friend ran a small grocery, with local specialties in front and a counter for beef buns and cabbage rolls in the back. There were a few men lounging on folding chairs, but nobody was eating, and I suspected the greasy beef buns had been sitting under a heat lamp for a month. This wasn't really a restaurant, or even a retail store. The friend hadn't even bothered to stock half of the warmers.

"On the house," Maltov said, as he gave us a plate of buns and took us through to the storage area. The room was half empty and filthy. There were meat hooks hanging from the ceiling, and bloodstains on the floor. I never thought anything would make me long for Karpenko's brown bread and lard, but it had taken only half a day to find something worse.

Twenty minutes later, Greenlees and I exited through the back door with a bag of pork rinds, neither having taken a bite of anything else. We left the car, but took the friend's Škoda Yeti. The Škoda was two years old, while the Opel was fifteen, but it was still a good deal for Maltov's friend.

"Three hours," Maltov said.

We spent the next two hours eating pork rinds and moving around Poltava, circling back a few times to watch Belenko's hotel through my field glasses. There were at least twenty-five men, assuming half on watch, maybe as many as forty, and they weren't trying to hide. They were moving between the building and the parking lot, packing and repacking two four-by-fours and two cars. It was nervous energy, not professionalism. They were eager. Or overeager.

Forty men. Four vehicles. Probably a few cars on patrol. The leader was a Maltov type: muscle, up from the ranks. They had the numbers, but we would arrive first. We could slow them on the entry road, especially on the curve, and bog them down in the parking lot, but I doubted we could stop them.

So it would all come down to timing.

"Let's go," I said, when the pork rinds were long gone and fondly missed. We drove slowly, taking extra turns, to a field south of Poltava, far from Karpenko's dacha. Maltov arrived an hour later with two friends and two delivery trucks. The writing on the side of the trucks was in Ukrainian, but the pictures told the story: one had fish on the side, the other potatoes. They weren't exactly what I'd had in mind, but they'd have to do.

"Any trouble?"

Maltov shook his head. "No trouble."

I gave him a stack of euros, and he passed it on to his friends, who left in the Opel. As soon as they were gone, I glanced at the sun, still high in the afternoon sky, and then out across the chaff from last year's wheat. It was a fallow field, unplanted this spring, and the blackbirds were hopping across it in a detestable fashion, their dinosaur claws beneath them. Stravinky's *Rite of Spring* ballet filled my head, with its insistence on grotesque beginnings. The "Harbingers of Spring" scene, especially, always made me feel unclean.

I looked around, trying to shake the unease. Maltov and his driver were leaning against one of the trucks. The driver looked like Maltov's younger brother, but of course all Ukrainian tough guys looked the same. If Maltov wasn't born with a grimace on his face, he'd spent half a lifetime developing one. I doubted he'd see much of the second half.

Greenlees, meanwhile, was slumped in the backseat of the Škoda with the door open and his eyes closed. It was a beautiful mid-May afternoon, sunny and warm, but it was wasted on the three of us.

You get what you get, and you don't throw a fit, I thought. It was something I'd heard my sister say to her four-year-old son the last time I'd visited her. A few weeks ago, the boy had turned nine.

I picked up the sat phone and called in the landing strip coordinates for the charter plane. The conversation took ten seconds. Ten minutes later, the sat phone rang.

"0215," Wolcott said.

"Done."

"It will work," Greenlees said, as I hung up the phone.

"I know," I said, even though I wasn't sure.

Only fools were sure.

CHAPTER 12

Brad Winters stood in the drizzling rain, driver's license in hand. In front of him stood a two-star army general and his aide-de-camp; behind him were three lobbyists chattering away about their pitch and a former congresswoman whose name he had forgotten. She worked on poverty now—but not in poverty, of course.

Two blocks away, he could hear the squeals of high school kids swarming around the tourist entrance to the White House. For a moment, he envied their ability to see the White House as something other than a pain in the ass, and this line as anything other than undignified. But he knew it was his height, and their puniness, that gave him a more accurate view.

"Brad Winters," he said to the gunny inside the checkpoint, as he showed his driver's license. They checked his name, printed a badge with his picture on it, waved him past the dogs and through the metal detectors, and in less than sixty seconds he was walking on White House grass.

He made his way to the Eisenhower Executive Office Building, a Second Empire colossus with marble floors and fifteen-foot ceilings. The EEOB, as it was called, was a classic signifier of historical importance. Official Washington, DC, from its offices to its bars and hotels, hated anything new. If it didn't look like something Thomas Jefferson would have designed, or even better, Julius Caesar, it wasn't worth taking seriously, so no one but tourists ever did.

Winters made his way up a grand staircase and down a hall lined with huge oak doors, each with a security keypad. He stopped at the one with a small placard, RUSSIA & CENTRAL ASIA, pressed a buzzer, and looked into the small camera.

"Hello?" A woman's voice.

"Hi there. It's Brad Winters for Naveen."

The door buzzed, and he pushed it open. It felt bombproof.

The Old Executive Office Building had once been a nice place to work, back in the 1890s, when it housed the State, War, and Navy Departments, and everyone had a polished wooden desk, a window, and went home for the sunset. But that was when the federal government was a few thousand people, Washington had malaria swamps, and the biggest foreign policy challenge was the western frontier. Now it was cheap cubicles stuffed with senior functionaries, their half desks barely fitting their two computers—one classified, the other unclassified—their half walls obscuring a towering window looking out over traffic. Even though it was lunchtime, the room was more crowded than a think tank intern pit. Nobody here ate, unless they made a dash to the vending machines. National Security Council staffers were vampiric; they worked twenty hours a day for two years straight, tethered to an in-box, and considered it the best two years of their lives.

"Naveen," Winters said, extending his hand as a lean young man in a wrinkled shirt and loosened tie came around the corner of one of the cubicles. Naveen Grummond was the CIA's lead analyst on EurAsia, seconded to the National Security Council to advise the president and other principals, making him one of the ten most powerful individuals in Washington in his area of expertise. It was a rare milestone few ever achieved. And yet, he'd only met the president once, in a receiving line at a White House reception, right behind a Hollywood starlet.

"Brad," Naveen said with a frown.

"They declared a day of mourning in Mariupol," Winters said.

"I saw."

"The local police refused to follow orders from Kiev. They went over to the Russians."

"The Russians want a land bridge to Crimea," Naveen said, searching for something on his desk.

"The Ukrainian military had to intervene," Winters continued. "Seven dead, right in the heart of Europe." Only Naveen would think eastern Ukraine was the heart of anything, but Winters was playing to his audience. "The Russian trolls are saying twenty, killed by Ukrainian tanks rolling down peaceful citizens who only wanted to rejoin their Motherland."

Naveen looked up, bags under his eyes. He'd lost hair, Winters noticed, since being rewarded with this godforsaken job. "What do you want, Brad?"

"Ten minutes with the president."

Naveen smirked. It was their old joke. Naveen was the one that wanted ten minutes, not Winters, even though Naveen was more aware every day how pointless those minutes would be. "What do you really want?"

"Five minutes with the national security advisor."

"Ha, me too," Naveen snorted, flopping into his chair. Winters leaned on a desk for want of a spare chair. The office was buzzing, the incessant noise of the incessantly busy, but they might as well have been at a private spa. Nobody but Naveen's five or six subordinates noticed the conversation, and even they didn't have time to care what was being said.

Winters's expression went from smiles to serious.

"I heard the Hill is forming a Friends of Ukraine coalition," he said. "They're going to ambush the White House during their opening press conference. It's going to be a full-court media blitz demanding military intervention to contain Putin."

Naveen sighed. "Who'd you hear that from?"

"Highly placed sources. I tried to knock them down with the usual talking points. Putin isn't al Qaeda. Putin has nukes and a massive inferiority complex. We're out of the nation-building business."

Naveen pursed his lips. "We're doing all we can," he snapped, "but sanctions take time, and the Germans have their own ideas."

"The Iron Bitch," Winters said, shaking his head. It was their pet name for German chancellor Angela Merkel, who had a soft spot for her neighbors to the east.

"Getting the military involved would make it more dangerous. Can't they see that? What would we do if the Russians sank a destroyer? Draw another line in the sand?"

"I just came to warn you," Winters said, knowing he had his man on the ropes.

"I know, I know," Naveen sighed. "I owe you one. When's the press conference?"

"In two hours. A few congressmen, Senator Addison from Texas . . ."

"Addison," Naveen huffed. It was a button. Naveen hated Addison.

"He's going to say we can't stand by, that we have to do something. He's going to use the term *pussy,* Naveen. Or at least strongly imply it."

"Christ, Brad. We're already at war in Syria."

"They're going to make a congressional campaign out of it. Energy security. Ukrainian pipelines. Freedom gas."

Naveen laughed. Policy wonks never understood propaganda.

"They're comparing Putin to Hitler and the president to

Chamberlain. It's Munich '38 all over again. It's going to launch a news cycle and make it to the Sunday news shows."

Especially after Karpenko's heroic moment on Saturday . . .

Naveen didn't say anything. Winters knew what he was thinking. The president was clear: no military interventions that could suck the U.S. into a shooting war with the Russians. The problem was that *any* intervention, beyond sanctions, could do just that.

"I'm sorry, Brad," Naveen said. "You know how it is."

Brad Winters held up his hands in surrender. "Understood." He had groomed Naveen for more than ten years, cleared his way to this so-called prestigious post. Naveen owed him, but the man was a true public servant.

"It's set in stone, Brad," Naveen said. "I'm truly sorry."

"Honesty, Naveen," Winters said. "That's all I ask."

He knew the value of letting Naveen think he let him down. He could use that guilt later. But the truth was, Naveen Grummond had given him exactly what he wanted.

There were wheels outside the government. Wheels with far more power and influence than Naveen could see from his narrow point of view. That was the world Winters was working in. And right now, all he wanted was to make sure that his biggest client, the U.S. government, stayed out of the way.

CHAPTER 13

"Thank you, my friends," Karpenko said. "From my heart, from my wife and daughter, and from my son, I thank you."

He held up his vodka. At the long table before him, set up in the barn with wooden benches for seats, thirty-five men lifted theirs. "God bless you," Karkpenko said.

The men dug into the food. It was a simple meal of brown bread, lard, bacon, and the remnants of everything else, but each place had been set with a candle, a napkin, and a stack of euros.

A last supper, I thought as I tore off a hunk of bread. I had eaten many last suppers. Some were in brocaded dining rooms with formal servants, but most were even more rudimentary than this: tins of sardines or whatever plants had been scrounged, a small group of men eating silently in some remote nowhere place in the hours before dawn. The Romans were wrong: Those about to die don't salute you. They care only about each other.

The plan was a good one. I had gone through it step by step, first with Karpenko and Sirko, then with Maltov. We had laid it out on this very table, using blocks of woods and stacks of euros as cars and buildings, a plank for the runway, hay for the trees. I knew the colonel didn't like it, so I had walked him through it carefully, noting the pros and cons, the possible evacuation routes and worst-case plans. I let him waver, change a few minor details, but it was too late for new ideas, and I wasn't backing down. The more serious conversation was with Maltov, who would lead the assault. It was a dangerous job, but Maltov didn't hesitate.

"I am Ukrainian," he said with a meaningful glance at Sirko. "This is my fight."

He was right. Everywhere I went, it was a local fight—over freedom and self-government, sure, but also over bread, and beer, and who got to fish which river, and how a society's energy would be spent. Even the evacuation of an oligarch's family, necessitated by a disagreement between rivals, was tied up in nationalism.

So I let Maltov call in the men on the assault team, in small groups, and explain their role in the operation. It was clear immediately that they were loyal to him, even more so than Karpenko; he must have brought them into the oligarch's service. Which was good. Maltov would be their leader tonight; when things went wrong, which they would, the men would have to trust in him. And the more times he explained the operation—the positions, the timing, the intent—the more he owned the plan. I didn't want Maltov to think about what to do when the enemy showed up. I needed him to know. Because I wouldn't be there with him on the front line. My place, as always, was with the principal.

I sliced off a lump of bacon, shoved it into a bit of bread, and stuffed it in my mouth. Maltov had risen to speak, but when Greenlees bent over to translate, I waved him away. I knew what was being said, even though I didn't understand the words. This is the moment. This is what we live for. Or maybe what we're paid for, I didn't know Maltov that well. Karpenko is a good man, he would say. He is our patron. Our future president. But this isn't for one man, it is for Mother Ukraine, or whatever they called this place.

There was some pounding on the table, a few shouts. It was either false bravado, or false ideals. Death should be respected, not shouted down.

I slipped out into the night and looked up at the sky, always there, almost empty. It was cold and clear, with a quarter moon. Too much light.

But this was what we lived for. This was what we did. And we had to go now.

I pulled out a cigar, an old habit I'd picked up in the army. I liked the ritual before an op: the snip of the tip, the careful burn, the slow char of the edges. It reminded me of General McChrystal, my first and best commanding officer, and Miles, my right-hand man, and every Special Operations Forces commander thereafter, until the day I left the organized world behind and stepped out into this unknown.

I heard a noise behind me, in the direction of the house. I turned and saw a woman's face framed in a window. She was holding a baby, so she must have been Karpenko's wife, but she was younger than I had expected, with dark hair like Alie's and the same penetrating eyes, the kind that hinted at other choices, other lives she might have lived. She didn't look scared. She didn't look any way at all. She just stared at me, not moving, and then, slowly, she disappeared.

In Kiev, Alie stared at Hargrove's ceiling, wondering how she had ended up here. Not that it was a bad place, this warm bed, and this warm body. It was better than an orphanage in Burundi. Better than a refugee camp in South Sudan or a backwoods cabin in south Alabama, where the screens don't fit the windows and the mosquitos are murder. It was better than a house in the suburbs, two kids, a yoga class, and a husband who either disappeared for months at a time or resented her for making him stay home and mow the lawn.

She got up and poured herself a drink. At least she was alive. At least she was here, where her efforts might matter.

Walk out, Alie, she thought. *Walk now. You still have time.*

The Wolf looked down at the map. He had marked five primary locations: two airfields, an industrial park, a large construction site, and the soccer stadium. The stadium was covered by a Chechen missile team. The airfields: too obvious. The industrial park and construction site: a problem.

Where was the helicopter? Where would they hop? Would they risk a short flight to a waiting plane?

"Reinforce the fire team, here," the Wolf said to Ivan, pointing to the airport. Ivan's men were shaky, but then again, they only needed to pin Karpenko down until the Chechens arrived. "Double the watch on the other. And from now until morning, no one is off duty. Everyone must be prepared."

"You think they will go tonight?"

"I would," the Wolf said, and he couldn't think of a better reason to be ready than that.

And Winters? What was he doing, safe in Washington, with his $6,000 suits and two-hundred-year-old townhouse? What was he thinking, now that his plan was on the line?

I stubbed out my cigar and looked up at the stars. *Forget Winters,* I thought. On a mission, the world was an oyster, closed in on itself. Winters was nothing. For the next four hours, this place, and these men, and these guns, were the only things that mattered.

CHAPTER 14

Grigory Maltov sat in the passenger seat of the lead Range Rover, impatient, waiting for the signal. It was after 0130. Enough talking. Enough planning. He hated the plan: too clever. But he had gone along. In fact, when Karpenko balked, and "Colonel" Sirko sat quietly, crapping his fancy pants, he was the one who had spoken up.

He hoped the American appreciated it.

"It's a go," Greenlees said into his earpiece.

"Finally," Maltov muttered in Ukranian, as he signaled the driver.

And then they were moving through the darkness, speeding down Karpenko's private road, a line of twelve Range Rovers and, near the middle, the family's two black armored Mercedes. They hit the main road and turned north. They were in black-out drive, all lights disconnected except the headlamps, which were taped with foil so that only a narrow beam shone on the road ahead. The drivers wore night-vision goggles, and they didn't slow for turns. The convoy would be gone before anyone knew they were there.

Eight minutes to the airbase, the American had estimated. Maltov planned to make it in five.

Let them come, he thought. *Let them bring everything.*

He was happy to be out of the dacha, after days of cowering behind the iron gate. Happy to have been given the most dangerous job. Happy to have been allowed to choose his own men. He had brought most of these men up from the mud with him. They were his brothers, in a way the Communists could never understand. They would follow no one else, at least not as they would follow him. The American understood that much at least.

"Twenty-five mikes." It was Locke, counting minutes.

"Copy." Maltov glanced at his watch: 0148. Twenty-five minutes until the plane was scheduled to arrive. Forty until it could be back in the air.

"0148," Greenlees said on the headset.

Maltov rechecked his kit. He wore a pistol in a chest holster, but he preferred his AK-47, with two magazines taped together at opposite ends for faster reloading. The Kalashnikov had greater firepower and made more noise.

They passed into a forest, the trees thick along both sides of the road. He had been in a firefight before, but not as often as his men assumed. He wasn't an enforcer. He had been the head of the local pipefitter's union at the ironworks in Kramatorsk when Karpenko had taken over the factory. He had fought Karpenko's thugs so brutishly that the boss had finally hired him. The other pipefitters weren't happy—until he brought the best along. Like Romanyuk, in the last car. And Poplavko. And Pavlo, his driver, who he had known as a boy. The rest of the pipefitters never understood. Unionism wasn't a path to better pay; it was a chance to impress the men who could give you a better job.

Now he was one of those men.

The entrance came quickly, with its small museum sign. Eleven vehicles, including the two family Mercedes, turned into the complex; three continued to the gravel road in the forest. Maltov leveled his AK-47. When the parked Škoda appeared, he fired. The Range Rovers behind him did the same as they passed. It was unfortunate. He knew Ivan, who led Belenko's men. He probably knew the two dead men in the car. They were Ukrainian comrades. They drank together, when their bosses had been friends. But their boss was on the wrong side now.

"We're here," he said, when they reached the gate. It was 0159.

"Sixteen minutes," Greenlees replied.

Maltov had argued with the American over the details, but the main components were never in dispute: two Land Rovers stayed to block the entrance from the main road, two stopped to guard the parking lot gate, the rest would form a ring around the parking lot. Locke had insisted on the exact placement of every man, including the ambush team on the entry road and the fire team in the forest. It was too much. Maltov had nodded along, but he no intention of fussing to that degree. These were his men. They were going to be taking fire. He trusted them to find the place where they felt most comfortable.

He stepped out of the Land Rover and stood in the middle of the parking lot, directing traffic. "Spread out," he yelled, at three vehicles bunched too closely together.

"Block that landing strip access," he yelled, as the family's two armored Mercedes pulled onto the tarmac and edged under the fuselage of the museum's Tu-160, a massive Soviet bomber. Even with the quarter moon, the plane dwarfed the two black cars, making them invisible.

"Set the ambush line there." He pointed with his rifle as armed men poured out of the Land Rovers and found shelter in the tree line. He looked around: he had men on three sides of the parking lot, and the enemy would have to cross between them to get to the landing strip. The American was smart. He had to give him that.

He lifted both arms. "Here is the kill zone," he yelled. "Wait for my shot. No one fires until I do."

"Nine minutes," Greenlees said in his ear.

"In position," Maltov replied, as his men locked the gate and deployed spike strips, covering them in dirt to blend into the ground.

"Is the area secure?" It was Locke.

Maltov looked toward the five Land Rovers parked in front of the runway. Two men were sweeping the grass and tree line with infrared scopes. No sign of trouble.

"Secure," he said.

The headset was quiet. It was 0206. Then: "Light up the landing strip."

Maltov picked up his radio. "*Svititi,*" he said.

Two SUVs broke the line and went speeding down the runway, dropping flares every hundred meters or so, making the mothballed war strip come alive.

"Seven minutes," he yelled to his men. "Positions!"

The men disappeared into the shadows, as Maltov slipped into the trees. The base grew silent. No movement. No lights but the parallel lines of red flares. He adjusted his night-vision goggles, as the two SUVs from the runway slipped back into line.

"Six minutes," he said over the radio.

But they didn't have six minutes. They had less than two before he heard automatic gunfire from the main road, and Pavlo yelling "They're here!" into his radio, followed by more fire as the enemy's vehicles passed into the ambush zone on the entry road.

"Wait for them," Maltov yelled, settling behind his Kalashnikov and aiming at the kill zone as a four-by-four careened into sight. It was shot to hell and running scared, the driver not even slowing down as he crashed through the gate. The spikes shredded his tires, the car fishtailed, and then the world burst open, gunfire pouring into the parking lot from three directions, even as a second four-by-four careened through the gate and smashed into the first.

Maltov could feel the AK-47 jerking in his hand. He could hear guns firing around him, a thousand bullets a minute, a deafening roar. It was unreal, as if the bullets exploding into the cars weren't from his gun, as if he wasn't the one tearing apart the men inside.

The fusillade lasted a minute. Maybe two. He paused, watching for signs of life. He could hear the echo of shots being fired, down by the main road, off to his right, but with no other targets in sight, he fired the rest of his clip into the decimated four-by-fours.

He didn't hear the diesel engine until he stopped to reload. He snapped in the fresh magazine and listened, wondering what was coming, until, *Shit!? How?* he thought, as an armored personnel carrier flattened the spike strip at fifty miles an hour and tore into the parking lot. It was a BTR-80, a tank on wheels with a heavy machine gun turret, firing as it came, splintering trees.

Maltov dove facedown in the dirt. By the time he looked up, a squad of soldiers wearing night-vision goggles were behind the BTR, firing in tight formation.

"They're not Ukrainian," someone shouted.

Maltov unloaded his magazine, half in a panic, the gun muzzle flashing green in his night-vision goggles. More SUVs were pouring in at high speed, swerving around the troop carrier and heading toward the landing strip. Maltov fired wildly, the whole tree line firing with him. An SUV took fire, flipped, and exploded. The SUV immediately behind crashed into it, sending bodies through the windshield.

"Don't let them through," Maltov shouted as he ducked again to reload, but nobody heard him over the gunfire. Another SUV was hit; it fishtailed and smashed into the concrete museum building. The car door opened, blood exploded, and a body fell to the ground.

The BTR lurched forward with a plume of diesel, its turret swinging in Maltov's direction. "Down!" he shouted.

"Kill that thing!" someone yelled. He heard the *fush* of an RPG and saw it zoom over the BTR and explode a tree on the other side.

"Reload!"

The vehicle stopped. The turret turned in the direction of the RPG as two men with AK-47s popped out of hatches on the top. Yuri and Danka, his RPG team, evaporated in a cloud of blood and dirt, the BTR advancing now, firing as it came.

We're being overrun, Maltov thought.

"Fall back," he shouted, wishing he'd gone over the evac plan with his men, as the American had insisted, but it was too late. Most of his men were already running or dead, and to hell with the landing strip, he'd done what he could. He turned to run, but a barrage of well-aimed bullets were slashing toward him. He dropped to the ground, but the man beside him wasn't as fast. Maltov heard the grunt, a thump, and the clattering of the AK-47. It was Poplavko, shot through the chest.

He couldn't look away. He heard the zing of the bullets overhead and the shouting. Chechen. He didn't know the language but he understood the rhythms. Belenko had hired Chechens. Maltov hated Chechens. Every Ukrainian did. But he couldn't see them. All he could see was his old friend, three feet away, lying dead in the leaves.

He started firing, his Kalashnikov propped on a fallen branch, his finger holding down the trigger. He fired through his magazines, two hundred rounds, until they clicked empty. He could feel the heat off the barrel, his hands going numb, but it only made him more determined. He wouldn't run. He would stand his ground. He didn't notice the screaming in his ear until he reached for Poplavko's last magazine.

"The bird is here. The bird is here. Detonate the C-4. Do you copy? Do you copy?"

He heard a plane, maybe, but then something exploded, a grenade, not close, but it knocked him on his ass.

"Detonate the C-4!" the voice was shouting in his earpiece, but he was paralyzed, on his back, there was nothing he could do.

Maltov tore off his night-vision goggles and stared at a sky cut by branches and leaves. He couldn't believe it. The stars were gone. They were overrun. Belenko had come with more than twenty men, a lot more, and an armored troop carrier, and there was no way he could keep them busy, or keep them in this parking lot, any longer.

CHAPTER 15

The Wolf stepped out of his SUV as the machine gun cut into Karpenko's men. He was surprised his old colonel had chosen this airstrip and staged an ambush rather than a classic security perimeter. Pretty cunning for a washed-out relic, and a perfect place for him to die. Here among the old Soviet bombers, in a provincial firefight between amateurs, the kind of men who dove for the nearest cover instead of the best, and emptied their magazines as quickly as possible rather than aim. The Wolf almost felt sorry for them.

Almost.

"Blow them up," he yelled to his Chechens, shooting a line of tracers at Sirko's two remaining SUVs. Two men shouldered RPGs, followed the tracers, and the SUVs exploded.

And then the rabbit bolted. It was a single black Mercedes, hiding under the biggest bomber, now tearing down the landing strip at full speed.

The Wolf leapt back into his vehicle and floored it. He didn't worry about the gunfire; speed would be his cover. Smoke poured from the dead SUVs, obstructing his view, until he cleared the wreckage and was on the access road to the landing strip, following the black Benz.

Wolf saw the BTR's turret turn, tracking its prey.

"No!" he yelled, but the car never stood a chance. The 14.5-millimeter machine gun tore through the Mercedes's "bulletproof" skin with such force that the vehicle flipped on its side and rolled end over end at ninety miles per hour. Two hundred meters later, it burst into flame.

The Wolf lowered his head. The only thing he could do now was hope to find something identifiable as Karpenko, once the car was cool enough to search. He needed DNA proof and pictures of the body to collect his reward.

Maltov heard explosions and saw the branches rattle above him. A twig fell, hitting him in the face, such a pointless thing. He sat up. A hundred meters away, SUVs were on fire, their gas tanks creating secondary explosions, and in the glare, behind the overturned four-by-fours, he could see the armored personnel carrier, its gun turret turning toward the fleeing Mercedes. He could hear screaming in his ear about the plane and the damn C-4, but it was no use, the Mercedes was flipping now, in slow motion, on fire, and the battle was over. They were pinned down, and they were all going to die here, and was there anything worse, really, than dying for a losing cause?

Then he saw it. The potato truck, plowing through the gunfire. For a moment, he didn't understand. Pavlo was supposed to block the exit with this truck bomb. He was supposed to be safe. Of all the men, he was supposed to be safe. He had promised the boy's mother . . . his sister . . . Pavlo was just a teenager. Maltov had been to his christening and bought him his first beer, it seemed like only yesterday. He had promised his sister he would keep her boy safe. But now Pavlo was racing toward the BTR, in a truck full of C-4 and ammonium nitrate . . .

"No, Pavlo," he said, as the truck slammed into the armored troop carrier, it's back end rising into the air with the force of the collision, then smashing down with a massive explosion that sent a pillar of fire into the night sky.

Maltov lay in the leaves, not firing, not moving. Watching. In the silence, he could see men scrambling away from the blast. Some were shot as they fled. Some stumbled, their bodies on fire. It was over now, truly over. It was time to go. He couldn't do anything more. Everyone was dead, including Pavlo, who had given his life for his friends.

"Firing," he said into his earpiece.

He pulled the detonator off his web belt, flipped the safety, and squeezed. He felt the first blast, a shock wave of hot air, and then the deafening bang. Six tall trees fell across the entry road, obstructing the exit. He squeezed a second trigger. The flight tower across the parking lot seemed to lift, then totter, then collapse to the ground, trapping the enemy's SUVs on the landing strip and buying precious time for his men to escape.

CHAPTER 16

I turned away from the radio, the C-4 explosion still ringing in my ears. "It's done," I said, pulling off my headset.

"God be with Maltov," Karpenko said, as he left the dacha's security office, where we'd been listening to the firefight. He hadn't liked the idea of a diversion. I had wondered why, since it was the only plausible plan against overwhelming forces, but I heard the reason in his concern. And it surprised me.

But then again, why should it? A rich man wasn't required to have a cavalier attitude about the deaths of those who worked for him.

I patted Greenlees on the shoulder. He was breathing heavily from the exertion of screaming into the radio. I could hear other explosions in the background, and Maltov ordering his men to fall back. We had twenty-five minutes by my calculations, even if Belenko's men reacted quickly, but I was hoping to be done in ten.

"When the plane lands," I whispered, "recheck the fuses around the house."

I grabbed a pair of night-vision goggles and headed out. Sirko was standing guard outside an open door in the family's private area. He tipped his head as I passed, and I nodded in return. Inside, I caught a glimpse of Karpenko. He was rocking a young girl, maybe three or four years old, on his lap, singing softly to her in Ukrainian.

Outside, it was cold and empty, but I didn't have time for more than a glance at the sky. I jumped into an SUV, drove down the long driveway, and pulled onto Karpenko's private access road. A kilometer down was a straight section 1,500 meters long and less than ten meters wide, not technically enough room for an An-12, but it was a calculated risk. The company always retained the best flight crews. I trusted them more with a tight landing than I trusted Karpenko's men.

A full kilometer from the gate, I pulled off the road and camouflaged the vehicle in a sea of shadows. I checked my watch: 0217. I did one last wind check and scanned the horizon, holding binoculars to my night-vision goggles. The pilots had radioed their approach twenty-four minutes ago. They should be in visual range.

"This is lima zulu bravo one niner, come in, over." The voice on the aviation radio in my hand had a thick Romanian accent.

"Roger, lima zulu, I read you lima Charlie," I replied. "Wind is twelve knots at two-six-zero. Track is clear."

I held up my infrared strobe to the night sky and gave it three bursts. It was invisible to the naked eye, but a beacon to a pilot wearing night-vision goggles. Then I took a small radio transmitter out of my breast pocket and switched on the infrared beacons that lined the dirt road. Through my goggles, the landing strip came alive.

"Confirm landing strip at three-three-zero."

"Confirmed," I said.

"On final approach," the Romanian replied.

I pulled off my goggles. I could hear the drone of turboprops, but the sound was roaring in my ears before I picked out the dark shape, flying low against the gray night. It looked impossibly large to land on this two-lane road, like a goose trying to land on a fishing line. The wings wobbled as the cargo plane slowed. It veered to the left, far enough to put it over the field, and then corrected and touched down in the road, its propellers churning dirt and rocks out of the fields, its number two engine passing so close over my head that I could feel the engine roar in my chest. The drag chute deployed and the plane pulled against it, slowing gracefully against a backdrop of trees, like a fat ballerina landing a perfect pirouette.

And then the winch truck tore past me, knocking me to the dirt.

"Fuckin' hell!" I said, spitting dust as I leapt to my feet. At least someone had a sense of urgency, even if they drove like shit.

"The bird is in," I yelled to Greenlees, as I raced to the SUV. "The bird is in."

I fired up the vehicle and raced after the winch truck, the plane still rolling along the road toward a soft curve, the engines powering down. In the distance, red star cluster flares arced above Poltava's commercial airport, the second distraction of the night. I was reasonably sure all of Belenko's men had been drawn to the airbase, but it never hurt to provide another false lead. It's amazing what a lone man with a motorcycle and box of flares can achieve.

By the time I arrived, the cargo ramp was lowered and four armed men were jumping out of the bay to form a perimeter around the plane. I recognized Boon, then Wildman . . .

"I thought this was a hot LZ," someone said.

I turned. It was Miles, smiling broadly, his face painted with night camouflage and his night-vision goggles perched on top of his head. He was suited up, but in desert camo instead of green. The team must have come straight from Libya.

"Ten minutes if you're lucky," I said, pointing down the road toward the iron gate just visible in the distance. "A quiet night if you're not."

Miles signaled to Boon and Wildman, who moved down the road. The other two men loosened the cargo netting and prepared to unload, while the flight crew hooked the winch truck's cables to the rear of the plane and began to pull it backward. The plane couldn't turn around on the narrow road; it needed to be hauled back to the airstrip's beginning for take-off. Once there, we unloaded it like a pit crew. Miles's team formed a human chain and passed rucksacks, weapon cases, communications chest, ammo crates, wooden boxes of explosives, and specialty gear illegal in most countries, cramming it into the fish delivery truck Maltov had sourced from his friend. The pilots looked on, smoking and talking among themselves.

"What the hell is that," I yelled, as a flatbed careened past. The truck skidded to a stop and backed up against the airplane's tail ramp. Beyond, in the darkness, I could hear the *chop-chop* of the helicopter, flying in blackout, carrying Karpenko's family from the dacha. It hovered next to the plane and then landed, blowing rock and dirt. One of the pilots ran toward the plane, yelling furiously in Romanian.

At the flatbed, two men had jumped out and were throwing boxes into the back of the plane. What was Karpenko thinking? We didn't have time to load cargo. It was time to go.

"Leave it," I yelled, jumping onto the flatbed as one of the men tore off the canvas cover of the biggest load. Underneath was a five-foot-tall cube of euros, shrink-wrapped in heavy plastic. It was wise to move money out of places like Ukraine, especially the illegal kind, especially if your assets were frozen. I had smuggled some serious stacks of cash in my day. But even I had to gawk at this pile.

"You have to go," someone said.

I heard the words in my head, like a voice from some distant part of my brain.

"I'm sorry, sweetie," the voice said again. "You have to go."

I looked behind me. It was Karpenko. He was crouching by the airplane's side door, his daughter clinging to him with one hand and her stuffed rabbit with the other. A Dora the Explorer backpack was slung over her shoulder, and her face was wet. To my surprise, so was Karpenko's. He didn't try to hide his crying. Instead, he pushed back her hair, hugged her, then kissed her in the center of her forehead.

"Daddy loves you," he said. "I will see you soon."

As I watched her mother take her hand, the baby boy in her other arm, I wondered if that was true. I knew this deal wasn't just extracting the family, and it wasn't just flying them back to Bucharest, or Berlin, or wherever this plane was headed. It was keeping them somewhere safe, maybe for a week, maybe three, until Winters's plan was complete.

Or we failed.

"We need to go, go, go!" I shouted, tearing myself from the scene. The plane had been on the ground for eight minutes already.

I pushed the men out of the cargo hold, then leapt to the ground as Miles and the flight crew raised the tail ramp. Sirko appeared out of the darkness, pulling Karpenko away as the ramp sealed. The trucks departed and the helo hopped a few hundred meters to the right, to avoid the plane's propblast. The An-12 pilots fired up all four engines simultaneously, and the sound, and the dust, and the pebbles beat against our skin, as the plane rolled down the road, raised its nose, began to lift, slowly, too slowly, and brushed a treetop as it cleared. I imagined a little girl inside, waving good-bye, wondering why her daddy wasn't coming, too.

"You know the coordinates?" I asked Miles, as he shouldered his ruck.

He nodded, lifted one of the SA-18 missile launchers we'd bought in Libya over his shoulder, and smiled.

"See you at the rendezvous," Miles said, climbing into the back of the fish truck and pulling the cargo doors shut behind him.

Three minutes later, the helicopter was in the air, carrying Karpenko, Sirko, Greenlees, and me. We swooped west over the fields, the brake lights flaring beneath us as Miles and the last of Karpenko's men scattered beyond the dacha's front gate, a few muzzle blasts visible off to the east where Belenko's men had broken free of Maltov's trap. There was a risk they would run into Miles's team on the road, but knowing Miles, he probably had a few antitank missiles ready for the Chechens. Miles despised cheap competition.

"Blow it," I said into the headset, as the helicopter peeled off to the north.

Karpenko didn't hear me. He was off in his own world, probably thinking of his family, maybe wishing he'd gotten on that plane. I thought of the woman in the window and realized I probably would have, if I'd had Karpenko's life, and she'd been there for me.

"Blow it," I said again, louder this time.

Karpenko took the detonator and squeezed. The fireball when the dacha exploded turned the night sky orange. There was no coming back. There was never any coming back.

"Winters was right about you," Karpenko said, as we watched his burning compound recede into the distance.

I thought about telling him the same thing, but I didn't know anything about oligarchs or Eastern European power struggles or even fatherhood. I was only an employee, and Karpenko was only my principal.

"Don't celebrate too soon," I said, Buddha calm, although inside, my adrenaline was pumping. I could never tell Karpenko, or Greenlees, or anyone really, even my closest friends, how proud I was pulling off a mission like this. Even if I could, they wouldn't understand.

I picked up my sat phone and punched in the code. Winters would understand. Maybe. He'd respect it, at least. But after this call, we'd never talk about it again. Never even mention that it happened. This was, in the end, a private victory in a private profession. The job was lonely that way.

But what did I care? Fuck the world. I knew what I'd done.

CHAPTER 17

A half hour after Tom Locke's call, Brad Winters pulled up to the security checkpoint. It was the third he had passed through already, each one a step up in prestige. The main purpose of this last one, Winters knew, was to keep out the lower-millionaire riff-raff from the first two rungs.

"Hartley," he said to the guard, showing his identification. "Seven six three."

The guard looked at his notes, then went into his booth and made a call. "Enjoy your visit, Mr. Winters," he said, handing back the driver's license and waving him through.

Inside the third gate, the lots were noticeably larger, with straight rows of trees and large stretches of green lawn. Riding mower territory, even for the full-time lawn crews. It was early evening—the golden hour, photographers called it—but there was nobody out. Hartley's house, number 763, had another gate at the entrance to the driveway, but it opened as soon as Winters pulled up. The mansion was Mediterranean meets *Gone with the Wind*, with white columns, a Spanish tile roof, and poplar trees. He parked in the circular drive beside the fountain. Glenn Hartley was waiting for him in Italian loafers and a bathrobe. Eight o'clock on a Wednesday night, and the man was in a bathrobe.

"Come in, Brad," he said, extending his hand.

They passed through a portico, past a double winding staircase, into a room with six couches. Texas wildcatters like Hartley made and lost more millions than a Vegas casino, so when they were up, they spent.

"Care to sit outside?" Hartley asked. The pool was visible through the floor-to-ceiling windows, with a waterfall at the far end. "The wife and kids are in Dallas for a lacrosse tournament. Saint John's School, they're a powerhouse this year. The boy plays defense and the girl's a cheerleader, if you can believe that."

Winters didn't know what was so hard to believe.

They took seats on the shaded porch overlooking the pool. There was a porch for sunbathing, too. Winters noticed the white sunglasses by the lounge chair and wondered whose they were. There was lipstick on an empty glass.

"Karpenko's in?" Hartley asked, as soon as they sat down. Winters noticed a bar, but Hartley didn't offer him a drink, not even iced tea. He had flown three hours from Washington to Houston for this meeting. He had raced to this godforsaken suburb as soon as he'd gotten the call from Locke, who was conveniently eight hours ahead. All Hartley had done was walk to his door. But the man still seemed inconvenienced.

"Karpenko's a rock," Winters said.

Hartley pursed his lips like he wasn't so sure.

"I've known him for ten years, Glenn. We meet at the Travellers Club in London. He has a Georgian rowhouse in Kensington. A ski chalet in Vale," though of course he didn't ski, that was for the horse riding, bear shooting, jet-ski-flipping Russians. Ukrainians were still in the acquiring stage. "Sir Gillingham goes way back with him. They own a brewery together."

"It's called a distillery, Brad. They make *artisanal* gin."

God, he hated this about the Houston boys. The way they chewed on words like *artisanal* with disgust. The never-ending kicking of tires. They were all self-made men who distrusted self-made men.

"Do you want to meet with him?"

"No. Of course not."

"If it's a moral issue, I assure you, we've dealt with worse."

"It's not a moral issue."

"Believe me, Glenn. The man is solid. And we have leverage. There's no amount of pressure Putin can apply—"

"It's not about pressure, Brad. It's about rights. International support for basic human rights. I mean, we were neck deep in Venezuela. Neck deep. We'd been working on that project for twenty years. We'd invested billions, Brad. Billions. Chavez took it away in a day. And what did our government do?"

Tried to assassinate him. Funded a rebellion. Undermined his government.

"Nothing," Hartley said.

Venezuela, it was always about Venezuela with these oil boys. What about Ghana? South Sudan? Nigeria? Hadn't Apollo proven itself there? They were pumping pure unadulterated profit by the barrel load, and all it cost was a few million a year and a bit of bad press whenever the starving locals tried to bunker some oil and incinerated their village in the process.

"Full faith and credit, Glenn. Just like I promised. Full United States government backing, guaranteed."

Hartley was agitated, like the very idea of Venezuela gave him hemorrhoids. "Where are we with that?"

"General Roberts is working State. Ray Brayburn, a former national security advisor, is working K Street."

"I know Brayburn," Hartley snapped.

"I've spent the last two days on the Hill. You saw the stories in the papers? Freedom gas. Friends of Ukraine. Elected officials are clamoring for action."

Hartley waved that away with a swipe of his hand. "Did you talk to Addison?"

"He's your senator, Glenn. We know he's onboard. I'm working on the ones who care about what happens in Eastern Europe."

"The idealistic bastards."

The opportunistic bastards.

"Don't worry, Glenn, we have the solution. We can push Putin back, promote democracy, and enrich America in one fell swoop. There's no reason to oppose it."

"My people tell me Addison might not go along. Too risky. Doesn't want America sucked into another war."

"Of course he wants America sucked into another war, Glenn. He's a hawk. And he's going to run for president."

"He wants cover."

"He wants to sound tough, Glenn, without having to take responsibility if the war goes wrong. That's the best part of being on the outside looking in. Besides, we both know the senators come last. Right now, it's a social call, keep them informed, so they don't complain when we need them."

Like you, Glenn.

It was almost eight thirty, the sun barely clinging to the horizon, but it was still hot. Winters could practically see the humidity hanging above the pool, and he could feel the dampness on the back of his collar. Houston was maybe the only place in America that made the stifling Washington summers seem pleasant. Two world capitals, both carved out of a swamp.

"Look, Glenn," he said. "I'm sorry about Libya. Sometimes you have to cut something loose when a better opportunity comes along."

"You cut fifty million dollars loose, Brad."

"It was only twenty million, Glenn, and half of that was mine—"

Winters stopped. Wrong direction.

He leaned back in his lounge chair and looked out at the swimming pool and the manicured lawn, a lacrosse net hanging limp in the corner. Nobody ever had enough money, especially in River Oaks, but Glenn Hartley came close. This wasn't about money. Hartley was a cowboy. He had loved the *idea* of Libya. But there were ideas he would love even more.

"Every time I come here, Glenn, I think of Prescott Bush, one of your famous oil men."

"He wasn't an oil man, Brad."

"No, Glenn, he wasn't. He was a dealmaker. He saw the opportunity to make a deal with the Saud family in the Middle East and supply oil to the United States for the next fifty years, when everyone else just saw Arabs in the desert. And you know what happened?"

"He made a pile."

"His son became president of the United States. And his grandson, too."

Winters paused to let it sink in. Opportunities to make money were everywhere. Opportunities to change the balance of power in the world for the next hundred years, and get filthy rich doing it, came once in a lifetime, if you were lucky.

"It's not just Ukraine, Glenn. That's a foot in the door. It's Kirkuk, Irbil, Azerbaijan, Turkmenistan. There's a hundred years of oil out there, just waiting to be set free. I can get you in there, and guarantee your safety. But if you aren't interested . . ."

"Brad . . ."

"We need a face, Glenn. Someone legitimate we can trust. If you don't want to be that face, I can find someone else. I can find someone in this very neighborhood—"

"Easy Brad. Easy," Hartley said with a languid smile, turning on the Texas charm. "I told you last year, and I'll tell you again, I like you. I believe in you. And I'm committed, even after Libya.

The team is together, and we're ready to go. You give us the call, we'll stick more holes in the ground than you can count." That was life with Glenn Hartley. Like other wildcatters gone corporate, he believed the world was his pincushion, and he wasn't truly happy unless he was driving in the needle. "Don't worry, Brad," Hartley said. "It's going to happen. One way or another, we are going to nail Putin's ass to the ground."

"I'm glad to hear it Glenn, because I've got a favor to ask."

Hartley laughed. "And here I am, licking your ass."

Winters smiled, just to show he was a good sport. "It's just a phone call, Glenn. I have a meeting with Karpenko's London bankers, the day after tomorrow. The ones who backed you in Kirkuk. I need you to put in a good word."

"What kind of word?"

"That you have my back 500 million percent." Five hundred million was the most recent valuation of Hartley's company, Valhalla Energy Group.

Hartley laughed. "Fine. So long as I don't have to sign that statement. Anything else?"

It was Winters's turn to laugh now. "I may have promised Addison you'd be a top backer of his presidential campaign."

"Hell, I practically promised him that fourteen years ago, when I made him a congressman."

Winters stared out across the pool, watching the evaporation burn off into the sky. Tomorrow morning, it would be back as dew. It made him wish for a tall glass of iced tea, one with a lemon wedge on the rim. What had happened to good old Southern hospitality?

"The boy's got a scholarship offer," Glenn said, looking at the lacrosse net in the gathering dusk, "and he's only a junior, if you can believe that. The University of Virginia, up in your neck of the woods. It's a powerhouse, I hear."

Winters felt it, the rush of adrenaline, something almost like joy. If Glenn was thinking of legacies, he was all the way in. All Winters needed now was the general and the bankers. And Locke, of course. All of this depended on Locke.

"Well send him on up, Glenn," he said. "You know we'll take care of him. Washington is always looking for promising young men."

CHAPTER 18

The Wolf wasn't happy. The fallen tower, the mangled gate, dozens of destroyed vehicles. He walked through the gate and down the access road to the blind curve. The Chechens had chained the fallen trees and pulled them from the road, but it had taken time. So had moving the burned remains of the delivery truck. And the Range Rovers blocking the entrance to the main road.

This wasn't Sirko. The Wolf was sure of that. This was too . . . modern. Too carefully planned. Too clever. Karpenko had brought in help. Someone connected. No amateur could fly a plane three hundred miles into Ukrainian airspace and out again. This was a top-flight operation, and the Wolf knew what that meant: the distant enemy. The West.

He wondered, briefly, about Karpenko's story.

Then he put it behind him. The story here, in this wreckage, was more important. He had sent the Chechens out onto the roads, chasing luck, but he knew they wouldn't stick with him for long, not if the bounty and his high-end extraction team had flown beyond his reach. They were in it for the money, nothing more, and there were many opportunities to make money in eastern Ukraine. Hell, Putin was basically paying mercenaries just to cause trouble.

But if the Wolf could find any proof of what had happened here, he could pay more.

He turned and looked back down the road toward the airbase,

running through the operation in his head. Black Range Rovers, two Mercedes. Ambush with AK-47s fired by Ukrainians, not professionals. C-4. Padlock. Delivery truck. Delivery . . .

"Professionals," Ivan said, walking up behind him.

The Wolf wheeled. Ivan was smiling, like this was nothing, even though half his men had been killed. Even though he'd been *beaten,* at the very thing he'd built his life around. Where was the pride? The professionalism?

"There's no way Maltov did this," Ivan said. The Wolf felt the urge to shoot him, right in his big blockhead. But then . . .

"Who's Maltov?" he said.

CHAPTER 19

Alie had gone to Bujumbura in 2004 for the same reason she had gone to the convent: to get away. Africa was as far from Anniston, Alabama, as you could get, after all, and even in Africa, Burundi was a backwater. It was small; it was poor (the fifth poorest country in the world, with a 65 percent Catholic population, Sister Mary Karam told her, a perfect place for mission work), and it was in the middle of the continent, away from lions, elephants, pharaohs, the Sahara desert, Nelson Mandela, and anything else anyone in America had ever heard of.

"Only the Nile River," Sister Mary Karam had said. "It starts there. And genocide. Burundi is the sister country of Rwanda."

Alie had stared at her blankly.

"The Rwandan genocide—where eight hundred thousand people were murdered. With machetes. In ninety days." Alie shook her head no. She hadn't heard of it. She had only been twelve. The sister threw up her hands. Literally leaned back and threw them up in despair. "You do Burundi some good," she said, "and it will return the blessing."

Burundi *had* done her good. She had thought her black grandmother's crumbling farmhouse in Hale County, Alabama, had prepared her for the worst, but Bujumbura was a city of desolate one-story buildings, squalid huts, and anorexic chickens. People were sitting on the side of the dirt road, selling three or four pieces of fruit. A woman pushed a canister of propane in a ratty baby stroller. The huts were cinderblocks or scrap metal, and there were gaunt people in doorless entryways watching their charity's Land Cruisers pass, just as people had watched when they drove their Lexuses down the backroads of Hale County to some shed where her black father had business, or knew somebody, or needed to chat in the backroom while kindly old men fed her pickled pigs' feet long after that Southern delicacy disappeared from the more prosperous gas stations along Route 411.

And Bujumbura was the capital of this country.

Eventually, they pulled up at a checkpoint staffed by two Africans holding clubs. She thought of the genocide in Rwanda, which she'd researched on the Internet, and the extreme violence of death by machete or club.

Barbaric, she thought, and instantly regretted it. She was smart enough to know that was racist, but she couldn't help it. Dear God, she prayed, as they pulled through the gate, have those men actually beaten someone to death?

The neighborhood on the other side of the concrete block wall was a different world. It was still dirt roads and chickens, but now there were electrical poles and oversized American-style houses on tiny lots. The driver stopped in front of a three-story cinderblock and plaster villa, centered on a trim green yard. In the doorway, another African lingered, this one dressed in formal attire, neat as a pin, with his hands clasped behind his back. When he reached for Alie's bags, she saw that he was wearing gloves.

"*Bienvenue à Bujumba,*" he said.

The first floor was wide, but through the back doors, open for the breeze, she could see a cinderblock wall with broken glass embedded on top. There were desks, papers, the sounds of activity behind doors, but the man didn't hesitate or inform. He carried her two small bags up the stairs—*I should have carried one of those,* she thought—and into a large room with a balcony and a queen bed. There was a ceiling fan, mosquito netting, African art, even a private bathroom. The air smelled like perfume and mosquito repellent.

"*Votre chambre, mademoiselle,*" the man said. Your room, miss.

"*Tout pour moi?*" she asked. All for me?

"*Oui, mademoiselle,*" he said, turning on his heels.

She opened the doors, walked onto the balcony, and leaned on the railing. She was looking out over the roofs, water tanks, and backup generators of maybe twenty similar houses, all within the compound walls. Beyond them was a startlingly large blue sky, bracketed by gorgeous green hills.

Africa, she thought, with a thrill.

"The Switzerland of the equator," someone said, and she turned, startled, to find a lean man in a white suit standing in her doorway. "That's what some call it, anyway. I'm not so sure. Maybe Alsace, I think. But the lake is beautiful." He walked onto the balcony beside her and stared at the view. Alie followed his gaze and saw the thin line, right in the middle of the blue. The sky wasn't bigger here; it was reflected in a lake.

"Lake Tanganyika. Over eighteen hundred kilometers long. The second deepest in the world. Over there," he said, pointing toward a hill, "was where Stanley found Livingstone and said, 'Doctor Livingstone, I presume?'"

It was the first story expats told newcomers, something Alie found even stranger now that she knew it probably wasn't true. She must have heard it three dozen times, or maybe three hundred. When she found herself saying it, she knew it was time to leave. But that was years away. On the first day, she was impressed.

"What's over there?" she asked.

"Congo," the man said. "You don't want to go there. It's dangerous." He extended his hand. "I'm Gironoux. I'm the secretary here."

She would see Gironoux almost every day of her stay in Bujumbura, or "Buj" as the expats called it, but never outside the compound walls. He was a sixty-year-old charity professional, tasked with handling the white part of the business: fund-raising, tours, parties.

She was a twenty-four-year-old fallen nun, who spent her days in the community. She sat with the sick and dying in crumbling rooms, quietly terrified of the legendary African maladies: the fly that laid eggs in your eyes and made you go blind, the worms that fed on your organs, HIV. She shopped with a guide at the Central Market (it burned down in 2013, she remembered sadly), where the meat was covered in black flies, and served humble meals out of a community center. She watched babies and filled out forms and helped women set up small market stalls, until she realized she was so ignorant of the local culture that she might actually be setting them back and begged to teach children instead. After that, she spent four days a week in an open-air, mud-walled church that reminded her of the one made out of old tires and broken windshields back in Hale County, watching small girls weave hot pads and pan holders out of scavenged wire.

I'm helping. I'm making a difference. I'm risking myself, she thought, even though every night she was back in the compound, and every Saturday afternoon she was at the embassy beach. It wasn't safe at night, they told her, and she believed it. There was electricity only in the wealthy pockets of town, and most of the city was dark by the time the rebels came out of the hills.

She heard the gunfire on the second night, while she was having dinner with Gironoux and three other natty Europeans at his villa down the road. They were eating goat stew (she was at that precise moment fishing out a few hairs, she recalled) and drinking Bordeaux when the popping started. She put down her spoon, but nobody else seemed to notice.

"Yes, it's gunfire," Gironoux said finally. "You'll get used to it. Now what do you think of Sister Mary Agnes?"

At least guns are better than clubs, she thought, although now, after ten years in war zones, she wasn't so sure. She met Locke two weeks later, right about the time she got bored with the place.

It was the Friday night party at the Marine House, a Buj tradition for young American expats. No, an African tradition. There was a Marine House near every American embassy, she understood now, and while the size and style varied depending on country, they were all the same: young men living in group rooms, in the kind of house none of them would ever be able to afford again. The United States embassy in Burundi was tiny and decrepit, but the twenty Marines sent to guard it lived in a mansion with a swimming pool, large-screen television, pool table, and barbeque. They had a butler for beer duty, a cook for meals, and maids for laundry. The frat boys at Auburn never had it so good.

Or partied so hard. These kids had gone straight into the Marines from high school, and now here they were, in one of the most obscure postings in the armed forces, where they could afford anything, even on their salaries, since everything was cheap. So they created a nonstop beer commercial: BBQ, music, women, satellite television for their favorite sports, a projector to show movies over the pool. She was squeezing through the crowded living room, trying not to spill her margarita, when she saw him, on the other side of the room, in the glow of the neon Budweiser sign.

It wasn't the first time. She had seen him around for at least a week, including that afternoon, at the embassy beach. It was a beautiful day. She was in her pink bikini, enjoying the tropical sun, even though her golden skin never needed a tan. He had been wearing pressed slacks and a linen suit coat; the man he was talking with wore fatigues. He glanced at her, but to her surprise, he didn't seem interested. Her mother always told her she was twenty pounds overweight, her mom told her a lot of terrible things, but she knew men loved her curves.

It was that cursory glance, or maybe just curiosity, that drove her that night. He was handsome, and sure of himself, but more than that, he was mysterious. In a community where everyone had defined roles—military, charity worker, debauched and/or bored diplomat—he didn't fit. He was older, but not old. Martial but not military. He seemed, somehow, to be all three at once, but also none at all.

When he glanced at her this time, she held his stare, and neither of them turned away. Ten seconds later, she was standing in the Budweiser glow.

"I'm Alie," she said.

"Um . . . Locke. Doctor Thomas Locke."

"Médecins sans Frontières?"

He laughed. "No, no. That was stupid. I'm sorry. I'm a doctor of international relations. From Harvard. The Carr Center for Human Rights." He passed her a business card. Who had business cards in Burundi? "I'm studying genocide."

"The civil war?"

"And a few others, all the way back to the Belgians. There's a long history."

"I'm an NGO worker," she said. "Catholic Relief Services."

"I know."

"Really? Did you look me up?"

"The indigenous shawl," he said, pointing to the light wrap she had thrown over her shoulders. "All NGO girls wear them."

She remembered that she and the younger women had gone to the market together, and she and Mary (and the other Mary) had bought similar wraps.

"You have a good eye for detail," she said.

He smiled. "I know what to look for."

Flirtatious. Maybe. "What do you think of Bujumbura?"

"It's a good place to study genocide."

They must have talked. She didn't remember now. She only remembered the end of the night, when she was half in the bag, wearing a sombrero with little tassels along the rim and fending off an overly persistent Marine.

"Let's dance," the Marine insisted, when the piano started. She had agreed. Why not? But the music was odd. It was wild, rhythmic, and toe-tapping, but . . . strange. Not Marine House style. She was about to complain, when she noticed it wasn't the stereo, but Dr. Locke on a battered upright piano covered with half a hundred empty beer bottles. Marine House had a piano? By the time he was finished, she had wandered over to watch.

"What was that?" she asked.

He turned, surprised to see her. "A fandango," he said.

"From Broadway?"

"No, Padre Antonio Soler. Baroque." He was clearly embarrassed. "You'd like him. A Spanish priest who liked to rock the harpsichord. Um . . . can I escort you home?"

She hadn't been thinking about leaving, but once they were outside, she was glad she had. The Marines had full-time staff, but the house was filthy. She had once made the mistake of going into a bedroom. The stench of floor clothes and sweat almost made her sick.

"I can't believe those guys went through Parris Island," Locke said, when they were outside.

She stopped, waiting, but Locke walked on. No one was allowed to travel in Buj after the sun went down without escort from cleared security personnel. Was Dr. Locke cleared? Where was his personal security detail, the one from the beach?

"I thought we might walk," he said, as if he didn't know this was dangerous.

It was a warm August night. The city was dark, so the stars were bright. She always found it odd to live in a city where you could see the stars. They were walking the ridgeline when the gunfire started somewhere in the darkness below. Someone was shouting. She recognized Kirundi, the native language. It was coming from a walkie-talkie hooked to Locke's belt.

"Sorry," he said, lowering the volume but not turning it off. "Someone reporting the shooting."

"Oh," she said. Most people wore walkie-talkies, since there were no landlines and the cell service had an annoying habit of cutting out for hours at a time. But the reports were always in French or English.

"Where did you learn to play piano?"

He blushed. "I was . . . a bit drunk," he said. "I shouldn't have done that." She didn't say anything. It was three blocks to the Catholic house, and she figured he'd answer eventually, if only to break the silence.

"I'm a classically trained musician," he said finally.

"On the piano?"

"Violin."

"That's an odd skill for a scholar in the middle of Africa."

"I had an odd childhood." He smiled. "How else would I have ended up here?"

She felt the truth in that. It was her own tough childhood that had pushed her into this forsaken part of the world.

"May I take you to dinner?" It was oddly formal, this idea of walking a girl home and asking her for a date, especially here. She wondered if he would give her an old-fashioned good-night kiss on the cheek at the door.

He did.

He arrived in a Land Cruiser the next evening. She hadn't been out of the embassy neighborhood at night, and she was surprised how dark the city felt. The buildings seemed to slink past, their cinderblock frames solid, but everything else sliding toward disarray, or toward the cooking fires fluttering in open windows and doors, like barrel fires in hobo movies. She found it exciting, so much more serene than the bustling days. It took courage to live like this, she knew, and somehow, out here, she felt that courage transferring onto her.

Eventually, they turned into the hills, and she started to see electrical wires, and then glass windows behind steel bars and lights behind curtains. They wove upward, the houses nicer at every switchback, and stopped in front of a wide brick building with a circular drive. A sign said THE BELVEDERE. The restaurant was mostly empty, but there was a flagstone balcony overlooking the city, the lights of Bujumbura so few and scattered they looked like constellations on the pitch-black lake.

"They say there's a huge crocodile named Leopold in there," Locke said, picking up on the otherworldly darkness of the water, "with a taste for human arms." They sat on the veranda. The hostess lit a candle. "I don't think it's a coincidence that the main form of punishment in the Belgian Congo was to chop off arms. Or that the Belgian king was named Leopold. The bottom of that lake is probably covered with human limbs."

"You are so romantic," she said, laughing, but despite the talk of severed arms, he was. They hovered near the edge of the balcony, the whole continent beneath them, and drank cognac, because that was what he ordered, and red wine, because that was what everyone drank with French food, especially coq au vin, the best she had ever had. She had dreamed of Paris as a teenager—why else would she have spent her Saturday mornings learning French in a strip mall on Choccolocco Road?—and while this certainly wasn't Paris, it was as close as she'd ever come. Paris, after all, wasn't a set of buildings, but an idea, or maybe a feeling, and being a thousand feet above a black lake, with an empty plate of classic French food in front of you and your hands intertwined with a handsome Harvard scholar's, was the essence of that feeling.

They went back to his hotel. It was a quaint guesthouse, twelve rooms around a courtyard, where hidden floodlights lit the undersides of the trees. He had brought a bottle of wine from the restaurant, and they drank it, alone under the branches, and kissed until morning. They hadn't slept together that first night, or even that next week, because when you're that swept up in romance, you don't want to spoil it with rolling and grunting. You want to spread it out, make it last forever.

"Why did you become a nun?" he asked eventually. "You obviously aren't very good at it."

"Simone Weil," she replied, with a laugh. She had always found it embarrassing that a long-dead writer had changed her life—had saved her, really, at the moment her violent, Evangelical mother had almost broken her down.

"*Oppression and Liberty*?"

She smiled. He knew Simone Weil. He had mentioned the wrong book. It was *Gravity and Grace*, Weill's tour de force on the redemptive power of mysticism, that had converted her, but Thomas Locke had struck closer to her true heart than any man or woman ever had before.

She should have known it was too good to be true.

Maybe she did know. Maybe she just didn't want to admit it at the time.

But no, she knew that wasn't true, either. Back then, she was too wrapped up in her story to worry about his.

And all the little clues? The mysteriousness of his schedule. The way he disappeared at odd times, for days on end. Sometimes he was distant, saying three words in a whole night. He seemed to go out of his way, after that first evening at the Marine House, to avoid the other expats, especially the Americans. And on that special night at the Restaurant Tanganyika, when their table was tucked away in the garden, under a flowering hyacinth, and she had thought, *He's going to tell me he loves me, that he can't live without me,* the words he actually said—"A former president of Burundi was assassinated right there"—should have tipped her off.

Instead, they made her fall in love with him even more.

She remembered the night they went to the street dance with Mary, poor, sheltered Mary, who was living out a fantasy of her own. The event was officially off-limits, and Locke didn't want to go, he was so tight about rules, but she was going, she told him, whether he came or not. So he had come, and she and Mary had danced for hours while he watched, sullen, a nothing night, until she stripped off his jacket on the car ride home and found the guns strapped to his side, and he had looked up at her, hesitated, and then kissed her passionately, truly passionately, until she fell backward on the seat beneath him. That was the first time they had sex, right there in the Land Cruiser, breaking her mother's first rule about boys, the one about never letting the first time be in the back of a car.

She wasn't a virgin, of course. That was obvious. But that was the end of her second chance, the night she took her clean slate and shattered it over her knee.

"You have to meet my family now," she had said, laughing at his shock. "Don't you know how it is with Catholic girls?"

She meant her work family, the twelve of them from Catholic Relief Services and the coterie of UN officials and NGOs who hung around them. All she was doing was inviting him for Sunday dinner, at least that was what she told herself, but he begged off that first week.

To her mild surprise, he showed up the next Sunday unannounced, in a natty suit that he and Gironoux spent five minutes discussing over predinner cognac. Gironoux was the most precise man in Buj (with the possible exception of their valet Prosper, the man who had carried her bags the first day), and he appreciated a sense of style. This dinner was his show, after all, and with Gironoux effort went a long way.

The conversation that evening was about Gatumba, a UN camp between Buj and the Congolese border, where 166 refugees had been massacred the previous day.

"It's not a lack of capacity," Neusberg lamented. "I know that's the official line, but I have to disagree. It's a matter of political will. There are plenty of UN workers here, not to mention our friends in charity, but what is the president willing to do for them?"

"The president is weak," Gironoux confessed.

"The president is lazy. He is holed up in his palace, drinking brandy, while the country slips away. That's what happens when you have professional politicians. They're like academics. They have no field experience. No offense . . ." he added, as he turned to Locke.

"None taken."

". . . but these are not men of action."

"It's preposterous," Weiss agreed, "that rebels infiltrate almost nightly. This is the capital city, for God's sake. If we can't be safe here, where can we be safe?"

"Perhaps if the military had better training and equipment,

they could push back the rebels," Locke suggested. He was politely ignored. Alie looked at him, saw his sincerity, and shrugged, *What can you do?* The humanitarian community would never condone such an idea, even after a massacre.

Later that night, Locke told her he was visiting Gatumba in the morning.

"Take me with you," she said.

"I can't."

"Take me with you," she said again, as she lay naked in his bed that night.

"It's a bad idea," he said.

"So is this. Obviously. But that hasn't stopped me."

He looked at her; it was chilly. "Some ideas are worse than others," he said.

She didn't know why he took her. Maybe it was her charm; maybe he really was in love. What did it matter? Gatumba changed her. The still-smoking remnants of refugee tents; the reek of unburied bodies. She had tried to turn away, but it was too late, she caught a glimpse of corpses being sorted like firewood.

"It's a UN refugee camp. How could this happen?"

"It happens all the time," he said.

"But we said we'd protect them."

Locke looked at his driver, the military man from the beach. He was American, early forties, angry. He hadn't looked at her once on the two-hour drive. He hadn't said a word until he replied, with disgust: "Who's 'we'?"

Locke pulled out a container of Vick's VapoRub. "Put it under your nose," he said. "It kills the smell."

He dropped her off at the Catholic primary school, four cinderblock buildings with a Burundian flag in the courtyard and an African nun, Sister Mary Clementine, to welcome them in

French. Had Magdelena been there that day? She was never sure. There were too many girls to remember just one: on the floor, in the desks, standing against the walls. Too many scared and terrified girls staring with empty eyes at the young American from lower Alabama, who had just walked into their hell.

She didn't want to leave. She never wanted to leave. She had told Sister Mary Clementine that. She had told Locke that when he came back hours later, jittery and unnerved, without his companion. But he had insisted, saying he was the last ride, saying it wasn't safe to stay the night.

"If it's safe enough for them, it's safe enough for me."

"It's not safe enough for them," he said. "Get in."

They argued on the way back. She demanded to know what he meant. He refused to tell her. She blew up over his lack of respect. What did he know about refugees? What did he care about altruism? He was an academic. Academics were cold. He saw statistics; she saw souls.

"I'm trying to help," he said.

"What does that mean?"

Silence. It was dusk. He was driving very fast.

"What the hell does that mean?"

He wouldn't say. He wouldn't treat her like a partner. Or an equal. Or an adult. They rode the last half hour in silence, the world darkening around them. They made the compound just as the nightly gunfire started in the hills.

"You don't understand," she said sadly, as she opened the door to leave. "You don't know who I am."

"Alie," he said. "Wait."

"Please . . ." she was fighting back tears ". . . don't . . . don't tell me what to do."

She closed the car door.

Three hours later, the rebels poured out of Congo and attacked Bujumbura in force. She stayed awake all night, locked in the house's safe room with the rest of the Catholic Relief Services workers, listening to the explosions down the hill toward the presidential palace, the gunfire moving back and forth across the city.

By morning, it was over. She slipped out and walked toward the center of town, where the worst of the fighting had occurred. She saw bloodstained streets, bombed-out buildings, burned vehicles. She smelled burned flesh; after Gatumba, she would always know that smell. There were men throwing bodies onto trucks, and others celebrating in the streets. The rebels had lost. Her boyfriend, the so-called scholar, had somehow been involved.

He left before she could ask him anything more. Disappeared. She never saw him again, not until a chance sighting in South Sudan six or seven years later. She had been so deceived, so embarrassed by her gullibility, that she had never even looked for him. She had spent the next nine hours helping the wounded of Bujumbura, and the next nineteen months in Gatumba, at the orphanage, wondering if she was doing any good. She thought she would stay there for the rest of her life, but when Magdelena, only thirteen, told her she wanted a better life in Europe, Alie agreed to help. She traveled with Magdelena and five other female refugees through Rwanda and Uganda, and up into war-torn Sudan. To document their journey, she had told them. To witness for them, so the world would understand.

It had taken almost a year, often on foot, often for weeks at a time in squalid smuggler camps, and for one long stretch on horseback, her whole body a raw wound by then. But she had stuck with it. To tell their story, to give voice to the voiceless. And because she believed somehow that her whiteness—her half-white Western-ness—was protecting them.

"Don't worry, Magdelena, I am with you," she told the girl on the loading dock in Bossaso, Somalia. "I am with you."

Then the boat's fake floor was fitted into place, the darkness descended on that dank hold, and she never saw any of them again. She had tried for years, working through slumlords and other refugees, through NGOs and networks of nuns, but she never found Magdelena, never discovered what had happened to that poor young girl in this civilized new paradise she had tried so desperately to reach . . .

Alie felt a hand on her shoulder and jerked up, her eyes flashing around the grubby hospital room in Kiev. A few feet away, a frail woman lay still on her bed. A nurse was standing between them, with her hand on Alie's shoulder.

"Don't cry," the nurse said in English. "Her pain will end soon. It is for the best."

Alie wiped away her tears. She fished in her pocket. She came up with a twenty-euro note. She held it out, but the nurse waved it away. Health care in Ukraine was free, but doctors and nurses usually required bribes, even if their patients were dying.

"Morphine," the nurse said, plunging the needle into the drip line.

Alie nodded absently. She had gone looking for information on John Greenlees as soon as Chad Hargrove identified him in the photograph. She hadn't expected that search to lead her here, to this dying woman. It was early, barely light outside, but even in the shadows Alie could see the pain. The woman was thin, ancient looking and brittle, but Alie knew that Olena Kravitz was barely a decade older than she was.

She had been a human rights lawyer. A decorated scholar. A lover of life and, apparently, her husband. There was the proof, in the photographs beside the bed: Olena hiking in the mountains, Olena and John Greenlees together. Happy. Healthy. In love. The kind of photographs Alie had never had.

And still those assholes at the U.S. Embassy called her a whore.

The nurse squeezed Alie's elbow and quietly closed the door behind her. The overnight was ending; the next shift would be arriving soon. Alie wondered if there were kind nurses on that shift, too, and if anyone would stay with Olena the rest of the day. *The husband comes every night,* the nurse had told her. *Just wait.*

He hadn't come.

She thought of the ride back from Gatumba, when she had wanted respect, and Locke had refused. When he shut her out. She thought of Olena Kravitz's husband, in the hotel lobby, yesterday afternoon. A man who stayed with his sick wife every evening, until Tom Locke walked into his life.

She touched Olena's hand. It was bones. The woman had days, maybe hours, to live. She crossed herself, the first time she'd done that in years. She thought of Magdelena, another woman left behind.

If there was one thing Alie MacFarlane hated, it was being left behind.

CHAPTER 20

I crouched behind a rusty hulk of machinery with my SCAR assault rifle, watching two boys explore the abandoned factory, a huge complex built in the Soviet heyday and later owned by Karpenko. This was the place, in fact, where he'd found Grigory Maltov, when the enforcer was acting as a union boss. The direct connection to the client was a risk, but worthwhile. The complex was a vouched location in an unknown city, and it was perfectly placed: two kilometers from Kramatorsk's city center, less than a klick from the target. Walking distance.

Besides, it was less than forty-eight hours until the assault, not much time for the enemy to piece together connections. We'd be fine, I was sure, as long as Miles's team arrived on time, and these boys were the only locals who happened to wander in.

As I watched the boys casually breaking glass, my thoughts drifted back to Burundi. I told myself it was the children—that both clients were fathers, that on both missions I had saved young lives—but I knew the connection was Alie. I thought of her confusion that day, when I left her at her doorstep and disappeared. Her effort not to cry, even though I was breaking her heart. That was her innocence, at the moment of being stripped away.

I pictured her three days ago in Kiev, the first time we'd spoken in ten years, and the hardness under her curves. I had dreamed of seeing her again, had followed her career from a distance as it rose and collapsed. I thought we would reconnect, like in the movies, *bam*, we were meant to be together, we've known it all along. I thought she'd remember the good times: my tiny room in the guesthouse, when I'd run my fingers over her scarred backside, and she'd flinched, and shivered, and finally relaxed under my touch. Our night at the Belvedere overlooking Lake Tanganyika, when we talked about Leopold the human-eating crocodile and her personal savior, Simone Weil, the Christian mystic who advocated a life of giving, and who died of self-starvation in 1943.

I should have told her then, that night, when I saw who she was, and who she wanted to be. I should have told her that I was a soldier-for-hire, but still a scholar. That I was in Burundi to stop a genocide. That the country was in danger, even the missionaries, and especially the women and girls.

I should have told her I took her to Gatumba to show her the real Africa, to prove that what I did mattered, to give her a way to access the purity of purpose that drove Simone Weil, who died in solidarity with Nazi victims. But I miscalculated. I thought the massacre at the UN camp was a crime of opportunity, when it was the beginning of the end.

I didn't know that until I dropped her off and crossed the border into Congo, twenty kilometers away. Our mission parameters forbade it, but Miles and I were tagging along with Gaspard, a trusted comrade in the Burundian Presidential Guard. We found the girl half a klick across the border, facedown and silent, with a grown man on top of her and three others laughing. She couldn't have been older than eight or ten.

Miles sensed my anger. My . . . foolishness. He put an arm out to stop me, but it was already done. A slash to a throat, two stabs to a left lung, a cranium crushed with a rifle butt. By the time I reached to help the girl, I was covered in blood. And she woke up. Somehow, she woke up to the pain, when she was safe, and started screaming.

The jungle exploded with shouts, vehicle engines, men crashing into underbrush. The FNL rebels were everywhere, in every direction. We ran. What else could we do? This was no raiding party. The FNL was massing for an attack. There were twelve of us, and probably twelve thousand of them.

Eight of us made the Burundian border. "Go to Bujumbura," I yelled at Gaspard, when we reached our SUV. "Raise the alarm. Make sure the men are ready."

"Where are you going?"

"Gatumba."

I saw Miles's mouth drop. I knew what he was thinking. *The white girl? Now?*

"I'll be there," I said.

How could I tell Alie any of this, on that long, rushed drive home? What good would it have done? Honesty would only have led to questions I didn't have time to answer and a conversation I didn't want to have. Not then, anyway.

But what about now? Could I turn our relationship around? Could I make her see that I had no choice, that it was fight that night, right then, or ten thousand people die, or a hundred thousand, or maybe more?

Could I explain that there are no medals for mercs? No celebrations. That I was on a plane out of Bujumbura as soon as the smoke cleared. That . . . that I could have said no to the flight . . . could have taken the time to talk to her, at least . . . but I was inexperienced, in over my head . . . and I've always regretted not saying good-bye.

CHAPTER 21

I was tired. I could feel the heaviness in my limbs, and this fuzzy nostalgia, these thoughts of Alie . . . I knew that was a product of exhaustion, too. The Poltava operation had been stressful, right up until the moment six hours ago when Karpenko's dacha had gone up in flames. We hadn't landed at the factory until four in the morning, and I was running on two hours of sleep. I needed to rest, gather my faculties for the next leg, instead of watching these young boys beating a steel chair to death with a pipe.

My knees hurt from crouching. My back was sore from the two-hour flight in the cramped helicopter, with Greenlees pressed against my side. Time was catching up to me, both in the short sense and the long. When the boys finally wandered away, I stood up, pissed in the bushes, and felt an obscene amount of relief.

I walked back toward our base. The factory complex consisted of eight large buildings with sidewalks between them, surrounded by a chain-link fence. It was a former industrial behemoth, now a rust heap of tendinitis and trash, with a dense forest of weeds and brush closing in. At the corner of our building—the seventh from the entrance—I stopped, scanning the area. The hangar-size front door opened to a paved area, where we had landed the helicopter that morning. There were clear sightlines for ten meters, to the trees and weeds on the other side.

I walked around the back and inspected the emergency exit,

our secondary evac route. There was a building overlooking the exit, and three meters to an eight-foot-high fence crowned with rusty razor wire. First priority: cut an evacuation route through the fence to the forest beyond.

I entered through the emergency exit, bolting the door behind me. The interior of the building was massive, four stories high with floor rails for supply carts, ceiling rails where smelters had hung, and a three-quarters catwalk. The windows started twenty feet up, so dirty they looked like stained glass.

The helicopter looked tiny, sitting in the center of that vast cathedral, the early morning light falling in square patches around it. We had pushed it inside last night before racking, so that wandering kids and scrap scavengers wouldn't see it. The factory had been filthy then, but Sirko had cleared space for our sleeping rolls and scrounged supplies for protective barricades: a few oil barrels, a wooden door, some pieces of rusted metal that had eluded the scavengers. Now he was sitting with his head down, exhausted, Karpenko beside him using a rucksack for a seat.

The only other comfortable seat was the helicopter, where Greenlees was slumped in the cockpit. The pilot was walking toward him yelling in Ukrainian, and then with the ease of a thousand flying hours he was lifting himself through the door. He pushed Greenlees out, the old man falling awkwardly a few feet to the floor. Greenlees lay there, not moving. Then he dusted off his sleeves, pushed himself to his feet, and turned to face the pilot, who had jumped down beside him. For a moment, the scene was iconic, two curved men facing off in the slanting morning light like a George Bellows painting of boxers, until the pilot slugged Greenlees in the face, knocking him to the ground.

"What's going on?" I said, running toward them. "What the hell is going on?"

By the time I was halfway there, Sirko had the pilot by the

shoulder and was dragging him away. He shoved the man against a wall and punched him hard in the gut. It was the "wall-to-wall counseling" of an old school military disciplinarian, and I had to admire the professionalism of his delivery. Effective, but within reason. Even today's soft army recruits wouldn't need to flash a stress card for that one.

"I shouldn't be here," Greenlees moaned, as I pulled him to his feet and dusted off his shirt. He felt spineless and slack. A welt was already forming around his right eye. If my back was sore, I could only imagine how he felt.

"I shouldn't be here," he said again.

"John."

"I'm too old. I've been out of the game ten years. When Wolcott called, I thought . . ."

He thought it would be like the old days: stiff vodka and cherries jubilee.

Greenlees was staring at me, as if trying to peer into my soul. He looked away. "You wouldn't understand," he said. "You don't know . . ." He stopped, sighed. "I should be with my wife."

He looked frail, almost white, and unprepared for hard beds and cold meals. It could have been alcoholism but it was probably age, not to mention a punch in the face. Greenlees was right. I shouldn't have brought him. But it was too late now. A helicopter flight was too risky, and besides, we didn't have enough aviation fuel left to get him more than fifty kilometers. And forget cars. There was no way out of Kramatorsk until Apollo's ex-fil sixty hours from now.

"Do you need a drink?"

Greenlees shook his head no.

"It's only two days," I said. "And it's only radio duty. You'll be fine."

I watched him shuffle off unsteadily, a serious liability to a difficult mission. What was it like, I wondered, to realize your best days were gone?

"What happened?" I snapped, turning to Karpenko. The oligarch was wearing the same suit and pocket square as last night, casually debonair, his hair slicked back. He looked like he was at the races—maybe horses, maybe charioteers. He probably hadn't slept on anything less than a mattress full of money for the past decade, but he seemed no worse for wear. It was clear he had packed his grooming products.

"The pilot said he was trying to use the radio," Karpenko shrugged. He lit a Dunhill blue and offered me one, but I declined.

"Did he?"

Karpenko eyeing me coolly, as if to say, That's your man, not mine. He exhaled smoothly. "The pilot's an asshole," he said.

Two hours until Miles and his team were scheduled to arrive. Two hours of holding these exhausted, frazzled amateurs together.

"Nobody touches that gentleman," I said to Karpenko. "Nobody."

I turned away. I was exhausted. I needed rack time, but I couldn't risk it until the team arrived. They couldn't come soon enough.

CHAPTER 22

Alie watched Chad Hargrove dig into a plate of pirogis. He wasn't a fan of Ukrainian food, but he had an inordinate fondness for their version of dumplings. Two months ago, when they had first gotten together to swap information and insinuation, Alie had to talk him into trying them. Now he was eating them for breakfast. Like a real Ukrainian, he said. Alie didn't have the heart to tell him these pirogis were Polish.

"So Greenlees's wife is sick?"

"She's dying."

Hargrove bit into a sauerkraut pirogi, his least favorite. He slathered the second half in applesauce. "I wonder what would make him leave when she was like that," he said, with his mouth full. "Money, probably."

"Or the chance to be back in the game." Men always talked like that: gotta be in the game, gotta win the game. Even if I have to leave the woman I love—or say I love—behind. In her experience, men rarely talked about money in the same way. "Sounds like Greenlees missed his old line of work."

"You mean because he hangs around the bureau? I suppose."

Their two nights together seemed to have loosened things up. Hargrove was no longer playing CIA, trying to keep everything just below the surface. Now he was buying her breakfast at her favorite diner, the one with good booths for private conversations.

Hargrove looked around, spy style, then reached into his briefcase and pulled out his laptop. "Came in this morning," he said as he logged on.

He turned the laptop to face her, and she read the report quickly. There had been a firefight at an abandoned airfield outside Poltava. An armored personnel carrier, truck, and multiple SUVs destroyed. Eight or nine trees knocked over, with extreme prejudice. Six dead, officially, all Ukrainians with criminal records. Pretty standard stuff, except . . .

"There was an airplane?"

Hargrove nodded. "Headed west. NATO logged it, and approved it, crossing into Romania."

"Locke," Alie whispered, and her disappointment surprised her. He had flown in for an assassination. To kill six people, not to mention blow up a house. Why did she care about this man again?

"What does Baker think?"

"He's at a meeting, probably will be for hours. But he won't think anything of it. If your friend hadn't been on my mind, I might not have looked closely, either. And that's how I found this." He pointed at the NATO flight report. "I checked back right before I came here. Already wiped from the system."

Our secret, Alie thought. "Good thing I left early, then."

He didn't answer. She had walked out at three in the morning, while he was asleep, and Hargrove was hurt. Puppy dog hurt.

"I'm joking, Chad," Alie said, reaching for her *pertsovka.* She always drank the local liquor, even when it was hot pepper vodka. Buying local was a point of pride. "I'm sorry about leaving. I just . . . I couldn't get Greenlees off my mind."

"Oh yes. Good old irresistible Greenlees."

Suddenly, she felt annoyed. "I'm not going to apologize."

"I'm not asking you to." He stabbed a pirogi. "And besides, you just did."

Had she really? Jesus. She didn't want to do this: the loaded banter, the relationship probing. She didn't want to have to work to keep this kid with the Colgate grin from feeling like he had the upper hand. He was just a mission boy, right?

She sat back. She realized the operation was probably over, and whatever Locke had come to Ukraine to do, it was done. But that didn't mean it was over for her. She was a reporter. She could find him. Or at least the mess he'd left behind.

"What's your relationship with Thomas Locke?" Hargrove asked.

First name. Official. Hargrove had done his homework.

"We knew each other ten years ago in Africa."

"Knew each other?"

"Slept together."

"Like us."

If you say so. "We left on bad terms. He was posing as a human rights scholar, but . . . he kills people, Chad."

It sounded so stupid when she said it. And worse, she wasn't even sure it was true.

"You saw it happen?"

No, never. "I didn't need to," she said, motioning toward the reports. "You've read about his work."

Hargrove put his hand on top of hers. He wanted to appear sympathetic, but Alie knew he was jealous. Locke was out there doing something. He was in the shit. And that was why Alie loved him, or hated him, or whatever these feelings were. Did she really feel this strongly about Tom Locke, even after all these years?

"What would happen if you saw him now?"

Alie took a sip of her *pertsovka* and eyed Hargrove, wondering what he was fishing for. What had she shown him just now?

"I don't know," she said. It was a stall, but it was also the truth.

Hargrove nodded, chewing his pirogi.

"I talked to Greenlees this morning," he said. "He called for Baker on an aviation channel. His coding was old but still valid. He wants a CIA emergency extraction. It seems he's lost faith in your friend."

Or he missed his wife. "Did he say where?"

"No. He was cut off. But I triangulated his location." Hargrove smiled. "Kramatorsk."

It struck her that Chad Hargrove was breaking his own rules. Just talking with a reporter about mercenaries was, as he'd say, *unprofessional.* Especially if you had feelings for her. But this was an opportunity for both of them. There was something big here: a story, a second chance, a promotion, an adventure, revenge.

"You have a plan?"

Hargrove nodded. "There's a CIA contract in the area. Training and advisement of a militia called the Donbas Battalion. They're overdue for an inspection, and with Baker ass-deep in paperwork. . . . It's three hours of official oversight work, at most, and then twenty klicks to Kramatorsk."

Klicks. Hargrove already thought he was a soldier. But he was clever, she had to give him that. He hadn't come up with this plan this morning. He must have been working on a way to get into the field for weeks.

"I can get us there, Alie," Hargrove said, the excitement clear in his eyes. "I have Greenlees triangulated to a tenth of a mile. My question is: can you get us inside?"

CHAPTER 23

Jim Miles pulled his sleeping bag up to his eyebrows and tried to stay warm. Usually missions for Apollo Outcomes were top-notch: first-class airfare, five-star hotels, stuff the army would never provide. Stuff you deserved, when you were risking your ass for the bottom line.

On this mission, they'd already flown the military transport "bus" overnight from Romania, after hightailing it from the Libyan desert. Now they were on their way to some industrial facility in some place called Kramatorsk in the back of a fish delivery truck. Most delivery trucks had transparent tops for light, but this one was refrigerated. The cooling unit was off, but it was still cold and dark, and the only reliable light came from four bullet holes Wildman had shot in the side a hundred miles ago, before Miles could stop him.

If not for Locke, he never would have taken the mission, Miles thought, but somebody had to watch out for the kid. Miles had been Locke's platoon sergeant in the 82nd Airborne Division, starting in 1992. Locke was a butter bar then, a month out of ranger school and one of the few officers in Division who hadn't received his commission from West Point. He'd gone to liberal Brown University, of all places. He was an opera zealot. He liked to quote some chick named Michelle Foucault and received an honest-to-God letter of reprimand from the CO ordering him to speak English at a sixth-grade level. Fucking Ivy Leaguers.

Still, the kid had potential, and Miles had wanted to get his claws in before the officer corps lobotomized him. So he took him to the one place they could talk undisturbed, a titty bar on Murchison Road, or "the Murch," as the men called it.

"You heard the term 'fragging'?" Miles asked, as young Locke picked up his Wild Turkey shot, tipped it down his throat, and almost coughed it back up.

"It means getting sabotaged by your own men," Locke said, sucking wind.

Miles ordered another round. "It comes from the Vietnam War," he said, "when arrogant and stupid lieutenants got troops killed." The bourbon arrived. They slugged back another round. "So troops would roll a frag grenade into an officer's tent, and problem solved."

"What are you saying?"

"I'm saying stop listening to Captain Franks."

"But he's the company commander."

"Doesn't mean you suck his ass," Miles said. "I'd hate to see you turn into one of those monkeyclowns." Then he gave Locke the only piece of advice a commander needed to follow every damn day of his life. "Take care of your troops, and they will take care of you."

Nice delivery truck, kid, Miles now thought with a laugh. *Glad you took my advice.*

Truthfully, though, Miles knew there was no place he would rather be. He'd dropped out of the South Hudson Institute of Technology (aka West Point, aka SHIT) after one semester to become a real soldier, sending his TAC officers into apeshit apoplexy, and he'd soldiered for twenty-four years. CAG, also known as "Delta Force." JSOC, *the* task force in Iraq under the legendary Stan McChrystal. Bosnia. Somalia. Afghanistan. Yemen. He knew more about Arabia at this point than he did about America. The only things waiting for him back home were two ex-wives, two kids he didn't know, and the equipment for his beer brewing operation stashed in a storage locker on the outskirts of Phoenix. The only thing he really wanted, at this point, were Rottweilers and the warm thighs of a woman who didn't ask where he was going, or why he couldn't stay. The only thing he cared about were his brothers-in-arms, and most of them were suffering in this truck with him right now.

"Roadblock," Jacobsen said in his earpiece.

Miles sprang out of his bag, his rifle in firing position. There was just enough light coming in through the bullet holes to see Boon, the best damn Thai ex-special forces op in the business, and Charro, El Salvadorean anticorruption death squad motherfucker, kicking out of their fart sacks and hunching over their weapons, too. Charro was a corruption of *Charral,* meaning "bush" in Spanish, because he had Moses' burning bush tattooed on his chest. Charro was a devout Catholic; he'd fled San Salvador after shooting up a drug gang that had taken over his sister's church. He had prayers for mercy tattooed halfway up his neck and all the way down to his boots.

"Lock and load," Wildman whispered, as the delivery truck started to slow. Miles didn't need to see him to know that Wildman was smiling. The man had a darkness in his soul; he'd once sent a goat into the officer's mess hall out of boredom, not to mention fistfighting several of his British 22 Special Air Service Regiment (SAS) comrades and almost killing a guy outside a gay bar late one night while on leave in Aberdeen. Even when not in the combat zone, Wildman was known to sleep with his SA80 assault rifle for a teddy bear and a block of C-4 for a pillow. The man had a serious relationship with det cord.

"Four," Jacobsen said, as the car slowed. "With Kalashnikovs.

Two on the driver's side. One on the passenger. Fourth man at the barrier with a radio."

Miles trusted the men with him in the back of the truck. They were outcasts, unfit for ordinary life, but they had found a home in the team, and they'd saved each other's asses so many times they'd stopped keeping count. But he didn't know Jacobsen, the driver, or Reynolds, his partner in the cab. He had needed a Russia-Ukrainian speaker on four hours' notice, and Jacobsen's two-man team was the best qualified available. And Jacobsen, the more experienced of the pair, fit the bill: an ex-Green Beret from Tenth Group, U.S. Army Special Forces, based out of Panzer Barracks in Stuttgart, Germany, meaning he'd been trained by the U.S. government in guerilla warfare against Russia. Plus he was qualified, meaning he'd been through six weeks of Apollo's training at the Ranch, just like the rest of them.

"Shit," Reynolds whispered into his headset, "they're nervous." Miles grimaced. Nerves were bad. Nerves meant amateurs, and amateurs did stupid things.

"Ahoy," Jacobsen said, hailing a man Miles would never see, and Miles couldn't help but think *¿Donde esta?,* the only foreign phrase he knew. The men were speaking rapid Ukrainian now, two voices back and forth. It seemed friendly enough.

Then the light went out of one of the bullet holes, and the tension increased with the darkness. One of the Ukrainians had put his finger over the hole, or maybe his eye, trying to see in. He shouted to his comrade.

It got so quiet, for so long, Miles could hear someone breathing, and knew it as Wildman, gearing up for a fight. The metal sides of the delivery van would never stop a bullet. If the Ukrainians got trigger-happy, the team was sitting ducks. And those ducks were sitting on a truckload of missiles, ammunition, and grenades. Wildman would be out the cargo doors before that happened, Miles knew. It was only a matter of a minute, at most, before he was firing, with orders or without.

A second hole went black, and Miles rocked onto his heels. The men were shouting now, back and forth with each other and Jacobsen, and Miles slowed his breathing, his finger resting a few inches from the trigger. They could shred the Ukrainians right through the walls, and be gone within seconds . . .

"Wait, wait," someone yelled in English. It was Reynolds, and it was a message for Miles. Reynolds knew the team could only sit in the dark so long. *Thirty seconds,* Miles thought, as the men outside grew quiet. *I'll give you twenty-five seconds, and then I'm opening up.*

And when Miles started firing, the rest of the team would start firing, too. And it would all be over then, one way or the other.

CHAPTER 24

Maltov pushed open the door and trudged into the club. It was crowded, especially for a Thursday lunch, but he hardly noticed. These people were insects, bouncing aside as he shouldered his way toward the bar. In the distance, a woman was onstage, under a bright light, dancing. He didn't turn to look. He didn't feel the halfhearted grip on his shoulder. He didn't care about any of these people. He was here for his nephew Pavlo, who his sister would never be able to bury, nothing more.

He saw the man in a corner beyond the bar and tilted that direction, not changing his speed. He slipped his knife into his palm, shouldered the last few people out of the way, and slid into the booth.

"Ivanych," he said, landing an elbow as he came in.

Belenko's bullheaded mercenary turned. "Grigory," Ivan said, without expression, like he was just taking whatever the world offered, without caring one way or the other. The piece of shit. "Let me buy you a drink."

"I don't think so. I had a rough one last night."

"So did I. That's why I drink today." Beer bottles covered the table, along with cigarette butts and ashes. The two woman across from them looked as strung out as the woman onstage.

"You brought Chechens," Maltov said.

The big man shrugged. "Not by choice."

"You brought a fucking armored personnel carrier."

"You drove a truck into it."

"My friend died in that explosion," Maltov snapped, leaning in.

Ivan stared at him halfheartedly. "That's what you get for having friends."

Maltov felt himself tense. They were only a few inches apart now, and he could taste the man's hot breath. One thrust, and this conversation would be over.

Ivan laughed. "Do you want to compare body counts? Or do you want to compare allies? You were not exactly alone, were you, my friend?"

Maltov eased back, realizing only then how coiled he had been. The knife he had been pressing in Ivan's side slid out farther than he expected.

"It's over, Grisha," Ivan said. He was smiling now. The moment had pulled him out of his stupor. "We are men for hire. Let it go."

Ivan was right. He was being unprofessional. There was the work, and there was the rest of your life. Your enemy in one might be your ally in the other, so you kept them separate. No malice. No revenge. Maltov had lived by that code since walking away from the iron works and into the world of men like Ivan. It was ingrained in him. It had to be, to keep the wolves from tearing each other apart. But he could feel it slipping away, maybe under the Russian military advance, maybe under the dirty squalor of that hooker's smile. Strong things on the surface, he thought, could be rotten underneath.

"Where did the Chechens come from?"

Ivan shook his head. "Chechnya, *urod*." Idiot.

"Why?"

"Because they were paid."

"For what?"

"Karpenko. There's a bounty."

"How much?"

Ivan shrugged. "A half million euros, I hear, although we were offered fifty thousand, as a finder's fee."

Maltov hesitated. A half million euros? That was nothing to men like Karpenko, and Belenko, and Putin, who was no doubt behind the bounty, but big money to a man of fortune. Five hundred thousand was enough to drink and tell stories on for the rest of your life.

"Who offered you the fifty thousand?"

Ivan smiled. "Why are you so interested, Grigory? Are you planning to turn on your boss?"

Maltov didn't answer.

"Oh, that's right, your boss has run away."

Maltov frowned. "Kostyantyn Karpenko would never run. Never. Unlike your traitorous boss Belenko."

Ivan smiled with all his teeth. He reached for his glass and drank half his beer in a long swallow. His hand was huge. Whatever had been pulling him down, he seemed out from under it now.

"It's a job, Grisha. For God's sake, don't take it so seriously. If you can't enjoy yourself—" he looked at the two women, one of whom smiled back "—what is the point?"

Maltov thought of the first job he and Ivan had done together. Ivan had shot a woman in the head—the reason was never clear—and then gone into a bar and sat down, blood on his shirt, and drank four beers. He had left a few-thousand-ruble tip. Generous, but in Russian currency, not the Ukrainian hryvnia.

"He calls himself *volk*," Ivan said. "*Chelovek-volk*. The Wolfman. What an asshole, right?" Ivan was laughing at him now, or maybe not at him, maybe just laughing. To Ivan, this was just another violent encounter in a violent life.

A month ago, it might have been the same to me, Maltov thought. He couldn't see himself drinking with Ivan, not here, not anymore.

"I've heard of him," Maltov said. "He's Russian."

"We're all Russian," Ivan said. "At least a little bit."

Maltov felt the passion flowing back. "No, Ivanych. We're Ukrainian. We're fighting Russia."

Ivan didn't notice the change in his companion's demeanor. "We're fighting death, Grigorivich," he said. "And poverty. And boredom. The rest . . ." The woman across the booth bared her teeth, and Maltov could feel legs at work under the table. ". . . let God sort it out."

Maltov pulled away and closed his knife. There was blood on the booth, but Ivan didn't seem to notice. It didn't matter. One way or another, the man was dead already. He was eaten up, Maltov could see, with disease.

"Good-bye Grigory Maltovovich," Ivan said, as Maltov eased out of the booth. "Say hello to the *americains* for me."

He watched Maltov disappear into the crowd, then turned back to his companions. He had a woman under his arm, whispering to her, by the time the Wolf's shadow fell over his table.

"Do you feel better now, *Chelovek-volk?* I told you he would come."

The Wolf didn't say anything. What did he ever have to say to a man like Ivan? He threw a thousand euros on the table, the agreed-upon price for information.

"Karpenko is still here," Ivan said, tapping the table.

"You are sure?"

"Almost. Follow that man, as I promised, and you will find out."

The Wolf threw another hundred euros on the table.

"What about the girl?" Ivan said, still tapping.

The Wolf rubbed the necklace in his pocket, his souvenir. He could feel his hand throbbing, but that was how it always felt, when his heart was beating this hard. He threw down another hundred euros.

Yes, he felt better, thanks for asking. But only for now.

He wouldn't really feel better until Karpenko was in Moscow, and all his accomplices were dead.

CHAPTER 25

"Any trouble?" I asked, when Miles stepped out of the back of the truck.

He had parked out of sight and sent a buddy team, Boon and Charro, to scout the area and facilitate the linkup. Once operation security was established, his driver, an American merc I'd never met, had pulled the truck into the building and through to the back corner, as far from the helicopter as possible. In case of attack, we didn't want to lose both transports to one grenade.

"Roadblock," Miles said. "About twenty kilometers southwest."

That would explain the delay. "Pay them off?"

"Didn't work."

"Take them out?"

"Almost. At the last second, Reynolds swapped some NYPD badges and a bottle of Johnny Walker Blue for passage."

"Risky," I said, checking out the merc Miles was nodding toward, although *stupid* was the more accurate word. Reynolds was young, probably late twenties, with a skintight buzzcut and monster arms full of tattoos.

"They were teenagers," Reynolds said with a shrug as he humped a chest of tag, track, and locate equipment from the truck. "Just scared recruits. I thought something rare and personal might keep them alive." I knew where he was coming from; I'd done the same many times in Africa, mostly with old airborne patches. "Besides," Reynolds continued, "they were pro-Ukrainian. On our side."

I glanced at Miles. It was one thing to kill; that was often the safest path. It was another to risk your life, and the lives of your team, on nonviolent options. Other commanders might complain about opsec, risk matrixes, blah, blah, but in my opinion Apollo Outcomes, and my missions, could always use a man with that kind of restraint.

"Welcome to the team," I said, extending a hand.

And that was it for small talk. These were my guys, closer than family, and Miles was my best friend, but we weren't the type for sentiments or hugs. This was a deadly business, and the team was already at it, unloading the gear they'd brought with them from Africa: three boxes of grenades, flash and smoke and incendiary; ammunition crates; several blocks of C-4 and four meters of det cord; blasting caps; white phosphorous, or "Willy P," that could create thick smoke screens or burn through bone and metal, depending on your need; night-vision goggles and flares; a case of freeze-dried provisions; a water filter; and six flats of bottled water, Kirkland brand.

"In arms reach," Miles instructed, as Reynolds and the older new guy, Jacobsen, carried four M90 grenade launchers, which were cheap, abundant, and wickedly effective against armored personal carriers.

"Back corner," Miles said, as Boon and Charro lifted out a couple of the SA-18 antiaircraft missiles we'd picked up in Libya. Miles had brought himself some toys.

"I could only slip out two," Miles said, smiling, "but it will be enough."

"More than enough," I said, "considering that we're assaulting a natural gas facility holding a hundred trillion tons of explosive gas."

It was a slight exaggeration, but Miles smiled even more. "We'll make sure the helos crash into potato fields," he said.

Wildman had set an old door on two grenade cases, and Boon was positioning two standard-issue Panasonic Toughbook laptops on the "desk." Add the portable generator and an 8 × 11 metal micro-antenna to connect to a satellite, and from there to Apollo's secure mainframe, and we'd be wired and untraceable on a simple system any half-competent Boy Scout troop could rig in an hour. The fancy stuff was the company's proprietary software, like the encryption codes and hyperaccurate three-dimensional maps of Kramatorsk. Many national militaries used Google Earth to plan missions; Apollo Outcomes had a private worldwide grid. The technology was worth millions, which was why a paper-thin layer of C-4 was hidden between the computer components and their hard-shell case. Airport security would never notice it, but insert a pin in the sides of these computers, and all that proprietary coding would be incinerated in an instant, with only the barest hint of visible smoke.

"Up and running," Boon said, as the maps flipped on the screen.

I looked at Karpenko, who was casually smoking another Dunhill, and Sirko, who was trying not to look impressed. It was either the technology, or the fact that my team had done more work in five minutes than he had done in five hours. Of course, none of the others layabouts had offered him any help

"We need to build better barricades?" Charro asked, as he unloaded and distributed ammo magazines and clips. Sirko and I had pulled a few scraps into position, but Charro was right—they wouldn't provide enough cover, and the factory wasn't an ideal defensive position. I'd chosen it for its concealment and proximity to the target.

"Up to you," I said, as Charro turned back to the truck for

another load, Mother Mary's hands upraised in bloody tattooed supplication on the back of his neck, "but I'm getting a couple hours of rack. We have thirty-six hours until the Donbas Battalion comes rolling into town, and as of right now, we've never even had eyes on the target."

"If they come rolling into town," Miles said. It was the mercenary's lament, working with amateurs.

"I don't know," Wildman said slowly, as he worked the chambers on his SA-80 assault rifle with a practiced eye. Mercs are mechanics, always tinkering. "I'm happy we're meeting the Donbas lads. Otherwise, this might all be too easy."

CHAPTER 26

It was nearly eight, and almost dark, as Alie crept through the streets of Lozova, Ukraine, looking for the Furshet supermarket. It had been a long drive from Kiev, but she'd kept busy evading the most personal aspects of Hargrove's questions. What had happened in Bujumbura? What had Locke done exactly? Why had he done it? How? Who with? He was excited, she could tell, not to confront Locke, but to meet him. But he was excited, mostly, to be out from behind his desk and in the field. Even if their first stop was a training school for the Donbas Battalion, this was war. Or at least a lot closer to it than Kiev.

"Have you been in a battle?" he asked, his eyes bright and his speech faster and more clipped than normal.

She thought of the villagers she'd seen slaughtered by the Janjaweed militia in South Sudan, and the bodies being stacked like firewood after the Gatumba massacre. She thought of her journey with Magdelena through some of the most violent regions on earth, trying to survive the gray market of human trafficking. She'd seen more rape and starvation than violent death on that underground railroad from African depravation into European slavery, but she'd seen deadly violence, too.

Women's stuff, the old boys scoffed, when she pitched those stories. Actual news, as she put it. About actual human beings.

But it wasn't war, so the old boy's network never understood. They would run those stories, but only two or three times a year at most. Otherwise, it was *too much, Alie. Too much. If you want to write here, write something else.* So she left.

"No. No battles," she said, knowing where Hargrove's sympathies lay.

"What about Locke?"

It was insulting that Hargrove was only scratching the surface of her life—a life more interesting than most, including Tom Locke's—but she didn't mind. She was used to it in military and CIA company, and she didn't want to talk about herself anyway. Nobody who truly lived this life did.

"There it is," Hargrove said, pointing to a store that looked more like a Food-4-Less than a supermarket. Ukraine, especially in the east, was more third world than European. Or maybe it was just more 1963.

They were late. The store was closed. There were only three cars in the parking lot, and a pimply kid pushing the shopping carts inside. At first, Alie thought he was the only person around. Then she noticed a man on the bench, waiting for a bus.

"Pull up next to him," Hargrove said. He rolled down his window. "Which way to the post office?" he asked in Ukrainian.

"Ten blocks as the crow flies. But it's hard to find."

"Perhaps you could show us?"

The stranger got into the back of the car, and Hargrove signaled Alie to drive. "Challenge and response authentication," he whispered.

What is this, 1959? she thought, unfairly. Her nerves, she realized, were frazzled from the drive.

"What's your name?" Hargrove asked the man in the backseat.

"Call me Jessup, sir. Take the right fork here. We're headed east." He paused, sensing Alie eying him in the rearview. "Who's she?"

"Nobody," Hargrove said.

"Nice to meet you," Alie replied.

The man didn't respond. He was her age, early thirties, and clearly military. He was also clearly unhappy. Alie wondered how long he'd been waiting at the Furshet, since Hargrove hadn't made any calls during the drive.

"How's the operation?" Hargrove asked, all smiles.

"I'll let the colonel answer that, sir."

They drove east for half an hour before turning off the main road. Alie assumed they were close, but after another hour, they still hadn't reached their destination.

"There isn't much activity at night," Jessup explained. "It's mostly daytime patrols, especially with the militias. But once you're in the valley, it's wise to stay off the main roads."

Alie was surprised this was the Donbas valley, since the word implied a low space between hills. Even in the dark, she could see this was flat farmland, with a few scattered forests and open-pit mines. Everything in Ukraine, it seemed, was flat farmland. These people were fighting over the Kansas of Europe.

I guess that's why the world doesn't care, Alie thought. But Kansas mattered, of course, if you happened to live in Topeka.

The destination appeared at first glance to be a rural elementary school on a two-lane road. Jessup directed them to a parking lot behind the building, where three cars were parked out of sight. There were six large camouflage-green canvas tents, further back at the tree line. They looked like they'd been bought from a World War II surplus store.

"The locals know we're here," Jessup said, "but there's no reason to advertise."

They walked to the front of the building. There was artwork on the walls and a long central hallway with doors along each side. Alie saw a monster with a misshapen head and five terrifying claws coming out of each forearm. The face next to it was perfectly round with no mouth.

Jessup turned into a small anteroom. The desk had a typewriter on it. The chart on the wall featured little gold stars. There was a door leading to another office. The principal's office. This *was* an elementary school. Or at least it had been before the uprising.

Colonel Barkley was standing behind the desk with his hands behind his back. He was in his late fifties, over six feet tall with white hair, a beer belly, and the ramrod bearing of a military lifer. He wore an olive-drab baseball cap, military fatigues with a wide black leather belt and brass buckle, and spit-polished Corcoran jump boots. When he reached to shake Hargrove's hand, Alie noticed an enormous Citadel class ring on the same finger as his wedding band. Behind him, on the top of a low bookshelf, was an old-fashioned slicer used to cut the edges off school projects and the fingers off people who double-crossed the mob.

"Welcome to the Dumb-ass," Barkley said in a thick Southern accent. "Take a seat."

Hargrove sat, and Barkley did too, his belly rolling over his belt buckle. He looked like a grandfather, and in fact, he was. Barkley had three messed-up kids back home in South Carolina—he hadn't been there for them, he had realized too late, but that was no damn excuse—and six grandkids he figured he was going to have to put through college himself. That was why he took a few of these six- to twelve-week jobs with Apollo every year, preferably when it wasn't Clemson football season. An operation would pay for a year of college. Twenty-four tours, and he might get them all through.

"No offense," he said, holding up his hand to Alie, "but who's the girl?"

"She's with me, sir," Hargrove said.

"Well, I know that, son."

Alie expected Hargrove to back down. Colonel Barkley talked like Foghorn Leghorn and looked like the executive vice president of a small-town rotary club, but he had served twenty-five years in Special Forces, and that was obvious, too.

"You can trust me, Colonel," Hargrove said. "I'm on your side."

Alie noticed Hargrove's slight Southern drawl and stiff back. He looked like he'd grown a spine. The colonel was rubbing off on him. Hargrove was so young he was still bending to the characters around him.

"All right," the colonel said, dropping the request. "What do you want to know?" He didn't say it with respect, but with a slight air of annoyance. He wanted to pass this spot inspection quickly, like a kidney stone.

Jessup arrived with a chair. Alie thanked him and sat down.

"So how's it going?" Hargrove said. He looked calm, but he couldn't quit looking around, as if there was something to see.

"What do you mean?"

"In general. How's the war going?"

"There is no war, son. There is an armed insurrection by pro-Russian forces, aided and abetted by little green men, courtesy of Comrade Putin. I hope you didn't come all this way to ask me about that, because that is not my job. I am not here to fight. I train men."

"That's true, sir," Hargrove said, taken aback. "But that doesn't mean you don't know how the . . . um, insurrection . . ."

Barkley did everything short of sighing. "You'll have to ask the Ukrainians. Or your CIA bosses. I don't do intel. I do combat. Next question."

Hargrove hesitated. This wasn't going as planned. Barkley

was disrespecting the partnership between the CIA and the men in the field. And even worse, making him feel like a kid. "How many men have you trained?"

"Fifty a week, for five weeks, that's two hundred fifty, give or take. About twenty percent wash out—" he paused "—and that's a conservative number."

"You don't know how many men you've trained?"

"Not exactly."

"But you get paid by the head."

"I get paid by the hour."

"But the Apollo Outcomes contract—"

"Son, my name is William Bedford Barkley. I am fifty-eight years old. I am a former full-bird colonel in the United States Army, Special Forces, and I have been training men in foreign lands to fight for their freedom since before you were born. And I don't count heads."

"But that's not what your contract says," Hargrove said. He wasn't challenging the colonel, Alie could tell, he was trying to gather his thoughts. This wasn't, as he would say, the *professionalism* a young go-getter had been led to expect.

"Jessup," the colonel barked. The soldier was in the doorway so fast it was like he'd been standing there all along. Barkley had his own five-man team. Jessup was the youngest, and thus the gofer, but he was valuable, because he knew his place.

"Yessir."

"Get this *operative* the numbers on how many men we've trained."

"Yessir."

Jessup left. Barkley stared at Hargrove. Waiting.

"I guess there's not any paperwork on the battlefield, right?" Hargrove joked, smiling weakly.

Alie rolled her eyes. "How about a drink?" she said, nodding toward the half-empty bottle of Bulleit Bourbon on a shelf be-hind Everly. "To show that we're all friends."

Barkley looked at her, then Hargrove. When the man didn't object, Barkley figured he had to oblige. He wouldn't be sur-prised if the woman was the boss. It was like that these days.

"What training are you providing?" she asked, when she'd knocked back a tumbler of Kentucky's eighth finest bourbon.

Barkley pursed his lips to show his distaste, but he figured he had to answer. "Physical fitness, marksmanship, individual movement techniques, battle drills, squad formations, first aid. The basics. That's why we call it basic training."

"You provide the weapons?"

"For those that don't bring their own," he said. "Who'd a thunk we'd be smuggling Kalashnikovs *into* Ukraine?" He let out a belly laugh as he poured himself another. He waved the bottle in midair, offering to refresh their glasses. No one de-clined.

Alie could see the headline: UNITED STATES ARMS MILITIA IN UKRAINE. But she wasn't going to write it. That was small beer. And besides, it was a good idea. She'd heard Ukraine was a mu-nitions desert, and the government was desperate for arms.

"How do you recruit?" Hargrove asked, having found his sec-ond wind.

"We don't. They've been coming since Cri-mea went red. Young, old, everybody. The paramilitary leaders split them into groups of fifty and send them here. Two weeks later, I send them back."

Hargrove gulped. "You think that will make a difference?"

The colonel sighed. He'd spent his career in "white SOF," covertly training indigenous forces to fight for U.S. interests. These two probably didn't even know the concept. It was all "black SOF" now, hallelujah for the scalp hunters. If these forever wars were to be won, Barkley believed, it wouldn't be through Americans martyring bad guys. It would be through men like him training others to fight for their God-given rights so that we didn't have to fight for them. Otherwise, it was terrorist whack-a-mole till the end of time.

"Young man," he said, "I believe not only in the right to bear arms, but the obligation to bear arms. I believe in the power of those arms, rightly respected and rightly used. A polite society is an armed society."

"I'm not sure I believe that," Alie said.

"I didn't ask what you believe. You asked what *I* believe. And I believe we are making a difference. Will it be enough in this particular case? I do not know. It would help if the United States government would provide additional funds, so that I can train twice as many men."

This was the standard line. Apollo Outcomes was a business; contractors were taught to always ask for additional funds to elongate the operation or widen the scope. Hargrove wasn't biting. He hadn't even seen the training grounds, and he was already worried he was going to have to write this colonel up.

Barkley shrugged. "The efficiency of my actions is not a calculation I have been tasked to make."

Hargrove started to object, but Barkley rose from his seat, his beer belly accosting them from across the desk.

"It's late," he said. "We start early. And we had very little notice of your arrival. We did not have the time to requisition a feather bed, I am afraid, but I can offer you a bunk in a classroom with my instructors. If the girl wants private quarters, she will have to sleep in a closet."

Hargrove looked appalled, but before he could object, Alie jumped in. "We can share quarters," she said.

Barkley stared at her, and he didn't look like a grandfather anymore, at least not the kind she remembered. He looked like a man who had tolerated enough.

"I bet you can," he said.

"I'm not going to give him a blowjob, if that's what you're implying," Alie said. She snatched the bottle of Bulleit and poured herself a glass. Then she laughed, and Bill Barkley did too.

"I have to admit, I'm disappointed," Hargrove said, raising his glass for another drink. It was a joke, but Alie knew there was some truth in there, too.

CHAPTER 27

Half a world away, and seven time zones behind, Brad Winters walked into the scallop-pink lobby of 1050 Connecticut Avenue, with its oversized plastic plants, and took the escalator to the second floor. He was wearing his civilian "dress blues"— a boxy suit with an American flag lapel pin, the exact same kind that had become a conservative cause célèbre during the 2012 presidential debates. He knew empty gestures were never as empty as they seemed.

He entered Morton's steakhouse, adjusting quickly from the overly bright atrium with the four-story American flag to the darkness of the steakhouse interior. There was a Morton's in every city in America. There were five in Washington, DC, alone. This was the only one that mattered.

"Your locker, Mr. Winters?" the hostess asked.

The restaurant had a long narrow vestibule, with wine bottles forming one wall and polished wooden lockers forming the other. Each locker was a square foot and featured a small silver nameplate. The hostess unlocked the one with "B. W." etched on the plate and stepped back. There was no one else in the vestibule, and if anyone had glanced around the corner, they would have seen that there was nobody in the dining room. There never was.

Winters removed a small box. "Thank you, Sheila," he said.

Sheila smiled. That was her job: to recognize and smile. "Your guest is here, on the balcony."

She walked through the crowded bar and toward a small glass door. Winters followed her onto the patio, a thin strip of concrete covered by a black awning. The patio was only one floor above Connecticut Avenue, so it was loud. The view was upscale chain stores and nondescript offices. For a high-end steak restaurant, the tables and chairs were cheap. Nobody came here for the ambiance, but everybody came. Even at 4:30 on a Wednesday, the tables were full of men in suits, puffing away on cigars. They came because it was a tradition. And because it was off K Street, and three blocks from the White House. And because, in a city that had banned almost all forms of smoking, this patio was one of the few refuges where you could indulge.

The general, Winters noticed, was already well into his indulgences, a half-smoked stogie protruding from his lips—a Cuban, for Christ's sake—and an empty glass of what used to be Scotch in front of him.

"General Raimy," Winters said, extending his hand. "Thanks for meeting me on such short notice."

"It's my pleasure," the general said, without standing. Normally he wore his uniform with all his pins and medals, including his four stars. Today it was a suit. His security detail sat three tables away, drinking soda water.

"Well, I know you're a man who loves his country."

"And his steak." The general smiled. It was true. The man liked his perks.

"Macallan 18, neat. Another round," Winters said, as the hostess slid the menu in front of him. "So how is the Pentagon?"

"Large," the general said.

"I spent half the week in the Capitol building," Winters said. "I could say the same thing." He opened the small box from his locker. "But it would be a lie. That place gets smaller every year."

He removed the cushion from the box and chose a cigar. Nicaraguan tobacco with a Connecticut wrapper. He was a patriot, and Cubans were overrated anyway.

"What were you doing on the Hill?"

"Meeting friends, specifically the Friends of Ukraine. You saw their press statements, I presume?"

The general laughed. "I should have known you were involved."

"That doesn't mean they lack conviction, General. This is Russia, after all. There are plenty of important people on our side." *Important,* of course, was a relative term. He was only talking about congressmen.

He worked the cigar, rolling the end in his fingers, loosening the tobacco. Then he worked his fingers down the shaft, squeezing delicately. Then he turned it around and sliced off the tip with the cutter.

The Scotch arrived, and he held up a finger. Wait. He dipped the end of the cigar in the whiskey and held it there for twenty seconds. "Bring me another, please," he said, handing the glass back to the waiter.

"You're a decadent bastard," the general said admiringly, puffing dramatically on his Cuban. Below him, cars honked. The light at L Street had turned red, and someone had refused to run it.

"You are what you smoke," Winters said as he toasted the end of the cigar with the torch lighter, turning it slowly, so that it darkened and dried evenly all the way around. He blew on the end, causing it to glow a hot red. Finally, he sucked in smoke and blew it out, satisfied.

"Let's order," the general commanded.

They ordered porterhouses, with a precracked lobster to share, and a bottle of 2009 Bordeaux, but not before another two rounds of Scotch while they finished their cigars. Winters asked the general about this family. He had been working with the general for a decade, and he still didn't know his wife's name. But he knew the general had a daughter up for promotion as a below-the-zone major, and his fatherly pride would keep the conversation going until the lobster arrived.

Eventually, the talk turned to business: Putin's next move, the future of NATO, al Qaeda, Pakistan, and how Apollo Outcomes could solve such problems. The usual. The general had been stationed in Germany for much of the 1980s, and was the commanding officer of the 66th Military Intelligence Brigade at Darmstadt when the Wall came down. That fortuitous posting had gotten him promoted to the Eastern European section of the Pentagon, just as its importance was being torpedoed by the Butcher of Baghdad. He'd been hiring Apollo ever since. Winters had all but promised him a seat on the board of directors, whenever the general decided he'd be of more use in the civilian world. It was a typical unspoken quid pro quo. Every four-star either had one or was angling. Air Force generals go to Lockheed; Navy admirals to Raytheon; Army generals to the mercenary companies. Federal law said they had to wait two years after retirement, but everyone was willing to wait, usually at some think tank.

"How deep are you in Ukraine?" the general asked finally, pushing away the last few bites of his steak. If you finished a meal, you hadn't ordered enough. Winters had barely touched his porterhouse.

"Training and equipping the Ukrainian army, as well as militias on the ground in the eastern oblasts and some intel collection," Winters said casually, as if this wasn't what he'd come here to discuss.

"Contract?"

"CIA." He actually had four contracts, all with different agencies, but honesty was no asset here.

"For counterinsurgency?"

"For peacekeeping operations. But the Russians have three times as many."

"Can we beat them?"

"Yes, if it was only pro-Russian militias. But it's not."

The general had read the top secret reports, and Winters, of course, had seen them, too. The resistance was homegrown, but the Russians had supplemented it with several brigades of professional soldiers. It was indisputable. They were even showing state funerals for fallen troops on Russian television, under the flimsy excuse that the soldiers had died in training exercises, just like in the old days of Afghanistan. The West wasn't in denial; Putin was openly daring them to act. The West was afraid. That was why patriots like the general were so important.

"Fucking Obama," the general said.

"Fucking Germans."

"Merkel has more dick than Obama and the French put together," the general snapped. Merkel was beloved for her economic austerity, but she had grown up behind the Berlin Wall, and she had a blind spot for Eastern totalitarianism.

"Too bad she's swinging it the wrong way," Winters replied smoothly, knowing the general would agree.

The general took a sip of his fourth Macallan. "What do you need?"

Winters shrugged. "Depends on where you want to draw the line."

The general took another sip. "We're willing to give them the two eastern provinces . . ." He wouldn't on principle use the Soviet term *oblast*.

Winters leaned in. "I didn't ask where our government's line was, General. I asked where *your* line was." He could tell the alcohol was working, although not enough that the general would, on reflection, find anything amiss.

"My line is where the damn line was three months ago," Raimy said.

Winters leaned back and sipped his drink, changing conversational gears. The ice had been broken. It was time for a deep dive.

"We can drive them back from Mariupol, General. That's Putin's immediate objective, to secure a land bridge from Russia to Crimea. We can drive them all the way back to the border, if that's what you want. But it's a commitment. The Ukrainian army isn't ready. Yanukovych spent seven years hollowing it out."

"Sabotage."

"Of course. But the core is solid. Good fighters. Disciplined. And most important, they believe in the cause."

This was the kind of talk generals liked. The kind that implied there was something right in the West and wrong in the East. It wasn't that American flag officers didn't respect the Russians. They did. The Russians were fierce adversaries. If you had said, "The just will prevail," the generals would have scoffed. History had proven that wrong a thousand times. And yet they always believed that, through some inherent defect in their belief system, the Russians were doomed.

"The problem is timing. The volunteers can't fight a trained army, and the Ukrainian army won't be ready for an offensive until June. The Russians are there now, looting the place. We can push them back in July, maybe, but by then, it might be too late. The eastern oblasts are historically Russian. Given a reason, or inevitability, they will revert to their old ways. And once the people are loyal, or at least not resisting . . ."

He shrugged. It was so obvious, even a general could see it. The Russians would use the popular sentiment as an excuse. They would bite off another part of the continent, and they would never let it go.

"What are you suggesting?"

"We cede Mariupol, but fight them like hell for the rest of the East. That gives Putin the land bridge that he wants and keeps the rest under the control of the West."

Including the shale gas fields. After all, a smart deal meant everyone got what they wanted, and Winters wanted the shale.

The general shook his head. "That means giving up territory."

"For now. But I've talked with Naveen at the NSC. The diplomats are working behind the scenes. Sanctions are coming, full sanctions, including freezing the SWIFT accounts for the Kremlin elite. They're going to work."

"As long as the Russians aren't in Kiev."

"If Putin had any balls, he'd be there already."

The general nodded. Winters was right. They were lucky Putin had lost his nerve. If Russia had steamrolled Ukraine, the Europeans would have folded like 1938.

"I'm not selling you on a war, General. Or a two-month solution. We all know how those promises turn out. I'm talking long-term containment."

"What do you need?"

"One hundred million for the eastern oblasts. To hold the line. Not at the border, but a reasonable compromise."

It was a concession. A new Cold War, with the line drawn west a few hundred kilometers. The general hated it. He even felt sorry for the bastards behind the line. But without a real commitment from above, it was the best he could do.

"Fifty million," he said, even though Winters's one hundred million was only a rounding error for the Pentagon's budget. Apollo Outcomes had an annual IDIQ umbrella contract for a billion. They didn't necessarily get a billion, but they were cleared for that much each fiscal year without having to get specific authorization, and it was only May. The general doubted they were at more than two hundred million this quarter.

"For one year, with two optional years," Winters said. "Scalable to, say, two hundred and fifty million."

"Two hundred."

"I have to stick to my number, General," Winters said. He knew the first number wasn't nearly as important as the second. Once Apollo men were on the ground, he could always find a way to expand or lengthen the contract to the maximum level. "I can't leave men behind. I have to be able to get them out."

The general understood. He was an army man; he believed in loyalty above all. "How long to be up and running?"

"Ten days?"

The general looked shocked. Winters laughed. "Do you think I've been sitting around waiting for your candy ass to come around?" he said with a smile, knowing the general would appreciate his aggressive braggadocio. "All I need is your word on the contract."

"It will have to be Title 10," the General said.

Title 10 contracts had a few more rules than CIA Title 50 work, which didn't appear on public records, even the ones Apollo filed with the Securities and Exchange Commission. Title 50 profits could be declared without any more explanation than "top clearance government work." It was Winters's preferred contract, by far. But his company already had four in Ukraine alone; he supposed he shouldn't be greedy.

Besides, Title 10 offered what everyone wanted: cover. Apollo received official government sanction for almost any and all actions in the area; the Pentagon brass received "plausible deniability." If caught, the generals would deny specific knowledge and blame a "rogue" company for breaking the law.

"I'll have our lawyer contact you in the morning," Winters said.

"Quietly," the general said. "I don't want this getting to the State Department."

Of course, Winters thought. That was always understood. "Just give us the tools, General, and we'll get the job done."

The general raised his glass. So did Winters. Once Churchill was quoted, a deal was struck. Everyone in the military-industrial complex knew that.

"To the last superpower," the General said.

"To the shield of the west."

The general looked around: at the other men, at the suits, at the waiters. His wife was waiting at home. It was bridge night.

"How about some cordials?" he asked.

"I'm sorry, sir," Winters said, "I can't. I have a plane to catch."

CHAPTER 28

Miles lay prone on a rooftop, covered by canvas he had scrounged
from the factory, peering through binoculars. It was 0300, almost exactly twenty-four hours before the scheduled assault,
and it was quiet. Two hundred meters in front of him was the
pipeline trunk station, two nondescript brick buildings and a
spaghetti of yellow and blue pipes, each about a meter in diam-
eter. Heavy machinery pumped the liquefied natural gas from
Russia through the eastern oblasts of Ukraine. At this station it
was compressed and consolidated before moving on to Europe,
making it a strategic choke point.

It also meant one stray bullet, and the entire facility would blow.
They had to be precise, which was why Apollo sent a Tier One team.
And the Russians had sent real troops instead of locals.

"I count three," Miles said. "Probably more inside the control
room."

"Roger. Three echos."

"Carrying Vals"—an assault rifle with built-in noise suppressor, issued primarily to Russian Spetsnaz special forces units for
undercover or clandestine operations. "Sexy, sexy."

"Roger," I replied. "Sexy arms."

I was hunched over the makeshift desk, with Greenlees beside me. Strewn across the desk were two Toughbooks, my GIS
tablet, radios, a flashlight, a half-eaten protein bar, water bottles,
maps, my equipment vest, and my FN SCAR-H assault rifle,

which I favored for its stopping power. Greenlees sat next to me, manning the radios. I was sketching the facility on butcher-block paper, and I didn't like what I was seeing. The facility's main defense was openness. It was on the edge of Kramatorsk, surrounded by open fields on three sides. The fourth side had fifty meters of standoff area between the facility wall and the closest building. An alert enemy would see us coming.

At least it will keep the civilians safe, I thought. Contrary to reputation, real mercs like to minimize collateral damage. It's cleaner and more professional, and I hated innocent people getting hurt.

"Alpha Two, what are you seeing?"

"Open ground," Charro said. "Too soft for wheeled vehicles. A few sniper holes." He was scouting the field behind the facility. I marked it off as no-go. We hadn't brought any sniper teams qualified for low-visibility operations.

"Alpha Five?"

"Quiet," Jacobsen replied. He was walking the mixed industrial and residential area near the facility, reconnoitering possible avenues of approach. For most of the night, the streets had been vacant, a sure sign of an active war zone. Even in the early morning, there should have been taxis, teenage lovers sneaking out, men coming off the late shift. Jacobsen had even wondered if the power grid was knocked out, until he noticed a few lights in apartment windows.

"Shit," he muttered.

Four men with guns slung over their shoulders appeared at the corner two blocks up. Local militiamen, out for a stroll. Jacobsen turned right, stopping in front of a window to watch them in the reflection. He could pass for Ukrainian, with his stubble and worker's jacket, but a good look and locals would know he was not from around here.

Best, then, to avoid closer examination.

"Four echos, 150 meters northeast of my position," he whispered. "Repeat four echoes, militia I think. Copy?"

"Roger that Alpha Five. Alpha Four, do you have eyes on?"

"Negative. Moving," Wildman replied. He was driving a four-door Škoda, hotwired several hours ago.

"Boon?"

"En route," Boon said. He was standing a few feet away from me in the warehouse, piloting one of AO's proprietary quadcopter drones. It was small, virtually silent, and could be flown from up to a kilometer away with a remote control and electronic glasses that allowed the operator to see through its camera.

"Got them," Boon said, as Jacobsen appeared on the second computer screen. Boon was a Buddhist, and a man of contemplation, at least until the Myanmar military junta came over the mountains and started burning monks alive, and he was still a man of few words.

But God Almighty, if he didn't have a steady hand. I watched the live feed on the laptop as Boon took the quadcopter below the roof line, so it wouldn't be silhouetted against the sky, then hovered it in the shadow of a chimney. The copter was only a few feet wide, so an unflappable pilot like Boon could fly it almost anywhere: up walls, through windows. *Boon could probably drop it on a dragonfly,* I thought, as the copter's camera zoomed in on the militia.

"Yep, that's four local gang members," I said to Jacobsen. "Ugly, too."

"Moving out," Jacobsen said, slipping out of view as Boon kept the camera on the thugs. They had probably been a small-time criminal enterprise, drugs and protection, but as soon as the shooting started, those kinds of men always found politics. And became more aggressive. These "military patrols" were the reason the street activity was dead.

Sirko said something. He was watching over my shoulder.

"Pro-Russian," Greenlees interpreted, "at least until it becomes more profitable to be pro-Ukrainian."

Wildman's Škoda turned into view, driving slowly to avoid suspicion. By the time Wildman passed them, one of the men was peeing on the side of a building while the others lit cigarettes.

"Confirmed, four local muscle, inebriated," Wildman said.

"Solid copy, Alpha Two," I said. "Charlie mike."

Wildman turned onto the road that dead-ended at the facility's front gate. He had already placed two surveillance cameras. The first was eight feet up a pole, hidden in a tangle of dangerous-looking wires. It watched the facility's pedestrian door. The second was buried in debris on a ledge above a trash container, with eyes on the front gate.

The last camera needed to be high enough to see over the wall into the facility itself. The quadcopter drone could take clear footage inside the walls, but only at night, otherwise it would be detected. They needed to know the movement of men, inside and outside, at all times of day.

He slowed the car and examined the building on his right. It was an apartment tower, two stories taller than any nearby building, and only three blocks from the entrance to the facility. *Perfect.*

He eyed the fire escape. It was an older style: ten feet above the street and not connected to an alarm. He took a right into the alley and parked underneath it. He got out, climbed on top of the car, and pulled himself onto the ladder.

The rooftop was flat, but there were air conditioners and an old pigeon coop for cover, so he wouldn't be highlighted against the sky. From the back, he could see the downtown square in the distance, where militants had set up tire barricades and were flying the flag of the breakaway Donetsk People's Republic. The flag was blue, red, and black, with a two-headed bird holding a shield in the center, but Wildman couldn't have identified it on a dartboard. From this distance, it looked like a rag.

He turned back to the pipeline facility. There were two small buildings, but most of the space inside the wall was open ground, pipes, or pumping equipment. He saw the three sentries smoking behind the larger building—he was close enough to see the flare of their cigarettes—and, less than ten meters away, dozens of pipes full of highly flammable natural gas.

The fools might blow themselves up, he thought, *before I have the chance. That would suck.*

Lying on his back, he pulled the small camera and transmitter from his bag, removed the adhesive tape from the bottom, and stuck it to the edge of the roof. He sighted it in on the facility, switched it on, and held his middle finger in front of the lens.

"How do you read me?"

"Fuck you, too."

He grinned and crawled back to the fire escape.

"Bollocks," Wildman said, looking down. Three armed men, weaving like drunks and singing what sounded like old Soviet marches, had stumbled into the alley and spotted the Škoda. The singing stopped, as they peered inside the car. One took his mobile phone from his pocket.

Not good, Wildman thought.

He crawled to the roof's center, where there was a trap door. It was unlocked. Thank God for teenagers smoking cigarettes. He dropped into the stairwell and ran down, leaping three or four steps at a time. Before he got to the exit, he unholstered his 9 mm pistol and screwed on the large noise suppressor. He concealed it behind his body, then walked out the front door.

The men were arguing when he appeared in the mouth of

the alley, but they stopped when they saw him. They spoke, but he kept walking toward them. The first yelled and raised his weapon. Wildman drew and squeezed off three rounds so fast it sounded like automatic gunfire, but a thud rather than a bang.

Two bodies fell to the pavement. The third man stumbled backward in a pink mist of blood. Wildman's shot had gone wide and struck him under his right clavicle, rather than at his center of mass.

"*Ey! Chto yebat!*" the man yelled in Ukrainian as he fumbled with his rifle.

Wildman corrected his mistake, and the man slumped forward, landing on his AK-47, then clattering to the ground. Wildman looked around. Nobody yet. Casually, he walked toward the car.

"Fuck," he said, as he stared down at the dead men. How was he going to fit all three bodies in the trunk?

CHAPTER 29

Brad Winters straightened his red Hermès tie in the bathroom mirror, then brushed lint from the right shoulder of his Brioni suit. He checked his shave. He hadn't missed a spot. He never did.

He brushed his teeth. He combed his hair to the point it looked sculpted, and put an American flag pin on his lapel. He walked into the bedroom of his Manhattan apartment—a one-bedroom on Sutton Place, owned by Apollo Outcomes, of course—then into the living room. There was a bar and a piano, but he hadn't touched either. He didn't turn on the lights. He never did. It was 8:30 P.M. EST. 3:30 A.M. EBS: Eastern Bloc Standard. He wondered, for a moment, what Locke and his team were doing. So much, after all, depended on them. He went to the window and saw, one hundred blocks down, the Freedom Tower. It looked like his mother's favorite cut-glass vase. It was ugly, but he didn't think it an embarrassment, or a sign that America had lost its way. The things that made America great were intangible, and always had been. But was there anything worse than spending billions of dollars for something that looked cheap?

Half an hour later, the town car pulled up to a skyscraper on Park Avenue, a few blocks north of Grand Central. The guards were still manning the desk, since it was only 9:00 P.M., and everyone here was putting in late hours. Occupy Wall Street had gotten it wrong; the banks had abandoned Wall Street for midtown decades ago. The hedge fund guys thought this hilarious. Dumb hipsters.

He gave the guards the name of the company. They called upstairs. A minute later, he was in the elevator, where he took off his security sticker and crumbled it in his pocket.

Blyleven was waiting for him when the doors opened. He was twenty-seven and thought he was Matthew McConnaughy. His coat and tie were off, his white shirttail was hanging out, and he had an extra button undone for chest effect. He was handsome, and confident, and rich, but he couldn't quite pull off the look. And his wingtips were out of style.

"Bradley," he said. Brad wasn't short for Bradley, but Winters ignored it. "Welcome home."

They passed through the small lobby. There was new art: two white squares on white walls. Winters knew the firm had paid a few hundred thousand at least, or they wouldn't be here. The corner office—his old office—featured a painting of a nurse by Richard Prince. He knew that because Blyleven pointed at it and said, "That's a Richard Prince." Winters didn't know or care who that was.

"Brad. Good to see you."

"Nice to be here, David." He shook hands with David Givens, his old partner, and took a seat in the most expensive piece of plastic money could buy. Hatcher was there as well. The venture capital firm had four hundred million dollars invested at ten times leverage, and this was half the staff. The other half was under twenty-five and in the cubicles thirty feet away, talking with Hong Kong or Singapore. Only Givens was over forty.

There were the usual pleasantries, and a bottle of Japanese whiskey, but it didn't take long to get down to business.

"What happened in Libya?"

"Growing pains."

"Just like Guinea."

"Not like Guinea at all."

"But with the same results."

"Process over product," Winters said, sipping his Yamazaki 18, the upper echelon's whiskey of the moment. "You know that."

"And what is the process?"

"We're putting the right team together: engineers, drill crews, suppliers, security. We're testing methods for staying off the grid. We're practicing for the right hole. We haven't found it yet."

"It's been three years."

Three years was nothing, but it was a dog's life on Wall Street. Three years ago, two of these partners were at Goldman Sachs, and three years before that, Wharton. Patience wasn't their deal, and he wasn't their mentor. Everything old was out, and here, Winters knew, he was old. So was Givens, if it came to that. They probably called him Yoda.

"We talked about a five-year time frame . . ." Winters started.

"So we're still two years away from striking gold."

"I was hoping for another five."

"Brad," Givens said, shaking his head.

"Thirty-eight million," Hatcher said. Hatcher was the numbers guy. He looked like a momma's boy, but he had a kink for BDSM. Winters wondered if he was wearing latex underwear.

"It's only twenty-five," Winters said.

"Up front, yes. But we've done the numbers. That's our opportunity cost."

That was what this was about. Hatcher, or more likely Blyleven, wanted to fund his own project, but this ancient investment was clogging the balance sheet.

"It's a lottery ticket," Winters said. "You pay a little for the chance to make a lot."

"It's not a lot. Not compared to Uber. It's just a lot riskier."

Kids. They had never lived in a world of ordinary valuations. They were always chasing the next technology, willing to pay a billion even before it netted a million. Except it wasn't even technological advancement anymore. That moment had passed. It was just business models now.

"I'm sorry, Brad," Givens said, and Winters could tell it was true. "It's a legacy investment in a legacy business. No one invests in oil anymore." That was clearly untrue, but Winters understood the point. He was moving too slowly. Or more apt, the firm was trying to move too fast.

"We appreciate the investment in Apollo Outcomes," Hatcher said.

Damn right, you insufferable ass. I made that investment, then moved over to the company and grew it a hundred times over. Apollo Outcomes was no software bubble. It was real. It was boots on the ground.

"If you were willing to take a little more of the company public . . ."

"I'm not." Ten percent already meant too much scrutiny.

"Then we're out of this side venture."

That was all. It was over in fifteen minutes. Hatcher shook his hand, Blyleven expressed his regrets, and the relationship was done.

"I'm sorry, Brad," Givens said, as they walked to the elevator. "But it's the right thing. No free rides. You would have done it yourself."

"No hard feelings. I knew it was coming." It was half the reason he had pulled out of Libya. To force their hand.

"If you want a personal investment—"

"I don't."

"Do you want to get dinner?"

Winters looked at his former friend, but he knew that wasn't quite the right word. More like former colleague. Or understudy. "I can't. I'm on my way to London."

"Well, tell Josey I said hi. And . . . I'm sorry."

Winters stepped onto the elevator. Givens wasn't so bad, he thought, as the doors closed. He was simply an idiot, only forty and desperate to keep up with the younger crowd.

CHAPTER 30

Alie stared at the enormous, pajama-clad ass of the man on the jungle gym. They weren't really pajamas, more like an ill-fitting ninja suit, solid black with a blue-and-gold ribbon tied around the upper right arm, symbolizing independent Ukraine. This was the uniform of the Donbas Battalion, although *uniform* wasn't exactly accurate, since every man was supplying his own. The sloppiness was not instilling Alie with confidence, but she'd seen worse. She'd seen half-naked kids with broken mirrors for jewelry charging tanks with machetes.

The man in the ninja suit swung for the next rung, missed, and went down in the sand, screaming and grabbing his balls.

"I don't know what to say," Hargrove said. "I seriously, swear to God, do not know what to say."

The trainers had set up a tire course for agility drills and six-foot wooden walls for the recruits—no, volunteers—to scale, but otherwise the operation was one officer in sunglasses watching thirty grown men on a playground. Jump the swings. Climb the ladder. Slide down the slide. Low crawl. High crawl. Make a circuit. Do it again.

Off to the side, a group of six was drinking water, two of them bent over with their hands on their knees. Behind them, another group of six was sitting on their rucks with their boots off. Alie recognized the squad assigned to march with their fifteen-pound rucks. Five miles, Colonel Barkley had said. It had taken them an hour and half.

"I don't know what to say," Hargrove said again.

It was the only thing he'd said all morning, but he must have said it a hundred times. Americans had seen videos of al Qaeda recruits training like this in the run-up to the Gulf War and laughed. We were going to fight these dogs? What a joke. And yet, right here, in front of him, American trainers were doing the exact same thing.

"Honestly, Bill," Hargrove said. "To say this isn't what I expected would be such a vast understatement, that I can't even say it. So what is left to say?"

Colonel Barkley didn't respond. He'd been around the world a dozen times, from Indonesia to Latin America, and this was how it was done. Every method had been tested; every exercise had a purpose. Even with the Iraqi security forces, this was the way it was done. The difference was time. In Iraq, the trainers had six months, and that still wasn't enough.

"I have to work with what I have," he said. "I have two weeks to train whatever comes my way."

"But these guys aren't even in shape."

Some were, some weren't. This was a representative cross-section of a modern society, not a CrossFit class. There was nothing substantially different about these Ukrainians than any other army Barkley had trained, and there was nothing substantially different about the way he was training them. He wasn't a scientist. He was a mechanic. It amazed him that the bureaucrats still hadn't figured this out.

"My job is not to get them into shape, *Officer*," Barkley said, emphasizing Hargrove's unearned title. "That is not going to happen in fourteen days. I assumed that would be self-evident. My job is to strengthen their minds. To give them the spirit of the bayonet, by which I mean the will to persevere. When I am through with these men, they may not be able to run a mile, but they will have the intestinal fortitude to fight."

"What are you talking about?" Hargrove asked.

"I'm talking about the warrior spirit, son."

"With bayonets?"

"With your bare hands, son, if that's what it takes." The colonel could feel himself getting hot. This was the mission: the lesson that had been taught to him in 1981, when he enlisted, and that he had taught to thousands around the world. Harden the mind. Control the fear. Trust the team. When you lived it, you understood. If you lived like a pussy, it could not be explained.

"I need to see your results," Hargrove said coldly. He'd lost the *sir,* and the respectfulness, of the night before. "Where is the Donbas Battalion?"

"At the front. *Sir.*"

Hargrove waited for more.

"Five miles up the road," Barkley spat. "Jessup will show you the way."

They argued halfway to the Donbas Battalion headquarters before Alie gave up. Hargrove insisted the training was a travesty, a swindle, a gross injustice to the American taxpayer and the CIA. She understood; this wasn't the world you imagined when you were at Camp Peary, running obstacle courses and reading field manuals. This wasn't how the military was portrayed in all those history books back in Hargrove's room. But it was how the world actually was. Alie had seen it before: in Sudan, in Kenya, in Niger.

"Locke trained security forces in Burundi, Chad. They prevented a genocide," she said.

"And?"

"They don't even have playgrounds. Three years in that country, and I never saw a single slide."

Hargrove stared out the car window. The guards for the Sloviansk Battalion appeared briefly, waving them through. Jessup, driving in front, had vouched for them. "I don't want to hear about Locke," Hargrove said.

She knew it was trouble when she saw the camp: men in mismatched black fatigues packing trucks, gear being tossed haphazardly, small groups of wandering militiamen. There were far fewer men than she had anticipated, maybe eighty at most, but that could be for tactical security. These days, nobody concentrated troops in camps. Too easy for the enemy to count, capture, or bomb. Except for traditional armies, most forces operated in small units now.

Twenty minutes later, they were gearing up to head out with a patrol. And Hargrove was fuming. The militia was sloppy, he said. The mercenaries—*his* mercenaries, the ones the CIA hired—had been curt. There was no respect for authority. His authority. The CIA's authority. The authority of being . . . right and proper in your work environment. Of being fucking professionals.

"They're going to Kramatorsk," Alie said. She had seen it in the master sergeant's eyes when she mentioned the city. It was only twenty kilometers away. That was why the men were gearing up. "They're going early in the morning," she said, when Hargrove didn't answer. "Mission early. Assault on the enemy early."

Hargrove wasn't listening. He was staring at a group of men smoking cigarettes and cutting up for a militiaman with a cell phone camera. This was the unit they'd been assigned to shadow.

"We're going to Kramatorsk," Alie said, grabbing Hargrove's arm. "That's why we're here."

"I'm going to do my job," Hargrove snapped. "I'm going to make sure these men get what's coming to them. And then, and only then, are we going to Kramatorsk."

Alie watched him stalk off. Of all the macho bullshit . . . of all the wrong times. Locke was out there, twenty kilometers away. How could this patrol possibly matter?

"I suppose you're a soldier," Alie said to the man beside her. His name was Shwetz, and he was their interpreter. He was dressed in black, with blue and yellow cloth tied around his upper right arm. A Kalashnikov was slung incompetently over his shoulder.

"I've been trained," Shwetz replied, handing her something black.

"At the school?"

"Yes. For two weeks. Two weeks ago."

She took the black item. It was a full-face ski mask, with only the eyes and mouth cut out. She shivered involuntarily, remembering the docks in Bosaso, Somalia, when they'd put her in a hood, when she'd lost Magdelena . . . there was no way she was putting it on.

"What did you do before?" she said, handing it back.

Shwetz smiled from inside his ski mask. "I was a teacher. Third grade." Alie could see it. He had a gentle disposition and fearful eyes. "But I guess, really, we are all soldiers now."

CHAPTER 31

Miles and I were sitting on our rucks, eating cold French field rations. One of the best perks of being a private sector soldier was that you didn't have to choke down American MREs— Meals Ready to Eat, aka Meals Rejected by Everyone. It was embarrassing, as an American, that the French version was so much better.

"Reminds me of Tamanrasset," Miles said, in the way other people might reminisce about their anniversary dinner at the Olive Garden or hearing Pachelbel's *Canon* yet again. I knew why he was thinking of Algeria. It was only Miles and me on that mission, and we had played backgammon for three days, while our local contact became increasingly unhinged with worry. We ignored him, and in the end, our man walked right into the line of fire and was killed, as we knew he would. If I recall correctly, I beat Miles 213 games to 62, although I wasn't convinced he was trying.

"Reminds me of Guinea-Bissau," I said, picking up a bite of freeze-dried navarin d'agneau with my ivory mission chopsticks, "when we left Tailor in the jungle." We were hunting a Colombian drug lord that had taken over this West African country, making it a transit point for cocaine going to Europe. Tailor had made the mission a living hell, constantly bitching about the local prostitutes and his scrotal infection, so when we accidently lost him on an all-night op, we weren't in a hurry to reunite.

"We tracked him for three damn hours," Miles laughed.

"We were a hundred meters away, and he never heard us."

"Because he kept bitching out loud about his scrotum, even though he was the only one there!"

"What a bonehead," I said, working the chopsticks with practiced ease, a calming ritual I'd been using for almost twenty years. Every outfit has boneheads, even the elite.

"I'm glad he washed out," Miles said. "But I feel sorry for his wife. She probably has the clap."

Greenlees came over and sat. "We're just talking about dick infections," Miles said to him, "but don't worry, Johnny, it's nothing you can catch from giving blowjobs."

Greenlees chuckled unconvincingly.

"What did he say?" I said, nodding toward Karpenko.

The helicopter pilot was the one reminding Miles of Tamanrasset, because he was becoming increasingly unhinged. He was a civilian. My guess was that Maltov had claimed to be hiring him for a corporate flight.

"He wants extra money," Greenlees said. "Hazard pay."

"What did Karpenko say?"

"He threw out a number, a good one, but he won't negotiate."

At least he had some spine. Karpenko was too willing to compromise, if you asked me, especially with assholes. Never compromise with assholes.

"Sirko should just punch him in the face," I said, thinking of the effective violence of their last encounter, after the pilot had gone gorilla on Greenlee's eye.

"Agreed," Greenlees said.

But Sirko wasn't going to do it. Not without word from Karpenko. I could tell the old colonel disagreed with his boss's generosity, but he'd spent a lifetime following the chain of command, and if this was how the boss wanted it, this was how

Sirko would act. It was disappointing. I thought old-school Russian commanders were bolder than that.

"*Mierda*," Charro said. "Two more."

Miles and I looked at each other, then pushed our meals away and swung around to the Toughbook screens. We'd gotten lucky. The edge of one of our surveillance feeds showed the industrial building where the local toughs hung out. The club was on the ground floor, front corner. It had probably been a workingman's club when the factories were flourishing, a place where shift workers gathered to knock off the rust. But the area had fallen into disrepair as the factories closed, and this protomilitia had taken over.

The club had been quiet, at least for a while, but since 0800 the members had been out in force, harassing passersby and looking for the three missing men. Around ten, they had congregated outside, smoking and arguing. Eventually most of them left, probably to sleep off their drunks. For two hours, almost nothing.

Then, five minutes ago, a low-end Mercedes had pulled up and two goons in ill-fitting, off-the-rack suits had gotten out. One went inside. One, with an AK-47, stood by the door. The second Mercedes, the one Charro had just spotted, was almost identical to the first.

"War council," Miles said.

"How many?"

"Five in the front door," Charro said. "Inside unknown. They've been in and out all day. And there's a back door."

I didn't like it. The muscle had gone home, but chances were, they were simply resting up for tonight.

"What do you think?" I asked Miles. He knew the calculus: leave them and hope for the best, or knock them out now. If we chose the latter, the next hour was our window of opportunity.

"It's a risk either way. When the dead men don't turn up for afternoon cocktails, they'll go looking for them. If they find the bodies in the Dumpster"—damn the Škoda and its small trunk, Wildman really hadn't had a choice—"this place will be crawling with ants. But take them out now, and the Russians may arrive, asking questions."

It was a matter of timing. We needed only a few hours without interference, but we needed them early tomorrow morning.

"Maybe we can distract them . . ." I started, when I caught sight of Boon, who was standing guard on the catwalk, raising his Israeli Tavor-21 assault rifle. Instantly, the FN SCAR was off my shoulder and aimed at the door. By the time we heard the car crunching on the gravel, the entire team was in firing position.

The sound stopped. Ten seconds later, there was a pounding on the door and shouting in Ukrainian. Karpenko relaxed. It was Maltov. When Charro opened the door, the enforcer walked in like a conquering hero, trailing seven tough-looking Ukrainians. The last of his loyal men.

I started to say something. It was ridiculous for Maltov to drive up unannounced, even if he was the one who had suggested this facility. What if he had been followed? What if someone else had been here? His lack of opsec was staggering.

But Sirko beat me to it. He was on Maltov in a second, yelling in his face, and I didn't need a translator to know that he was up his ass about professionalism.

Maltov didn't care. He brushed Sirko off with a wave of the hand and went directly to Karpenko, who gave him a hug. They hadn't seen each other since before the assault, I realized. Until this moment, Karpenko might have thought he was dead. And I hadn't even given the Ukrainian a second thought.

Sirko started to say something else, but Karpenko turned away, his arm on Maltov's shoulder. Maltov was his guy. It was

Maltov and his men, I was sure, who had saved Karpenko from the palace coup three days before my arrival in Poltava. Maybe Maltov had always been the inside man; maybe that moment had thrust him there. Either way, Sirko was out. Maltov was Karpenko's man now.

"Double the watch," I snapped to Jacobsen, since we'd still been compromised by the enforcer's stupidity. No sense taking our operational security for granted. But there was a positive side here, too, because I could always use extra muscle, and because Maltov had proven adept at sourcing supplies from locals, and he knew Kramatorsk . . .

I turned to Miles with a smile, thinking of the club. "Third option," I said.

CHAPTER 32

They passed into a town, Alie driving in the rear, following two sedans and a minivan that comprised the official vehicles of the Donbas Battalion patrol. The town was scattered houses, then apartment blocks and small businesses, and finally, a one-story building next to a park.

"We're here," said Shwetz, the teacher, taking a deep calming breath.

He jumped out of the car and started toward the building, as twelve men jumped out of the other cars, their weapons drawn. Several stopped behind a planter, a few against the front wall of the building, while three rushed to the door and burst through. Alie could hear yelling from inside, and then gunfire, and then all the militiamen began to converge, swiftly, as if they were being sucked through the front door.

Alie followed the teacher, figuring it was safer that way. Inside the small building, it was a scrum of bodies. Men were swinging guns, and screaming, and one man was down on the floor holding a wad of bloody paper to his face. A police officer was rushed by, two militiamen holding his arms behind his back, his face covered with blood. Two policemen were on the floor, their hands on their heads. Two more were cornered in a front room, where a man without a hood was yelling in their faces, spittle flying, the militiaman with the cell phone camera close enough to capture the veins bulging as he barked. One of the two policemen was nodding absently. The other was staring out the window.

Alie grabbed the teacher, who was on the edge of a scrum. "What's he saying?"

"That they are prostitutes," the teacher translated. "That Ukrainian citizens have been paying them with taxes. That they are not getting what they paid for because the police have gone over to the separatists. That he is an unhappy customer."

A complicated message, Alie thought, as more men surged into the room holding policemen, knocking her against the wall. She could see a dozen fresh bullet holes in the ceiling. Intentional? Or was someone about to get accidently shot in the face?

She saw Hargrove in the crowd, recognizable under the hood, as two policemen were knocked aggressively to their knees. The cell phone cameraman caught the triumph, then switched to another corner. There were eight policemen in the front room now, their hands behind their heads. They were not resisting. They had experienced this kind of harassment before, Alie figured, probably from the other side.

The mission leader stepped forward, berating and lecturing along with the civilian, whose voice was starting to crack. The militiamen nodded along. The policemen had their heads down, avoiding eye contact.

"They are shamed," Shwetz said.

They are waiting it out, Alie thought.

The speech seemed interminable, but eventually the men started to chant. "Putin is a motherfucker," the teacher translated with a smile.

The leader chose two policemen, and the militia moved into the street, shoving the policemen before them with their AK-47s. Hargrove made eye contact with her as he passed, but Alie couldn't tell what he was thinking. At this point, after the disappointments of the last twelve hours, his brain might be totally fried.

"Where are they going?"

"To victory," Shwetz said gleefully, heading out the door.

The street was quiet. There was no one on the block except a few militiamen swinging their AK-47s and the knot of men leading the policemen toward the park. It was a few hours after noon, and the sun was shining. Three trees were in bloom. The police station had felt claustrophobic, but out here, the operation was a stroll. A block away, a small crowd of people on foot and bicycles had stopped to watch.

Really? Alie thought when she saw the Ukrainian flag.

The flagpole was in the middle of the park, but the cord was too high. *It must have been cut by the militia that raised the Donetsk Republic flag,* Alie thought. After a few leaps, the Donbas men stopped and stared. They signaled for an older man, who was wearing an antique World War II infantry helmet, and tried to lift him. No good. Finally, someone ran back to the police station for a table. It took a moment to get it straight. Then the old man —now the symbolic everyman of the group—climbed on top and hauled down the Donetsk Republic flag. Another man tore it off the cord, stepped on the corner, and ripped it in half, or tried to—flags are hard to tear. When three men couldn't do it, they stomped on it, kicked it into the street, and lit it on fire as the man with the cell phone tried to direct them for his propaganda piece. The fire also failed to take. The spectators at the intersection started to fidget.

The cameraman turned to the park. The new flag was on the cord, but the leader wanted to make sure the ceremony was filmed. The man in the antique helmet gave a thumbs-up, then started to raise the flag. The Donbas militiamen began to sing the Ukrainian national anthem, while the cameraman zoomed in on the limp flag as it inched its way bravely toward the top.

And then something cracked, loud enough for Alie to hear it from half a block away, where she'd stopped outside the police station. Even from that distance, she could see the old man totter. A leg had snapped off the table, but the men were holding him steady now, the group precariously balanced.

The singing started again. The flag started to move. And then another crack, and this time the whole group went down in a heap.

It's gunfire, Alie realized, as a third bullet struck the table. The old man was lying on the ground, his crazy helmet beside him, the other three men crawling and tumbling backward to get out of range.

They're beaten, Alie thought.

But then a man stepped forward from the body of the militia, walking in the direction of the hidden gunman. There was one more shot, but it banged off the flagpole with a resounding gong. The spectators scattered, and Alie saw a man with a deer rifle slide out from behind a parked car and start to run.

The militiaman pointed, waved for his colleagues to join him, and started to run. Behind him, the militia poured out of hiding, following him into the breach. It was the sands of Iwo Jima, on some unnamed Ukrainian square.

The lead runner fired. It was a tinny shot, because he wasn't carrying a Kalashnikov. He was carrying a pistol.

Oh Christ, Alie thought. It was Hargrove.

Maltov stepped up to the door of the club at precisely 1700 hours. It had taken him more than three hours to assemble the equipment the American needed, but he had done it gladly, thinking through each request, so that he would understand how the pieces fit. He was even the one to suggest the garbage truck—a stroke of genius, the American had to admit.

"*Davaite pohkovorymo,*" he said calmly, as two guards leveled their AK-47s. Let's talk.

Inside, the club was dank. There was one room with a hallway, clearly leading to a back door, and two windows: one in the front to the left of the door, one on the right wall looking out on a side street. A few lightbulbs hung overhead, throwing a feeble light. Three men sat at a table in the center of the room. One was Vadim, a local tough Maltov had known since childhood. The second was the Russian who had arrived ten minutes ago in the bulletproof Mercedes. The third was simply in the way. Behind them, three bodyguards had their guns drawn. There were cigarettes and glasses scattered on the table.

"*Da?*" the Russian said.

Maltov continued to look around. Bar in the back left corner with a man behind it. A pool table blocking access to the side window. Empty right front corner.

"*Chto ty khochesh?*" the man continued in Russian. He turned to Vadim and said, again in Russian, the prick: "Is this your man?"

Maltov placed his hands in his pockets and the three guards raised their guns (they already had rounds chambered, the muscle always had rounds chambered), even though he'd been searched for weapons outside. Two more men came from the back hallway, rubbing their noses and pointing their guns like amateurs. That would be all of them.

"I am Maltov," he said in Ukrainian. "Vadim knows me, and he knows my reputation. I am from Kramatorsk."

Vadim nodded. They had been a few years apart in school, and they had run in similar circles ever since, sometimes as enemies, sometimes as friends. Maltov hadn't seen him in almost a decade, but he wasn't worried about Vadim. The man was small. He always had been. This filthy club must have been his, because it was about his speed.

"I hear your boss went down," Vadim said. It was almost a sneer. After years of watching his old acquaintance rise, Vadim thought he had the upper hand.

"I have a new boss. He sent me to apologize."

The Russian looked up with interest. He was young. Too young to be somebody. His guards were young, too. Even if they were connected in Moscow, they were nothing more than thugs on the make.

"We mean you no harm," Maltov said. "We have a long-term interest in this city, and a long-term interest in your friendship. The three men last night, that was an accident."

Let them think what they want: drugs, arms, as long as it was lucrative.

"Are they dead?" Vadim asked.

"How much?" the Russian said.

"I am authorized to give you five thousand euros."

The Russian snorted. "Not enough."

"Per man."

Vadim tried to hide his smile. He would sell out for too little. The small-timers always did.

The Russian sneered. "Why should we settle?"

Why should you *get a piece?* Maltov thought. *You just got here.*

"This country is at war," the Russian continued. "That's an opportunity. If you have operations here, cut us in. We can protect you from the separatists."

It was what the Americans wanted. They had sent him to cut a deal that would buy them one day of peace. That was all. But Maltov had a longer interest in Kramatorsk. And he still wanted revenge for Pavlo.

"I won't cut you in," Maltov said. "And I won't give you the money. The payment is off the table. I deal with Ukrainians, not pig fuckers."

"Maltov . . ." Vadim said, always a coward. "Be reasonable. We don't want trouble."

But I do, Maltov thought.

"I will be back in three hours," he said. "If the Russian mercenary is gone, I will give you ten thousand euros, as a peace offering. If he's not . . ." Maltov shrugged. "I apologize again, this time in advance."

He turned and walked out. Behind him, he could hear the Russian laughing. Outside were the three Mercedes and two guards. He scratched his pen, then pushed down on his lapel to switch the microphone on. *Too bad the Americans didn't hear what was said inside,* he chuckled to himself.

"Eight," he whispered, without lowering his head or changing his stride. "Two on the door. Target is young. Black hair. Black tracksuit. Table inside the door."

CHAPTER 34

Hargrove sat down on the curb. Collapsed onto it, really, his muscles already starting to seize up. He could feel his blood pounding in his head. He needed water, but he didn't have any, so he stared at the street beneath his feet, sucking wind.

How far had he chased the man? Maybe half a mile. Not far.

But it wasn't the distance that exhausted him. He could run half a mile in his sleep. It was the firefight. The zigzagging and sprinting. The tension. The excitement.

He hadn't expected that. The compulsion to keep going. The excitement, once the enemy turned their backs. How many had there been? Maybe five. Six. He had only seen them in glimpses, hiding behind cars, running up the street. Militiamen without uniforms but heavily armed. Like his men. Like *these* men, the Donbas Battalion, the ones who followed him.

"Good work, guys," he said. "Great work."

Eight militiamen had joined him on the corner, but none responded.

"They don't speak English," someone said finally.

It was the interpreter. The man from the car. He was a teacher, right? He had a baby . . . a baby girl, was it? It didn't matter. Whatever his life had been, it didn't matter here. They were strangers, heaving on a corner with their guns in their hands. Because of the hoods, he had never seen most of their faces. But they were his brothers. *Blood brothers,* Hargrove thought. First blood. His first firefight. He hadn't hit anybody, but nobody on his side had been hit. Had they?

"Is anybody hit?"

Nobody responded, even Shwetz. The one in the back, the short one, was filming. He wondered if the man had filmed the whole battle—how long did it last, half an hour? He looked at his watch. Eleven minutes! He would have loved to get a copy, but he wasn't supposed to be here, and he wasn't supposed to engage the enemy. It was a serious breach of protocol. But it was spontaneous. An intuitive act. They had shot first. It was self-defense.

He felt for his hood. Still on. Good.

He took a deep breath, his pulse slowing. It had been a while since the last shot was fired, so he could relax. Take a moment. The hostile militia had been driven off. People were starting to drift back into the street. An old man shuffled past, a bag over his arm. Going shopping.

A kid on his bicycle rode by, looked, circled back. Twelve. Maybe seven. Hargrove couldn't tell his age, only that he was young. The boy stopped and stared. He looked nervous, until one of the militiamen started chatting with him—the older man with the antique helmet who had led the chant about Putin.

The man stood up and went into the shop. They were sitting in front of a shop. Hargrove was surprised he hadn't realized that. He looked around. They were in a residential neighborhood in a small town . . . what town were they in?

He heard yelling, and instantly, he was alert, clutching his pistol.

It was only the militiamen, saying good-bye to the boy on the bicycle. The boy was pedaling away, waving, a smile on his face. *An odd kid,* Hargrove thought. He hadn't said much. But then Hargrove realized what they must have looked like, nine men in masks with AK-47s, sitting on a neighborhood corner. It had taken courage to come up to them. He never would have done it when he was a boy. But then again, he never would have seen masked gunmen in Centennial, Colorado.

A bell rang, causing Hargrove to jerk his pistol into firing position. It was the chime on a door, the old man coming out of the store. One of the militiamen was following the kid, shouting for him. The man was holding a bag, but the boy was gone. It was a backpack, the kind Hargrove had carried himself, in elementary school. The boy must have been in elementary school. Was it a school day? No. There was no school. School was cancelled.

"Is that the kind of kid you taught?" he asked the interpreter-teacher.

"I can't tell," Shwetz said sadly.

They were doing the right thing. The boy was proof. The Donbas Battalion may have seemed out of shape and poorly trained, but they had charged into gunfire. They had cleared this neighborhood of separatists. He watched the man with the backpack. He watched the older man look down at the bottle of Coke in his hand, obviously intended for the boy, but all that was left of him was the backpack and a cell phone. The boy had left his cell phone.

They would give it back, Hargrove decided. They would find the boy and return his backpack and cell phone, because they weren't just fighters. They were liberators. They were fighting for these people. Not for ideology, or politics, but for the ordinary people and their ordinary lives.

He looked up at the Soviet-style apartments. The buildings were dull, yes, but the people were proud. He could see their colorful curtains. Their freshly painted shutters. There were flags, mostly Donetsk Republic, but that was to be expected, they had only five minutes ago liberated this block, using the spirit of the bayonet, of course, Sergeant Barkley had been on to something there, but also the spirit of compassion. And freedom. And self-determination. Everything he had learned in his CIA training program.

He never saw the missile. He saw the old man with the antique helmet holding the cell phone, walking toward him. Then a shock wave, a huge noise, and the man was gone, and Hargrove was rolling on the pavement, covered in glass and blood, the ringing in his ears erasing the cacophony of car alarms.

He never made the connection: the tracking function on the cell phone, the targeting mechanism of the missile. He felt the blast, saw blood spray a building. The windows were blown out. He was lying in blood. There was blood on the sidewalk, blood in his hand, and a hand under the curb. How could a severed hand be under a curb, and what had happened to the curb? He looked away. The top of the Coke bottle had been torn off, and it was lying in the street, the liquid pouring out, foamy and brown.

He sat up. There was a man screaming into a radio. The car alarms were pummeling. There was a car, its tires flattened by shrapnel, with five men crouched behind it. His men. The Donbas Battalion. They were firing, and there were bullets coming back, but his men were in a perfect firing formation, holding their ground. They were real soldiers, brave men who stood and fought for their country.

The old man was dead. So was the teacher. He was lying on his back in the road, with a hole in his head.

No, it wasn't Shwetz. Shwetz was behind the car, firing at the enemy. It was some other teacher. Or butcher. Or baker. Someone else whose family would receive a video of their last moments. If the cameraman made it out alive.

And he would, Hargrove was sure of that. The Donbas men

were disciplined. They were *right*. There was no way a separatist militia could push these soldiers back.

Then he saw the T-72 tank come around the corner, crumpling a car in its path.

"Get outta here!" he yelled in English to no one in particular, frantically searching for something to take out the tank. He tried to grab an assault rifle from the dead man, but it slipped out of his hands. He tried again, and again it was jerked away. It was still strapped to the man's shoulder.

He tried to run. He tried to pull away and get the hell out, but his feet kept slipping on the blood, and then he was falling backward, falling . . .

No. He was being dragged backward. Someone was pulling him. He could feel the hand on his throat, and he couldn't breathe, until he was in a car, in the backseat, being taken away. Kidnapped. Tortured because he was an American, because he was CIA . . .

He kicked the door, but his knees buckled. He tried to grab the seat, but his hands were slick. He grabbed for his CIA service pistol but fumbled it. His shirt was slick. His stomach was covered in blood. He'd been shot.

"I've been shot," he screamed. "I'm covered with blood."

He heard the brakes, and he was thrown violently forward, then bounced back onto the seat. He had time to see the fist a half second before it hit his face.

"Shut the fuck up," the man said. Then they were moving again, faster this time. Hargrove didn't know what to do. He couldn't move. He was too stunned to talk, or think, or even make a sound . . .

"Quit screaming. You're not hurt."

Hargrove complied. He didn't even know he'd been screaming. He felt his stomach. He didn't know what he was feeling for, a hole maybe, but there was no hole. He was sore, but not split. *It's someone else's blood,* he thought.

"Alie," he said.

"Shut up," the driver said again.

"You speak English."

"Don't be an asshole."

Hargrove sat up. The driver spoke English. The driver was . . . Sergeant Barkley's go-fer, what was his name? Jesus. No, Jessup. What was Jessup doing here?

"You're Jessup?"

The man didn't answer.

"What are you doing here?"

"Rescuing you."

What about the other men? "What about the other men? The Ukrainians."

Jessup shook his head. "Can't be done. Only you."

"But I'm not an asset . . ."

"No shit. You're a liability."

They drove in silence, Hargrove wasn't sure for how long. He kept thinking of the old man with the bag. The kid on the bicycle. The missile. The Coke.

"Good men got killed because of you," Jessup said.

It was true. Hargrove knew that, and he felt ashamed. "And Alie?"

Jessup didn't say anything for three or four blocks, until the town started to recede. Hargrove was sure the man wanted to punch him again. Was it the ambushed men? The botched mission? Or was it him? Was he asking the wrong questions? Was Alie dead?

"Your girlfriend left you fifteen minutes ago," Jessup said.

CHAPTER 35

"It's a go," I said into my headset, as I watched Maltov walk away from the club. I had hoped the payment would work. Truly, it was the best option. But luck wasn't on our side. At least we had given them a chance.

I started humming Verdi's *Requiem* as I moved into position. It was an instinct, a desire to find something that calmed me. For some guys, it was heavy metal. For others, the Lord's Prayer. For me, today, it was the terrifying "Dies Irae" from Verdi's death mass, a work that defined the relationship between man and his mortality, and thus his maker. This music, like so many classical works from my violin playing days, was etched into my soul. It made me feel like death incarnate.

I lifted my SCAR rifle and prepared to run. On the eighth note, the garbage truck accelerated past Maltov, who was a block from the club and still walking away, and then past my position in the alley, one of Maltov's boys at the wheel. The guards had their eyes on Maltov; by the time they realized the garbage truck wasn't stopping, it was too late. Twelve seconds into the *Requiem,* the truck smashed the club like a battering ram, collapsing half the front wall.

We were shock and awe before the dust could settle, throwing flashbangs and smoke grenades of various colors as we poured into the breech. Charro pounded a guard in the head, Boon high-kicked the second in the solar plexus, and we leapt inside as the music frenzied at thirty seconds, our gas masks on and laser scopes dancing in the smoke. *Pop. Pop. Pop.* I could hear precision shooting, incapacitating the guards.

I looked for the black tracksuit, my laser scope flashing through the smoke, the violent music in my head focusing my mind. I found the Russian on his back behind an overturned table and put a bullet in his shoulder, close enough that the muzzle flash would sear. I stomped his shoulder, snapping his clavicle, and he shrieked in pain. Killing the leader would incite the pack; hearing him screaming in pain would terrify them. I dropped a playing card on his chest. The King of Hearts. It didn't mean anything; it was just meant to confuse. And it was some badass shit.

"*Nastupnoho razu,*" I said. Next time. The only two words I knew in Ukrainian, taught to me by Sirko an hour ago.

I stepped past the Russian. The smoke was thick, the music in my head winding down. It was time to go. I looked for my team, found them, and fired one more shot at a bodyguard moving in the smoke. Then I was in the back hallway and out the back door and running down the street, following my evac route.

Two minutes, and everything was finished. Death had passed, the shadow moving on. The entire team was at the rally point, safe and accounted for. I nodded to Miles; he nodded back. We moved out in formation, silently, down the alley and out of sight, and before anyone could figure out what had happened, we were gone.

CHAPTER 36

Winters picked up the phone. "Yes," he said.

It was Wolcott. It was 1000 EST, so Wolcott was in. That was a rule at Apollo: Wolcott was always in. "It's getting ragged," Wolcott said. "Extracurricular activity a few blocks south."

"Is everything on schedule?"

"For now."

"Let me know."

Winters hung up. That was another rule of the company. Winters hung up whenever he felt like it.

1500 London time, *two hours until the meeting,* he thought, instinctively straightening his tie, cobalt blue with yellow parachutes, in honor of this club. He had flown overnight from New York to London, five hours' time difference, and he was feeling the lack of adequate rest. He should be napping. But he couldn't sleep, not with this much on the line, so he had fallen back on his familiar routine, and that meant a drink at the Special Forces Club.

There was a time when gaining admittance to this redbrick row house on a quiet street in central London was an honor. It was the social hub of the international mercenary community, and at that time, he had enjoyed the exclusivity. The history. Now he could see how shabby it was: threadbare furniture, a stain on the carpet. Imperial decrepitude.

He looked up. There on the wall, staring down from his portrait, was Sir David Stirling, the father of them all. The founder of the SAS in 1941 and, more important, Watchguard, the first modern mercenary company. Under the portrait was the SAS motto: "Who Dares Wins." It was catchy, but he preferred the photo in the entry lobby of Churchill giving his famous "set Europe on fire" speech. As the Navy SEALs said: "The only easy day was yesterday."

1800 Ukrainian time, Winters thought, counting time zones. Ten hours until the Donbas Battalion arrived. Eleven until the press junket flew in.

Eleven hours, he thought. Eleven hours until Karpenko's victory speech, and then he could leave this fraying place behind. For a higher place. A more powerful place. Or maybe he should say, a deeper state.

CHAPTER 37

It wasn't hard to find Kramatorsk, since it was only about twenty kilometers from the little town with the police station. Alie had expected roadblocks and soldiers, but the road was empty, the farmland punctured by two rusty factories with grasping pipes and defiant smokestacks, like south Alabama without the mosquitos. Actually, she wasn't sure about the mosquitos.

She rubbed her temples, fighting the headache. She felt cotton in her mouth, and she wondered about the last time she'd eaten. Early morning at the elementary school, she remembered, long before Hargrove had gone cowboy in the park. He was a good guy. Smart. A true believer. He wanted to work his way up in his country's service: recruit spies, defeat enemies, and defend the flag in the pat way history books and novels portrayed.

But he was impatient, as young men often are. He wanted to be Bill Donovan, the legendary head of the OSS during World War II, but act like Tom Locke, the mercenary, because he thought Locke was changing the world. *Maybe he is,* Alie thought, although she wasn't so sure.

To be like Locke, though, you had to understand where he came from. You had to know the scars, the bullet hole in the back of his left shoulder and the cut across his ribs, and all those fucked-up places in his soul. Hargrove was too fresh and innocent. His only scar was the tooth he'd chipped doing a keg stand in college, and even that had been immaculately repaired.

She hated leaving him behind. It felt like Locke and innocent Alie in Burundi, with the roles reversed. But she knew that
wasn't true. She'd see Hargrove again, probably tonight, after
he'd gotten his cowboy fix and rejoined the main body of the
Donbas Battalion.

She could have waited with the milita for whatever was coming. She could have found Locke that way, she was sure of it. But
she had a feeling the militiamen were on the outside of whatever was really happening here, and she wanted to be inside. She
wanted to find Locke before the action went down. It was the
only way to get the real story, and that was what she was here
for, right?

Maybe she was impatient, too. Maybe she should have waited.
After all, Hargrove knew where Locke was. He had him triangulated to within a hundred meters. But he had refused to tell
her the location, even on their long drive together. Maybe Hargrove suspected that, with enough information, Alie would take
the car and run.

Funny, because she didn't realize that herself, until it was already done.

She pulled into a bar. Bars were a good place to collect infor
mation, but this one was mostly empty, even at 5:30 on a Friday
afternoon. It was tidy, with strings of yellow flags advertising
Obolon, a local beer. There was an unused Obolon dartboard,
and two pensioners drinking out of Obolon glasses. The bartender cheerfully wiped a spot with an Obolon towel, chatting
in rapid Ukrainian, but his smile didn't diminish the depression
that hung over the place.

She ordered a pint of Obolon with a *horilka* back. When in
Ukraine, drink as the locals drink. She drank. The bartender had
lost his enthusiasm when he realized she didn't speak Ukrainian,
but she called him over for a second round.

"Food?" she said, miming the act of eating.

The bartender pointed to a display of Lay's potato chips.

"Ukrainian?" She moved her hands like she was holding an assault rifle. "Militia?"

He didn't understand. Some people, when they don't know a language, don't even try. The formerly cheerful bartender was one of them.

She made the motion of a gun again. "Kiev?"

He shook his head. "Donetsk."

She showed him the picture of Locke on her phone, taken in the Kiev hotel bar two days ago.

"American?" she said, motioning to ask if he had seen him.

The bartender shook his head no.

Alie drank her second round of local beer and liquor and ate the bag of chips. She left hryvnias on the counter along with her contact information—in case he saw "the Americain"—and got back in her car.

She drove, trusting her instincts. Kramatorsk was a midsize city of five-story apartment blocks, but off to the west she could see larger apartments, and off to the east, a bristling black factory. The train station bridge, crossing ten tracks and several abandoned red and green engines, afforded a perfect view of the smoking colossus. No pedestrians, the town was quiet, the billowing smoke the closest thing to a social life.

Beyond the train station, the pavement was scorched and windows blown out. At the river, she turned north. The trees were yellow and white, the green grass broken up with black mud. Monet would have loved the waterlillies, but Alie could see slag in their tendrils. She imagined the fish, nibbling at the corners of plastic bottles. The river made her sad for the people who lived here, although she couldn't say why, it just made her feel like nothing would change, like this would go on and on until it was forgotten. But the white church with the gold metal onion domes, the one she caught only in glimpses—that was lovely.

A few blocks later, she saw a mortared building, the front sloughing off like a rockslide. She passed a burned bus left in the street, the electric wires cut or blown off their supports. More shattered windows, more scorch marks, more metal hanging perilously off façades.

She pulled off the road near a makeshift memorial, dying flowers and a photo of a young man. The damage here was extensive. Three burned buses were flopped down on their bellies, their melted tires stolen. A block ahead, she saw a barricade, mostly tires held in place by barbed wire. The two men at the barricade were wearing skeleton ski masks.

She turned into a package store and bought a bottle of vodka in a brown plastic bag. It was the only open store on the block. She showed the photo of Locke as she paid. "Americain?" No. She left the man her card.

Outside, she turned back the way she had come and went down a side street, avoiding the barricade. There was a barricade on the next street as well. She saw the handle of a baseball bat sticking up from the pile—how strange, did they play baseball here?—and men in masks, mostly stocky, with bushy beards. They were wearing camouflage, as if they were in a forest, even though they were standing in front of a coffee shop. It seemed to be open. She wondered if the Cossacks paid for their coffee.

There was a small park, like the one Hargrove had charged across. There was a flagpole flying the colors of the Donetsk Republic and a statue of Stalin, which was surprising—she thought they had all been torn down decades ago. An armored troop carrier was sitting on the far edge, no doubt stolen by separatists from the Ukrainian army, and men were wandering around with guns. A young woman was sitting against Stalin's pedestal, a sandwich in her hand, a handheld video camera beside her.

"Reporter?" Alie asked, handing her the brown paper bag.

"Doing my best," she said. Alie had thought she was American, but she was European, Dutch or a Scandi probably, judging by the accent and glasses. "Who do you work for?"

"Independent," Alie replied.

"The *Independent*?"

"No, I'm independent. I work for myself. I've had some stuff in the *Guardian*." Three years ago.

"A liberal," the woman said crookedly. She took a sip from the vodka bottle and grimaced, handing back the bag.

"I publish anywhere that will take me. What about you?"

"*Vice*."

"The website?"

"YouTube channel. More traffic that way. We file dispatches under the heading Russian Roulette."

Alie took a long pull and settled in beside her. "Anybody else around?"

"A couple Germans. One Brit. Locals, of course, they have a thriving press here. Professional and independent." She smiled at the word. In this context an independent meant anyone with a cell phone and the ability to upload to the Internet.

"Any Americans?"

"You're the first I've seen."

Alie wasn't surprised. The American news agencies never came this deep. They were barely even in Kiev.

She showed the girl the picture of Locke. "How about him?"

The kid shook her head no. "Is he in town?"

Alie took a drink. "Probably." The bearded Cossacks were intimidating, but they weren't even looking at her. It was tough to stay on alert. "If he is, he doesn't want to be found. I figure if I make enough noise, show his picture around, he'll have to find me."

Silence me, in other words. It wasn't much of a plan, and it had its risks, but it had worked before, in much worse places and with much worse men.

The young woman understood. Maybe. She didn't ask any questions.

"It's quiet," Alie said, taking another drink.

"The fighting has moved on. The separatists have held this part of town for a week. The battle is out at the airport and the television tower."

She had read about the Ukrainian army offensive at the airport. The one runway had been rendered useless by the first mortar attack last month. It was purely symbolism now. Not Locke's type of gig.

"Television tower?" she said.

"I know," the young woman said. "Crazy, right? But television still matters here."

"Military or militias?"

"Official Ukrainian military," she said. "We're going this afternoon, if you want a lift."

Alie drank and handed back the bottle. That didn't sound like Locke's spot, either. The U.S. wouldn't send a merc for a television tower, would it? There must be something else. "What about local militia?"

"Which side?"

"Ukrainian."

The vice reporter shrugged. "There's the Donbas Battalion about twenty minutes away, if you have a car."

Alie shook her head. "I want something here, in Kramatorsk."

"Well, it's mostly Donetsk."

"What do you mean?"

"Most people are for the separatists. I'd say 75 percent."

"Seriously?" Kiev was running 90 percent the other way, from what she could tell.

The young woman pointed across the street. "See the holes in that building? And the apartments with the front blown off? That was the Ukrainian military firing mortars toward these barricades." Poor propaganda. Bad for winning hearts and minds. "I doubt the support lasts long, though. It's going to get worse for these people before it gets better."

The young woman was maybe twenty-two, younger than Hargrove, but she knew what she was talking about. The idea of an insurrection was easy to support, especially in a poor region, because there were always legitimate grievances, and nothing bad had happened yet, and the future was sunshine and lollipops. The reality of an insurrection was usually hell.

"If you want pro-Ukraine," the kid said, pointing to her left, "take that road. Keep going until you see the flags. It's about a kilometer." She took a long drink of the vodka and wiped her mouth. "Or you could try that," she said, pointing in the other direction.

Alie looked behind her. Smoke was rising from the west. "When did that happen?"

"About an hour ago." The young woman smiled. She looked exhausted, filthy, but convinced this was her calling, because it was the greatest experience of her life. Alie envied her youth.

"Be careful," the young woman said. "The separatists kidnapped a female reporter a few days ago. They let her go, *untouched*"—an emphasis on the word Alie understood too well— "but she was local, so it's not necessarily a precedent."

"Don't worry. I've done this before."

"In Ukraine?"

"In Africa."

"I knew it," the young woman said. "You're Alie MacFarlane, right?"

Alie looked at her. Who was this girl?

"I saw you speak at a refugee conference in the Hague a few years back. You're a legend. Sort of. To a few of us diehards anyway." Okay kid, *legend* was nice. Quit qualifying it. "That refugee series, when you traveled with those women from Burundi to Bosaso. . . . It's obscure, sure. You have to take a deep dive to find it. But that's where the good stuff is, right? Down in the depths."

It's not down there to be cool, Alie thought. *It's down there because I couldn't verify it. Because I didn't organize my sources, some of whom might have killed me. Because I lost my subjects and lost the ending and didn't bring it home with a bang.*

"That series was brilliant," the young woman continued. "I read it when I was a junior in upper school. It changed my life."

That series was a failure, in every way.

"How is Magdelena?" The young woman sat up even straighter. "Is she here? In Ukraine?"

Alie felt the lump in her throat. She couldn't say it. Magdelena is missing. It hurt for her to even think it: Magdelena is almost surely dead.

"I'm working on a bigger story," Alie said, and she wished she hadn't. Why did she need to impress this kid?

"About Ukraine?"

"Nobody cares about Ukraine. This is about the USA."

She knocked back another gulp of vodka, then handed the young woman the last of the bottle. She felt tired. "I'm going to check on that smoke," she said.

It wasn't even a decision. At this point in her life, what else could she do?

CHAPTER 38

The Wolf stood outside the smoking building, staring at the back end of the garbage truck, the only part not buried in the wall. There were policemen on the scene, but they seemed mostly intent on extricating the stolen city property and getting it back on duty.

It's a tank, he thought, as he stared at the hard metal frame.

"It's a miracle no one was killed," an older man was saying.

It's not a miracle, the Wolf thought. *It was intentional.*

Eight wounded, none dead. It would have been easier to wipe them out. One incendiary device, fired or planted. Boom. Nothing. No worries, no risk. Killing people was the simplest act in modern warfare, if you simply wanted them dead. That was why the world had spent the last hundred years figuring out how to make better munitions. No, this was specialized, like a laser-guided missile.

"They were pro-Russians," the old man is saying. "They were wearing separatist uniforms."

Unlikely, the Wolf thought. This was a professional team. The combination of brutality and precision. The spectacle of the garbage truck and the staged "clumsiness" of the shooting. They missed from point-blank range! No, they didn't. This was a message.

Or a distraction.

"Why here?" the old man was lamenting to no one in particular, or maybe to the Wolf, who wouldn't even turn toward him. "Why in my building?"

Good question, old man, the Wolf thought.

He walked around the side of the building. Witnesses had seen six men run this way. They had been wearing gas masks, the old-fashioned Soviet kind with the greenish-brown face cover and the alien-like breathing hose. Masks that could be sourced locally, and were ghoulish enough to distract from any other details.

Maybe they were separatists. Maybe. But he didn't know anyone else at his level working the area.

He thought of the Ukrainian. Maltov. He had tracked the man to Kramatorsk, where his henchmen had dropped him off for the night. Somehow, he had slipped out during the night. The safe house turned out to be his mother's apartment. Nice lady. Excellent blinis. Far too trusting for this day and age.

Karpenko was here, and so was his hired team. There were too many coincidences to think otherwise. But why? What was their objective in this nothing town?

The Wolf walked the side street, checking the surroundings. He walked to the front of the building. A gas facility was five hundred meters away, its pipework visible behind the surrounding walls and two low houses. The guards were wearing militia uniforms, but the Wolf knew them immediately for Russian Spetsnaz. He had worked with them for decades, all the way back to Afghanistan. They had stormed the Crimean parliament, in a similar disguise. They were the tip of the spear. The pressure point . . .

"Americain?" he heard someone say.

"No, no." It was the same old man, muttering, still in his pajama bottoms, the Wolf noticed, at four in the afternoon.

"Americain?" the foreign woman said, turning to him and holding out her phone for him to see.

CHAPTER 39

"Shit," I said, as I watched the surveillance feed of the crowd outside the club.

"What?" Miles said, appearing at my shoulder.

In America, there would have been a crowd of news crews and gawkers. Here, two months into the street fighting, there was already a weary acceptance. If the insurrection lasted another year, this kind of tragedy would be so commonplace, even this sparse crowd wouldn't bother.

I pointed to Alie.

"An American." Miles said, leaning in. "What's she doing? Charro, can we get a closer look?"

The camera zoomed in, but I didn't need to see what was on her cell phone. I knew it had something to do with me. Why else would she be in Kramatorsk?

"She's looking for me," I said.

Miles looked up, confused. I could tell he was trying to put this together.

"You know this woman," Karpenko said. It didn't sound like a question. For a boss, he had a way of slipping into the edges of conversations. Dangerous.

"From an old job," I muttered, glancing at Miles, wondering if he remembered her from Burundi. It had been ten years, after all. "I ran into her in Kiev four days ago. She knows what I do."

"How does she know you're here?"

Exactly what I was wondering. "I don't know," I admitted, "but I think we need to find out."

Miles was shaking his head no. I tried to turn away, but he pulled me aside. "Is that who I think it is?" he hissed. "The white girl from Burundi?"

"Half white," I said.

"The one you risked everything for at Gatumba?" I knew by *everything*, he really meant everything: the mission, the country, thousands of lives, his respect. He hadn't forgotten.

"She's a reporter," I said. "We can't leave her on the street."

"She's an emotional attachment," he snapped. "You have to let her go. We've already risked too much."

He was right. The operation at the club looked like a success, at least in terms of spooking the local thugs back into their holes. But if it brought too much attention, if it spiraled into other loose ends I needed to tie up . . .

"Mission focus," Miles said, his arm on my shoulder, his head close so no one else could hear. "I don't care about your past. That's over. You know that."

It should have been over. I promise, Miles, I thought it was.

"She's smart, Miles. She's making noise. She knows I can't have my picture shown around."

"Ten hours," he said. "And we're done. We're out of here."

But it wasn't done. And I wasn't out.

"Actioning her isn't personal," I said.

"It isn't professional," Miles countered with bite. "We're warriors, Locke. We're here for a mission. We don't do damsels in distress."

She wasn't a damsel, I wanted to say. And she wasn't in distress.

"I determine the mission parameters," I said, turning to the computer monitor to let him know this discussion was over. Miles was my NCO, my second, but I was still the unit commander.

Miles didn't like it, but he took it. Like a professional. I almost turned to say something to him, to say I appreciated his support and his trust, not in a dickish way, but sincerely, because it really did mean everything to me.

But I didn't. I let it go. I leaned in toward the monitor, watching my old love show her cell phone to a stream of Ukrainian men. *Are you thinking about opsec, Locke?* I asked myself. *Is this about maintaining secrecy?*

Or is it about Alie?

The Wolf stepped into the shadows, where he could keep an eye on the attractive American without being seen. You never knew, after all, who was watching. He took out his cell phone. One of his Chechens answered.

"He is here. Yes. Karpenko. Kramatorsk. It's a town. No. With a gas facility." The Wolf looked at his watch, a Soviet military model he had been wearing since Afghanistan. It was 1923. "Yes. Fine. The whole million. For as many as you can bring, but only if you can get them here by midnight."

The Wolf hung up. He would give the Chechens the entire FSB million-dollar bounty on Karpenko's head, assuming the oligarch was actually in Kramatorsk. Karpenko didn't concern him, as long as it got the Chechen hunter-killers here.

He wanted the American special forces team, the one that had outmanuevered him in Poltava. He wanted the reward for them, and for proof of an American invasion, and knew it could set him up for life.

And revenge? Well . . . there was nothing wrong with that, either. Once a mercenary reached the age of the Wolf, everything felt like revenge for something.

CHAPTER 40

Now this is a room, Brad Winters thought, as he eased into a large leather chair next to a massive fireplace mantel, probably Renaissance Venetian. Across from him was a huge carved desk from the 1700s with the ancient crest of England carved into its front. An old-fashioned brown globe in a ponderous metal stand sat nearby. The walls were dark red silk damask, with old paintings hung by wire from the ornate crown molding. The ceiling was coffered, with gold leaf detailing; palatial Persian carpets overlapped to cover the floor. The leather club couch was so deep you could knife a wayward assistant (or willing secretary) without disturbing the adjacent office.

The building, like the Special Forces Club, was a row house, but not the American kind, a hundred years old and built for the upper middle class. In the London neighborhood of Belgravia, the stone buildings were three hundred years old and built by those in the process of conquering the world. Nothing in the New World could compare. This, after all, was the real thing: the seat of Empire. It was what the inhabitants of Washington, DC, aspire to, and what New York hedge fund managers had never understood. To them, the world was now. How can I make unfathomable money, and spend unfathomable money, before I die? In America, three months was a window.

For these men, three decades was a first step. They were connected to power, and wielded power, in ways Winters could only imagine. Their bank was not listed in any phone directory; it's true holdings not recorded in any database. Most of its clients' wealth was older than the desk. If you worked here, you thought in generations and centuries, not quarterly reports.

He had stepped out of the gutter, Winters felt, when he started to think that way, too. But he had no illusions. He was little more than a curiosity here, an ambitious nouveaux man on the rise. Still . . . he was here.

"Mr. Winters," a man said, extending his hand as he entered the room.

"Mr. Cavendish," Winters said. The great irony, he supposed, was that Eastern European oligarchs, who made American hedge fund managers seem like long-term thinkers, were now these bankers' richest clients, because they were now the richest men in England. It was through Karpenko, in fact, that Winters had entered their circle, albeit on the fringe. That was how he knew Ukraine mattered: because these men cared.

"My associates," Cavendish said.

Winters shook hands with the other two men. One was classically British, Sir Hyphen-Something, no doubt followed by a string of letters for arcane knighthoods. The other was Indian subcontinent by race, English by every other measure. No doubt his ancestors had been among the collaborators who made the Empire possible. Despite his dark skin, he was as British as Cavendish, from his facial expressions to his pointy shoes.

The last man in the group, who didn't seek or receive a handshake, was younger than the others, but impeccably groomed and attired. No doubt he was next in a line of private bankers that stretched back to the Glorious Revolution of 1688 and forward as far as London's existence. He took a seat in the back. He was empty-handed, without a pad of paper or cell phone. Winters hadn't noticed electronics anywhere, even though he knew this bank was connected.

"Have you given up on North Africa?" Cavendish asked.

"Temporarily."

"Why?"

Winters shifted, already off guard. How did the bankers know about his North African operation? "There's more opportunity in Eastern Europe," he said.

"I doubt that."

"A better opportunity, anyway. For me. And you." He had to be careful here.

Cavendish turned and walked past the large brown globe to his desk. Winters could taste the skepticism, but then again, it could have been the British mannerisms. These men had a way of looking down their noses at everything, including their own noses. He wouldn't have brought his partners, Winters assured himself, if he wasn't interested.

"I know you have interests in Ukraine," Winters said.

"We have interests everywhere."

"Yes, but Ukraine is special. There's enough shale gas there to power Europe until Putin retires, and enough infrastructure to get it here within six months." It wasn't the right word, men like Putin never *retired*, but he had shied away from *expires*. Look how long Castro had held on. Putin would outlive Sir Hyphen for sure, and probably a few others.

The bankers weren't impressed. They hadn't agreed to meet him for his philosophy. It was time to be American.

"I know you secretly backed the Nabucco pipeline," Winters said, shifting into direct mode. "It was a smart idea. Bring gas directly from Turkey into Europe, castrating Gazprom and dimming Russia's influence. I know that, in retaliation, Putin began a pipeline of his own, South Stream, from Russia through the

Black Sea. It was an old-fashioned arms race, with pipes instead of nukes, and it killed Nabucco. You took a haircut. A big one. Do you know why he did it?"

Nothing.

"Because he could."

Cavendish breathed deeply. Or maybe he just breathed. "Your point, sir."

"I can change the dynamic. I can put Putin on his heels, and Europe in the driver's seat." He was mixing metaphors, losing his edge. *Jesus, Brad, get a hold of yourself.* "But it's more than that," he said, moving quickly past the momentary stumble. "It's more than business deals or a few billion dollars." Let them chew that number. "It's victory, gentlemen. I'm talking about taking Russia off the world stage and snuffing out its last chance to rival the West. The end of an era." He glanced around the room for effect. "The end of an enemy."

The bankers stared at him in silence, but Cavendish must have signaled for the meeting to proceed, because after a few seconds the younger man rose from his seat and walked to the credenza, where an ornate crystal decanter of Scotch was perfectly positioned on a silver tray. He poured four glasses, and added a few drops of water to each. Winters took his with a nod. Nobody else acknowledged the young man's existence.

"Tell us," Cavendish said.

It was a blunt statement, but Winters could read the significance. *We are listening.* These men knew war. They had profited off everything from the Boer War to Afghanistan. He wouldn't be surprised if they had backed the winners at the Battle of Hastings. But they rarely started wars; they finished them. That was why they endured. He was going to have to make them stretch.

"We have the power, gentlemen," Winters said. "The West is distracted by the Arabs, and our citizens are tired, but Russia is worse. It is hollow. Their economy is one-dimensional, dependent on oil and gas, and any rupture—supply, transport, price drops—will cripple them. Their military has spent a decade feasting on children—Georgia, Chechnya, Azerbijan—to hide its inadequacy, but their officer corps is thin and their soldiers poorly trained. They couldn't even control a third-tier shithole like Georgia without the help of mercenaries."

"And America couldn't control a second-tier shithole like Iraq, even with mercenaries," Sir Hyphen huffed, but for business purposes—the business purposes only—Winters let it slide.

"They are a paper tiger, gentleman, fatally flawed on two fronts. All we need is a spark, and they will go up in flames."

"And the invasion of Ukraine is that spark," Cavendish said, in the dry British way that made it impossible to tell questions from answers.

"My firm has three hundred top military professionals operating in the Balkans. I've trained hundreds of fighters in the region. Within three months, I could have an army of thousands, well trained, heavily armed, and under elite command. And that doesn't include the official Ukrainian army. With minimal effort, we could hold Russia in a stalemate for years. That's not an opinion. That's a fact. But why settle for that? It gains us little. Why not destroy them instead?"

"How?"

"First, we break their military in Ukraine. It is easier than you imagine, and more effective than you might think. Putin has wrapped Russia in the symbolism of strength. A proud nation resurgent, a northern bear reborn. When we shatter that image, we shatter the people's faith. Then we break them economically."

"With oil."

Winters nodded. "Once we roll back the Russians, I will install my own man as the Ukrainian Minister of Energy. We will control their shale gas reserve in the East, which only the violence has kept Shell from exploiting. We will control the pipelines between Putin and the West. Ukraine has enough untapped natural gas reserves to become Europe's main supplier of energy within two years. That will make you powerful, gentlemen. And better, it will make Putin poor."

"It could also cause a devastating spike in energy prices," Sir Hyphen said with unprofessional fluster. He was probably a legacy. "Just the threat of all-out war could cause a market panic that could crater the world economy."

"That's the fear Putin counts on," Winters said calmly. "It's his currency of power. But the window here is small: only two years before the East—*our* East—is pumping enough oil to make Gazprom dispensable. There is easily enough oil output amongst our other suppliers: Norway, Venezuela, Nigeria, Saudi Arabia . . ."

"The Saudis hate Putin," Cavendish said thoughtfully, "because Putin is propping up Syria and Iran."

"Exactly. It's to the Saudis' advantage to fill the supply gap. And you have the contacts"—Winters glanced quickly from man to man—"to show them why."

Cavendish nodded. Winters was coming to them with a different kind of proposal: a request to use their influence, instead of their cash. At least, Winters assumed it was a new kind of proposal, because it was unlike any he had made before.

"This all hinges on your man in Ukraine," the Indian said languidly, speaking for the first time.

Exactly, Winters thought, hoping the change of direction meant they had bought the oil argument. "As you probably know," he said, "I have been grooming Kostyantyn Karpenko for some time."

The Indian sipped his Scotch, as if he'd never heard the name. But these men not only knew Karpenko, they owned him, or at least the part of him not currently listed on the London Stock Exchange. Karpenko had told Winters as much.

"You are invested in him, I believe, to the tune of a billion or more. So am I, but in sweat equity and personal reputation. Right now, in fact, his future is in my hands. Which practically makes us partners."

The Indian scowled, and Winters regretted his flippancy.

"Tomorrow morning, Karpenko will lead an assault on a Russian army unit that has taken over a strategic natural gas facility in the city of Kramatorsk. Karpenko's forces are Ukrainian patriots, all men who have volunteered, a citizen army . . . with a bit of professional help, of course. It will be a small battle, but an enormous symbol. These are Russian troops, threatening a major energy hub, a hundred miles from the Russian border. When Karpenko climbs on a troop carrier to proclaim his victory, he will show the world not just proof of an invasion, but his personal resolve to fight for Ukrainian freedom. This will be his Yeltsin moment."

"You have press, I assume?"

"Two helicopters, thirty passengers each. Reporters, photographers, video, Internet and traditional outlets, from Europe and the United States. We will manufacture a CNN effect, and drive the news cycle until it gets enough airlift. After Kramatorsk, it is a short drive to the next pipeline trunk station, and an even shorter one to the next. Within a week, Karpenko will become a national hero, my army will make sure of that."

"And then?"

"Ukraine will rally to him, and so will the West."

Another long pause. The Brits were masters of feigned disinterest. "The Americans will never go for it," Cavendish said.

"Do you think I would come," Winters said slowly, "if I didn't have that angle covered?"

He saw Sir Hyphen squirm. Was he impressing them, or had he gone too far? The only way to find out was to plunge on.

"If you've seen the news from our Congress, you know the United States is looking for a point of entry"—this wasn't true, they were looking for a way out, but there were layers under the administration with more insight and courage. "The congressional resolution in support of Ukraine introduced this week; the war hawks on the talk circuit. Freedom gas. The timing is not an accident. There are many who agree with my plan, even if they don't know the details, and we have been carefully amplifying their voices. Karpenko's triumph will prove they were right to demand action, and give them a way to respond."

"Obama will never agree to military action."

"He doesn't have to. I have Houston, gentleman. I have the Pentagon and cover in Congress. I have five current contracts with the United States government that can be rolled into a private military offensive under Ukrainian army cover. All Obama has to do is stand aside and let me work, and he will, because he always avoids hard choices, and that is the easiest choice."

In the silence, Winters realized he was leaning forward, and that he'd spoken with more passion than he'd intended. He wanted to say, Fuck it, this was years of work, this is my big chance, I'm not going to come in half-cocked. But instead, he sat back and adjusted his cuffs, to signal his casual reserve.

"You're absolutely right," Winters said. "The U.S. won't intervene to help us. But they won't stop us either"—as long as we're winning—"not with my business, military, and Congressional coalition. If you can simply rally the EU, publicly or privately . . ."

He left them the opening, but the bankers didn't respond. They could rally the British—they could make the British government do almost anything—but they wouldn't commit. Yet.

"Are you sure Karpenko will do as you ask?" It was the Indian again.

Winters nodded. "We're partners. He has agreed to everything."

"And when he starts to believe his own press?"

"I have leverage." Personal leverage. Family leverage. The best kind.

"What about the current government of Ukraine?" Sir Hyphen asked. "What if they don't want him to be the Minister of Energy?"

"Why would they refuse? It is a low profile position for a national hero. It strengthens their government, instead of threatening it."

"And when Karpenko is in place?" It was the Indian, cutting to the crux.

Winters smiled. "Pipelines, oil fields, leases in the Black Sea, anything you want. Anything you have desired. It must be a fair price, of course, but gentlemen . . . how can you place a price on a country's freedom?"

The Brits didn't even nod. They simply looked at him, as if they'd never seen him before. Winters had heard of stiff lips, but this made concrete look like Silly Putty.

"And if Putin returns?"

"That's part of my fee, gentleman, a long-term lease on a private military base in eastern Ukraine: airstrip, training grounds, fortified installations. From that base, I will not only keep your investments in Ukraine safe, I will keep Putin on the defensive, and I will keep the peace from Belarus to the Balkans. Think of it, gentlemen, a new Eastern Europe, free from Russian tyranny.

And all of it, or at least the military portion, paid for by the United States government."

"You have that guaranteed?"

Winters shook his head. "No, but that is the least of my concerns." Once he had sent Putin scurrying, he'd be up to his elbows in Title 10 contracts. He would be so in demand, he could write them himself. And he would.

The Indian leaned back, as if trying to see him at a new angle. He had a regal nose, and bushy eyebrows, and a stare that told Winters this was the man he needed to impress. And that he was listening.

"You've split with your New York bankers," the Indian remarked.

Winters swallowed his surprise. Of course they knew. "I think you know why."

Cavendish nodded. Everyone understood this room was an upgrade over New York. "What is the other part of your fee?" he asked. Sharp. These men never missed anything.

"A partnership with you, on a gas field in Eastern Ukraine. Preferably a big one." Winters had no intention of stealing oil leases from potential allies in Houston, but there were fields still available, especially just across the border in Russia, because why would he stop at the border, gentlemen, once he had Putin on the run?

"We secure the lease for your congolomerate—"

"—and you share the profits as silent partners."

Cavendish sniffed. "At what percentage?"

"I need 40 percent. The rest is unimportant to me."

"That is a remarkably poor negotiating technique."

It wasn't about negotiating. In New York, yes. But not at this level.

"It's enough to keep our mutual friends in Houston happy

and heavily invested in the democratic future of Ukraine. I'll make my stake on the security contracts." With a tidy taste off the top of the shale profits, of course. "It's not just the Balkans, gentlemen," he said, lifting his glass. "A base in Eastern Ukraine is the perfect staging area for the Middle East, Russia, the Caucuses, Iran. As I said at the top: from Ukraine, together, we can"—he almost said *control,* but caught himself—"change the world."

He sipped his Scotch. It was strong and smoky, straight out of a peat bog. Fifteen years in a barrel, at least. In the scope of things, that wasn't long.

"You are asking for nothing up front," Cavendish said.

"Nothing," Winters confirmed, "until Karpenko is in Kiev. Then I will need your influence, as well as your money, to make sure Europe and the markets go along."

"What are the chances of success?" the Indian asked.

Winters grimaced, but only to hide a smile. "It depends on *your* determination," he said. "With your help, greater than 90 percent. And that's to secure Ukraine for a generation."

Or plunge Europe into war. Those were the stakes. And still, the bankers didn't react. Was there anything that could make them flinch? What if he told them their wives had been murdered? Or their mistresses?

"And if the assault on the gas facility fails? That is the first step, is it not?"

Winters smiled. "The assault won't fail."

Cavendish and the Indian glanced at each other, but Winters couldn't read their expressions. He hated not being able to read expressions.

"You said tomorrow, if I'm not mistaken," Cavendish said.

"That's right."

"Okay," the Indian said slowly. "What time?"

He hadn't known how the bankers would react. They had kept him waiting, alone in the office, for an eternity, and beneath his cool nonchalance, Winters was nervous and cold. The world on a string, and he was sitting in a London office, counting the minutes until these starched-collared bankers returned. Was his plan too bold? Had he chosen the wrong partners? He didn't worry if the plan would work. He only worried that he wouldn't get the chance.

A half an hour. An hour. And then, finally, Cavendish and the Indian returned, this time without Sir Hyphen. "We need you to meet an associate of ours," Cavendish said. "Now. Before your operation."

Inside, Winters relaxed. He had thought, only half in jest, that they were going to have him arrested for off-the-books ballsiness. Or worse, exiled to Virginia.

"An honor," he said.

"A car is downstairs. It will take you to Farnborough."

Winters hid his shock. Farnborough was the corporate airport where London's superrich stowed their private jets. Maybe they were going to take him to a secret CIA prison in Poland after all.

"Who am I to meet?"

"All will be made plain soon enough," the Indian said.

Winters bowed. "Thank you, Mr. Beckham."

The Indian smiled. "Please. Call me Kabir."

CHAPTER 41

Alie tried not to panic. She tried to think straight. How had this happened?

She had stayed outside the shattered social club for an hour, maybe more, making notes and talking with citizens, trying to piece together what had happened. She had seen the Ukrainian, or Russian, maybe he was Russian, as she walked back to her car three blocks away. He was big, scowling, watching her. But it had only been, what? Two minutes since she'd left the site of the attack. God, they were fast.

Which meant Locke, right? Wasn't that what she wanted? To force him to grab her and get her off the street.

But the hood. Why did they need the hood?

She took a breath. She felt the cloth clogging her mouth, and she tried to slow herself down, tried to focus on her breathing. She thought of people with hoods over their heads: those being led to executions, their anonymous executioners. She thought of the ship captain all those years ago in Somalia, when she was trying to escape with the girls . . .

She jerked her shoulder, trying to chase away the memory, but her hands were tied. They hadn't tied on the hood, but her hands were tight behind her back, and she couldn't reach it. She couldn't move more than a few inches. She had known that, but feeling it was different.

Breathe, Alie, she thought, trying not to panic. *Alie, you have to breathe.*

The captain's face came to her, unwanted. The beautiful green eyes, the filthy brown teeth. She felt the warmth of his room in the Bosaso flop house. "Sorry to pull you aside, sister, we don't get many white women here," he had said, as he shoved goat into his mouth with his fingers. "We can't let you ride with the others, of course, we aren't savages, we'll give you a room on deck, my second mate's cabin, he had an accident anyway, here, have some of this." It was the worst liquor she had ever tasted. Why had she kept drinking it? Why had she listened to him lying, saying, "Don't worry, we'll take care of the women. We always do."

Breathe, she thought. *Alie, you have to breathe.*

She had to focus on these men, here, now, the ones who had grabbed her off the streets of Ukraine, not the ghosts from Bosaso. There were three of them. The big Russian who met her on the street, and the two who jumped out, grabbed her, and tossed her, literally, onto the delivery truck's cold metal floor.

Forget the hood, Alie. Forget the African captain and his teeth, and your stupid relief when he laughed and said, "We'll take you to the ship now, you can see your friends, they have to hide in the hold, but they will be fine."

She jerked again, trying to wrench her hands out of the cuffs, but a hand was on her shoulder. "Be calm," someone barked in accented English.

She thought of the hood back in Africa, her dizziness as the sailors covered her, and the captain saying, "For secrecy, you understand." Then the short walk to the docks in total darkness, or so she had thought, until she felt the blow to the back of her head, and the ground rushed upward to meet her, and then the captain was leaning over her, saying, "We cannot take you, we must leave you here, but don't worry, sister, I won't rape you. I am a Christian, just like you."

She screamed, the sound muffled by the hood and the truck. She jerked wildly, an animal instinct. Something was grabbing at her. Something was holding her face down, pressed into the floor, *and you can't breathe,* her mind told her, *when your mouth is facing the floor.*

"We're not going to hurt you," the voice said.

But she was losing consciousness, losing her ability to understand.

"Your friend sent us," the voice said, as a hand pulled her up.

Locke, she thought, but distantly, because the darkness was rushing in, and she could feel it filling the hood like blood, and the last thing she remembered was the foul goat breath of the captain, whispering, "I'm not going to rape you, sister," *but when you wake up tomorrow, alone, in a filthy bed in a Bosaso boardinghouse, you are going to wish that you had died.*

CHAPTER 42

I hardened myself when I saw the Ukrainian carrying the unconscious body like a cord of firewood. I needed to keep cool, like Karpenko or my first commanding officer, General McChrystal, the epitome of grace under pressure. This was not the time for dissent in the ranks.

"She fell," Maltov said, laying her down.

I pulled off the hood. It was Alie, all right, her curly hair damp with sweat and plastered to her face, blood in her mouth where she'd bitten through her lip. A bruise was forming on her forehead, distending her golden skin.

"Crazy bitch," Maltov said.

I couldn't stop myself. I lashed the man for his cruelty, as savagely as I could. Maltov simply looked down from six inches above me, his eyes uninterested, waiting for me to finish. It was thirty seconds before I was back in control.

"Bad ju-ju, American," Maltov said, something he must have heard in a third-rate movie. "You told us to use the hood."

That stung, because I couldn't argue.

"Leave her to me," I snapped, signaling for Miles. We carried her to a far corner of the warehouse, for relative privacy, and laid her gently on the ground.

"Increase the watch," I said.

Miles nodded. He was thinking the same thing. Maltov had only been gone twenty-three minutes. He should have driven around for at least half an hour after snatching Alie to see if he was being tailed. Instead, he must have come straight home.

I should have sent Colonel Sirko. But no, this was proper thuggery, not a military operation, and Kramatorsk was Maltov's turf. He had the local knowledge and the respect of his men, both things Sirko lacked. Besides, I could sense the colonel's distaste for kidnapping women. He would do it if ordered by Karpenko, but he wouldn't like it. I admired his honor, but it saddened me, too. His rigidity wasn't practical for this world; he was a man outside his time.

Alie groaned, and I bent a knee beside her. She started to retch, so I turned her onto her side, so that she wouldn't choke, and put a hand on her hip, hoping my touch would calm her. Her body was shaking.

Seven hours, at most, until we had to be on our way. And shit tons of work left to do.

Bad ju-ju indeed.

Alie started to come around thirty minutes later, so Greenlees and I propped her on the ammo crate against the back wall of the warehouse. Greenlees had taken care of her while I went over the final details of the operation with Miles. The older man, it turned out, was a natural nursemaid. He'd wiped the grime from her forehead, and the blood and vomit from her lips, with a surprisingly delicate touch.

Now he gave her a shoulder to lean on, as she rolled her head, trying to lift it. Her curly hair was matted from the hood, her eyes closed, and I felt strangely nervous as I watched her coming around, not daring to touch her. I had rarely seen Alie in repose. Only once, in my bed in Bujumbura, when I was alerted to the slaughter at Gatumba at 0200, and I had taken a moment to relish her before strapping on my guns and heading out . . .

Eventually, her eyes opened, and she began to look around. Greenlees gave her a sip of water, then stood back to give her space. Alie's eyes roamed the warehouse, resting on everything briefly, before finding me. For a moment, I thought she was still in a daze. Then she tried to tear her hands out from behind her, as if she expected them not to be bound, and her momentum threw her off balance. Before I could grab her, she crumpled to the floor. Greenlees started to rush to her aid. I signaled him to stand down. Let her lie there, undisturbed.

"You son of a bitch," she muttered.

"What are you doing here, Alie?" I said coolly—professionally—as Greenlees and I lifted her onto the ammo crate.

"What are *you* doing here?" she said, as her eyes flicked to Miles and a few others who were gathering behind me.

"Work."

She was angry. Of course. She was lost, bruised, no doubt worried, and shaking from the physical exertion of the last few hours. She'd be sore in the morning, but by then, sadly, I'd be gone.

"I need a drink," she said.

Greenlees offered her water. She laughed and refused it.

"Does anyone know you're here?" I said.

"You can't shoot me, Tom."

Of course I could. But she was the last person I'd shoot, and I was surprised she didn't know it. "I'm not going to shoot you, Alie, but we're leaving, and we can't take you with us. Do you have someone to pick you up?"

She looked past me, at the helicopter, the hasty defensive positions we'd made out of piles of metal scrap, the drone. She looked up at the roof of the warehouse, at the cracked windows, the rusted beams. "So this is what it's like," she said, "on the inside."

She checked me up and down with her fiercely direct stare. I could see Alie coming back. Not the girl I knew in Africa, but the woman I had met three days ago in Kiev.

"You look like shit," she said.

It was true. I'd ditched my action slacks and blazer in Poltava, and my fatigues and ballistic vest were carrying three days of grit and sweat. I hadn't washed since Kiev, and I had mission stubble from my chin to the bottom of my neck. I smelled like the rest of the team: body odor and gun oil. It probably hung over the place like a fog. But I was sporting duel thigh holsters for my nine mils, with my SCAR slung over my shoulder, and my Gerber knife strapped upside down over my left pectoral. Four grenades were rigged to my vest, so I could pull and throw with one hand. And I was jacked, like you get before a mission, when the adrenaline is pounding, even though on the surface you're calm. I looked like a motherfucking badass, come to think of it, because only back-benchers went into battle looking like a recruitment poster.

"Hello, Mr. Greenlees," Alie said, turning to him. "I bet you're wishing you never had that drink in Kiev. I should have warned you that Locke leaves people behind."

Greenlees looked sick, and I almost pitied him. He was wearing his same retiree-casual attire, but it was as filthy as my battle gear, and surprisingly frayed. He was coming apart seam by seam, and Alie could always sense a weakness.

"Let it go," I said.

"Who's he?" Alie said, nodding toward Karpenko.

"None of your business."

She smirked. "Then he must be yours." She turned to the oligarch. "I hope he kills the right man."

I felt a hand on my shoulder, and I knew it was Miles. "That's enough," he said, stepping toward Alie. "I guess you think you're a reporter now . . ."

"And you're his bodyguard?" She paused. "Even now. Ten years later."

Miles never lost his cool. Never. But he was close. "This isn't the job, Alie. This isn't what reporters do, flashing photographs around, attracting attention. You don't endanger people. You don't compromise the mission . . ."

"And what is the mission, Miles, if that's even your real name? Secret warfare? Targeted assassination? Stealing oil rights?"

I flinched. Was that really what Alie thought I did? But the shot seemed to have missed with Miles, who looked calmer now.

"The mission is what we are sent here to do," he said.

"And I'm endangering that mission?"

"You're endangering men's lives. *My* men's lives," I said.

"Good. Then I'm probably saving someone on the other side."

Out of the corner of my eye, I saw Karpenko shift his weight and Maltov reach for his gun. Alie was lucky the other Ukrainians didn't speak English, because she had gone too far. She knew it, I could tell, but she was moving now, letting go, so she pivoted and pressed forward, too stubborn to turn back.

"I know this man," she yelled, so everyone in the warehouse could hear her. "I knew him in Africa. In Burundi. He will not bring you peace."

I wanted to say I stopped a genocide in Burundi. I stopped a fucking genocide. What have *you* ever done? But I breathed deep and swallowed the Apollo line. "I was never in Burundi," I said.

"What about Darfur then? Were you ever there?"

I could see Miles out of the corner of my eye, ushering people away. It was no one's business what we did for the company, and the less people that knew anything, the better.

"I was never in Darfur," I said, stepping closer so that no one but Alie could hear me.

"I saw you, you lying bastard," she hissed. "Outside Garsila." I could see the emotion in her face, and it surprised me, because it wasn't anger, it was . . . disappointment. "I know you could have stopped it. You had the men. But you watched. You watched as an entire village was slaughtered by the Janjaweed. You watched children being chopped down, men shot for sport, women stolen on horseback never to be seen again."

"It wasn't the mission."

"It wasn't the mission to save innocent people?"

I didn't answer. I'd already said too much, and Alie was rolling, maybe with stuff she'd been saving up for years, maybe from the adrenaline rush of surviving death in a black hood, maybe because she realized she had a moment, only a moment, before she was gone from my life, maybe for good.

"The mission," she scoffed, like it was a dirty word. "Do you only save innocent people when someone pays you to do it?"

"I saved that orphanage," I said.

"Don't you take my—"

"I gave you Gatumba, I gave you those girls, because they were in war's way, and without me they would have been dead before you even arrived, them and their nuns, too."

She hesitated. Never hesitate. "So who have you really saved?" I pressed. "Not those orphan girls. Not those women in Darfur. Not those refugee families you wrote those articles about so many years ago."

"You don't know anything about that."

"I know everything about that," I said. "I know you went with them to Bosaso. I know you bribed a UN official to find a worthy ship captain, and paid him a thousand American dollars to smuggle the girls out. And I know you wouldn't go any further, Alie. In the end, you wouldn't submit your white girl virtue to the hold. You booked passage above deck, over dinner with the captain."

"You've been following me."

"And you still missed the boat. You missed the fucking boat—" I was snarling now, and she knew it was coming, I could see the horror in her eyes "—because you were drunk."

"I wasn't . . ." she tried.

And then she broke. I could see it. And it only made me more vicious. "It was your idea, wasn't it? You wanted to take them to Europe. You wanted that story, as a memorial to your own past: two women and three little girls escape lives of abuse by crossing the ocean in a sweltering hold. But they didn't make it, did they, Alie? Did they?"

She cracked. She would never admit it, she would fight like hell to deny it, but I'd beaten her.

"Or even worse," I said slowly, "you don't know. You don't know what happened to them. And that's why you're here. You're looking for penance. You're trying to rescue all the lost girls, in Darfur, Somalia, Ukraine. But being a reporter fixes nothing."

"You've been spying on me."

"I've been protecting you," I snapped. "I'm protecting you now." It wasn't true. Ten years, and I'd never done shit for Alie, never had the balls to be anything to her, except for tonight.

"I don't want your protection," she said, rising out of her self-loathing, like I knew my Alie would. "I hate your fucking protection."

I leaned even closer, I don't know why. Maybe to punch her. Maybe to comfort her. Maybe, I don't know, to kiss her. But before I could figure any of that out, Miles stepped in and slammed me in the shoulder, knocking me back. It was more of a shove than a tackle, I'm sure, but it felt like stones colliding.

"Take it easy, brother," Miles said as he pulled me away, his arm around my shoulder, his head close to mine. "Take it easy."

He punched my chest, hard, like he was giving me airborne bloodwings. He was reminding me who I was, reminding me to breathe, which I did, slowly.

"Mission girl," I said, even though both of us knew it wasn't true.

He smacked me, flat hand, even harder this time. "Mission focus," he said.

He was right. I couldn't lose control. Ever. But especially now, with men's lives on the line, and only a few hours left. "Mission focus," I said.

I looked back at Alie. She was slumped on the ammo case, exhausted, and Karpenko was talking to her almost like Miles was talking to me. Close, with his arm over her shoulder.

"I'm going to tell her," Karpenko said, looking up at Miles, but talking to me, "what this man has done for my family."

His children. Poltava. Whatever. What was done was done, what was coming was coming fast.

Miles nodded his approval.

Karpenko turned to me. "I will take care of her," he said.

Fuck her, I thought. But I didn't mean it. I didn't know what I meant. None of this had gone like I'd expected. On this mission, nothing had.

Alie felt the Ukrainian's arm around her, soft as a habit, hard as a rosary. She thought of her time in the cloth, weeping before the statue of a virgin. She was a fraud, she thought, as the Ukrainian led her away, saying, "Let me tell you a story" quietly into her ear. She'd chickened out. Sold women and children out. Then wrote the story like that part, the dark hood in the alley in Somalia and everything after, had never happened at all.

She was a fraud, she thought, as the Ukrainian took her under his arm. But so what? Everybody was a fraud. Everybody.

CHAPTER 44

Brad Winters sipped orange juice from a champagne flute and eased back in his off-white leather seat. The whole airplane was off-white and gold, except for the teak, but in true *ancien régime* style it managed to be understated. The attendant rose when he swiveled the teak table to the side, but he waved her away. He only wanted to stretch his legs. In the last twenty-four hours, he'd flown from DC to NYC to London, with an eight-hour time zone change and only three hours of sleep. Now he was heading east. But he wasn't tired. Luxury like this will do that for a man. But so will adrenaline, and the pressing need to figure out the next move.

The bankers hadn't even bothered to ask him any questions, not important ones anyway, like how much natural gas went through Kramatorsk? What percentage was that of the total that passed through Ukraine into Europe? Who would be affected? What effect would taking the facility offline have on the broader economy? Could Europe be wounded? How badly? For how long? Could he guarantee any of this, or was he playing a hunch?

He could have given answers confidently. Cited numbers proficiently. Yes, this was the right pipeline station. Yes, this was the right time. He'd done his homework, that was why he had spotted the opportunity. He knew the cubic liters of gas involved, of course, but he was much less clear on the ramifications on the interlocking global market and industrial infrastructure of a postunification austerity EU, not to mention the internal politics of an oligopoly like Ukraine, where only money mattered. The bankers knew that. They kept a spectacularly stiff upper lip, but they were men of the world. They knew any numerical discussion was speculative at best, so they didn't bother.

It was the idea that mattered. The idea on a broad level, not in the specifics.

Ukraine was a Gordian knot, an interlooping factional hive of actions, threats, and consequences. The West had been trying to unravel it for years, decades in fact, even before the Cold War or the Russian Revolution. And what do you do with a Gordian knot?

You don't untie it. You slice through it, as quickly as possible.

The idea had come to him two days ago, like that legendary sword through that mythical rope. He knew Karpenko was only half an answer on his own, but he had seized the opportunity after the assassination attempt in Poltava. It was a time-tested strategy: bring in the player, put him in motion, figure out how to use him later. Bringing in Locke from outside the conflict zone was equally orthodox. Locke was the perfect combination of excellent at his job and unknown, at least in Russia and the Eastern Bloc.

Align the pieces. Apply pressure. Look for the angles, as he had always done. Push with a steady hand. He had engineered the assault on the facility, the Donbas Battalion, Karpenko's press. He had done the same many times before. He was doing it in other parts of the world right now.

But then, for the first time in his life, he had burst through. He had flashed onto a masterstroke and gambled on intuition.

Why were the Russians guarding the pipeline facility? To protect it. From whom? *From everybody.* And what your enemy fears most: that is your greatest asset.

Anyone can play the odds. But you can grasp the moment, Winters thought, only when you've mastered the game. When you've studied all the moves; when you understand them in your bones.

It was a long rise from being the only white kid in that poor black neighborhood in south Baltimore, with his broken family and his hippy single mom. Altar boy, even though he wasn't religious. Principal's pet and "special project," even though he wasn't well behaved. Then the army. It broke his mother's heart, but she signed the enlistment papers when he was sixteen, and that was when he lost respect for her, when she supported him in something she despised. Officer School. Airborne. Wall Street. Private banking. Ivy League MBA, even without an undergrad degree. The Pentagon. Back to Wall Street. He caught a lucky break when the planes hit the Twin Towers, because he was already in the private military business, but he had worked it from there, making himself not just a beneficiary of government largesse, but a creator of it. He devised the policies, through the K Street two-step, that put armed contractors on the ground. Then he cashed the checks.

But this was different. This was beyond money, beyond the place where people were impressed by billions. He had felt it the moment Karpenko introduced him to the London bankers. There was another layer, a deeper level of power. Anyone could turn a billion dollars into ten billion. But how many could shape the next century? Rothschild. Carnegie. Rockefeller. Prescott Bush, but not his offspring. Jobs . . .

The bankers were insiders, workers for those who moved the world. And like all employees, they had expected a business plan. Instead, he had given them a solution. Ukraine can struggle on for a generation, savage and inefficient, or we can change the dynamic. Force the pussies in Europe to act, as self-preservation.

Force the Americans to strike the death blow to Russia they should have delivered in 1992. He would break Eastern Europe, he might break the continent, but in the end, he would remake it, exactly as it always should have been.

And then, as he neared the final moment, the bankers had changed the game.

Winters sipped his orange juice, feeling the jet throttle back for its initial descent. He looked out the window, past the blinking light on the tip of the wing. It was dark, but beneath that darkness, and those clouds, was the place he had never anticipated going, at least not on this trip.

Russia. The home of the enemy.

Great men develop great plans, he thought. *Truly great men can improvise in the arena, even when they don't know the rules. Are you a truly great man, Brad Winters?*

He laughed to himself. *You're about to find out.*

At least he'd been smart enough to hide an ace up his sleeve.

CHAPTER 45

The rusty fishing boat bobbed in the Black Sea, which on this night wasn't living up to its name. The moon was waning gibbous, almost full, and it threw a bright path of light from the boat to the horizon. It was so bright, Jacob Ehrlich could see the patterns of their nets in the water, rocking on a gentle breeze.

The moon didn't matter. There wasn't anyone else out, not this deep. Ehrlich had been out here every night for the past twenty days, and there never was. He had taken this job for the adventure, but he had quickly realized it was even more boring than sitting in a motor pool, changing the oil on Stryker combat vehicles. At least it was thirty days on and thirty days off, with twice the pay of a warrant officer.

He turned back to his work, running his scanner over the wing of the drone, then the body. Usually, his primary duty was to make sure the cameras were in place and working. They were worth more than the drones, and besides, it wasn't any good to send spy drones over Ukraine and the Balkans if the cameras weren't in proper order. Apollo Outcomes had some sort of overlook contract, tracking troop movements, probably, although Ehrlich didn't know. He didn't even fly the things. That was done thousands of miles away in Michigan, if the rumors were true, or maybe Minnesota. He never even saw the footage. He just maintained, launched, and recovered them from this rusty scupper.

Six a night, every night. Always the same: except for this one.

"It's a banger," Johnson said, as he finished his inspection. Johnson was the other tech, and the only other company man on the job. The six fishermen were locals, hired for cover and trained in firearms. Ehrlich didn't entirely trust them, but he assumed Apollo paid them well. More than they could make fishing, anyway.

"Previous generation," Ehrlich said. "Not as fast, but at eight thousand feet, still invisible. And I guess they don't have to worry about pretty pictures." There were no cameras on this drone, but it had a special nose cone, bulkier than any he had ever seen.

"I wonder what's up?" Johnson said, nodding to the cone.

"None of my business," Ehrlich shrugged. "I just get them in the air. You clear?"

"Clear," Johnson said, stepping back.

Ehrlich looked at his watch. They were eight miles south of a remote stretch of Ukrainian coast, and it was midnight on the dot, as specified. He punched in the launch code, telling the boys back in Michigan the bird was ready to fly. Maybe if he had realized the nose cone was a blasting cap filled with a pound of C-4, and that almost fifty pounds of C-4 were laced through the interior of the drone, making it a bomb big enough to blow up a building, or an entire factory, especially one filled with natural gas, he would have paid closer attention.

But he didn't, so Jacob Ehrlich didn't think anything of it as he watched the massive drone bomb lift into the air. Thirty seconds later, it was invisible, even in a moonlit sky.

"Bring up the next one," Ehrlich said.

CHAPTER 46

Almost three thousand miles away, the Gulfstream-V corporate jet touched down at Pulkovo Airport outside St. Petersburg. It was 0100 local time, three hours ahead of London and one hour ahead of Ukraine.

The door opened, and Brad Winters stepped off. He had never been to Russia. He'd never done business on this side. The Berlin Wall had come down decades ago; Wall Street had arrived five seconds later; but in the mercenary business, there was a barrier between East and West. Apollo would work for almost anyone, anywhere, if the mission and money were right, but it had never worked for the East. Putin was an ex-KGB officer; he had his own private armies. And he was the enemy.

But Russia was warmer than he expected, at least for May.

Below him, a black sedan pulled onto the tarmac and parked four feet from the airplane stairs. Winters walked down and got inside. There was a man in the backseat. Early forties, neat as a military bedsheet, clearly British from the cut of his hair to the lack of a chin.

"Welcome, Mr. Winters," the young man said. Young for private banking, old for private equity. He must be out here in the hinterlands, Winters figured, working his way toward the London office.

"Thank you, Mr. . . ."

"Everly." They didn't shake hands. As soon as Winters's bag was loaded into the trunk, they started moving.

"I've been briefed on your plan," Everly said. "You are here to communicate it to our contact on the other side, Mr. Gorelov. Have you ever dealt with Russians?"

No comment on the plan, Winters noticed. Everly knew the company rules. "I've met a few," he said.

"They are tough," Everly said. "Blunt, even by American standards. You are not here to finesse the details. Nor are you here to negotiate. You are here to break legs. I understand you are a military man . . ." Everly looked at him for the first time and smiled, although it looked pained, due to his lack of chin. ". . . I assume you know what I mean."

Ambush him. Keep him in the kill zone. "No offense, but what are you expecting from this?"

Everly side-eyed him. It was as close to an emotion as the banker's had ever given him. "You're the first person that's ever presented a plan for Ukraine that might work. That has . . ." the banker searched for the right word ". . . testicular fortitude. We expect you to convince them, just as you've convinced us. Do you understand?"

"I understand." He didn't. Not entirely. But he was working on it.

"Good. The meeting is at 5:00 A.M. It is 1:09 A.M. local time. I will take you to a room. I advise you to get some sleep."

0500 St. Petersburg time. 0400 in Kramatorsk. That left only two hours before the Donbas Battalion was scheduled to arrive and four, maybe, before he lit his secret weapon and blew Russia's excuses, not to mention her precious gas lines, into a fireball half a mile high. If it came to that. And Brad Winters was finding that, increasingly, he hoped it did.

"Not much time," he said.

Everly smiled, sort of. "Pressure," he said, "is our ally."

CHAPTER 47

I stood over the sand table, a five-by-eight-foot mock-up of the gas facility and surrounding area that Miles and I had created on the warehouse floor, as Miles gathered the team. As the noncom, it was his role to call the men to order. As officer, it was my role to devise and brief the plan. We weren't strict about protocol in Apollo, but the team was former military, and old ways die hard.

It was a big group. The seven men on the team: myself, Miles, Charro, Wildman, Boon, Jacobsen, and Reynolds. Then Greenlees, looking a thousand years old. And the three Ukrainians: Colonel Sirko, Maltov, and Karpenko, who had come out of the back of the warehouse, where he had been talking with Alie for most of the last hour.

He'd convinced me not to cuff her and, reluctantly, I'd agreed. Now, with Maltov's men on guard duty and Alie falling toward an exhausted three-in-the-morning nap, I was happy he'd talked me out of it. He was taking care of her, just like he'd promised, so I could keep her off my mind. I wasn't particularly happy to have Karpenko at the sand table, but it was the client's prerogative to sit in on the plan meeting, and we had a good working relationship. I knew he'd respect my authority on military matters. But . . .

"Only the principal and team members," I said, pointing my broken broomstick at the pilot, who was skulking over Karpenko's shoulder.

Karpenko turned and snapped something in Ukrainian. The pilot started to object, but Karpenko took him by the collar, pulled him close, and muttered something that made the man turn pale.

"'One more word, one finger,'" Greenlees translated in a whisper to Miles and me, as the pilot backed away.

I locked eyes with Miles, and I could tell he was impressed. Karpenko knew when it was time to get down to business, and he could swing the hammer. If I wasn't mistaken, that hammer was Maltov. Maybe Winters was on to something. Maybe Karpenko *was* the right man for Ukraine.

"This is the target," I said, pointing with my broomstick to the bricks and cardboard that denoted the facility. The sand table looked haphazard—bricks or concrete chunks for buildings, cardboard and other scraps for walls, copper wire for the tangle of natural gas pipes—but Miles and I had rendered every distance and size as carefully as possible, since lives depended on accuracy. Of course, when I wasn't looking, Wildman had painted the words "slags KIA" at the spot where he took down the three thugs and tricked up one of the wooden block "cars" with a racing stripe. I had to laugh. Soldier humor was puerile, but important. Every unit needed a clown.

"This is north," I said in my command voice, pointing. "East. West. South." I touched each one.

"North is fallow fields. No good avenues of approach, if they have thermal imagers. East is the same. On the south is the industrial park and two entry points, each with a metal security door: one vehicle, one pedestrian. Parking lot in the southeast corner. Road along the front." I traced it out. "Fifty meters of open space between the road and two industrial buildings, here and here. Two-story industry buildings along these three blocks. Apartment buildings here, including the tall one where Wildman set the camera. Good for overwatch, but be alert for slags."

I glanced at Wildman. He was nodding, looking serious, as if I was simply recounting useful information, but a couple of the other guys laughed.

"You all know about the pub thugs here," Miles said, taking the broomstick and pointing to the club we had hit a few hours ago. "So far, they are scared back into their hole, but we should avoid this part of the AO." Area of operation.

I took back the stick. He who has the stick has the floor. "Inside the facility are pipes, a small equipment warehouse, and a control building. They are surrounded by a six-foot brick wall, with embedded broken glass and rusty concertina wire on top." I traced the wall with my pointer. "The entry points are monitored by closed-circuit cameras and floodlights here, here, and here. We are ghosts. We are not here. We avoid the entry points and lights unless our lives depend on it."

Only Karpenko nodded. It was standard operating procedure for the rest of us.

"The enemy are Spetsnaz." I paused and looked at the men. That word had gotten their attention. No joking now, except for Wildman, who was smiling like this was the funny part. "Random three-person foot patrols inside the facility, no discernable time or pattern. Single-man overwatch from this roof." I tapped the control building. "Also random times. It's designed to look sloppy, right down to the fake militia uniforms, but it's highly professional. Miles and I estimate a squad-size element, as many as twelve men, although only three have ever appeared outside at the same time. They are heavily armed and well trained, but bored and not expecting us. Those not on patrol will be here"— the control building—"probably on the first floor, but that's best guess. We have no eyeballs inside."

Nodding. Half blind was not ideal, but common.

"There are two civilians on the overnight shift. Engineers.

They are monitoring the pipeline from here, the control building. They are to be unharmed and incapacitated. We'll hand
them over to the Donbas Battalion on linkup, and they won't see
the light of day until the operation is over." Meaning the press
has departed and Karpenko is a national hero.

"Got it boss, no molesto," Wildman affirmed. "Civilians sleep
like babies tonight."

What did Wildman know, I wondered, about babies?

"The facility operates 24/7 and the day shift starts at 0700.
Workers arrive as early as 0630, so we need to have the little
green men flex-cuffed by then or we're fucked. Questions?"

Silence.

"Good. Our objective is to capture Russians. I repeat, capture not kill." I tapped the copper wires. "Fire discipline is para-
mount. One stray bullet here, and . . ."

"Kaboom," Wildman whispered, like it was a forbidden love.

"Kaboom," I agreed.

I looked around. Everyone was alert, especially Karpenko.
His eyes were gleaming, and he was grinning like a carnivore.

"At 0430"—I looked at my watch—"that is two hours and
thirty-three minutes from now, we move out on foot, and approach the facility here." I traced our route from the factory to
the facility's northwest corner. "Use available concealment from
the surrounding forest and BMNT." Before Morning Nautical
Twilight, military speak for twilight, a good time to catch un-
aware soldiers in their rack.

"We scale the wall here," Miles said, taking over the tactical
portion of the briefing, "on the far side, where the pipes come
out of the ground. Locke and Charro carry the folding ladder.
Charro, once the ladder is up, I want you to cut the wire and
lay the blanket over the glass." Miles tossed him a thick wool
blanket, scrounged by Maltov's crew.

"Boon will fly the drone, so we're not blind." Earlier, we'd had tryouts to see who could walk and fly at the same time. Boon smoked everyone. Jacobsen almost flew the damn thing into a tree.

I took back the stick. "Object is to catch all men inside, so we maintain cover through the pipes to here." I pointed. "It's cover, but it's also insurance. Spetsnaz aren't stupid enough to shoot at us in the pipes." I hope.

The team nodded. Incineration would be excruciating, but instantaneous.

"If we mistime, and there's a patrol, we hunker down in the shadow. Whoever is closest, take them out. Silently. Assume one Spetsnaz on deck at the control building, so hug the dark."

"The drone's noise may alert them. I'll park it here," Boon said, pointing to the center of the maze of pipes. "Once the op is finished, I . . . or someone else," Boon said calmly, at peace with the idea that he might be killed tonight, "can fly it out before the workers arrive."

I could feel it now, like I always could at some point during the briefing. I could see the movement in my mind, and I was walking the steps, picturing myself there. The adrenaline was pumping, but I knew how to control that. Movement to contact would take seven to eight minutes, the same length as "Mars: The Bringer of War" from Holst's symphonic odyssey *The Planets*. I could already hear the rhythmic beat of the music, its trajectory toward total obliteration. By the time we were on the ground, it would be an inferno in my mind.

"We split into three teams," Miles said, pointing at the control building with the stick. "Jacobsen and Reynolds provide overwatch. Sniper anything that moves. If shit gets bad, use the M90 rocket launchers." We had five, tough enough to kill tanks and blast through walls, but we could realistically only carry two. "Civilian collateral damage is authorized but discouraged. And don't forget the drone. We'll rig a block of C-4 to it, as a backup kamikaze, if the shit gets thick."

Everyone nodded. They were feeling it, too.

"Wildman and I will breach the building's east door," Miles said. This was the most dangerous part. Close-quarters combat was the trench warfare of the modern world. But Wildman held up his det cord and duct tape with a grin, like it was a gift, and this mission was Christmas morning.

"Boon and Charro, take the west door. I'll synchronize detonation over comms. I leave it up to each team how you stack and sector for room clearance. Watch your corners, and clear room by room. Hit tangos, spare civvies, and don't bother with sensitive site exploitation. This is a snatch-and-grab, with prejudice."

"Nonlethal takedowns?" Boon asked.

Easy for him, I thought. Boon was fast as a cat and could break black belts like he was swatting mosquitos. He was so quiet, they usually didn't know he was there.

Me? No so much. Not anymore.

Miles nodded. "Nonlethal if possible, but no unnecessary risks. Locke and Sirko will be backup . . ."

Wildman and Charro fidgeted. Sirko wasn't one of us; they weren't comfortable with an outsider. I could see Maltov scowl, and Sirko smirk. The enforcer wanted to be there, but he was going to man the radio with Greenlees back here in the warehouse.

I guess you shouldn't have manhandled Alie, I told him telepathically.

"Sirko and Locke will be second in the east door," Miles said, raising his voice to drown out any objections, "providing firepower where needed. Sirko will be our interpreter. You can talk to each other, but only Sirko talks to the prisoners."

"Remember the mission," I said. "The more live Russian special operators Karpenko can parade before the cameras in flex-cuffs, the better."

"What do I do?" Karpenko asked. He was no doubt thinking of his moment standing in front of the world, imagining himself there, the impending king of Ukraine. It always seemed so clean and easy on the sandtable.

"We'll call Greenlees when the facility is secure. You walk down with Maltov and his men and scale the wall. If this all goes down right," I said, turning back to the team, "we lock it down in eight minutes, and hold the objective until the Donbas Battalion arrives, expected 0600. The press birds arrive at 0700."

More than two hours inside. It was a risk, especially in an active war zone.

"And if it goes sideways?" Jacobsen asked.

I pointed to the fish truck in the corner of the warehouse. Maltov's men had welded scraps of steel to its side for protection, like something from Mad Max, and loaded it with three drums of gasoline wired to a few kilos of C-4 and a blasting cap.

"Maltov drives the truck," I said, "and blows the front gate. We improvise from there."

Wildman smiled. I hadn't noticed before that he was missing teeth. "Now you're talking, boss," he said.

CHAPTER 48

It took another ten minutes to finish the briefing—almost fifteen minutes total—but only because Maltov and Karpenko had to be walked through their part three times, even though it was straightforward.

If I call Greenlees and say "green," walk down and act like you just kicked Russian ass.

If I say "red," drive the fish truck to the front entry gate of the facility as fast as you fucking can. Park it there. Light the fuse. Run.

No shooting. That was the hard part for Maltov to understand: that the last thing I wanted was a Ukrainian cowboy running into a gas facility with guns blazing. That was why the Russians had sent Spetsnaz, their best-trained troops. That was why Winters was sending a Tier One team before the militia arrived.

"And if the Russians send reinforcements?" Jacobsen asked.

A good question, and a distinct possibility, given that the camera crews weren't scheduled to arrive until 0700 and would probably be late.

"If the Russians roll in, I call the boss," I said, meaning Winters. "I'll see how far he wants to take this."

"And if that doesn't work, we blow the place up," Wildman exclaimed, clearly liking the idea. Thank God Apollo provided a place for men like Wildman. Thank God he was here to cover my ass. But there was no way I was blowing the place up. I'd have rather run than take that chance.

"It's 0213 zulu time," I said. Shit, it was late. "Rack out. We're up at 0415 to sanitize this place, and then move out. Let's hit it."

The team dispersed. They had two hours for last preparations and personal rituals before sleep: pray in the case of Charro, meditate in the case of Boon, listen to music in my case, sculpt bunny rabbits out of C-4, if you were a certain Welsh ex-SAS son of a bitch.

I kicked the sand table apart, making sure that no one could figure out later what had been planned here. I piled the few things we would leave behind on top—rations, spent batteries, ammo crates, excess equipment. One of Maltov's men would burn it with white phosphorus after the op was done. Take only the objective; leave nothing behind, not even footprints. That was our mission, every time.

I needed rack, but instead of heading to my sleeping bag, I found myself drifting to the far corner, where the Ukrainians were holding Alie. She was asleep near a crate of smoke grenades, and even from across the warehouse I could see the curve of her neck, the soft golden skin of her cheek.

I heard angry voices and turned toward them. Maltov was shoving the pilot, who was gesturing toward Boon, who was siphoning helicopter fuel into one of the truck's barrel bombs. Smart. Aircraft fuel was extremely explosive.

When I turned back, Alie was watching me. I expected her to get up, the better to confront me, but she only pushed herself to a seated position as I approached. Behind me, the loud Ukrainian curses crescendoed, until they turned into a single voice. It sounded like the pilot pleading.

"Hello again, Alie," I said, as a scream ripped through the warehouse. Someone had lost a finger.

"Asshole," she muttered to me, without her previous conviction.

"How do you like Karpenko?"

"I like him, of course," she said wearily. "He's a rich man. That's how rich men get rich, by being smooth. Telling you what you want to hear. It's called manipulation." She paused. "He seems to have taken a genuine shine to you, though."

I shrugged. "Nobody's perfect."

"You saved his children. Or at least that's what he thinks. He told me he doesn't know where they are."

"They're safe," I said, but I could tell she wasn't convinced. Who did she think I was working for? The mafia? "I don't know where they are, but I know who they are with. They are safe."

"I guess you have to think that way . . ."

She trailed off. She was tired. Her hand was shaking. I noticed Karpenko's label-less bottle of booze from Poltava, now empty. Perhaps they had been toasting better times. But the better times were in the past, and all we had was right now.

"We're leaving before dawn. You're staying here with Greenlees. It will be your job to get yourself to . . . wherever it is you want to go." I felt bad for her, and I felt lost, although I wasn't sure why. Perhaps because, after this was over, I didn't have anywhere else I wanted to be. "You can take the bird, but I wouldn't advise it. There are antiaircraft batteries between here and . . . everywhere. And the pilot . . . I think he's lost some blood."

She didn't question me on that.

"I'd take the Škoda, since it won't attract attention. Drive with Greenlees back to Kiev. I can't guarantee your safety, but it's the best I can offer."

I stopped. I was tired. I knew she would write about what had happened here, but I also knew it wouldn't matter. We had her cell phone, so there were no photographs, and no one would corroborate what she'd seen. It would just be more rumors from the front lines, on an Internet already swimming with them. Worse things could happen. People were "disappeared" in war zones everyday.

"You shouldn't have come," I said, more tenderly than I expected.

She looked up at me. She was fierce, and then she wasn't.

"I'm sorry," I said. "For . . . you know."

She wouldn't take her eyes off mine, so I was the one who stood up and turned away, giving her a last small victory. It was the least I could do.

"Tom," she said after I'd taken a few steps, causing me to turn. She was smaller than I had ever seen her before, but she was still everything I wanted . . . in some other life. "Don't leave me here."

Bam. A frag grenade to my heart.

"You can't come with me," I said.

She didn't argue, so I turned around, started walking, and didn't look back. What else could I have said? She couldn't break me. I was far too hard for that, no matter how much she meant to me. I needed this mission to work, and she had to know that. I needed to do it right, so that everyone would walk away alive—including Alie.

Karpenko caught up with me a minute later, as I was pulling my sleeping bag over me like a blanket. He pulled up an ammo crate and lit one of his blue Dunhills. He crossed his legs, so that his $5,000 shoes were hovering near my face. I knew he had worked on this pose, maybe for years. It was his signature move: dominant indifference.

"I'll take care of her," he said. "I'm going to take her with me."

He was the client. Fine.

"I've told her my story. I want her to write it."

"Leave me out of it. And the team."

"She knows. This was Ukrainian, purely Ukrainian. It is better for both of us that way. Especially me."

He smoked his cigarette slowly. He was the only man in the warehouse who still looked clean. Never let them see you sweat.

"What is your father like?" he said.

"My father was Miniver Cheevy," I said. Cheevy was a character in a poem I'd read in sixth grade, a hopeless romantic who dreamed about the past.

"He was a minister," Karpenko said, nodding, as if that explained something.

My father was a drunk and an amateur historian, a lover of the doomed romance of the Confederate cause, not slavery but chivalry, for which our ancestors fled south across the Maryland border to fight with the Army of Virginia. He always wished he'd been born then, he said, but if he had, he'd just have pined for some other, earlier cause. The time period didn't matter. You were either a man of action or you weren't. Or as his hero Teddy Roosevelt once said, a "man in the arena," or a nobody. That was why he pushed me, in his absentee-father, show-up-once-every-six-months way, into military service. Or maybe I'd done it to show him I wasn't going to be the loser he'd always been.

"He named you Thomas after the prophet?" Karpenko mused, still misunderstanding.

Thomas was a disciple, and a doubter, not a prophet.

"He named me Jubal, after an American Confederate general" and patron saint of lost causes. "Thomas is my middle name."

Karpenko puffed his Dunhill and recrossed his legs. "You have no doubt heard about my father," he said. I hadn't. "How I came back from college in Kiev after the Soviet Union collapsed and liberated the steel plant were my father worked. How he came out, covered in slag, and I handed him a check like all the other men, six months of unpaid wages. How we hugged, the first time since I was a boy. And then every worker hugged me, a long line of dirty men, crying as they poured out of that hole."

"Yeah, something like that," I lied. I had never heard a word about his past.

"It isn't true," he said, flicking away his butt. "It is propaganda. I don't know who started it, maybe me, I honestly can't remember."

He lit another cigarette. It was his way of creating drama. Or calming his nerves.

"My father died when I was eight, soon after the Russians moved him to the steel plants in Poltava. It was a promotion, perhaps. Or a punishment. He may have been a nationalist. We were ethnic Cossacks, and the Soviets didn't trust us. I hated the Russians after that, because my father never recovered. He only lived six months. He was sick, and the foreman never allowed him to go to hospital, even on the day he died."

I thought of what Alie had said, about Karpenko being smooth, about his ability to manipulate you into liking him. I admit it. I liked him.

"I want my son to know me," he said, blowing a big lungful of smoke. "I want him to understand that I did this for my country. For our country, because Ukraine is his, too. Is that too much to ask?"

I didn't know. I didn't have a son. "Your children are safe," I said, eyes closed.

"Yes, but I am not."

I was tired. I had a mission to run in less than two hours, and time was ticking down. Besides, he wasn't asking if he should risk his life for his cause. He'd already made up his mind.

"You shouldn't smoke," I said. "Nobody smokes anymore. It will kill you."

CHAPTER 49

They met in a restaurant, one with a bare concrete façade and burgundy curtains closed over the windows, a type very common in the East. The inside was ornate, burgundy and gold, with abundant curlicues and lurking cherubs in the old Russian style. Even in the deserted quiet of 4:45 A.M., or maybe because of it, Winters felt like he'd stepped inside a Fabergé egg.

But if the restaurant décor was delicate (and it was), their contact seemed designed to counteract it. The Russian sat heavily in the back corner of a back room as if made of a thousand pounds of lead, his neck bulging over the collar of his too-small Italian suit. He was sixty, perhaps, and rough, with loose jowls and a shock of unnaturally black hair, a cigarette between fat gold-ringed fingers, a five o'clock (A.M.) shadow crusted onto his slumping face. On the table in front of him were a pack of cigarettes, a bottle of vodka, espresso in a glass cup with an ornate metal holder, and six cell phones.

I always expect Russians to look different from the stereotype, Winters thought, *but they never do.*

"Mr. Gorelov," Everly said, extending his hand.

Winters had studied Putin's inner circle, and a few outer ones too, but he'd never heard the name. He didn't like that. It put him on shaky ground. Who was this man?

"This better be good," Gorelov grumped. Behind him, a couple of bodyguards were frowning. Winters had counted eight in the restaurant, all armed, smoking on the job.

"I don't know if it's good," Everly said. "But it's important."

"I hope this isn't about the transfer agreements again," Gorelov grumbled. No formalities, Winters noted. And no espresso for his guests.

"Any change in your position?"

"No change."

"Have you discussed it with your superiors?"

"I have no superiors," Gorelov said.

"Of course," Everly replied, dipping his nonexistent chin. "But I assume the right people know of our proposition. Our clients expect . . ."

"I don't give a damn about your clients," Gorelov said, burying his head in his coffee. He was stonewalling. Winters wondered if it was personal, or personality. About 110 Russians owned 40 percent of the country's wealth. Winters suspected more than a few were Everly's clients, and Gorelov's enemies. Stereotypes suggested that Russians were men of titanic grudges.

"So who is he?" Gorelov sniffed, jerking his head.

"This is Mr. Winters."

"Pleased to meet you," Winters said, extending his hand.

The Russian drank vodka from a short glass. He looked anything but pleased. "An American," he said.

"An expert on Ukraine," Everly replied, only slightly exaggerating.

Gorelov turned toward him for the first time, his eyes bloodshot. "You have something for me?" he asked in gruff, accented English. He was a man, Winters could tell, who liked to dominate the conversation.

"I have an opportunity," Winters shrugged, almost as if he regretted it, "created by you." There was no point in being coy.

"Let me guess. You think you can use Little Russia for your advantage." A derogatory Czarist term for Ukraine, meant to irritate him.

"We must protect Western interests," Winters said.

"And expand them, because you are takers. But Ukraine is ours, Mr. Winters. It always has been, and it always will be. When the czars ruled, Ukraine was a province, just like your California. When the Soviets came to power, they marched through Kiev, just like Moscow. *Ukraine* means 'meadow' in Russian—did you know that?—because they grow our grain. They feed our mothers. They nourish our factories with coal. They speak our language, with an atrocious accent, yes. They are not our most sophisticated region, but they are ours."

"That's not what the international community says."

"International community. What does that mean? The West? What is the West, in the face of hundreds of years of history?"

"What about the will of the people?"

Gorelov scoffed. "The people want to be Russian. That is why they fight."

"They want to be free."

Gorelov waved the suggestion away. He drank vodka, then coffee, then dragged on his cigarette. One of his phones buzzed. He ignored it. "They want to be happy. They want to be free of this violence brought on by the meddling of the West."

"The West didn't create the crisis."

"But you believe you can exploit it."

"I know I can," Winters said, switching to the first person.

Gorelov laughed, one of the least joyous sounds Winters had ever heard. It sounded like a cat choking on a brick of coal. "You think a businessman," the Russian said with disgust, "can face down the greatest nation on earth."

That's our phrase buddy, Winters thought, and no kleptocratic petrostate is going to steal it. But he wasn't offended. He was intrigued. It was going to be brass balls and bullshit, he could see that. No wonder France buckled like a Peugeot under a tractor-trailer when Putin dared them to intervene.

"It's not a matter of facing down," Winters said. "This isn't intimidation. I plan to beat you at your own game."

"And what game is that?"

"Military exploitation."

Gorelov grunted, or maybe it was another laugh. "I am a bureaucrat, Mr. Winters."

Good to know, Winters thought. "And I'm a military man, with a private army."

The Russian glanced at Everly and frowned. This was new. Winters saw his advantage and moved in, cornering the Russian with his eyes.

"For years, you have counted on our passivity," he said. "On our refusal to meet you with force. No please, don't insult me by objecting, you know it's true. You support our enemies—Iran, Syria, even Afghanistan—in order to grind us down, to make our Deep State interests weary of war. But I am different, Mr. Gorelov. I feast on war. Conflict is my business, and business is booming. But it can be better. My dream, unlike the men you bully, isn't peace. It is war. The type that grinds you back, the way you have subdued Georgia and Chechnya, the way you will try to grind down Ukraine. In other words, I am what you fear most, without knowing it. I am a Putin of the West."

Gorelov visibly recoiled, as Winters knew he would. "You are no Putin," he grunted.

"No. I am not a monster."

Gorelov pounded the table, making his vodka glass rock. He curled his hand around a cellphone, his weapon of choice. "You insult me, Mr. Winters."

Winters smiled. He had hit the big man where it hurt. At this level, every Russian worked for the state, and that meant Vladimir Putin, because in Russia, Putin *was* the state. He had reined in the oligarchs with ex-KGB muscle and crushed all political opposition. If you opposed him you died, went to prison, or, if you were lucky, into exile. If you worked with him, he gave you whole cities or entire segments of Russia's economy, bringing unfathomable wealth and power. It was institutionalized mafia—Nigeria with nukes and snow. It wasn't much different, in all honesty, from how the country had been ruled for the last thousand years, except for brief interludes from 1917 to 1921, and most of the 1990s. At those points, the country was chaos.

Putin created his order, Winters had to admit, as he watched the Russian fume. Too bad he was such a shit.

"Don't worry," Winters said, when he'd stretched out the silence and Gorelov was sufficiently rattled, "I am not merely talking. I will show you how like Vladimirivich"—he used the honorific for Putin, a serious breach of etiquette for outsiders—"I truly am."

"You're going to attack Ukraine," Gorelov snorted.

"Only the parts you want."

"We'll stop you."

"At what cost?"

"It doesn't matter the cost," Gorelov said smugly, "because we control it all, and the Russian people are with us. The Russian people, the ones you call Ukrainians, will never accept you. They will curse your name."

"Do you know who I am?" Winters said smoothly.

"I know everyone, Mr. Winters," Gorelov said, leaning forward. He looked ready to bite. "And I have never heard of you."

"And the Ukrainians won't either, Mr. Gorelov. Even when my man is king of Kiev."

Gorelov blinked. He sat back in his chair, his hand cradling a cell phone. He hadn't considered the power of anonymity as a choice, and now it was his turn to be thrown off balance, to think, as Winters had only minutes before: who is this man?

CHAPTER 50

I grabbed my SCAR and rolled into position. Miles was laying prone a few feet away, his Bushmaster ACR up and aimed, the safety unlocked. I dropped my weapon to my side and kicked out of my sleeping bag beside him.

"There's someone at the gate," Miles said. I looked at my watch: 0352. I'd lost only a few minutes of sleep.

"Ukrainian?"

Miles shook his head. "He looks homeless, but he's speaking English. Yelling in English, actually."

"Grab him."

"We already have. There will be blood."

"Good," I said as I slipped on the earpiece of my headset. From the way Miles was looking at me, I knew he was worried about my breakdown with Alie. Poor form, and not just in front of the troops. As the old commercial said, never sweat. "Mission focus," I assured him, as I strapped on my pistols.

"Warrior spirit," Miles said, fist thumping his chest. Meaning: For the mission, for your brothers. Get your head on straight.

The prisoner looked terrible. Boon had zip-cuffed his hands in front of him, and he'd taken a few "shut the fuck up" punches to the face, but I doubted he'd looked much better when he arrived. He had a crusted bandage circling his head, half-covering one eye, and dried blood on his clothes. His hair was matted from blood and sweat. He didn't look like a threat, unless he was rabid. But he was here, and that was dangerous.

"Who are you?" I said.

"CIA."

"What does that mean?"

"Central Intelligence, Kiev, Operations Officer Chad Hargrove." Like he was reading off a dog tag. Was this what they taught at the Farm these days?

"How did you get here, Hargrove?"

"Stole a car. From Jessup."

"You parked on the road?" Miles exclaimed in disbelief.

The man nodded. He didn't seem to understand the implication of the highly visible car. I punched him in the face, for his stupidity. He took it pretty well.

"What are you doing here?" I said.

"Looking for Alie."

Miles glanced at me, but he didn't need to worry. Mission focus. "Who is Alie?"

"Alie MacFarlane." The man looked around. Wildman kneed him in the back of the leg. He buckled. No looking around, asshole. Eyes front.

"Who is Alie MacFarlane?" I said, my voice rising. This was a serious problem. This was becoming a compromised operation an hour short of the assault.

Nothing.

"Why the fuck are you here?" I yelled, resisting the urge to punch him again.

He looked up. "Are you Locke? The mercenary? She was looking for you."

I drew my pistol. I never drew my pistol unless I planned to use it.

"Don't," Miles said, just as Alie's "Shit" echoed through the warehouse. She was coming out of the shadows, Karpenko beside her. They were probably best friends by now.

"Alie," Hargrove muttered with relief.

"What the hell happened?" she said, taking in the bandages.

"Jumped. By Russians . . ."

"What the hell?" I said, lowering my weapon. "Alie, what is going on?"

I watched as she walked toward us, everyone on edge. She knelt beside the prisoner. He looked up at her tenderly. Thankfully. He was missing a tooth, a recent loss judging by the amount of blood on his gums, but he was no Wildman. "Let him go," she said.

I laughed, but nothing about this was funny.

"He's a CIA officer, Locke." She was speaking softly, as if that would make her sound more serious. "He's a United States government employee."

"Don't care."

"He's been injured."

"Don't care."

"He's a kid." She looked at me. I looked at the so-called CIA officer. She was right; he was young, maybe midtwenties. And he was scared.

"He's not here on Company business," she said, meaning the old company, the CIA. "He was just trying to find me. Make sure I was safe."

"Why?"

"I ditched him."

He was in love with her. I could see it in his face. "You used him."

Alie frowned. The truth hurt. "Would it help if I said yes?"

No, it wouldn't.

I turned back to the kid. "Is there anybody else?"

He took his time, probably contemplating his odds, or maybe his relationship with Alie. Not as easy as you thought, is it?

I punched him again, right in his Aryan nose. "Is anybody else coming?"

He shook his head no. I could tell he had settled on the truth.

"Does anybody else know you are here?"

"I'm an American," he said. "I'm on your side."

It doesn't work like that, asshole. "Does anyone else know you are here?"

He hesitated, then sadly: "No."

I put the gun to his head. "How did you know we were here?"

This was the big one, but Hargrove wasn't answering. He was a coward who hoped his silence made him a hero. I turned to Alie and put the gun to her head. "How the fuck did you know we were here?"

"I told him."

I turned. It was Greenlees, of course it was Greenlees, looking more pathetic than usual, looking exactly, in fact, like the man he was: a relic. If this was a le Carré novel, he'd be the hero, but that was what had gotten him in trouble. Too much faith in the power of the past.

"I called for an evac," Greenlees said. "That first morning. After I was punched." He glanced at Karpenko, as if to apologize. To Karpenko. Not to us.

"You gave up our position over a punch?"

He shook his head. It wasn't the punch, I could see that, but Greenlees knew that didn't matter, because right now I didn't give a fuck.

"I know that kid," Greenlees said. "He's a newbie, still on a leash and answering phones for the Deputy Chief of Station. He must have intercepted my radio call—"

"I never told anyone," the kid said frantically. He was starting to get it now. "Except Alie, I swear. I never told Baker."

Who is Baker? I wanted to scream. Who the fuck is Baker?

Miles must have sensed my frustration. "You don't want to shoot him," he said calmly.

The hell I didn't. Hargrove was young, a hell of a lot younger than Alie. Maybe he was just a kid in over his head, in love with an older woman, the possibility of an adventure, an ideal. But he was a kid who knew my name.

"Gag him." I looked around. "Attach him to that pipe," I said, pointing to the far end of the warehouse. "If he gives you any problems, kill him. We'll leave the body." Let the CIA sort it with the Russians.

"Tom," Alie started. Since when did she think she could use my first name?

"Don't worry, Alie, you can cut him out when we're gone. If you can find a strong enough blade."

I could see Greenlees slump. He'd mined harbors in Central America; he knew the game. The kid was resigned. Alie was going to fight, I could see that in her face, even before she grabbed me.

"Tom," she said quietly, really looking me in the eye for the first time, or at least for the first time since that night in Burundi when we'd fallen in love.

And that was when my world exploded.

My ears pressurized. Then I felt the shock wave, like a physical assault. Time stopped, and I saw the windows above me blowing inward, glass shards and debris hanging in the air. I sensed, but didn't hear, the *crack* of the explosion, and then time caught up with the RPG, and the glass shattered against the far wall.

Instinctively, I pushed Alie down and rolled flat, groping for my weapon. My vision was blurry, my breathing hard in my ears.

Two more RPGs slammed through the front wall, the concrete exploding toward me, and I buried my head in the floor as the shock waves passed above me.

Another rocket came through the breach, hissing across the factory and blowing out a chunk of the back wall, leaving a thick smoke trail hanging in the middle of the room.

My senses came back.

"Cover!" I heard Miles shout, as Boon vaulted from the catwalk.

Two grenades hurtled through the smoke into the center of the warehouse. I heard a *clink clink,* as they bounced off the concrete floor a few meters away. I pushed Alie behind our makeshift barricade and leapt on top of her. Successive blasts shook the building, and automatic gunfire raked the room, shredding the computer workstation and exploding a box of smoke grenades.

It had only been seconds since the windows blew out, but I'd already lost Miles in the smoke. I'd lost most of the team. Half the front wall was gone, sections of the ceiling were collapsing, but the building was holding together. This was a commando raid: fast and vicious. *Survive the first minute,* I thought, as the first man leapt through the blasted wall. *Must. Survive.*

"Tangos East wall!" I shouted into my headset, as a second man leapt a pile of shattered concrete, moving like a pro.

I glanced at Alie, crouched beside me. Behind her sat Hargrove, his eyes wide in terror. A few feet away I saw a body on the ground. It was Greenlees. It looked like he'd taken one in the head.

Get off the X, I thought. *Escape the ambush zone.*

"Suppressing fire," I yelled. "Everyone out."

Alie nodded, but I wasn't talking to her, I was talking to the team. They were already at it, laying down a wall of lead and tossing grenades, adding to the chaos. I swiveled. A figure rose on my right—Boon, I think—and headed toward the back. A third man appeared through the hole in the front wall. I leveled my SCAR, acquired the target in my sight picture, exhaled, and squeezed the trigger twice. Target down.

I took my time, finding the space in the fury of my team's massive counterbarrage. Slow is smooth, and smooth is fast. I melted behind a pile of metal scrap and slowed my breathing, steadying my nerves. Buddha calm. My SCAR was a precision weapon, unlike their AK-47s, and it shot 7.62 mm body-armor-piercing rounds. So I waited for a silhouette, and dropped it with a double shot, center of mass. Two more came through the crumbling wall, and I took them down, buying time for my team. The goal was to withstand the first wave of an assault, but this first wave was withering.

"Fall back," I barked, this time at Alie, but she wasn't there, only Greenlees, still dead.

I turned back to the attack, as the familiar smell of gunpowder filled the factory. The Škoda was on fire. My barrel was hot from too many rounds, making precision shooting difficult, so I flipped to automatic and fired three-round bursts. There were plenty of targets now, but most were behind cover. I tossed a grenade toward the breach point and ducked behind the barricade to reload, wishing I'd taken the time to build it right, as Charro had suggested.

Two more explosions rocked the building and put me on my ass. The first was an RPG. The second was the Škoda's gas tank. I looked up. Half the roof was blown out. The corner of the warehouse had collapsed. I could see the sky through the smoke, with only one blinking star, maybe a planet out there on the edge. I followed the cracks along the metal ceiling. It was safe. For now. I turned to fire again, as two figures rose from our side of the barricade and started to run. I spotted the Ukrainians on the left. Sirko was laying down impressive lead, holding his field of fire, but Karpenko was still crouched beside him. He should have fallen back.

Too bad. Too late now.

I shot another magazine on semiauto as two hostiles jumped the barricade. Someone—Charro—was in hand-to-hand combat. I ran without thinking, leapt into the void, and plunged my knife into the enemy's back, slamming him to the ground. Charro was under him, struggling, but my knife was an eight-inch blade; it didn't penetrate all the way through the chest cavity.

I pulled out the knife and rolled off into firing position, as Charro rolled the dead man onto his back. We locked eyes, he nodded, and then, as he popped into a firing position, a bullet ripped into his throat, and right out the back through Mother Mary's tattooed hands.

"Watch out," someone yelled.

A gunburst, close enough to shatter my hearing, and a man fell dead on top of me. I could hear the bullets whistling over me from both directions, and I knew I was in no-man's-land, so kept my head down. I could see hostiles—Russians? Spetsnaz?—struggling to hold their positions. *Get up. Get up now,* I thought. *Move to the evac route.* And then, just as I was about to run, a figure leapt up and sprinted through the fire. It was the pilot, racing for the helicopter. What was he doing? Where did he think he was going, up through the hole in the ceiling?

Time slowed, as the pilot loped across the last five meters, leapt over a pile of debris, and exploded. It was as if the door handle had been rigged, but it was an RPG, screaming in from beyond the breach, hitting the helicopter and hurling body parts and aluminum through the back wall a moment before the concussion caught up with the carnage and knocked everyone down.

"Pop smoke!" I heard Miles shout over the headset, as three smoke grenades plunked onto the factory floor, filling the warehouse with colored smoke. I crouch-ran for the back door, following someone—Reynolds—to the evac route. We passed Boon, hunkered behind a broken smelter, and laid down suppressing fire while Reynolds kicked the exit door at a full run, almost taking it off its hinges, and burst out into the open space beyond.

The air lit up, the lead ricocheting off the warehouse wall, as Reynolds danced a foot in front of me, the bullets tearing him apart. I grabbed him by the upper arm and hurled myself back through the door. My face was coated with Reynolds's blood; his shoulder was disintegrating in my hands. The enemy had all the exits covered. The enemy had a machine gun trained on the alleyway, the fucking pros.

"Alpha Four down. Alpha Four down. Back alley a no-go," I shouted, dropping Reynolds's body and making a throat-slashing gesture at Boon. The smoke grenades had done their work, and visibility was zero in the red-and-purple haze. The enemies' laser sites danced in the smoke, marking our targets. No time to reload the SCAR. I reached for my twin pistols and moved down the factory floor, popping skulls. A nine-millimeter pistol can sound like an air gun in battle, but it packs stopping power at close range, and three hostiles didn't get up. I missed two more, as they slipped behind cover and turned off their laser sights.

"Fire in the hole!" someone shouted, as a satchel charge thrown from the Russian side landed in the center of the storm.

I leapt behind the smelter with Boon and covered my ears. Several kilos of C-4 cratered the floor and sent a shock wave that knocked the smelter over and stunned and deafened everyone within thirty meters. I stumbled away, right into a Russian, his muzzle pointed at my chest, and it was over, all over, until someone opened up on automatic—it was Jacobsen's M249 SAW machine gun—and the Russian collapsed.

"Thanks Jake," I said as I turned, still stunned, but it wasn't Jacobsen. It was Alie, gasping for air and staring at the body, holding Jacobsen's gun.

"I fucking pissed myself," she said.

I looked down. She had. I almost said it was a good look, but instead I told her to fall back, this isn't over. "Is Jacobsen dead?"

"I think so."

The gunfire had stopped. In the smoke, the hostiles were falling back, consolidating their position outside, using the remains of the front wall as cover. Five meters in front of me, a wounded Russian attacker lay on his back, breathing heavily. His head swiveled toward me, and I put a bullet through his brain.

"Who's hit?" I screamed into the headset, my ears aching and hearing mostly gone.

"Charro, Jacobsen, Reynolds," Wildman said. "KIA."

"The old man, Greenlees. KIA."

"A couple Ukrainians . . ."

"Three dead," Maltov said, crawling up next to me. "One wounded."

I could see a young man a few feet away, slumped against the wall, sucking air. The other three living Ukrainians were near him, along with Sirko and Karpenko.

"Fuck." The voice snapped from the back of the warehouse. "Holy fuck, get me out of here. Get me out of these." I couldn't find the voice. I was looking but . . .

"It's me . . . It's Hargrove."

He was lying on his side ten meters away, breathing heavily.

"Get me out of these cuffs," he said. He smelled like shit, and his eyes were wild with fear.

"Miles is wounded," someone said.

"Get me out," Hargrove said.

I turned away.

"Locke. Please. Locke . . . don't leave me."

"Shut the fuck up," I said, resisting the urge to smash his skull in with the butt of my rifle. This was his fault. The enemy had followed his car.

I surveyed the scene before me. We were cornered in the back of the warehouse. Smoke clung to the air, and half the building was on fire. Bodies littered no-man's-land, piles of broken concrete and glass, but no movement; the enemy had withdrawn to the other side of the flames. But they were out there, waiting. They had the tactical advantage, because they had the only exits covered, and we were stuck inside a burning building going down like a torpedoed ship.

Think fast, Locke. Think. These motherfuckers won't wait long.

"Call your dogs," I said to Maltov, tossing him my sat phone. "Anybody you know. Get them here."

I scrambled to Miles. He was on his back, gasping. He had taken three shots to the ballistic vest; its ceramic plates had been destroyed, saving his life but breaking ribs. Another shot in his left arm had missed the bone but rendered the arm useless. But the real problem was his left leg, torn and soaked with blood, a tourniquet tied around his thigh.

"Femoral artery," said Boon, our medic, as he tied on a second tourniquet. "He's bleeding out."

I'm not going to let him fucking die, I thought.

But a hospital was out of the question. Even if we got him there, anonymously, the FSB would pick him up, interrogate him by torture, and dump his body in a beet field. The Geneva

Conventions didn't extend to mercenaries, not that modern soldiers benefitted much either.

"Morphine," Miles gasped.

He clenched his teeth. He knew the bargain: no extraordinary measures that could get others killed. But I had one chance. A desperate one: Winters. We just had to get out of here first.

"Ten minutes," Maltov said, handing me back the sat phone.

Shit. Too long. I figured we had two, at the most, before the Russians came knocking again.

"Two teams," I said, as Boon jammed the morphine into Miles. "Out the back and into the woods. Get far away, and get there fast. We'll link up in town, on the roof of the building where Wildman killed the slags. If I'm not there by 0700, head to the extraction point and wait. I'm taking Jimmy"—I could see Miles shaking his head, but I ignored it—"and the Ukrainians and the girl—"

"We're not going."

I turned. It was Maltov, his three healthy men crouched behind him. "We're not leaving," he said. "We're here to hang Russians."

"Chechens," Sirko snapped. Of course. The Colonel was right. They were mercs, not Spetsnaz.

Maltov turned and barked something in Ukrainian. Sirko spat back, then raised his rifle and stepped toward the enforcer, his finger on the trigger. I could feel the tension in his glare and the ferocity of his voice. Sirko had been pushed too far by Maltov. Sirko hated the man's recklessness and lack of finesse. But we were part of it too: Hargrove, Alie, and me. From Sirko's perspective, and it was a fair one, our carelessness was about to get him and his client killed.

"Enough," I said, cutting through the heated exchange.

Sirko didn't lower his bullpup, but Maltov laughed, even with the rifle in his face. He turned to the three men beside him, who laughed in turn. The Ukrainians were young and hard, but I could tell only Maltov's force of will kept them together. They were terrified.

"True Ukrainians will fight," Maltov said, turning toward me. "This . . . Russian will follow you."

"He follows me," Karpenko said.

The oligarch stepped forward and whispered something to Maltov. It looked like a business tip, not a good-bye. If Maltov survived, Sirko was out. He was probably out anyway. But I doubted either would survive.

Focus, Tom, I thought, looking around.

The fish truck was in the corner, untouched. It was packed with high-octane helicopter fuel.

"Please . . ." someone said.

The drone was next to the truck, also untouched. "The SA-18s?" I asked.

"Punctured," Boon said, shaking his head. Useless.

But still, a thought was coming together. Maybe even a plan. It wasn't much, but it was something, and I'd lived through worse . . . or almost as bad.

"Please," the voice pleaded again.

It was Hargrove.

"Please," he said.

He was on his back, crying and holding up his zip cuffs. What was I going to do with Hargrove? What was I going to do with the man who had brought this down on us, our extra baggage, our bad-luck charm?

Alie grabbed my arm. "He's CIA," she said. I had seen her vicious, and I had seen her passionate, but I had never seen her this determined. "He's a walking international incident, Tom, not to mention congressional investigation."

She was right. I had to bury Hargrove deep. The Russians could never find him, dead or alive. I knew which option I preferred. So I pulled out my knife, thinking through the steps—and at the last moment, decided to cut him loose.

"Wallet," I said with my hand out. "Keys. Badge. Anything that can identify you."

Hargrove emptied his pockets. I ripped off his dog tags. Why would a Case Officer have dog tags? He probably bought them at the mall. Everybody thought they were soldiers now.

"Find a gun," I said, reaching for my ruck.

It wasn't his fault. He didn't kill the guys on my team. He didn't kidnap Alie. He didn't hurt Miles.

I did.

CHAPTER 51

The Wolf stood in a copse of trees thirty meters from the front of the warehouse, watching it burn. The Chechen machine gun crew had reported only one kill behind the building; the rest had gotten the message and retreated. Part of the front wall had collapsed, enough to glimpse the wreckage inside: a shoddy barricade, a burning car. He could see five or six bodies scattered inside the building, the KIA of his first assault. The survivors were outside, surrounding the building.

He was glad it wasn't Colonel Sirko, his old commander, who had snatched the American girl in Kramatorsk. The Wolf might not have been able to resist shooting him on the spot. Instead, it was the Ukrainian Maltov, and he had been able to follow the fool straight back here. He had scouted the warehouse quickly, planning the assault in his head. He had gone in blind, as soon as the Chechens arrived, but there hadn't been a choice. He couldn't afford a "wait and see" strategy with quarry this elusive, or this good. He'd been burned that way in Poltava, and he wanted payback. These Chechens were hardened fighters, men who had hunted Islamists door to door, like dogs, from Damascus to Tbilisi. This time, the plan had been pure firepower, the old Soviet way. Hit hard, hit fast. Leave corpses.

He had made two errors. The first was not killing the loud American when he arrived in the car. The second was not attacking the mercs when they opened the door to pull him inside.

But his men weren't in position, and launching a raid prematurely could have been disastrous. The Westerners could have slipped the noose.

As things stood, the Wolf wasn't worried. He hadn't lost. He had taken casualties, but so had they. Now they were trapped in a burning building, with wounded, and their exits were covered.

The Wolf slid the action on his twenty-year-old Steyr AUG bullpup assault rifle, his life's true friend and companion. He stared down the scope and saw movement in the depths of the warehouse, men crouching and moving, but no clear shots.

He dropped the rifle to his side. "Be ready," he said to the ten-man secondary assault force around him in the trees.

The enemy was cornered, and they would either roast or run. It was that simple. All the Wolf had to do now was wait.

A thousand miles away, Gorelov put down his phone. Another was already ringing. "We have no troops in Little Russia," he said with the arrogant bravado of a man used to lying in the face of clear evidence. The Russians were even showing funerals for "martyred" soldiers on state television.

"You have a brigade in Severdonetsk," Winters replied calmly. "Three units outside Sloviansk. Not to mention the Spetsnaz near Mariupol, and the brigade helping the separatists hold the line to the west."

"They are volunteers," Gorelov growled, spouting the party line. "Patriots on holiday."

The man was grasping. Winters could see it. Gorelov didn't know military strategy. He didn't know mud—not the business variety, but the actually stinking, bloodstained dirt. If Winters could keep the battle on this terrain, guns not numbers, then he was confident he could break his man.

"They are Russian military units, under Russian command," he said, slowing down as Gorelov quickened his pace, "and I'm going to prove it. By this time tomorrow, the whole world will see you with your dick in the cookie jar."

Gorelov spoke abusive Russian into one cell phone, grabbed another, shouted, then put it down. He stubbed out a cigarette and lit another. Smoke was circling his head. He grinned.

"You think a private militia can defeat us?" He laughed. "You think a man like you can defeat Russia? The mightiest empire on earth?"

Wrong move. You already said that, my friend.

"No," Winters replied, "nor do we need to. I simply have to break you, at the point where you are weakest."

Gorelov refused to look away, staring his opponent down as he spoke rapidly into one cell phone after another. Winters didn't know what the Russian was saying, but he knew he was relaying threats to others further up the line, government officials, maybe military men. Good. He was probably trying to confirm the positions of Russian troops, and whether there was a Western private military company operating in east Ukraine. Let him try.

"My man will break you once, two hours from now, and then he will break you again, and again, until the world knows his name," Winters said, feeling it now, watching the military and media campaign unfurl in his mind. "By tomorrow, he will be Nikolay Karpenko, the savior of Ukraine."

Winters saw Everly swallow, then hesitate, and he knew he'd made a mistake, even before Gorelov slammed down his phone. He had become overconfident, Winters realized. He'd swerved back onto Gorelov's terrain, names, and power structures, when he should have stayed in the mud.

"Karpenko?" Gorelov snorted, with a laugh that sounded like

a cat caught in an industrial crushing machine. "Kostyantin Karpenko? The baby oligarch? The so-called businessman of the West? *That* is your man?"

Winters started to answer, but Gorelov stubbed out his cigarette, violently, snapping off the unsmoked barrel. "Karpkeno is *nichego*," he barked. Nothing.

"He is a leader," Winters said, pressing forward, knowing it was all he could do. "He is a symbol . . ."

"He is, what, maybe the sixtieth most powerful man in Ukraine?"

"Who was Stalin, before he changed his name to Joe Steel?" Winters barked, with more confidence than he felt. *Press on. Right the ship.* "Who was Lenin, before he murdered the czar? Who was Putin before the Wall fell? Who were you, for that matter, before your godfather lifted you to this position?"

"I was a violinist," Gorelov smiled. He was a good one, in fact, trained at the Saint Petersburg Conservatory. "Karpenko is *zhaba*." A toad.

But Gorelov was the toad, squatting in his smoky backroom, puffing out his chest. "And besides," the Russian croaked, knocking back a short glass of vodka for effect, "Karpenko is dead."

CHAPTER 52

We moved fast and stayed low, throwing Hargrove's personal effects onto the burn pile of equipment we were leaving behind. Then we gathered the bodies—Greenlees, Jacobsen, Reynolds, and Charro—and tossed them on top. We left the dead Ukrainians for the police, or whoever came next. Those bodies would tell the right story and, if the dead men were lucky, maybe even find their way home to their mothers for last rites.

I thought about saying a few words, but there was nothing to say. Boon took Charro's cross and kissed it, as Charro often did, but nobody knew Jacobsen or Reynolds. They didn't have anything that would identify them, and they didn't seem to be carrying mementos. They were strangers.

I turned away and scrambled over to the fish truck, where the Ukrainians were gathered. "Ready?" I said.

They had been slamming vodka from the bottle, particularly the injured man, who was strapped into the driver's seat. He was half drunk and half delirious, and he was saying something slurry and serious to each man in turn. His wound wasn't fatal, but apparently he didn't know that. I wondered if Maltov knew. If this was the sacrifice required.

"Good luck," I said to Maltov, as the driver finished the bottle and smashed it on the factory floor.

"No luck necessary," he said. "Only pride."

The driver started the engine. I noticed he was crying. Fuck pride.

"Take her up," I said to Wildman. He nodded, and our drone-copter whirred up through the roof and into the night. It was met immediately by gunfire.

I walked to the pile. "Adios, brothers," I said.

"Wait," Alie said, running from the back of the factory, where the team was waiting at the evac door. She stopped at the pile, reached in, and carefully removed Greenlees's wedding ring, as if she didn't want to pull his finger too hard. She touched his cheek, then slipped it into her pocket. "Okay," she said. She wasn't crying. She wasn't showing any emotion. It only made her look sadder.

"Diving," Wildman said.

I signaled to Maltov—go time—lit the fuse, and ran. The white phosphorous, or "Willy P," would eat through the bodies and the equipment and wouldn't stop until it had eaten two feet into the concrete floor. In ten minutes, there wouldn't even be a tooth.

"Let's go," I said, as the truck crashed through the front wall, the driver's desperate scream disappearing into the void.

The Wolf heard the motor, then saw the small quadcopter slip through a shattered window and bank upward, losing itself in the sky. It was a spy drone, probably used to scout their objective. Now it was scouting his positions. So what.

"*Yego shit*," The Wolf said. Shoot it down.

The first barrage missed, as the copter zigzagged across the dark sky. Lousy Chechens.

"Take it down," he said more forcefully, as the drone dipped toward them.

A kamikaze run, the Wolf thought. *Or a decoy.*

"Oni idut," he yelled. They are coming.

A flash from the warehouse. A blinding white starburst. Phosphorous fire. The Wolf grabbed a rocket-propelled grenade launcher. The whirring of the drone faded to gunfire, the world faded into ten men firing, but he kept his eye on the target and his finger on the trigger and, just as he anticipated, a truck burst out of the warehouse. What he hadn't anticipated, as he lined up his shot, was the explosion a few feet above them, right in the middle of his men.

Everly sucked in his breath, a small sound, but from the London banker, it might as well have been a gasp. He had seen the look on Gorelov's face, too, Winters realized. For the second time that morning, Gorelov had blinked.

He was bluffing about Karpenko being nothing. He had either been told Karpenko was dead, or he had created the lie himself and forgotten. There was no reason for either to be the case, unless the Ukrainian mattered, not just in Kiev, but in Moscow, too. Gorelov had been cocky as he gloated over Karpenko's death, until he saw the look on Winters's face, and knew that he was wrong.

Winters pounced. "Call your friends," he said and gestured to the Russian's phone bank. "Tell them that Karpenko is alive. Tell them he is coming."

Gorelov grabbed two cell phones, as if on impulse.

"Call someone important," Winters laughed. "By all means, call someone who matters. I hope they are early risers."

Maltov opened up with Jacobsen's M249 SAW machine gun as soon as the white phosphorus grenade strapped to the drone exploded. He was behind a barricade near the center of the warehouse, too far away to target with any hope of accuracy, but close enough that he could see, through the burning front wall, the Russians squirming in the starburst of the blast, like earthworms in bleach. He kept firing, pointing the gun toward anything that moved, as the fish truck barreled through the hole in the front wall of the warehouse, Yevgeny at the wheel. Poor Yevgeny, who had once played three consecutive games of eight ball without missing a shot. Who always received a card from his mother on Valentine's Day, meaning he was a perverted bastard, sure, but also that his mother knew where he was, and what he was doing, but not that he was already dead, that even now, as Maltov fired, a Russian RPG was ripping into the truck, exploding the fuel drums and C-4, making the kamikaze drone look like mere fireworks.

The SAW machine gun clicked dry, out of ammo. Maltov let go and grabbed the AK-47 from his shoulder. He ran toward the Chechens and their Russians overlords. He didn't think of death or country or burning to nothing, not even ash, in unholy flames. He simply got to work.

Gorelov slammed down a phone. "You don't have the men," he said brusquely.

He had been talking with military commanders. Winters heard the name Karpenko several times. Good.

"Stalin said there's a certain quality in quantity," Winters replied slowly, with affected ease. "I disagree. I believe in actual quality. That's why my soldiers are the best."

"Even the best soldier is nothing when the ammo runs out. How many could you possibly have?"

"Almost a hundred," Winters lied.

"We have thousands," Gorelov lied in return. "We have troops in every oblast in eastern Ukraine. We can be anywhere in minutes."

"It will take an hour," Winters said confidently, "once you factor in the time to mobilize."

Gorelov shrugged. "An hour is nothing. You can't change the world in an hour with a hundred men."

"Maybe," Winters said, "but in an hour, it will be too late for either of us to turn back."

"You're bluffing," the Russian said dourly, but Winters could almost taste the fear.

Winters smiled. "Go on. Make calls. Waste time. I'm a conflict entrepreneur. I have spent years planning this operation. It is my life's work. But if you wish to gamble on my incompetence, be my guest."

The Wolf lifted his head. His men were burning around him, the white phosphorous eating through their flesh as they screamed. The truck was a crater, its fire burning hot, but he had been ready. He had blown it apart before it reached the trees, and there wasn't much firepower behind it, only four men with Kalashnikovs, if his count was right. The rear guard, clearly untrained, fighting a hopeless delaying tactic out of adrenaline and pride. No Colonel Sirko, his old commander, no oligarch, and certainly no Western mercenaries.

The Wolf shook his head. He lowered his rifle, considering his next move. *Ukrainians,* he thought with contempt, as one of the rear guard fell. *History's fools.*

Wildman lunged into the back alley, wheeling three steel doors on a truck dolly in front of him as a makeshift shield. Behind him, Boon bent to a knee with the first M90 rocket launcher. The M90 could take out tanks, not to mention a machine gun crew on a roof only fifty meters away. Within seconds, Boon had pulled the trigger. The rocket's backblast scorched the pavement behind him. The shot went high, over the heads of the gun crew.

"Next!" Boon yelled, and I tossed him the other M90. Machine gun fire rained around him, slamming into Wildman's steel shield with thudding force, but Boon sighted calmly, adjusted for the weapon's arc of fire, and squeezed the trigger. *Fwoosh.* The rocket hit just below the machine gun nest, collapsing the wall.

Wildman screamed and tossed aside the shield in favor of his British SA-80. Sirko jumped through the door beside him, letting rip with his bullpup ASh-12 as the enemy struggled to right themselves and return fire. Next came Karpenko, then Alie and Hargrove, pulling Miles behind them on an improvised litter. The Chechens were scrambling, pulling the machine gun from the pile of bricks and bodies and readying it for firing. *Ten seconds,* I thought. I kicked Hargrove like a mule to get his ass in gear, practically knocking him across the open area and through the hole we'd cut in the fence directly beyond the door.

Within seconds, we were in the forest, with Boon and Wildman laying down cover behind us. I sprinted past Karpenko ten meters into the twilight and underbrush, then dropped to a knee in the leaves, signaling the group to pass me, then cut to the left.

I knelt, breathed deep, and scoped the Chechens through the trees, their guns up now and firing, but raggedly. I squeezed the trigger and laid down heavy covering fire. Seconds later, Sirko sprinted passed me and cut left. Boon and Wildman cut the other way, heading right into the forest. They were the diversion. If they couldn't draw the enemy off, they'd circle back to cover us.

"Pick up the pace," I whisper-yelled, moving past Hargrove and Alie as they struggled through the underbrush.

"The blood . . ." Alie huffed.

Jimmy Miles was delirious and bleeding through his bandages; Hargrove's incompetent jostling of the litter was killing him; but it was the best I could do for him. My gun was worth more than Alie and Hargrove put together.

"Fuck the blood," I said. "We have to move."

I heard Maltov's machine gun fall silent in the distance, out of ammo. I heard his AK-47. It was met by a vicious barrage. The Chechens had survived Maltov's best shot, which had always been a long shot at best, and they were hammering him.

"Move fast," I said. "Light and noise discipline." No shots, unless lives were on the line. We needed to move silently and rely on stealth, not firepower.

"Don't stop," I said, turning to Alie and Hargrove before double-timing ahead to take point. "No matter what."

"Thanks," Alie said, but I didn't know what she was talking about.

There was a gully a hundred meters to the east. I'd scouted it as a possible evac route the first morning, and I was heading for it now. It was first light, bright enough to silhouette us against the horizon. If we could make the dry creek bed, we'd

have some cover to run or, more likely, find an ambush spot
for a last stand.

I dropped into the gully and paused, the rest of the group
filing in behind me, Miles grunting as the litter slipped down
the short incline into the rocky ravine. In the distance, Boon
and Wildman were firing, drawing the enemy away from us.
Beyond the warehouse, Maltov and his men were still in a firefight, but for how long? We had passed five of the seven buildings in the complex, dark squares behind a fence, blocking our
access to the road, but even here, I could see the warehouse fire
lighting the sky.

The road.

I moved quickly to Hargrove. "Do you have your keys?"

"What?" He was huffing. It had been a long day.

"Do you have your car keys?"

"What?" He grimaced. Behind him, Jimmy grunted. I didn't
dare look.

"Can we take your car?" Alie snapped.

"I think so," Hargrove said. "I think . . . Yes. I have the keys.
I left it at the front gate."

I moved past Karpenko to Sirko, who was crouched behind a
fallen tree, listening for hostiles. I heard an Israeli Tavor, Boon's
gun. Then Wildman's SA-80. Then half a dozen AK-47s. They
were a few hundred meters away.

"Around the incinerator," I said to Sirko, pointing toward the
small building on the far edge of the factory complex, "then left
toward the road." The fence was done at the far end of the complex. If we could get past the incinerator, we would have cover
all the way to the road. I just hoped Hargrove's abandoned car
was unguarded and in one piece.

I heard Boon's Tavor, closer now, but not Wildman's SA-80.
I heard gunfire from the direction of Maltov's men. Somewhere,

something exploded. Something large collapsed. My ears were ringing, but I felt attuned. I tried not to think of Miles bleeding out. He had half an hour; that was what I had told myself when we left. I couldn't doubt now.

"Now," I said, signaling Sirko to lead. He bolted up and crouch-ran toward the incinerator, trailed by Karpenko, Alie, Hargrove, and Miles on his litter. As I'd hoped, the old colonel was a skilled operator in the right conditions, so I waited six beats. I expected the enemy to come quickly, if they came, and I might be able to catch a few before they knew I was there.

No one came, so I moved out. The others were halfway to the incinerator, fifty meters to go at the most. There was an open area in our direct path, so Sirko skirted the widest part and hit a narrower clearing at speed, his ASh-12 bullpup rifle level before him. I saw Alie pass into the open area and, suddenly, I knew she would be gunned down—almost anticipated it, already feeling the shock—but she was through before I could react, with Hargrove beside her and Miles's litter dragging at their heels and me a few paces behind, my SCAR rifle ready. *Not much farther now*, I thought, as Sirko passed into the partial concealment of high weeds.

And then the guns opened up, *pop, pop, pop,* and the dirt danced. Something struck me, and I fell headlong, my shoulder slamming into Miles, and then my face into the ground.

Reflexively, I pulled my Beretta pistols and rolled. I wasn't hit. It wasn't a bullet that knocked me down. It was Hargrove, spinning backward, knocking me onto Miles. I saw Alie falling, pulled down by the force of my weight on the litter. The SCAR was gone, lost in the tall weeds, but I had my pistols, one for each hand, siting for targets, when I heard someone bark: "Kapitan Sirko."

"Leytenant Balashov," Sirko hissed, jerking his bullpup upward as a shadow stepped out from behind the incinerator and shot him in the face.

I sighted the man's head with the Beretta in my right hand. Five meters. High percentage shot. I started to squeeze the trigger, but Karpenko stepped into my line of fire. His back was to me, his arms partially raised in supplication. Fuck. I twisted around, trying to I get an angle with the Beretta in my left hand, but a Chechen appeared to my right, his AK-47 trained on my head, his finger on the trigger.

Silence. The world was silence, except for gunfire in the distance, meaningless to us now. There was no motion, there was nothing at all, until Sirko's killer spoke in Russian, first to the corpse, then to Karpenko.

"I knew that man," he said in rough English, for my benefit, and I knew then he was my counterpart, the mercenary leader who had engineered this ambush.

"Do you who I am?" Karpenko said in English. The Russian merc's Steyr AUG laser sight was dancing on his heart.

Nothing. No reply.

"I am Nikolay Karpenko," he said calmly, again in English. That was smart, to use a secondary language. It forced the Russian to focus on his words. "I believe there is a half million euro bounty . . ."

"One million," the Russian interrupted.

"I will pay you two . . ." Karpenko stopped. "No. I will pay you five million euros for safe passage to Vienna."

The Russian didn't say anything.

"To Krakow then. No . . . Lviv."

"Vilnius," the Russian said. Lithuania. Due north. He must have friends there.

"Fine . . ."

"*I ihk?*" the Russian said. And them?

Karpenko hesitated, and in his silence, I heard death.

I lunged hard, clearing my lines of fire, and squeezed. I felt the recoil of both pistols and heard two shots. The left, aimed at the Russian, went wide, but that was my weak hand. The right connected and spun the Chechen sideways, causing him to spray his fire above our heads as Boon leapt from the trees, a savage ghost, and plunged his knife into the man's sternum, burying it in his heart.

I ducked and turned hard, trying to find the next shot, trying to locate the Russian merc, but nothing was moving. No shadows. No sounds. Even the shooting in the distance had stopped.

Then I saw him, dead on the ground, with one blue hole in his chest. I followed the direction of entry and saw Karpenko, standing motionless, holding a six-shot Glock.

He turned and looked at me. He wasn't stunned or shaken by what had happened, at least as far as I could tell. He dropped his gun hand to his side, his arm steady. His hair was barely mussed.

"I've sacrificed too much," he said slowly. "For my children. For my country. For *their* country, because they are Ukrainian, too. I'm not going to fucking Vilnius."

He stopped. He glanced at Miles. Suddenly, I could see the strain, not just of this moment, but of everything.

"*You've* sacrificed too much," he said, turning toward me, and I didn't care if it was manipulation or sincerity, I knew he was right.

"Charlie Mike," I said, nodding. Continue mission.

I turned to Boon, who was crouching over the dead Chechen, wiping his knife clean. "Out of ammo?"

He nodded.

"Where's Wildman?"

"In the wind."

They must have gotten separated in the firefight. At least Wildman wasn't KIA. Maybe.

I looked at the Russian merc. He was old, that was the first thing I noticed. Older than me. Jimmy Miles's age. And this was a young man's world. I thought about throwing his body in the incinerator, out of respect. I knew he didn't have anyone who would miss him. After a certain point, very few of us did.

I looked at Jimmy. He was thrashing, delirious and in pain, probably spiking a fever. His leg was covered with blood down to his boot.

"We've got to go," I said. "Now. We've got to make the car."

"Hargrove's down," Alie said. I looked. He'd been clipped in the shoulder, nothing more.

"Leave him. I got it," I said, grabbing Miles's litter and moving out. Ten steps, and Miles and I were into the shadows behind the incinerator, putting distance between ourselves and whoever might be following. Ten more steps, and I was gasping. *Hang in there, Jimmy.* Twenty more to the road. But the car wasn't there. The car wasn't fucking there.

"The car isn't here," Alie said. She had her arm under Hargrove's shoulders, and she was carrying him, dragging him out of the dark, when only his will was broken, not his legs.

We moved to the tree line, and I laid Miles down. I pulled out my sat phone and dialed Apollo's twenty-four-hour tactical operations center. They picked up without a ring. They always picked up without a ring.

"Man down," I said. "Mission abort. Need immediate medevac."

"Authenticate."

I didn't have a password. "This is Locke. Thomas Locke. My team is down, mission fail. I have a man bleeding out. I need a dust-off."

"I have no Locke on record."

You fucker. You know me. "I need an extraction. Now!"

"Authenticate."

I tried a few passwords from old missions, but I knew they wouldn't work. This was a kite. No calls. No records. They hung up. I dialed Winters. He had given me his private number.

He'd said I would know when to call.

CHAPTER 54

Brad Winters reached into his pocket and put his cell phone on the table without taking his eyes from Gorelov. He knew who was calling. Only two people in the world had this number. It would be gone by tomorrow. "That's my guy," he said. "That's the man who is right now setting this whole thing in motion. So tell me, have you figured it out yet?"

Gorelov's jowls quivered, as much from rage as confusion. *Pressure,* Winters thought, *is our ally.* The Russian took a slug of vodka. He hadn't touched the coffee since Karpenko's name had come up, but he'd smoked through half a pack of filterless Marlboros.

"Suddenly, ten thousand men doesn't seem like so many, does it?" Winters said. "Not to cover a thousand miles."

He was toying with him, daring the Russian to figure it out, and it was crushing him. An unsolvable puzzle wasn't pressure. When the answer was in your grasp, but you couldn't put the pieces together: that was when you broke down.

"Here's a hint. Tell them you already have Russian troops in disguise on location," Winters said with a smirk, as Gorelov snapped rapid Russian into his cell phone. By now, he had no doubt reached high up into the Kremlin and the FSB.

"Why would you tell me this?" Gorelov said. He was agitated, and not hiding it. "Do you think we won't reinforce our position?"

"I know you will. You might even bring more Spetsnaz, since they were recently spotted only twenty kilometers away."

Gorelov barked in Russian, relaying the latest information.

"Of course," Winters said casually, "there are Spetsnaz all over Eastern Ukraine, so that might not help much."

Gorelov slammed down the phone and poured more vodka. "We won't fall for a trap," he said, knocking back an unhealthy slug, "especially not one based on threats."

The cell phone rang again.

"Do you even know what the trap is?" Winters said, placing his hand over Gorelov's phone so that he couldn't answer. He knew Gorelov didn't. The Russian had no idea what a man on the cusp of his dream was capable of. Time to push this confrontation to its conclusion and see what happened.

"Bring too few men, and I'll capture them, parade them on camera, and show the world who you really are," Winters said. "Bring too many, so many that the world media will see without a doubt that the Russian army is attacking a Ukrainian natural gas station . . . and I will blow it up."

Everly's chin disappeared entirely, like a turtle retreating into its shell. Gorelov looked stunned.

"That's right," Winters said, nodding, as he saw the light coming on in Gorelov's weary eyes. "The big bang."

"You're going to blow up a transfer station."

"And your invasion will be blamed."

"But that would cripple the European economy . . ."

"And make the world realize what a threat you are," Winters said. "Isn't that what you fear? Not that this little invasion of yours blows up in your face, but that it blows up in Western Europe's face, in a way they can't ignore."

Gorelov didn't know what to say. Was this man, this

Mr. Winters, really crazy enough to escalate the confrontation between Russia and the West into outright war?

"That's mutually assured economic destruction," he muttered, buying time.

"The West can weather it," Winters shrugged. "But you can't, not with an energy-dependent economy."

"The Russians will do what they must," Gorelov said. "They always do."

"No Yuri," Winters replied calmly, using Gorelov's first name for the first time. "I'm afraid you misunderstood me. When I said 'you,' I didn't mean Russia, although that certainly applies. I meant you, Yuri, the man who has been waking up half of Putin's senior advisors at dawn to tell them how badly you're mishandling this situation. When they see this story fire-hosed across international media, and they realize that you knew and could have stopped it . . ."

Three or four of the Russian's cell phones were ringing, as they had been for the last twenty minutes. Now Winters's phone joined in again, and Gorelov glanced at it, almost with dread.

"Pick up your phone," Winters whispered, ignoring his own call. "Figure it out. But remember: I don't need a military victory to defeat you. All I need is . . . testicular fortitude."

"These men," Gorelov said, nodding his fat jowls toward Winters's ringing phone. "They must be fanatics, to blow themselves up for this crazy plan."

"Oh Yuri," Winters chortled, shaking his head. "I said the assault and explosion would be linked, in the media, in the eyes of politicians and Deep State players around the world. I never said they'd happen at the same transfer station."

Winters felt a hand on his arm, pulling him gently backward, and Everly leaned forward into his line of sight for the first time.

"You can't stop him, Yuri," the banker said calmly. "I think you see that now."

Gorelov looked beaten, slumped into his Italian suit, a cigarette turning to ashes in his fist.

"Yuri . . ." Everly said, getting him to focus. "Yuri . . . don't you think it's time we made a deal?"

CHAPTER 55

Somewhere out there, eight thousand feet beyond the clouds, in the cold upper reaches of the atmosphere, the drone was cruising on its appointed path. It was nothing more than a cold machine, invisible to eyes and instruments, transporting a large amount of explosives inside its protective shell.

There were other ways to destroy a natural gas transfer station. You could send a Tier One team, or a sniper with an incendiary round, but odds of human error were higher and tracks were harder to cover. You could destroy it with a cyberattack without leaving your command center, but every cyberaction was traceable, no matter how much you covered your tracks.

That was why when Apollo Outcomes wanted to send a confidential message, it sent a man to deliver it verbally, even when that meant a trip halfway around the world. When that wasn't an option, for whatever reason, the company sent a fax. The fax system was so out of date that no one bothered to monitor it, and so low-tech it was untraceable after the fact.

It was the same thinking that made the kamikaze drone work. Who would suspect? Who would be able to trace it? The drone was an emotionless piece of equipment with no cybertrail, designed to incinerate on impact, and that made it the perfect weapon to set off a chain reaction that would be felt around the world.

The Russians were prepared for atom bombs. Brad Winters had thrown a stone.

CHAPTER 56

I almost threw the sat phone into the undergrowth. Winters was supposed to answer. Winters always answered. That was the bare minimum of his guarantee: I risk my life, he answers the phone. Why would he give me the number, if he wasn't going to answer the phone?

I stared at the forest, frustrated and betrayed. We were in a thicket of bushes, half a klick from the warehouse, the trees providing some cover and concealment, even as the deep purple sky made dark spikes of the branches and leaves. The mission was a kite. I knew that. This was how kites worked. I knew that, too. But this wasn't how our kite was supposed to turn out. Jimmy Miles wasn't supposed to bleed out in a scrubby forest in Eastern Europe. Jimmy was supposed to die in a bar fight in Juba, or on the African savannah wrestling lions, or behind a Vulcan machine gun, mowing down a legion of machete-wielding fanatics. Or jumping on a grenade to save his team. Or with a wife, goddammit, one of those after-sex heart attacks that we always joked about, what a way to go. Not that either of us had a wife, but still . . .

I pushed past Karpenko, who was quietly sitting on his heels, and examined Miles's side with my Maglite. The bandages were soaked through, and blood was pulsing from his artery. But weakly. Too weakly. I shone my light on his face. His eyelids fluttered involuntarily, but his eyes didn't open. He was alive, but he wasn't going to make it, and it was going to be a painful death. It might take an hour, but out here, without an evac, it was death, guaranteed.

I started walking, pulling Miles behind me on the litter, Boon moving ahead to walk point and Hargrove leaning on Alie in the rear. Hargrove murmured, every now and then, but otherwise, no one made a sound.

I stopped twenty minutes later on the edge of a potato field a half klick north of our intended route. It was almost sunrise, the first blue tinge on the horizon, and the world was quiet. Nobody was following; we'd left the firefight behind. Alie was behind me in the trees. Hargrove was in the shadows. But this was our hour, Jimmy's and mine. We'd watched the sun come up on dozens of successful missions. We'd smoked a hundred cigars in tight-lipped triumph. We'd told a million stories of these mornings over bourbon, while I played the "Toreador" aria, the macho bullfighter's song from Bizet's opera *Carmen,* to celebrate being alive—I mean really alive, not lives of quiet desperation—for another day.

But not today.

I signaled to Alie. She nodded. She understood that this was Miles's last stop, and she knew I wanted to be alone. She rounded up the company and moved off into the morning. I waited until I couldn't hear anything but Jimmy's shallow breathing, and the hundred thousand legs crawling out of the forest, coming for Jimmy, coming for all of us.

I remembered the way my grandfather signaled for me to come closer. He was ninety-eight, laid up in a hospital bed with a broken hip. He whispered, "I'm done." I helped him pull the oxygen tube out of his nose, because he was too weak to remove it on his own. He died that night.

How do you kill a friend?

We were out of morphine, so I did it with my bare hands on his neck, in the classic style, choking him out.

Then I knelt beside him, not wanting to wipe the blood off my hands. I unbuttoned his shirt pocket. Jimmy always carried a heavy metal ring; he'd picked it up on a patrol in Bosnia, a lifetime ago. It was industrial, made for some broken off bolthole, but Jimmy used it to rap skulls and open beer bottles. The perfect piece for the perfect job, he'd say, but now there were no more skulls to rap. Nobody would ever use that brewing equipment in his storage locker outside Phoenix. They'd just, some day soon, stop paying the rent.

"Vive la mort! Vive la guerre! Vive le sacré mercenaire!" I whispered over his body. The mercenary's battle cry, or maybe his lament.

I put the metal ring in my pocket. Then I pulled the pin on the white phosphorous grenade and gently placed it on Jimmy's chest. A funeral pyre, the Viking way. The enemy would see it from a kilometer away, especially in this dim light, but by the time they got here, if they got here, we'd be gone, and so would Jimmy Miles.

This wasn't supposed to matter. None of it. None of us. That was how we did this job, by believing we would beat the odds. I'd seen a thousand men die violent deaths, many at my own hand. I shot a man in the head in Nigeria because he wouldn't sell land to an oil company, and I couldn't remember his face. Alie was right. I'd watched a village full of women and children gunned down from the back of Toyota trucks for sport, the gunners laughing and counting kills, something I'd sworn I'd never do again after the massacre in Srebrenca. I had burned four good mercs and a retiree less than an hour ago, and left three Ukrainian allies dead in the dirt, and who was going to remember them, or know what happened to them, or care? We were walking tombs of unknown soldiers, trying to make a difference, trying to do some good in the world.

By the time I reached the others, the rim of the earth was blue. They were standing in shadow, in a canebrake, looking out on a field of cow manure and crops.

"Charlie mike," I told the team, or whatever was left of it. "Let's move. We have a mission to complete."

It would have been what Miles wanted, because he was a soldier. But more important, I didn't know what else to do.

CHAPTER 57

Brad Winters listened closely, as Everly and Gorelov hammered out their deal, sometimes in Russian, other times in English. Everly's first concern seemed to be transfers from Bank Rossiya, Putin's bank. Bank Rossiya had gone from $1 million in assets in the 1990s to more than $100 billion in 2011 by serving the needs of the Russian Deep State. Now it was a pariah institution, locked out of SWIFT, the international banking consortium, by sanctions imposed after Russia's annexation of Crimea two months ago. Everly wasn't trying to skirt those sanctions, not explicitly, but the Londoners clearly had clients and projects caught up in the mess, and they needed Gorelov's reluctant help to free them.

Half the conversation—the half in Russian—went over Winters's head. The other half mostly bored him. He was more intent on watching the men and understanding their relationship. When he and Everly had arrived, Gorelov was arrogantly dismissive, the man in control. Even now, he appeared the same, gruffly rebuffing his more urbane counterpart between slugs of vodka, rejecting aspects of every request.

But Winters could see the shift in power. He could tell that in his stiff, unflustered way, Everly was a bar brawler, and he was pounding the Russian into submission, piece by piece. He could see it in the way Gorelov shifted in his chair, in his reluctance to make the phone calls required to seal certain deals, in the way he grimaced at odd moments like acid reflux was tearing his insides apart.

Ukraine was, in the end, little more than incremental business opportunities. Everly was less concerned with the fate of the country, Winters soon realized, than in making sure that current agreements—especially for the big energy companies, but for other clients, too—were honored no matter what happened in Kiev. Winters had offered the London bankers the chance to change Eastern Europe; they had chosen the status quo.

He daydreamed, briefly, about upending the relationship. During one long exchange in Russian, he even pictured the drone, floating downward out of the heavens, and then accelerating into the massive chamber where natural gas was compressed into liquid for concentrated delivery, the C-4 ripping the drone's skin apart like so many treaties and alliances and exploding it into a million worthless burned-out shards.

But Brad Winters was practical. He had seen this coming when the Indian banker called him on the private jet and told him his destination was Saint Petersburg. So when Everly and Gorelov offered him minor shale oil fields on the edge of Eastern Ukraine and free passage to operate, he accepted gracefully and then said, "And Azerbaijan."

Gorelov scoffed. "That's not our country."

Winters ignored the obvious lie. "I'm not talking ownership of the oil fields. I'm talking about a partnership, with one of your smaller national subsidiaries. My people will explore and extract the oil, and your people will ship it."

"It's a dangerous region, an unstable investment."

"I'll build a private military base, for the protection of your shipping lines, and for other work in the region. I'll keep you appraised of our activities, of course, and rest assured, you will find our services profitable."

Gorelov squinted.

"And Georgia and Armenia, too," Winters said, offhandedly, although he was not going to walk away without a piece of all three. "If we are going to be working together in the region, we might as well dominate it, right, Yuri?"

Those three countries formed the bottleneck between Russia and Southwest Asia. They had been a battleground between Deep States, dating back to the "Great Game" between Russia and England for control of central Asia in the 1800s.

"The Kremlin would never agree to that," Gorelov snapped.

"Yes they will," Winters said, "if you explain it to them correctly. It's better to have me inside the tent pissing out, after all, then outside pissing in."

Gorelov stammered, but Winters held up his hand. When a man was beaten, there was no point in indulging his concerns. "I must insist," he said. "That is my price, and it's a onetime offer."

He was thinking of the drone, and of Thomas Locke and his men, no doubt creeping up on the facility right now. He tapped his watch. *Time is running out, Gorelov. I'm not a patient man.*

"I require proof of your goodwill," Gorelov said, squatting like a toad. He seemed to have spent the last hour sinking into his chair, as if it were mud. The air was foul with his smoky stench. "The Near East for Karpenko."

"No."

"And your men."

CHAPTER 58

I lay prone on the roof of the apartment building where Wildman had planted the last camera, watching the pipeline facility through my scope. It was a clear blue morning, almost full light, and I was pinpointing heads, trying to grab that rush you feel when you have a man's life in your hands and he doesn't know it, but it wasn't coming. I had been angry after Miles died, and then brokenhearted. Now I wanted to feel angry again, but I couldn't muster it. I felt wrung out. Not just exhausted, but empty. The only thought that kept running through my head was, *What am I doing here? How did it come to this?*

I wasn't surprised the Donbas Battalion didn't show at 0600. Everything had gone to shit so far, and besides, militias were notorious for being late. By 0630, I was agitated. My body was locking down, my brain curling up on itself, my stomach wanting to vomit, except I hadn't eaten anything but a single energy bar since Miles and I ate MREs in the warehouse twelve hours ago and talked about old times.

Then three military trucks screamed up to the facility gate, and dropped their tailgates.

Whiskey Tango Foxtrot. What the fuck?

Russian reinforcements poured out, shouting and gesturing, and my heart dropped into my boots as they covered the exit points and swarmed into the facility, fanning out in search formation. I scoped the Spetsnaz commander, and I could practically read his lips when he saluted the officer in charge. *No one is here but us, sir!* Of course, he was speaking Russian, so that piece was in my head. But I could read the signs. We'd been sold out.

If the militia had been hit, prisoners might have been captured and interrogated. Had someone, under duress, given up the location of the assault? But no one outside my team knew about the mission, except for the Apollo men with the Donbas Battalion. They wouldn't crack. And they wouldn't have told the Ukrainians. This mission was blacker than black.

Two minutes later, a call came in on my sat phone. I hit Talk on my earpiece, still scanning the facility through my rifle scope.

"Mission abort. What's your sitrep?" Winters's voice.

"Three hundred meters south southeast of the objective," I said, giving him a false locale. "We ran into trouble. I called—"

"Is the client with you?"

"Affirmative."

Winters paused, long enough for me to sight the Spetsnaz leader's head in my crosshairs. It was a clean shot.

"Roger," Winters said. "Make your way to the extraction point ASAP. Bird en route. Watch your fourth point of contact, and wait for the signal."

Two seconds later, the Spetsnaz commander reached for his radio, listened, then frantically waved his men to get into one of the trucks. *We have them!* I imagined him saying, as I watched his lips move. The vehicle belched black smoke and lurched forward, heading east, toward the extraction point. That was the signal.

"Wilco out," I said, ending transmission.

Brad Winters had done the worst thing any commander could do: he'd betrayed his men.

Maybe. Because he was also trying to save us. The five points of contact for landing after a parachute jump are (1) balls of feet,

(2) heels of feet, (3) thighs, (4) ass, and (5) shoulder blades. So when Winters said "fourth point," he was telling me to watch my ass, in a way that no one without jump wings would understand. Somebody outside the military had been listening, forcing him to make the call.

Maybe. Because if everything had gone as planned, and Alie and Hargrove hadn't screwed the pooch, we'd have been inside the facility, waiting for the Donbas Battalion, when the Russian reinforcements arrived. There was no way Winters could have anticipated the Chechen mercs . . . or contacted them . . .

Don't get crazy, Locke, I thought, scoping the Russian commander's right cheekbone to calm my nerves. Winters didn't know where we were holed up. He thought we'd be in the facility as planned. The Chechens had followed Hargrove. In a way, Hargrove had saved our lives . . .

"What now?" Alie whispered, sliding up beside me on her belly so the Russians wouldn't see her silhouetted against the morning sky.

There were only five of us left: me, Boon, Karpenko, Alie, and Hargrove, who was wrapped in bloody bandages and nearly comatose from shock and exhaustion. I thought about what I had in my ruck: field jacket, night-vision goggles, a small amount of ammo, four nutrition bars, water. Around my neck was the gold chain Wolcott had given me last week in Washington, so I could snip links if I needed funds. In the map pocket of the ruck was about thirteen thousand euros in a Ziploc bag, the last of my Apollo cash. Boon and I could escape and evade, but what about the rest?

The smartest move was to leave them and run. They were war tourists, after all. Alie and Hargrove, at least, would probably survive. Karpenko, though, was wanted by all sides.

"We wait," I said, without taking my eye from my scope.

One shot to the cheekbone, and the Russian commander's head would blow out like a Jackson Pollock painting. I breathed deep and thought about the shot, the trajectory, the windage. I probably wouldn't hit him from this distance, at least not a clean kill, and I was glad. For the first time in a long time, the thought of killing made me sick.

I didn't realize Alie was still beside me, until she put her hand on my back and started rubbing it gently. I had a scar; I don't know if she remembered that. Maybe she could feel it. I had a brief, horrible thought that I might have been crying, but my scope was clear. My eyes were dry. Mercs don't fucking cry.

"I'm sorry," she said, but it didn't move me. She'd said that before. "I'm sorry I compromised your mission. I didn't realize it would be like that. I didn't realize that people would die."

Did she mean Miles? Or did she mean everyone?

"I'm sure you've seen it before," I whispered.

Alie was tough. She'd been in back alleys and slave brothels and God knew where else in pursuit of her truth, places even I wouldn't go. Anyone who thought she wasn't a hardened warrior was a fool. But I knew she hadn't seen anything like the last four hours before. I had never been in a worse battle, or on a more devastating mission, so how could she have been? We were lucky to be alive.

"I don't understand what you do," she said. "I don't see how you can live like this." She paused. The carnage was catching up to her. "But I respect it, Tom. No one would go through that if they didn't believe in the cause. Right? I didn't realize that before. I guess that makes you think I'm naïve."

It made me wonder what I think. It made me wonder why it had come to this, why I made all the decisions I'd made—leaving grad school for Burundi, turning down Winters's offer to climb the executive ladder, walking away from the one woman I never wanted to forget. Why bother, if all my choices only led me here?

"I would have married you, Alie," I said without turning from my scope. "In some other life. I would have taken an office job, and bought a minivan, and we would have raised our children on ice cream and spy novels, even the girl. We would have been happy."

I felt Alie's hand moving down my back, and then falling away. "Oh Tom," she said sadly, "what makes you think I would ever have wanted that?"

I thought she'd leave me then, alone with my weariness and regret. But she didn't. She lay beside me, not touching me, not moving. Was she watching the Russians below us loading their trucks, getting ready to ambush us at the extraction point? Or was she thinking what I was thinking: that there was still a place for us, a bed somewhere and happiness, at least for a night, until one or both of us left to save the world. Maybe Paris. Why not? The place didn't have to be large or fancy, it just had to be there. One bed and one window would do.

"What do we do now?" Alie asked again.

"We keep waiting," I said. "Play for the breaks. Something will come up. Something always does."

Twenty minutes later, we heard the helicopters, two Mi-17s, each capable of carrying thirty people. At first, I thought they might be Spetsnaz reinforcements, about to fast-rope into the facility from a hover. But the Russians were screaming and scurrying out of sight, like roaches when the kitchen light flicks on. *The choppers are with us*, I thought.

"News crews," I said, as the two birds came into view, black against the morning blue. "My boss lined them up for Karpenko's victory speech. It must have been too late to recall them back to Kiev."

"So they'll be going back soon," Alie said.

I took my eye away from the rifle scope and looked at her. She was smiling.

"I can talk my way on," she said.

I believed her. Alie could talk her way out of a sunburn. "What about them?" I said, nodding toward the others.

Alie looked over her shoulder, at Hargrove with his bandages, and Karpenko, lying faceup in the sun, smoking a cigarette. "Are you asking if I'd risk my life for Hargrove?"

I laughed. "You already have."

"Then it's my call."

I heard it then, even above the blades of the choppers setting down two blocks away in front of the gas facility. It was a jaunting whistling, "God Save the Queen." I turned, knowing exactly what that meant. *Don't shoot my head off, assholes.* Sure enough, Wildman appeared at the top of the fire escape thirty seconds later, carrying his SA-80, a rucksack, and an RPG. Splattered blood stained the front of his shirt.

"It's a proper shit show down there," he said with a twisted smile.

"I have to go," I said to Alie. This was no time for moping, and no time for regret. We had miles to go, hundreds of miles, and most of it would be on foot.

"Call of the wild," Alie said, but she was smiling.

CHAPTER 59

"They aren't going to find them, are they?" Everly asked, as the black Benz limo pushed through Saint Petersburg's early morning traffic.

"Unlikely."

Everly pursed his lips, pushing his lackluster chin deeper into his neck. "Did you warn them?"

"I didn't have to."

Winters had come up through army airborne, and he'd kept his military mind-set: never leave a man behind. Not an Apollo man. It was a guiding principle behind Apollo Outcomes. It was literally chiseled into a stone that someone had given him as a paperweight, which he'd passed down to the man who replaced him as the leader of the paramilitary wing of the firm. He felt wrong about what he had done, deeply wrong, but maybe, he reasoned, that was the price of success: to lay down a few of your core convictions in pursuit of the greater good. At least he had warned Locke.

"It wasn't necessary," Winters said, with steel in his voice. "Karpenko, maybe. But my team?"

"It was currency," Everly replied bluntly. "Gorelov needed to save face in order to pitch our deal to his superiors."

They were quiet. Brad Winters was hardly ever quiet.

"I admit," Everly said, with a snuffling laugh, "I enjoyed seeing Yuri so . . . incontinent. I'd like to thank you for that."

"It was my pleasure. Sincerely." Winters liked sticking it to a Russian, any Russian. He was Cold War that way.

"He may try to use this . . . escape as an excuse," Everly frowned. "To back out on your part of the deal."

"I don't think so," Winters said. "They had their chance at the facility, they have no one to blame but themselves. And this is a smart deal for the Russians." Winters had planned it that way. He knew the power of mutual benefit. "That's the real way Gorelov will save face. And besides—" he smiled at Everly "—I have the same protection as everyone else you negotiated for to-day: your bank and its backers."

Winters had long known the game. He knew the Deep State wasn't a powerful cabal. It was a ruthless jungle of apex-predators in a zero-sum contest of conquest and annihilation, where every alliance was temporary, and everyone, even the largest players and power brokers, could be destroyed. Gorelov could fall out of favor with Putin all the way to a prison cell, or a grave. Karpenko could be sold for assassination. The London bank could fail, if it stopped being useful to the right people at the highest levels of influence. At the Deep State level, everyone was both predator and prey. That wasn't a defect in the system, but its survival mechanism; competition kept everyone's claws sharp.

What Winters hadn't realized was that East and West no longer mattered. The Deep State, as seen through the bankers, penetrated across the great divide, from London to Moscow. Its interests didn't track with normal geopolitics, or even official government positions. He had been raised a patriot, always believing that it was us versus them; that national interests trumped business; that flags were, in the end, more than cloth.

But that was twentieth-century thinking, and as he'd just learned, the modern world was much bigger than states, and much more dangerous and profitable, too. Yes, there was negotiation left to do, but Glenn Hartley and his partners were now looking at three times as much drillable land as he'd promised in Ukraine. The security environment was worse, sure, but Apollo would roll its Ukrainian security contracts into Azerbaijan, either with the financial backing of the U.S. government or some other partner. Within a few years, his conglomerate would be pumping millions of barrels, and Apollo would be the best military force in the hot zone between Russia, Iraq, and Iran. And then, if and when the time was right, Gorelov would learn what Winters had taken to heart: that all strategic alliances are temporary, until the next opportunity comes along.

"I hope you're not disappointed," Everly said, misinterpreting the silence. "It was a brilliant plan, in its way. Expose the Russian military invasion. Blow up our energy network. Pressure the world into war. Jolly good as bluffs."

If you say so.

"But the world doesn't work that way, I'm afraid," Everly said. "It is not remade, all in one whack. History is a series of carefully applied pressures, moving things incrementally toward where you want them to go. It's managing crises, not creating them. That is our business, Mr. Winters. The steadying hand. That's how we'll push Putin into line. And you gave him a mighty big push today."

Everly was wrong. History didn't work like that. It was a constant collision, a series of catastrophic breaks and long repairs. Bin Laden had changed the world in a moment, when his men flew airplanes into the World Trade Center. George Bush had remade the world in three weeks, when he blitzkrieged Baghdad. Bush had intended to break the Middle East so that he could build back: newer, modern, and better than before. The first part worked; the second part . . . not so much. But that was a failure of execution, not vision. It didn't mean the idea was wrong.

"Cheer up, old chap," Everly said with a knock on the shoulder and fresh British pip. "We did a good thing today. *You* did a good thing. It was impressive indeed."

"Thanks," Winters said, without much conviction. They were approaching the airfield. He could see the private jet on the tarmac.

"We'd like to express our appreciation," Everly said, turning serious. "We'd like to buy back your firm's stock and take you private, through a shell company, of course. You'll have complete managerial control, and once your firm meets our clients' needs, you'll never have to depend on another government contract again. The possibilities are greater, Mr. Winter, than even you can imagine."

He was talking about a 10 percent stake in a $1.8 billion company at current valuations, probably more once the hedge funds got wind of the rumors and drove the stock through the roof. It was more than payment in full. And it would correct Winters's most foolish error, when he had listened to his New York banker friends and decided fifty million in his pocket was better than the anonymity of being privately held.

"Take your time. It's a big decision, I know. We don't expect an answer right away."

"I accept," Winters said.

Everly raised an eyebrow. "To our partnership, then."

"To our future."

Winters smiled, and whether the smile was false or how he truly felt, even he wasn't sure. This wasn't how he had hoped his Ukrainian gambit would turn out; but maybe, if he played this opportunity right, it was better. The London bankers thought they were buying him, but Winters knew that if you were going to climb a man to power, you had to stand close.

Everly snuffled his nasal laugh, and Winters realized that, in his way, the man was truly enjoying himself. Today was a major victory; maybe even bigger than Winters understood.

"It was clever, you know, what you said about nobody knowing you."

"It's the truth," Winters said. "It's my code."

"It's *our* code," Everly correctly him, "but you can rest assured, my friend, Vladimir Putin is going to know you now."

CHAPTER 60

The pilots were back in the cockpit by the time Alie burst onto the scene. The helicopters had been on the ground for more than forty minutes, and the reporters were eager to leave this dry hole in a dangerous war zone. They had been up since 5:00 A.M.; they had four-star food and expense accounts waiting for them back in Kiev; and the only people going in or out of this pipeline facility were employees.

Alie took advantage of their eagerness to slip past the thin line of spectators that news cameras always attract and grabbed one of the women by the arm, a low-level on-air personality, although Alie didn't recognize her, since she had long ago given up watching American television news. She was risking a pistol-whipping from the so-called protection, but Alie knew her looks would save her. She wasn't a desperate damsel in distress, but she knew how to play it for TV.

"Please," she begged. "Take me with you."

The newswoman turned, startled. She was young and beautiful, the right kind of woman for the post-Internet news, and Alie knew she'd have no sympathy for a freelancer in a bind.

"I'm an American," Alie said, with flagrant despair. "Take me with you. Please. My husband. He's hurt."

The woman looked at the bloody rags covering the man's face and his staggering steps. He looked like he was about to fall over.

"My name is Alie . . . Alie Jenson. I'm from Missouri, USA. My husband . . . he's a minister. We're Christian missionaries.

We've been stranded for a month. Please. My husband needs medical attention. The Russians . . . they beat him. They beat everyone at the mission . . . even the children."

The woman eyed her, but not with compassion. With greed. Behind her, a cameraman was calling for her to get onboard.

It took her only a second to decide.

"It's against the rules," the reporter whispered as she ushered them into the helicopter. Alie knew the woman smelled a story, but she was going to be disappointed when they got back to Kiev, because there was no story to be had.

"What's his name?" the reporter shouted over the rotors, as they rose into the air, but Alie tapped her ear, pretended she couldn't hear her. The reporter turned away. Alie leaned into her husband, settling into the flight.

"It's only Kiev," she said into his ear, "but it will have to do."

Karpenko smiled, although nobody could see it under the filthy bandages. "Better than Vilnius," he said.

Eight hundred miles away, the drone eased out of the blue sky and came to rest on the deck of a rusty scupper in the middle of the Black Sea. Jacob Ehrlich sighed and began the postflight inspection. This was the last one of the night, so he went quickly, like a Hertz employee looking over a just-returned rental car at the end of a long shift. Fifteen minutes later, the drone was packed up and hidden in the hold.

Ehrlich took off his hat and wiped the sweat from his forehead. The sun was up, the deck was rolling beneath his feet, and there was nothing in any direction but water, as far as the eye could see.

Just another boring nothing day in paradise, he thought, as the engines kicked in for the long boat ride home. *But at least I'm getting paid.*

EPILOGUE

British Virgin Islands

July 4, 2014

I should have known, I thought, as I watched him take a seat at the beachside bar, like a man who owned the world. He was wearing a Panama hat and Bermuda shorts, and was puffing a nice cigar, like the ubiquitous middle-aged white man on vacation that crowded every beach north of the equator, and quite a few south of it, too.

But he wasn't on vacation; he was here for me.

After Boon, Wildman, and I had humped it out of Ukraine, we spent a few weeks on the run, watching our six for an Apollo hit team, but it never materialized. Maybe Winters had decided we weren't a threat; maybe we were just that good. By the time we reached Ankara, Turkey, my money was running low, so I saddled up and flew to the British Virgin Islands with the last of our stash. I knew the company would find me if they wanted to, since I was flying on my real passport, using my real name. So when I didn't see anyone at the airport, I thought they might let me go, and I was disappointed. Was that all I meant to them? Then I spotted a stiff loitering across from my bank. Apollo

Outcomes knew everything, apparently, including where I kept my secret emergency cash and safety deposit box.

So I pulled back and waited to see what happened. Two days later, the boss arrived and hit a bar at the beach. He wasn't hiding or planning an operation. He was here to be found. There was nothing to do but oblige.

"Wolcott," I scoffed, as my shadow fell over his table.

Wolcott lowered his *Financial Times* and squinted. He hadn't even bothered to watch if anyone was coming. "Thomas Locke," he said, as if I was expected, which of course I was. He gestured to the empty seat. He could tell I was angry. "I know you were hoping for someone else."

"I thought he might want to apologize."

Wolcott laughed. "Our friend doesn't apologize or explain. You know that." No names. Fine.

"He burned me, Wolcott."

"I don't think so."

"He sabotaged the mission. He tried to have me killed."

"I don't know what you're talking about," Wolcott said, "but I assure you, Thomas, whatever happened, it wasn't personal."

"Men died, Wolcott. My friend Miles. Your friend Greenlees . . ."

"I know. I am sorry."

Sorry meant nothing, especially from an empty suit. I needed to talk with the man himself.

"Why are you here?"

"To close the loop," Wolcott said. "To make sure we're square."

He really had a way with words. "We're not square."

"Don't make this hard."

My hands wanted to reach for my Berettas, holstered in the small of my back under my Tommy Bahama shirt and linen blazer, but I restrained myself. "You think this is hard? Sitting on the beach drinking . . . what? A cherry margarita?"

"It's a Singapore Sling. You should try one." Wolcott called the waiter. I glared at the young man, which wasn't fair, he was just doing his job.

"Fine," Wolcott huffed, turning to the waiter. "A piña colada for my friend."

He drank. I've always had issues with multicolored drinks garnished with tiny umbrellas, but this one looked right in Wolcott's chubby hand.

"I assume you're not coming back," he said between slurps.

"No."

"Then take this as a severance package." He slid the folded *Financial Times* across the table. Inside was a sealed envelope thick with cash. "Consider this your exit interview."

There was an old joke at Apollo Outcomes: the exit interview was the funeral. I looked out at the water. It was strikingly blue. There were a few white sailboats bobbing on the swell.

"You going to the competition?"

Half of me wanted to hunt Winters down, figure this out, and deliver the kind of moral justice my job at Apollo had always promised, but rarely produced. The other half wanted to disappear.

"Tell him I'm going solo. Low-key. Starting a company with a couple of friends. Preventing genocide. Taking down tyrants. Disrupting the disrupters." That was a Brad Winters phrase, from our time in management together. "Tell him not to worry about competition because this will only be missions worth killing and dying for." I thought of Miles. We should have done this years ago, together. "Tell him Ukraine was the last time I work for someone I don't trust."

Wolcott let the trust issue slide. He was a corporate jockey, a company man, but he was sympathetic, I think. "Then you're definitely going to need this," he said, shoving the envelope of money closer.

I looked out at the harbor and thought, *I like white boats*. I used to make them out of scrap paper when I was a kid. Sometimes they'd float a few feet, before they sank.

"Did you see the article?"

He meant Alie's article about Karpenko, "The George Washington of Ukraine." Apparently, the oligarch was holed up somewhere in London, in a town house whose windows were two-way glass. Most of the article was standard hagiography, but part five was a detailed account of his family's rescue and the "Russian aggression" in Kramatorsk, from the point of view of the client. It read like a *New York Times* puff piece on Navy SEALs, as if my team was all supermen, especially Miles. I appreciated that.

"Cut her some slack, Wolcott. Everything was true. And she didn't include names, including Apollo Outcomes, and you know she could have. Our employment records can be found."

"We killed it, anyway. That's why it ended up on a website out of Amsterdam, with no office and no assets, instead of the *Atlantic*. We had it taken down, of course, but not before it had been copied into the ether a hundred times. It's still causing us grief."

Not enough, considering.

"But our litigators will find her." He switched gears, but not artfully. "Have you had any contact? I hear you two used to be close."

He knew I hadn't. But did he know that was why my return flight was routed through Amsterdam? "No."

"Did you hear about the CIA kid, the one that stumbled back from Kramatorsk?"

"No."

"He got a tongue-lashing. Then he got a medal for bravery. He was promoted to Islamabad."

My piña colada arrived, but I ignored it. Wolcott noisily

sucked up the last of his Singapore Sling. He was sunburned on his nose and the back of his neck. Why was he even bothering to wear the hat?

"Am I free?" I asked. Boon and Wildman were waiting in Bosaso, and I needed to get back. For the sake of the local Somalis, of course. You don't want Wildman haunting your bar district for long.

"We forgive you, if that's what you mean. Assuming you forgive us."

Nothing forgiven, Wolcott. Nothing forgotten. The loop wasn't closed, and the circle wasn't squared.

"Look, Thomas," Wolcott said, leaning forward confidentially as another Singapore Sling appeared on his cocktail napkin. The Breezy Point Inn, the napkin said. "This isn't right. I know that. But there's nothing I can do. Men like Brad Winters . . . we spend a lot of time wondering about them. What are they doing? Why are they doing it? Why are they doing this to me? But the fact is, guys like Winters, they never think about guys like us."

"He asked for me, Wolcott."

"And you think you're the only one? He asks for everyone, every now and then."

Wolcott sat back. He looked out at the boats. He took a deep drink, like he was on a long weekend with the family at the Jersey Shore.

"You might be right, Locke," he said finally. "You might be special. That might be why I'm here. He's never sent me, he's never sent anyone, like this before. Usually, it's just adios, and a burn notice or a body bag. Sign the confidentiality agreement and get off my lawn. But for some reason, he cares about you."

I took the money.

"Tell him I'm . . . disappointed."

I almost said, *Tell him I'll see him soon.* But why let him know I'm coming? Winters would understand my message, just as I understood his. He would know I wasn't going to let this lie. And now I knew he wouldn't, either. That was what made us different from men like Wolcott, I suppose, and the billion other middle managers slugging it out in an office every day.

"I have to go," I said, standing up.

I left the bar and didn't look back. What would be the point? I had a world to save, and two friends to meet in Ankara. And before that, a small bed in a small room in the Jordaan neighborhood of Amsterdam, and a single night, for now, when I knew it would be warm.

A C K N O W L E D G M E N T S

Thank you to Jessica, my wife, whom I met while writing this book. I'm sorry I spent so many late nights laboring over these pages.

Thank you to my agent, Peter McGuigan and everyone at Foundry, including Emily Brown, Kirsten Neuhouse, and Richie Kern. And to all the great people at HarperCollins: my editor, David Highfill, Chloe Moffett, Mumtaz Mustafa, Kaitlin Harri, Danielle Bartlett, David Palmer, and Mark Steven Long. And, of course, my co-conspirator, Bret Witter. None of this would have happened without you guys.

This book is a result of what seems like a lifetime in combat, and I am grateful to all those who served with me and helped along the way, especially Gifford Miles, my platoon sergeant from the 82nd Airborne Division, who has always been a big brother to me.

Thanks as well to those who helped me get it right. A CIA friend (you know who you are). Fred Kagan, a great muse of international intrigue. Henry Escher, a seasoned thriller reader, who showed me what good dialogue looks like. Elena Pokalova, my Russian/Ukrainian friend who helped with the slang and feel of the place. Deanne and Jim Lewis, Jay Parker, Corinne Bridges, Brett Duke, Elizabeth Butler, and Robert "the firewood guy," who read my drafts with keen eyes.

Lastly, I wish to acknowledge all those professional warriors out there who serve in the complicated shadows of world politics. You will never be left behind or forgotten.